WRITERS AT BAY

Short Stories by the Forthwrite Writers

iUniverse, Inc.
New York Lincoln Shanghai

Writers at Bay

iUniverse books may be ordered through booksellers or by contacting:

iUniverse
2021 Pine Lake Road, Suite 100
Lincoln, NE 68512
www.iuniverse.com
1-800-Authors (1-800-288-4677)

Because of the dynamic nature of the Internet, any Web addresses or links contained in this book may have changed since publication and may no longer be valid.

ISBN: 978-0-595-47086-0 (pbk)
ISBN: 978-0-595-91368-8 (ebk)

Printed in the United States of America

CONTENTS

Introduction

The Forthwrite Writers' Group was formed several years ago by three persuasive scribblers. It is now an eight to ten-strong mix of enthusiastic and somewhat more advanced but still variable writers. The members of the group aspire to be added to the enviable list of accomplished Fife authors. They meet about once a month in the Dalgety Bay Library to read, critically assess, and enjoy each other's latest effort. In this collection of short stories they try to improve on their last effort, **Ripples Across the Bay**, which was well received by their captive audience. The initial theme selected for this volume was "Scottishness", but indiscipline and creativity managed to break through this limitation during the course of the year. Still, for the most part, the stories are set in Scotland and reflect the Scottish nature and character.

In this volume the reader will find nostalgia for the good old days, reflections on ancient Scottish history, pure fantasy, social critique, and above all, much humour. Nessie is in here, as is St Columba, a ghost, and a fox that speaks in the Scottish dialect. Where else could you find such a collection of weird and wonderful characters? We have tried to avoid clichés in these stories. Nevertheless, there is one that is true: There is something in here for everyone. We hope that the reader enjoys the reading as much as we have enjoyed the writing.

William Clinkenbeard, the Editor

The Kickstart

By Maureen Brister

Morag opened one eye and stared sleepily at her alarm clock. 5.30 am. What had she heard? She listened again. Someone was crying in the cold dark December morning. Someone was trying unsuccessfully to stifle their sobs and Morag knew exactly who it was. She sighed and slowly swung her legs out of bed.

Peggy Simmons was not taking her daughter's broken engagement and shattered wedding plans well. To be fair Morag had not expected she would but it was worse than she had anticipated. Her mother had gone into one of her depressions, always her reaction to things not going to plan. Her plan that is.

There had been no choice in the matter. When Morag's best friend Alison told her that she had seen her recently affianced Bill having a "cosy and intimate" lunch with another woman only a few days after their engagement party there was no hesitation on Morag's part. The engagement was off!

Peggy Simmons had revelled in the very successful engagement party. Both parents had been overjoyed that their daughter was to be married in less than a year to an up and coming newspaper reporter. Bill Gordon was already well known in the Scottish town where he had served his time on the local rag, but he had gone on to bigger and better things. He was now a senior reporter with a Scottish daily newspaper based in Edinburgh but hoped to move on to a National soon. Morag's mother had been prepared to see her only daughter move to London after the wedding. She had been completely bowled over by Bill. He always brought her flowers or chocolates and had little bits of gossip to impart. In fact now that Morag thought about it, he had known just how to win her mother over. Her father had not said much, but Morag knew if her mother was happy then so was he and they both knew that having a wedding to organise was just the thing to keep Mrs Simmons busy for the foreseeable future.

Peggy's world had been shaken with the news that the engagement was off. Hence the depression, sleepless nights and tears. It was not exactly what Morag had planned either, but her mother could not see past the humiliation of telling her sisters and close friends that there would be no wedding.

By the time Morag reached the living room her mother's tears had stopped. She found her sitting staring at the unlit electric fire, wrapped in her dressing gown, cradling a cup of what looked like cold tea in her hands. Morag put her arms round her shoulders. 'For heaven's sake Mum, you need to get over this, you'll make yourself ill and have to go back on medication if you keep this up. How do you think I feel about it all? It isn't exactly what I wanted either, but I had no choice. Better to find out what he is like now than later. Life goes on.'

Mrs Simmons looked up tearfully at her tall, slim, bespectacled red haired daughter. Morag was no beauty. That mop of curly hair! There was still time to fix these protruding teeth though, but at 33 years of age it would not be easy to find someone else. Bill Gordon had seemed quite a catch. She had so much wanted this wedding. Now Christmas was rearing it's head and what kind of Christmas would it be this year? They always spent it with her sisters, their husbands and families. Peggy knew what her sisters would be saying. It was about time she got taken down a peg or two, always did have ideas above her station etc. She didn't think she could face it.

Morag put a cup of hot sweet tea into her mother's hands. 'Come on Mum, drink this, there's still time for you to get an hour or two's sleep. I expect Dad has slept through it all, has he?' Over the years Mr Simmons had grown used to his wife's little depressions. He thought it best to ignore them as far as possible, though he privately thought this one might be worse. He slept on.

Her mother safely back in bed, Morag made herself some toast, poured herself some tea from the pot and switched on the electric fire. She settled on the couch. There was a good hour before she needed to leave for work. It was not the perfect start to her busy day as a medical secretary in the local district hospital, but she would cope. She always had.

Morag Adelaide Simmons was born to Peggy and George Simmons following ten years of marriage. When they met some four years before their marriage, a meeting which she was sure her father had long forgotten but which her mother had most definitely not, she had known instantly that this was the type of man she wanted to marry. Morag had been told this story many times. A friend, a fellow salesperson in one of the two ladies' and gents' outfitters in their local town, had introduced her mother to George when he came in to buy a suit for work. He was introduced as an insurance salesman who was going places, and indeed that is what he had achieved. George was now a very successful insurance salesman, in charge of a small team, and the family unit had lived in Dundee, Glasgow and now Dunfermline. Peggy had to do all the chasing according to her, and that hadn't been easy as George had not been one for spending his hard earned money on visits to the local cinema or dance hall, but Peggy was persistent and in the end she got her man! Peggy herself was the eldest of six sisters and Morag knew what her aunts thought of her mother. Marrying George was seen as a major coup in Peggy's opinion. Not for her the factory workers, grocers and removal men who were her brothers-in-law. An insurance salesman, and a successful one at that, was more her style. A cut above. They always had nice houses, no council houses for Peggy. There had, however, been a price to pay. George's tightness with money had really set in once they were married and he and Peggy did not get along. Arguments about what he saw as her over-spending and his attempts to curb that spending, became the norm and Morag had grown used to hearing her parents berating each other over the years. As she grew older she had become a peacemaker of sorts. She loved her parents dearly but had to admit the thought of marriage and a move to London had excited her. She could finally escape the claustrophobic atmosphere of their current home. She knew her mother thought she would never marry, but she had just never found the right person. Bill Gordon had not been the right person either but he had bowled her over when he approached her at a local dance and he had well and truly won over her mother. She realised that was his way. He loved being the centre of attention. He had been annoyed when she had confronted him about his lunch date and tried to bluff his way out of it, but she knew at heart it was his nature. Deep down she had always known. Morag, and her mother, had been carried along with the brief whirlwind courtship, the engagement and marriage plans.

She finished her tea, put her dishes in the sink and went off to get ready for work. Morag was a very efficient and hard working secretary. Work was her saviour at the moment. The busier the better. She was meeting Alison after work for a bite to eat and a chat. What would she do without Alison? Her sounding board. Alison of the long blonde hair, the sparkling blue eyes and the impressive figure that she, Morag, had always secretly envied. One thing was certain, she didn't intend to be around to face this coming family Christmas. Her mother was not the only one who felt humiliated. Changes had to be made to her life and the quicker the better. She had gotten used to the idea of leaving home and still intended to do that. How had yet to be determined. Between them maybe they could come up with something over their pizza and wine tonight!

A quick phone call home during her coffee break that morning ascertained that Mrs Simmons was up, dressed and had arranged to meet a friend that afternoon. Someone who would sympathise with her plight no doubt Morag thought grimly. There was a letter for her from her Aunt Meg in Canada according to her Mum. God, had the news reached there already, the family drums really had been beating!

Later that evening, despite two bottles of red wine with their pizza, Morag and Alison had still not come up with an escape plan. Apart from suggesting they both went in search of some sun over the Christmas and New Year period, Alison had not come up with anything more substantive. That wouldn't work as Alison herself was hoping to get engaged next year to her long-time boyfriend John and though it was good of her to suggest the holiday, she knew Alison would rather be at home in Dunfermline. Who could blame her?

Morag got off the bus and walked slowly home. No lights on in the living room and just a hint of light in one of the bedrooms. Good, her parents hadn't waited up and hopefully her mother was in a sound, medicinally-induced sleep.

The letter was lying on the hall table. Morag took off her coat and shoes and padded upstairs to her bedroom, taking the letter with her. Once in bed, hot water bottle tucked at her feet she opened the envelope. Her Aunty Meg, Uncle Ted and their three sons had emigrated to Canada some six years previously. Ted was a surgeon at the Montreal General Hospital and apart from one visit to their home town during the boys' summer holidays they had never shown any inclination to return to Scotland. They loved their life in suburban Montreal. Large house and country club membership. The boys couldn't get enough of the outdoor life, taking to skating, skiing and ice hockey like ducks to water in winter, and stars of the local baseball teams in summer.

Morag's eyes widened as she read the short two-page letter. Aunt Meg was sorry to hear of the broken engagement and wondered if spending Christmas and New Year in Canada would cheer her niece up. Tears filled Morag's eyes. This could be the answer to her predicament. OK, she would have to come back in the New Year and face things, but at the moment all she could think of was flying away from all her troubles. Her mind raced. She had two weeks holiday saved, there was still time to book flights. Her tears changed to a broad grin. Thank you, thank you Aunt Meg!

After a restless night Morag was awake before the alarm went off. Her "to do" list had been made over and over during her sleepless night. First on the list was telling her parents of her plans. Not easy, but the quicker she got it over with the better, give them time to get used to the idea.

They were sitting watching breakfast television, tea and toast at their sides when Morag appeared dressed for work. 'Hello dear, want a lift in to work this morning, it's pouring down out there,' said her father. 'OK Dad, if it doesn't take you out of your way thanks.' Morag poured out her tea. She would pass on the toast for now. The next half hour would be difficult enough. Her mother was still in her dressing gown but there were no puffy eyes this morning. A good sign!

'I need to talk to you both,' she said. They looked up warily. Her mother opened her mouth to speak, but Morag interrupted. 'Before you start Mum, what I am going to say is not up for discussion. OK?' They both nodded slowly. 'I'm going to Montreal for Christmas and New Year. The letter from Aunty Meg was an invitation to spend two weeks with them and I intend to take her up on it. I'll phone her today once I have confirmed things with work and booked my flights.'

Her mother's face became paler as she slowly shook her head from side to side. Morag moved quickly and put her arms round her Mum. 'Look, this is a difficult time for all of us, but I need to get away for a bit, you must see that surely. Get my thoughts together, and come back ready to face the New Year. What do you think Dad?' Mr Simmons drained his cup and stood up. 'I can see your point of view Morag and yes, I think it is a good idea. Your mother and I will join the family as usual, it isn't as if we will be on our own, will we dear?' Mr Simmons stared intently at his wife. God alone knew how he would deal with her after Morag had gone, but this was the right thing for his daughter, that he did know.

'Come on then, coats on, time to head into town.' He grinned at Morag. 'You have a busy day ahead of you.'

Morag stared at her Mum. 'I'll give you a ring this morning, OK?'

There was no reaction as they headed out the back door to the car. 'Will she be alright Dad?' 'Of course she will, I've only got two appointments today so I'll pop home between them just to make sure. Don't worry about her Morag. Your Mum would have to face up to a Christmas without you at some time or other, we both would, we'll cope.' He smiled at his daughter and patted her knee as she took her seat beside him in the car. 'Just you get on with your plans.'

By lunchtime that day Morag's head was reeling. Her boss had agreed her leave, she had texted Alison with the news, and the travel agent confirmed there was still availability on the flights from Edinburgh to New York and the onward connection to Montreal. She had not forgotten to call her mother who seemed to be coming to terms with things, though how much of that was due to her father's visit home that morning and whatever words has passed between them Morag was not sure.

She had a week to prepare for her trip. She would leave Edinburgh on 21st December and return on 4th January. A phone call to her Aunt had left her in no doubt she was doing the right thing. They couldn't wait to see her and she couldn't wait to be there! The boys were planning all kinds of things, mostly involving outdoors and snow. Her Aunt had warned her to be sure to pack her warmest clothes and boots. The temperature had already plunged below zero and was unlikely to rise much above that in the foreseeable future. There had been several snowfalls too. Well this would certainly be a different Christmas Morag thought. She had never experienced cold like that, nor as much snow. Looked like she would need to visit one of these outdoor shops in Edinburgh to see what they had for that kind of weather. She shivered excitedly and texted Alison again. A shopping expedition with lunch in Edinburgh could maybe be fitted in!

The journey had been bumpy but Morag's travelling companions had kept her mind occupied during both flights. She had learned a lot about life in North America from the natives returning home for the festive break. The couple on the New York leg of the journey were spending two years in St Andrews where they were travelling professors at the University, and being avid golfers were loving every minute of their time in Scotland. The single girl she now knew as Marnie, like herself, travelling from New York to Montreal worked for the United Nations as an interpreter. All three were open, friendly, outgoing people and she had really enjoyed their company. She had not bored the first couple with her circumstances but Marnie had managed to get a bit of the story out of her. She had asked Morag why she didn't think of applying to work in the United Nations as a secretary. Apparently there were always lots of opportunities there, and sometimes on quite short-term assignments. Morag had promised to follow up on that.

The plane was touching down in Montreal. She could see the snow covered ground as they got closer to the airport but the skies were clear blue. Marnie smiled as she saw Morag's eyes widen. 'Hope you've brought your winter woollies Morag, you'll need them. Are you going to try your hand at skiing?' 'That's the plan Marnie. My three cousins have all sorts of outdoorsy things planned. I just can't wait, really I can't.'

They had already exchanged addresses and phone numbers. 'I know you'll be busy with your relatives, but if you get bored and want some company, don't hesitate to give me a ring. Really Morag, I mean it. There are lots of great eating places, bars and clubs in downtown Montreal. No disrespect to your Aunt and

Uncle but they probably don't take in that scene. I still come home regularly enough to keep up to date with it all and I'd be happy to show you around.'

'That sounds just great Marnie and I will probably take you up on that. You're right, two weeks of snow, snow and more snow may just be too much!'

They both got up as the seatbelt signs went off, hugged each other and moved forward to disembark. Morag had a good feeling about this, it was right for her, she knew it was.

The cold hit her as she linked arms with her Aunt and Uncle. They were walking to the car park over icy snow covered surfaces. She took a deep breath and coughed as the cold air hit her lungs. They both laughed. 'Hope you are prepared for this Morag. It really is very healthy once you get used to it,' Ted said with a smile. Morag nodded.

'It's great to see you here. The boys have told all their friends you are coming, so expect to be inundated with offers to take you here, there and everywhere. Don't think you have to do it all though, they will settle down after a few days,' said Meg. 'There are lots of social events this time of year too, mostly connected with the hospital and we would be happy to take you along to some of them if you feel like it, introduce you to some of our friends, maybe even a young doctor or two, or is it too early for that yet?' Meg smiled ruefully. 'Just tell me to shut up. Really there is no pressure on you, we just want you to relax and enjoy yourself. I can just imagine what your mother will have been putting you through recently. Turned things into her usual drama I imagine and everything will be your fault of course.'

'Got it in one Aunt Meg. It has *not* been easy. At least Dad has encouraged me to do this, he seems to be on my side. Your invitation was so perfectly timed. As soon as I stepped on the plan I felt so relaxed for the first time in weeks, like every muscle in my body smiled and said "About time too." Does that sound stupid?'

'Not at all and hopefully after all the outdoor exercise you are about to get these muscles will stay relaxed.' Meg turned to Morag and all three of them laughed.

Morag had managed to briefly introduce Marnie to her Aunt and Uncle at the airport, there had been time for handshakes all round before Marnie was surrounded by her family. 'You should try to meet up with Marnie too Morag, she will be able to show you a side to Montreal that we won't be familiar with. She seems very friendly.'

Morag nodded. 'We got on like a house on fire, amazingly we had a lot in common. She encouraged me to find out about secretarial jobs at the United

Nations. Apparently there are always opportunities there. I 'm going to follow that up once I get back home.'

'Sounds good,' said Ted, pulling into the driveway, taking care not to clip the banks of snow on either side. 'Here we are, let's get you settled Morag.'

Morag slowly got out of the car, staring around at the feet of snow everywhere. She could see her three cousins standing at the front windows of the house and she waved to them. Well Bill Gordon, she thought, I hope you are looking forward to your Christmas and New Year break as much as I am. Wherever you are. You may just have done me the biggest favour by kickstarting the rest of my life!

School Daze

By David Cruickshanks

There was a girl who rode to my school every day on a motorbike. She would park it right beside the teachers' cars. When I heard the *ging ginging* of the screeching gears, silenced by the squeaking brake and the swift turn of a key, I would take a detour past the car park on my way to the red ash football pitch. I longed to see her taking off her red white and blue helmet, before swishing her perfumed hair around like the slow motion girl on the hairspray advert.

I was twelve years old, small for my age and had recently engaged in a sticky and one sided relationship with my new found raging hormones. It was good so long as it lasted.

One crisp bright morning I stopped and stared as she slivered out of her leathers to reveal her grey school skirt and matching tights. The pleated skirt had ridden up to reveal the dark band of her shiny grey thigh. She caught me looking and creased her forehead. I jerked my neck as I looked away, my face as red as the ash on the football pitch. My heart though, had leapt at that sight.

I kicked my ball, staining it red on the moist ground, panting around the ash until the bell summoned me to classes. I stared at a jungle of chalk on the blackboard, almost unnoticed, through Mr H's lesson in engineering science until the chalk symbols began to fuse into the shape of a girl, then fully formed into Motorcycle Girl. She peeled off from the blackboard and floated out towards me. Her body shivered as a blast of hot air caught it. I thought I could smell apples and cinnamon but as she drew closer, it smelled like bad breath.

A high-pitched voice ejected me from my sexual Nirvana. 'The—answer—is—what—David?'

My face burned as I realised I was being interrogated. The question however, wasn't what colour were her tights when she removed her leathers? It wasn't how many stripes on her helmet? It wasn't even, who would you like to go out with, the Hairspray ad Girl or Motorcycle Girl?

Mr H's bulging eyes threatened to burn through my retinas into the wood of the desk.

'Well—Cruickshanks?'

I looked up at Mr H and though I was terrified of this boggle-eyed praying mantis with Halitosis, I just couldn't resist the temptation to be funny.

'Is—it 42—sir?'

He poked out his neck at me like a tortoise that's just heard the words "lettuce dead ahead," then he drew himself back to his full height becoming "mantis man" again, lifting up his scraggy vein ridden limb sheathed in a wrinkly white coat before bringing it back down, cracking the desk with the pointer stick.

There was a synchronised thud as everyone's bottoms left their stools before rebounding on the hard wooden surfaces.

'Are—you—trying—to be funny—son?'

Of course I was, I was the class jester. Everyone *expected* me to make them laugh in return for not getting my head kicked in. That was my job. Bullies would "claim me" for a fight just to listen to me wriggle out of it by making them "double up". That was my number one weapon; if that didn't work there was my ability to run fast for hours.

'No sir,' I replied, scratching a newly formed itchy nose.

Mr H, who had obviously never heard of *Hitch Hikers Guide to the Galaxy* and the fact that the answer to Life, the Universe and Everything was indeed 42, screwed up his face as if he had caught the full force of a farting cat. I thought he would devise a singular punishment for me, seeing as how everyone had shit themselves when he cracked the desk, but maybe he was surprised at his effect on the rest of the class and would file it away under "unexpected effects of punitive techniques" to use when the next class came in. He leaned back, as if an invisible wire had saved him from falling over with rage, then folded his arms, his nose wrinkling; perhaps the farting cat smell had lingered.

'Next time pay—attention—boy.'

He turned away, his gangly gait heading back towards the blackboard, then glanced over his bony shoulder as if he expected me to disappear. His raised eyebrow confirmed my suspicions; he *had* expected me to disappear and seemed genuinely pissed off that I was still there. The whole class stared at me as if they too were in on the "teacher makes naughty boy disappear" trick.

I couldn't disappear I so just sat at my desk, a small, red necked, tousled haired, freckle faced joker, with a wet dream.

The next night was the end of the first year's school disco. I cradled my chin and peered at the wiry hairs springing up like weeds on a putting green on my top lip. My dad's razor jutted out of his bright orange plastic shaving cup. I looked down to see a couple of curly black cousins between my shiny white legs. I dipped dad's razor in the water and scythed at the invading fuzz. The ones on my top lip were given a reprieve.

The thumping bass drew me up the school assembly hall steps. Halfway up I froze as I met the narrow eyed gaze of 'Daz', his head cocked to one side like a Rottweiler sizing up a puppy. He put his hand onto the collar of my pink shirt, creasing it with his fingers, stained yellow with surreptitious smoke.

'A bit poofy isn't it?'

'Is it?' I stammered, looking down at his dirty finger nails scrunching my bright pink wing collar. My neck stiffened, still sore from staring at Motorcycle Girl. Daz was still talking; his breath could give Mr H a run for his money. Daz's long nose and tiny black eyes reminded me of Dad's obsession with Sharks on the telly. Maybe Daz had swallowed a shoal of herring. I fantasised about sticking my fingers in his eyes like some brave Australian diver had done with a Great White, or so my dad said. *My* fingers were stuck by the invisible glue of fear to the side of my Bri-Nylon trousers.

'Too right, a widnae be seen dead in it, eh Greig?'

Greig, Daz's reluctant sidekick, who was trying to watch paint dry, looked at me and then shrugged his shoulders; then he looked at Daz who stuck his face against Greig's.

'Aye, Daz, a wee bit poofy ah suppose.'

'There ye are, even Greig says so."

I turned and headed back down the stairs. At the school gates I broke into a run, reaching my own back door in four minutes flat.

'Is that you David?' My mum called up the stairs.

'Yip'

'I thought you were at the disco.'

'I forgot something.'

'What?'

'Nothing, I'm away now, see you.'

'Don't be too late and mind; enjoy….'

My mum's words trailed after me in the darkness but I out ran them.

The school assembly hall, a draughty shell by day, where rows of silent stone faced uniformed kids listened to dried-out teachers telling them how important it was to do well at school, was now an ocean of glowing faces flashing orange, blue, green and purple. Tentacles of hair floated in the flashing lights, hips wriggled like tickled jellyfish, feet flipped intricate patterns on the parquet floor. Bright eyed girls shoaled and shimmied, their shiny dresses catching the light like silver darlings.

I looked up and a girl smiled at me, she actually bloody smiled. I glanced behind me in case it had been a mistake, as I turned back she thrust out a hand and grabbed me, sucking me into the depths of the dance floor. All the girls that pervaded my waking thoughts and unconscious dreams danced around me. I nearly tripped over a handbag but caught my balance. The girls giggled, their kaleidoscopic faces drew me to them like bubbles to the surface. The music drowned out their gossip as they cupped hands over ears, then drew back, laughing. A tall slim girl with shiny black hair and eyes like a Siamese, held her palms up in a motion, which I translated as *dance here*. Her long Aquamarine silk dress clung on as she shimmered, tossing her hair up and down like a cork in a storm. I stood transfixed in my yellow shirt, having dumped my 'poofy pink' effort on the bathroom floor. I started to move my feet; the effect was like a statue coming to life inside a museum as the clock struck midnight. The girl with the cat's eyes laughed but I didn't care. My feet felt the rhythm and I had watched Michael Jackson's *Thriller* video twenty times in one go; after all, your face could only stay red for so long and in this light nobody would know *what* colour it was. After a few minutes the girls were forming a circle around me; my hips were giving Elvis a run for his money, and I was moonwalking better than Neil Armstrong. The girls started to whoop and squeal. I had scattered their bags around the floor, but they were oblivious. I was possessed by the music, lifting my head up to gauge their reactions to my new dance moves. One or two of the girls pointed to my feet and laughed. I couldn't care less if they were taking the mickey. Then, some of the girls moved back; a few boys had decided to see what the commotion was. Daz was standing amongst them, his arms folded. He was laughing, and then jabbing at the shoulder of one of the girls in the circle—mocking, like only bullies can. But the girl moved and came closer to me. She started to dance with me, she was so close I could smell her hair; it mixed with my sweat, forming a deliciously heady cocktail. I closed my eyes and drank it all in.

When I opened them I saw Motorcycle Girl looking straight at me. This time I didn't look over my shoulder. It burned the back of my neck but I forced myself to look back at her. Sweat began to trickle down my forehead; my shirt was sticking to the small of my back. I smiled; her face was closer now, she smelled of bubblegum and candyfloss. Fantastic! A girl that smelled like a sweetie shop.

She pulled me close to her and slinked her warm arms around the back of my blood red neck, nestling her nose under my bum-fluffed chin. I almost pulled away, my heaving chest pressed against her satin dress, my face burning again. The music had softened. The frantic disco lights, their bulbs now cooling down to the encroaching darkness, cocooned us together in the gloom.

Feeling brave in the darkness I lifted up my smooth shiny chin, turning my head an inch, then a few inches more. The parquet floor was a jungle of entangled black bodies, swaying, holding onto each other like dancers on a ship's deck.

As I inched my head around to get a better look, my lips brushed something wet soft and warm. I opened my eyes. Motorcycle Girl's lips were pressed against mine. I prayed that my hairy top lip wouldn't tickle her, then snapped my eyes shut and concentrated. Now I *knew* what two limpets shagging felt like.

Ten; eleven; twelve seconds as her warm breath filled me up, her lips seemed to be searching for something underneath mine, chewing gum maybe. As far as I was concerned she could look forever. Our necks made little circles. I held on, the music faded and I thought that was it. Death could come anytime now, things were never going to get any better than this. I tried to break away, but another slow record started up. She pulled me back towards her and searched for my neck again with her soft warm nose.

I had a peek out again; I just had to have a look around the dance floor, in case this was to be the best dream I would ever have. Bodies were still draped over each other. I caught the shape of a grey shirt skulking on those jaggy wooden chairs that kill your bum in ten minutes. There he was, Daz, leaning forward, elbows resting on his thighs, a knuckled hand strangling a can of Coke wedged under his spotty chin. His eyes were attempting to climb inside his eyebrows, while scanning the sea of dancers. His other hand picked at a jaundiced tooth with a finger that had been up his nose more than once. I turned quickly back in case he caught me looking. Motorcycle Girl took this as a signal and fastened her lips back onto me. This time her tongue probed between my teeth before letting itself in. I slumped against her sweating silky body and tried to ignore my rousing rush of blood pressed against her warm belly.

'So ye think yer Michael Jackson dae ye?'

I opened my eyes; Motorcycle girl had another head sticking out of hers. Daz's head. I pulled away from my warm soft embrace and felt a familiar bony finger digging into my collarbone. A large black stain on his shirt signalled a battle lost with a can of coke. Now he was looking for payback.

'Naw' was all I could muster; my tongue was numb after exploring every molar, incisor and bicuspid of Motorcycle Girl's beautiful mouth.

'Ah'll see you the morra, yer're claimed!'

And with those two words clanging in my ears, he turned and was gone.

'Just ignore him David, he's an arsehole.'

Motorcycle Girl had called me by my first name; she actually knew who I was. This was my chance to talk to a girl that I actually fancied and who might even fancy me, but Daz had dried up my patter. Fear of tomorrow had struck me mute.

'Am away hame, see ye.'

I couldn't even look at her.

In three minutes fifty two seconds and with only one shoe, I turned the key of my front door. I wiped my eyes and dragged the oyster-like snotters away from my top lip.

'Well did ye have a good time son?'

I sat in my jammies, hugging a mug of cocoa, as some toast cooled on the coffee table. The telly mooned at me from the corner, causing mum's face to flicker.

'No bad'

'Yer face is a wee bit red, is it cold outside?'

'No really.'

'Whit happened tae yer shoe? Yer sock's soakin.'

'Dinnae worry, I'll find it tomorrow.'

'Yer sure yer alright?'

'Mum, jist leave me the now will ye?'

'Right, I'll see ye in the morning son, mind and pull aw the plugs out.'

'Night.'

She was gone in a melange of creaking stair, toilet flush and squealing door.

I turned the telly over and there she was: Hairspray Girl, her head thrust back by invisible reins, her eyes closed, mouth slightly parted, poised for kissing just like my Motorcycle Girl. I touched the collar of my shirt and rubbed it. I could still smell her. A tear fell into my cocoa cup, landing on the wrinkled chocolate skin. It was then I had an idea. I pulled the plug from the telly and thought about Daz.

The school hall smelled of yesterday's custard, floor polish and treacherous cigarettes. It took me nine minutes to arrive at the entrance from my house, a puddle of mud spewed from my shoe, which had shrunk from hypothermia. I looked up at the clock: 8.57 am. The bell would be going soon. Double maths, what could be worse? Then I felt fetid hot breath on the back of my neck.

'Surprise surprise, look who it isnae.'

I turned to see Daz, flanked by Greig and "Baldy" Nicoll. I had made "Baldy" helpless with laughter many times, so I had never felt his scuffed shoe leather on my face. But his granite clad fizzog froze in a look that said 'I am only following orders; nothing personal wee man.'

Someone had replaced my stomach with the waltzers and my heart was banging on my chest demanding to be let out. I must have looked like the Scarecrow, Tin Man and the Lion rolled into one.

'A don't see ye dancin' noo, ya wee poof.'

My mouth was still dry from last night. I felt my chest tighten and I braced myself for a fist, but Daz liked to string it out, a bit like the baddies in James Bond films. Their fatal flaw was always to tell Bond how they were going to kill him, when they were going to kill him and what they were going to kill him with. By that time Bond had undone the rope, disarmed a platoon of baddies, shagged the token female and drunk three Vodka Martinis without breaking sweat. I gripped my hand around the canister in my trouser pocket, popping the pink plastic top.

'Ah'm gonnae wipe that smirk aff yer ugly wee kisser Cruickshanks, so the lassies are no gonnae be looking at you fur a while.'

'If ever,' Baldy's Granite fizzog chipped in.

I sneaked the canister out of my pocket, holding it behind my back while Daz did his Blofeld impersonation.

'And when ah'm finished wae ye Greig's gonnae ...'

I let him have it.

Pow!

'... agh whit wiz that? Ah ma eyes ah cannae see, jesus ah cannae see!'

I turned the hairspray onto Baldy but he backed off. Greig had grabbed Daz, who was shaking like a man in the electric chair, tears streaming down his face. Peering through little piggy eyes, he broke free of Greig, his hands grabbing my throat and squeezing hard.

'You're gonnae die ya little shite.'

There he goes again, tellin' me what he's going to do to me. I felt the blood thrumming in my brain, then nausea came before the stars began to twinkle as his grip tightened. Maybe I was going to die after all.

'Ugh.'

Daz dropped to the floor; this time he moaned and whimpered. His hands clutched at his crotch and his purple face glazed over. The bell clanged just as his nose got intimate with the smell of floor polish. Greig was off and running, throwing in the towel. Baldy just turned and walked away, shaking his head.

The second sense to return to my brain caught a whiff of bubblegum and two stroke Castrol. I turned to see Motorcycle Girl standing, her helmet glinting in the morning sun. A Harley Davidson biker boot had done the damage to Daz. Motorcycle Girl took my hand.

'Are you all right David?'

It was the way she said it; it came out like *voulez vous couches avec moi*?

'Aye, thanks. Em, eh ah cannae mind yer name, sorry'

'Frances, you know your kissing partner for all of last night, the one who lost his glass shoe running away.'

I was about to say something witty when the Praying Mantis appeared. He hunched over Daz whose face had gone from purple to lilac.

'What's going on here?'

'Ugh, mmmm,' moaned Daz.

Frances answered for him, hands on hips; all she needed was a Wonderwoman costume.

'Sir, David stuck up for me when this boy tried to steal my bike helmet. That's all.'

'Is that right, Cruickshanks?'

'Em, yes sir,' was all I could manage, still waiting for my brain to register. Oxygen was on its way again.

'Well done son. I hope you can continue this vigilance in our next class, and you—Darren—Edwards, get yourself along to the Rector's office.

'Ugh'

'Get a move on son, that'll teach you to pick on a girl.'

Daz pulled himself up and shuffled off to the Headmaster's. 'H' stalked off to scrutinise a puff of smoke coming from the bike sheds.

'Thanks Frances; my god where did ye learn that from?'

'Karate Kid 2,' she smiled at me. I looked at her and felt the familiar rush of blood to my neck. This soppy stuff was harder to do in daylight, but I was determined not to bottle it. I took a deep breath.

'The dance was good eh?' I mustered.

'David?'

I braced myself for the line that goes: "It was only a bit of fun, it didnae mean anything, in fact I did it fur a bet. All the lassies bet me that I wouldnae kiss a scrawny we turd like you in fact...."

'David?'

'Sorry, whit were you sayin?'

'I've got a spare helmet. I'll drop ye off tonight and then we can go bowling if ye like.'

I beamed back at her; butterflies and the rest of the insect population had a party in my stomach. I checked that I wasn't still in my pyjamas, that this feeling wasn't a dream. I looked straight into her eyes, her smile was like an invisible force drawing me to her. I was putty but I couldn't resist a one liner. I let out a big sigh and folded my arms.

'Well, I don't know Frances, ye see Friday's my night fur washin' ma hair.'

THE EXCLUSIVE

By William Armstrong

'... in your own words,' I said carefully. First rule in police interviewing. Let the suspect talk.

'Well, when I opened my eyes there he was, in that damned rubber suit, just where you are now. It gave me quite a turn. I mean ... when you've spent years steering clear of humans, you don't expect one of them to turn up in your lair at the bottom of Loch Ness. However, I tried to be civil.'

'Who are you?' I said. After all, it is my lair.

'I'm a reporter,' he says, bold as brass, 'and I was hoping you'd give me an interview.'

'I'll have to think about that,' I said cautiously. 'What's in it for me?'

'What do you mean?' he queried.

'You surely don't think I'm giving an interview for nothing. Oh no. The seagulls tell me that celebrities make millions from their stories. Awful well read the gulls are, you know. It's all those newspapers lying about. Who do you work for anyway?'

'I'm a freelance,' he says, 'and an exclusive from you would really kick-start my career.' These newspaper chaps talk awful funny.

'So, you're going to make a name for yourself at my expense are you?' says I.

'Well,' he said quickly, 'we could come to some arrangement. What had you in mind?'

'Ach, nothing much,' I replied. 'Some fish maybe. Oh, and two or three sheep.'

'Sheep!' says he, looking startled. 'I didn't think you ate meat.' He edged back slightly.

'Oh aye, there's nothing like a nice piece of mutton. Of course after the 1933 sighting, when that couple in their car saw me crossing the road with a sheep in my mouth, I've had to be a lot more careful. Ach, I wish the motorcar had never been invented. In the old days I could come up for a breath of fresh air and nobody noticed. Well, fishermen sometimes, but who believes fishermen anyway? Nowadays I've only got to show my back and traffic on the A82 comes to a stand-still. On top of that there's the teams with their tracking devices. They never seem to think that all these electrical gadgets give me a headache. Then you have the tourists with their video cameras. They're everywhere. A monster is entitled to some privacy you know, just like everybody else.'

He nodded. 'I see what you mean,' he said. 'Supposing I had a word with the Highlands and Islands people. They might come up with something.'

'I should hope so,' I said, sharply. 'After all, I am THE Loch Ness Monster. I've kept the tourist trade going for years. Oh, just the odd appearance you know, but by jove it does wonders for the local economy.'

'Are you the only one?' says he, scribbling away like mad.

'In Loch Ness? Aye. Mind you, there are still a few of us scattered about the world. I've a cousin in Loch Morar, but I haven't heard from Morag in years.'

'Did you ever have a mate?' says he.

'I wondered when you'd get onto that subject,' I snapped. 'Yes I did. He was a Norwegian monster. Lived up in one of these fjords. Rolfe, his name was. His family had died out, just like mine, and he came across looking for a bit of company.'

'And did you …?'

'You mean, were we an item? Indeed we were and I must admit it was nice to have a male in the loch.'

'Any family?'

'My,' says I, 'aren't you the nosey one. Aye, we had three. Lars, Rory and Fiona. Fine youngsters they were too.'

He looked at me curiously. 'What happened to them?'

'Ach, it was Rolfe's fault really. Said the loch was too quiet, so he did. Anyway, he went off to Norway for a visit and never came back. I still hear from him occasionally. So there I was, on my own, with a family to raise. Of course, once they were older they left home. You know what youngsters are like nowadays.'

'Where did they go?' says he.

'Well now; Lars and Rory went off on a round the world trip. The last I heard of them, through the seabirds, was that they were going to explore the Marianas Trench. You know, that awful deep bit in the Pacific, just off the Philippines.'

'And Fiona?'

'I was coming to her.' I said shortly. 'She went south to the Antarctic. Fair taken with the place she was. Decided to stay there. Oh, she keeps sending word that she'll come home for a visit, but she never does. Aye, aye.'

'Well,' he said, putting away his pad and zipping up his rubber suit. 'I think that'll do for a start. Later we might even have a regular column. We could call it Nessie's Newsletter.'

'I'd like that,' says I. 'Mind how you go in the tunnel.'

'Oh, I will,' he said. 'I've finally got an exclusive.' Then he waved and went off. That was the last I saw of him … alive.'

I pondered for a moment. There was a ring of truth in the rambling statement. Still … 'He never surfaced,' I said pointedly.

The monster hesitated. 'Well you see, it was all a terrible mistake. Fiona came back, just as he was leaving. She thought he was a seal. It seems she'd got very partial to seal meat down south.'

'You mean …' I said slowly.

'Aye. It took two days to get the rubber out of her teeth! Then I sent her packing. "You've brought shame on this family," I said. 'Oh, she'll be well on her way to Antarctica by now.'

'So what do I tell them up top?'

'Accidental death would be best I think. Now, if you'll excuse me; I've a lot to do. I'm leaving for Norway shortly. It's time Rolfe and I had a reconciliation. Besides, they couldn't extradite a monster … could they?'

THE PAGODA

By Robert Kirk

'What's wrong, Mum?' asked Jenny as Mrs Thomson gently replaced the telephone on its rest.

Jenny's mother said nothing, just stood looking at her daughter while her chin trembled and her eyes filled with tears. Then she dropped to her knees and pulled Jenny into her arms. 'Oh Jenny,' she sobbed. 'Your gran's gone.'

Jenny's mind pretended not to understand, but her heart seemed to know. She felt a sadness there. It was a bit like last Christmas when she'd swallowed her pudding too quickly and it stuck half-way down. Only, this time, it was a cold feeling.

'Gone, Mum? Gone where?' As she said it, she swallowed, blinking away tears that stung the corners of her eyes. 'What's happened?' she whispered. 'What's wrong with Gran?'

Her mother took a deep shivering breath and held Jenny away from her. Her heart leapt, as it always did, when she saw how pretty her daughter was. Almost ten now, Jenny was a bright, talkative child. She was small for her age, but as several had discovered to their cost, she would let no one bully her.

She's so much like her gran, thought Mrs Thomson, with her mousy brown hair, her determined chin. She brushed a rat's tail away from Jenny's eyes and felt sorrow well up in her again. Everyone said that Jenny had her grandmother's hazel eyes.

'Why are you sad, Mum?' Jenny asked.

'I'm sorry, pet. Your gran has died.'

And her mother began to cry again. This time though, she sobbed loudly and huge wet tears ran quickly down her cheeks. She pulled Jenny to her and Jenny stayed there while her mother patted her gently on the back.

Over the next few days, Jenny began to feel better. Her mother had assured her that Gran would be in heaven by now, chatting to the angels. Jenny had formed a picture of what that would be like and imagined her gran walking round the living room table, topping up everyone's cup from her huge porcelain teapot that had a duck's bill for a spout. All the angels would have a big slice of chocolate cake on their plate and a smile on their face.

After the funeral on the Wednesday, her mother came into Jenny's room carrying a small black and gold box.

'Jenny,' she said. 'This belonged to your gran, and I know she wanted you to have it.'

Jenny took the small cardboard box from her mother and opened it. 'Oh! It's the pagoda,' she breathed excitedly.

The pagoda had been one of gran's favourite things. It was a glass case about twelve centimetres tall. And inside was a little Chinese temple. From the temple, a bridge arched over a stream to another island, and on the bridge, stood the figure of a Chinese girl with a beautiful red apple in her outstretched hand, as if she was offering it to someone. The girl's dress was gold and she carried a red parasol. Everything else in the scene was unpainted, left in plain brown. Because everything in the case, including the Chinese girl, had been carved from cork.

Jenny treasured the pagoda and kept it by her bed where she could watch it. She made up little stories about the tiny oriental girl; who she was; why she stood on the bridge; and to whom she offered the apple.

She must be a princess, Jenny thought. And her cruel stepfather is keeping her prisoner on the two little islands linked by the bridge. Or perhaps she hoped the apple would tempt some large, beautiful bird. When the bird bit the apple it would turn into a handsome prince who had been under a witch's spell.

Jenny often peeked into the little cork temple. She peered closely at the small building whose roof turned up at the corners, hoping to see some furniture or even people inside. Somehow, she never could.

The part of the ornament she loved most was the Chinese girl's shoes. They were blue high-heeled slippers, exactly what Jenny wanted for her birthday party next week. She knew her mother couldn't afford to buy them for her. Still ... maybe ...

It was two days after the funeral that Jenny had a strange dream. She dreamed that she had shrunk to the same size as the oriental figure and was standing on the outside of the glass case. The tiny Chinese girl had come to life and was calling to her; 'Please let me out! Please help me!'

Then she turned back to cork and Jenny drifted into another dream.

But Jenny remembered the dream and it disturbed her all the next day. Every so often she would go upstairs and look at the Chinese girl, but every time she looked, all she saw was a cork figure on a cork bridge. Real though the vision had seemed, Jenny eventually resigned herself to the fact that it had been no more than a dream.

Now it was only two days before her birthday and Jenny took a long time to fall asleep, she was so excited. But when she did, the dream of the little Chinese girl in the pagoda came to her stronger than ever. And this time, instead of drifting away into some other, happier thoughts, she awoke and lay there in her darkened room. She turned her head and saw the little pagoda, bathed in a soft beam of moonlight that slid past the edge of her curtain. Then an idea came into her head. If she could get closer to the little cork figure on the little cork bridge, maybe, just maybe, she could speak to her. Ask her why she was imprisoned there. Perhaps there was something that she, Jenny, could do to help her.

Moving slowly so as not to waken her parents, Jenny slid out of bed and turned on her bedside lamp that had a picture of Sleeping Beauty on the shade. She eased open her dressing table drawer and found the zipped-up pouch that contained the manicure set she'd got from Aunty Sharon last Christmas. She tucked her hair behind her ear, and using the edge of her nail file, she twisted off the lid of the glass case.

It opened with a popping sound and the air filled with musty smelling dust.

Her heart in her mouth, Jenny reached trembling fingers inside and touched the small cork girl.

She was dry and hard.

Well, what did you expect? Jenny thought as her heart plunged to the bottom of her chest. She is made of cork, isn't she?

She carefully replaced the glass lid and pressed it into place.

The night before her birthday, the dream came again and Jenny tossed and turned all night. Two or three times she woke up and switched on her bedside lamp to study the pagoda. But each time she saw that the little figure was only cork and lay down to sleep again.

In the morning she opened her eyes and waited while the room drifted into focus. She rubbed her eyelids to remove the stickiness and looked at the pagoda. She wasn't sure what it was, but something was different.

Then she looked closer and gasped. The Chinese girl had gone. Jenny lifted the glass case and shook it; turned it upside down in case the tiny figure had broken off and rolled into a corner somewhere. But finally she was certain. No one stood on the bridge. The little cork girl had vanished without a trace.

Jenny jumped out of bed with the intention of telling her mother what had happened. Then she stopped, excitement rising in her chest. There, on the floor, was an apple; a bright red gleaming apple! That certainly wasn't there last night, she thought. Her heart seemed to have moved into her throat, so loudly did it thump in her ears. She bent and picked up the apple. It was a strange apple, so round and so red. It was exactly how an apple should be, except it was so very light and there was a curious, jagged split on one side.

Without thinking, Jenny lifted it to her mouth and took a huge bite.

'Phew!' She spluttered and spat the mouthful out again, rushing to the bathroom for a drink of water.

The apple was made of cork.

Disgusted with herself, and angry that she'd been taken in by a make-believe apple, Jenny started downstairs. This particular apple was going straight in the bin.

Then she saw the slippers.

They were blue and beautiful, and stood together at the top of the stairs, as if inviting her to step into them. Jenny stood, balanced on one foot and stared suspiciously at the slippers. They didn't look like cork. But then, neither had the apple. She stretched out a toe and nudged them. They felt heavy, real … not at all like cork.

Okay, she thought. I'll risk it. And sitting on the top step, she pulled on the slippers.

They *were* real.

She rushed back to her room and twirled in front of the mirror. Oh, they were fabulous. And a perfect fit. Downstairs she hugged her mother and father who wore big smiles, telling them how happy she was and how much she loved her birthday present.

That night, preparing for her party, Jenny dressed in her best clothes, pinned up her hair and put on her favourite bracelets and pendant. Not until the very last minute did she step into her beautiful blue slippers.

She greeted the guests as they arrived, hugging each one and pretending not to be too excited about the presents they brought.

Then her mother called to her. 'Jenny. Come and meet someone. You have a surprise guest!'

A surprise guest? Who could it be?

Jenny skipped out to the front door then stopped with her mouth open, her eyes wide. Her parents were chatting to Mr and Mrs Parsons from next door. And standing shyly beside them was a little girl. She wore a shimmering gold party frock that was even prettier than Jenny's and her black, shining hair was pulled back into a ponytail. On her feet, she wore blue, high-heeled slippers, just like Jenny's. But there was one thing really special about the girl that made Jenny gasp in wonder.

She was Chinese!

'Jenny,' her mother said, 'this is Lin Chu. She's come to live with Mr and Mrs Parsons.'

'Hello,' said Jenny nervously. 'Do you want to come in?' All of a sudden her nervousness disappeared. 'We're just about to start Pass The Parcel. And later on we're going to have jelly and fruit and dad's going to play some music and we'll be having games and ...' Jenny realised she was talking too much again. But this time her mother didn't scold her, just smiled.

When the children were safely out of earshot, Jenny's mother said, 'You were telling me about Lin Chu, Mrs Parsons.'

'Yes, so I was.' She took her husband's hand and squeezed it. 'Her parents were killed in those awful floods that swept China a few years ago.'

Jenny's mother nodded.

'We found her in an orphanage out there,' Mrs Parson went on. 'Nobody wanted her. She was so thin and ...' Mrs Parson's eyes began to fill.

'That's right,' Mr Parsons said, slipping his arm around his wife's shoulders. 'But that's all over. She's our little girl now; we've adopted her.'

Inside, the party was a merry affair. After pass the parcel, they played Musical Chairs and The Grand Old Duke of York. But, no matter what game they played, Jenny's eyes strayed again and again to where her presents lay in the corner. One present sat slightly apart from the others. A very special gift, the one given to her by Lin Chu.

It was a glass pagoda! And on the little cork bridge that arched between the two cork islands, stood a little cork princess and a little cork prince.

Absence makes the heart grow fonder

By Anne Ewing

Grace's immediate reaction had been one of stunned incredulity. He surely couldn't be serious! Could he? Further explanation on his part made it abundantly clear that he meant every word of his dramatic declaration: 'I'm going to have a gap year when I retire!' A gap year? A year out of his—and more to the point—her life? Surely gap years were for young people trying to 'find themselves', travelling the world before settling down to serious reality. Her initial response of, 'Don't be ridiculous, you're nearly sixty-five years old!' remained unspoken in the face of his barely concealed excitement and obvious enthusiasm.

On reflection later, she realised that it was a long time since she had heard that tenor in his voice or seen that gleam in his eyes. And it soon became clear that this was not something she could just shrug off as a passing fancy on his part. His plans were advanced to the point where his application to Voluntary Service Overseas had been accepted and his date of departure was even decided, exactly one month after he was due to retire from work in August, giving him just enough time to make final preparations for his great adventure. He explained that V.S.O. was no longer designed for school leavers or new graduates, but the preferred candidates were those people at the other end of their working lives who could bring a lifetime of experience to contribute to projects in the developing world.

She privately felt quite hurt that he had kept his plans secret from her. Could it be that he didn't particularly care what she thought of his ambition, or that the short time span of only weeks would make it hard for her to affect the *fait accompli* he presented her with? She had to admit to herself, in her typically rational way, that they had increasingly lived separate lives over the last years of their marriage, especially since the children had left the nest and they had both reverted to a single-minded approach to their work. Even their social lives tended to move along parallel lines, converging only at the occasional dinner-party with long-standing friends, the holidays they habitually went on twice a year, or family occasions which had become less and less frequent as the older generation died off and the younger one led lives increasingly independent and geographically distant from their parents.

Her acceptance of his decision was taken for granted, not only by her husband but by their friends, who were unanimously impressed with what they saw as an altruistic and laudable intention.

'How wonderful to be able to put his wide experience to such a worthwhile cause!'

'A great way to round off a successful career!'

'You must be so proud of Tom!'

'Don't you wish you could go with him, Grace?'

So she felt it would be seen as churlish at best and disloyal at worst, if she were to show anything but whole-hearted approval of Tom's impending departure for the 'dark continent'. He had signed a one year contract with an option to extend beyond that, to help build a dam to generate electricity and ensure water supplies in Murawi, a former British dependency in Africa. This was a country with a fledgling democracy and faltering economy, whose name had previously barely impinged on her consciousness before her husband's shattering announcement had sent her scurrying for the atlas!

Tom's momentous decision was entirely out of character. Until then, his—and indeed her—life had followed very conventional paths. They were both only children, he the son of an eminent advocate, she the daughter of a successful surgeon. While there may have been a hint of disappointment from their fathers when they chose engineering and general practice respectively, ultimately they were gratified when their offspring became very successful in their careers, and equally satisfied with their choice of each other as life partners. Neither of their mothers had ever worked after marriage, and were less concerned with their children's careers, but nevertheless quietly proud of their achievements and those of their grandchildren. Privately, Grace's mother was delighted that her daughter was on equal terms with Tom in earning power and independence. Both sets of grandparents had enjoyed a sense of a job well done and the future in safe hands when they all four died within three years of each other, causing their families none of the angst or difficulty that can so often come when parents reach old age, and leaving their children and grandchildren very well provided for.

Meanwhile, Grace and Tom's children were also suitably compliant and co-operative as they grew up. Schooling at one of Edinburgh's most venerable private schools, followed by good degrees at Oxbridge assured them of success in their futures. As it turned out, their son George was now working as a meteorologist in charge of one of the teams studying climate change in the Antarctic, of all places. It was felt that he was destined for great things, as his return from the ice-face would no doubt coincide with the government's and media's belated but fervent pre-occupation with global warming reaching fever-pitch, when he expected that his expertise would be in great demand. He was often on his parents' radar, but they were seldom on his.

Their daughter Jane had followed in her grandfather's footsteps in studying law, but had married soon after graduation and had never actually worked. Her husband, considerably older than her, was an important cog in the machinery of the Council of Europe in Brussels, where they lived a luxurious lifestyle with their burgeoning family of four, and one more on the way! They saw her only occasionally as time would allow, but Tom and Grace had brought up their children to be confident in themselves and comfortable in any company. They had shown them much of the world and encouraged them to avail themselves of whatever opportunity came along, so they could hardly be surprised that they were both far away and in less and less need of, or contact with, their parents. In those rare moments when they missed their boy and girl and longed to be with them, they might also have reassured each other of this, had they ever been able to admit to such feelings. But, as they couldn't or wouldn't, one more emotional tie that had held them together was lost as they drifted inexorably further and further apart.

Tom and Grace were very much part of the Edinburgh establishment. He worked for one of the oldest engineering companies in Scotland as a design engineer, and counted some of the most high-profile projects in Scotland amongst his achievements. Fortunately, as it turned out, almost the only hiccup in his career had been the failure of his team to secure any part in the design and building of the new Scottish Parliament. Having thus happily avoided that particular fiasco, his firm went on from strength to strength and were being favourably considered by the right political and business connections in the capital for the forthcoming construction of the new crossing over the Firth of Forth.

It had been something of a disappointment to him when he realised that his impending retirement would rule out any involvement for him with such an exciting prospect, and perhaps that was one reason why his mind turned to a new project of his own. For a long time, he had regretted that his career had never involved a more hands-on approach to engineering. His hard-hat had only ever been worn with a smart suit, shirt and tie and shiny shoes on site visits. Never since his earliest days as a student or newly qualified engineer had he ever been able to wear a donkey jacket, get his boots muddy or his hands dirty on the job. If the truth be told, Tom had always felt like a bit of a fraud, claiming to be an engineer, but only really involved with the conception of an idea, hardly at all with its gestation and only ever in at the birth as an invited guest. On these occasions when foundation stones were laid, buildings topped out or bridges and roads officially opened, he would often glimpse eager young engineers, surveyors and labourers in the watching work-force who had clearly been far more involved in the job, and could feel more justified pride in its completion than he ever had. Even his design skills were utilised less and less as he was increasingly involved in management, and the public relations and financial aspects of running the company. He was like a father who helped to conceive a child but didn't see it born and never helped to bring it up. So he looked forward to being associated with a job from the beginning to the end, to see it through and feel it was part of him and his efforts.

If he was more than ready mentally to embark on a fundamental change of direction, Tom was also physically very fit for a man of his age. Weekly golf and tennis matches, in addition to getting maximum benefit from his membership of an exclusive health club had all helped to keep him in trim and there was little or no evidence of the regular business lunches and formal dinners that he had attended over the years. Grace couldn't help but notice in the month leading up to his retirement, a new spring in his step and when they attended his presentation dinner he cut an elegant figure in his evening suit and was the epitome of good humour and affability as he made a witty and well-received farewell speech to his colleagues. She could see that Tom had clearly resolved any lingering regrets about the end of his career because he had new horizons to set out for, and as the remaining four weeks sped by, Grace began to feel that he couldn't get away fast enough.

It was hard for her to understand how Tom could leave his work behind with hardly a backward glance, because the prospect of retirement was to her an alarming and dreaded one. Eight years younger than Tom, Grace comforted herself with the thought that there was still time left before she would have to confront the issue. As the senior partner in a well set up health centre in a fashionable area of west Edinburgh, she acted as gate-keeper to private specialist medical care for many of her patients, and for their more mundane ailments, had initiated programmes of preventive health care and offered a wide variety of minor surgical procedures, alternative and complementary medical services. These were held up in the world of general practice as a shining example of what could be achieved, much to the annoyance of other group practices in the city, struggling with the mental and physical ill-health of patients who were dogged by poverty, addiction of various kinds and the worst effects of the general malaise and depression that accompanies social deprivation. It had been many years since the health issues that so often accompany physical and financial hardship, compounded by poor education had affected her, and she was blissfully complacent about her highly privileged medical environment.

Grace was also unaware that she had become the kind of boss so resented by her when, as a young G.P., she struggled to look after her family and run a home in addition to coping with the demands of her job. The significance of barely suppressed sighs and exasperated reactions whenever she suggested changes and developments that were guaranteed to add to the workload of the more junior doctors, nurses and ancillary staff at her health centre, failed to register with her. As she no longer had the care of her own family to occupy her mind, and she and Tom shared less and less of their lives, she became narrowly focussed on work and increasingly unable to see the effects this was having on her personal and work relationships. Dr Grace Lawrie was no longer the popular and well-respected colleague she had once been, and even more seriously, had become an increasingly detached wife, mother and friend.

Having very little interest in anything but work, she was failing as a human being and barely succeeding as a doctor in any of the ways that really mattered. Her accountants and primary care trust were more than satisfied, but her more vulnerable patients and immediate colleagues were feeling increasingly frustrated and disappointed in her. Because she was totally blind to how she had changed, it came as even more of a shock when her husband of nearly forty years announced his intention of leaving her in favour of an engineering project in a far off country, the future of whose people he would appear to be more concerned with, than that of his own nearest and dearest!

She suspected in her heart of hearts that it was a long time since she had been either near or dear to Tom, or, to be fair, he to her. Material and professional ambition and success and the power to influence almost everything that happened in and around their lives, had gradually but surely blinded them to the things that really mattered. Despite her misgivings, unspoken and barely acknowledged even to herself, years of self-control and training came to her aid. As Grace recovered from the initial shock of Tom's decision and had time to rationalise the situation, she saw that there was nothing to be done but accept it, and she threw herself into helping him to make the final plans for his departure: shopping for suitable clothing and gear for his new life, inoculations and health and travel insurance, familiarising herself with all the household finances and paperwork that Tom had always dealt with, took up most of their time. He was certainly anxious to ensure that she would manage without him in a practical sense, but they never once broached the real essence of what being apart for such a long time would mean.

It was only on the morning of his leaving that the full implications of his impending absence suddenly dawned on her for the first time. After a night of little or no sleep, by five o'clock Grace had become consumed with a certainty that she had to do something to stop this imminent madness from consuming them both. As Tom slept peacefully beside her, she came to the decision that she would simply tell him he couldn't go. It was utterly preposterous that things had gone so far. How dare he think that he could abandon her and embark on such a risky and dubious venture? He was going to the back of beyond and would have to be self-sufficient, in terms of his daily needs. For the last forty years—indeed for most of his life—he had been looked after: he never had to think about what he was going to eat, or how he was going to have clean clothes to wear. There would be no one to see to all that where he was going, not in the way she had for their entire married life. He had always lived in a safe and clean environment, with expert medical advice on hand whenever he needed it. The best travel insurance would be of no use in a place where even the most basic amenities were lacking.

But as he continued to snore gently, Grace knew what she was really feeling: It wasn't that she was worried that he wouldn't manage without her, it was that she couldn't bear to face living without him. As she lay there trying to control the rising panic she felt, she knew that she could never tell him how she was feeling, so she resisted the impulse to wake him and instead told herself not to be such a wimp, and to pull herself together. By the time Tom woke she was once again a model of self-control and brisk efficiency as she oversaw Tom's last minute preparations. It was with a sense of relief that they left for the airport and she was grateful for the fact that Tom had insisted on the minimum of fuss, forbidding anyone else to come to see him off. As they said goodbye, Grace felt herself begin to weaken and longed to cling to Tom and beg him to change his mind, but with a supreme effort, she was able to hold everything together as they kissed and hugged briefly and then he was gone through the departure gate with one last cheery wave, before walking smartly away with what seemed to be an anticipatory eagerness in his stride.

Somehow she made it back to her car and automatically went through the business of paying the parking fee and negotiating her way to the exit. But as she left the airport behind, Grace found that she was trembling in every limb and felt powerless to continue driving. She stopped in the first lay-by on her way back into the city and sat there for what seemed a very long time as she struggled to gain control of herself. Arriving home at last, she aimlessly wandered through the echoing, empty rooms of her home. It was elegant and well cared for: some very good antiques from their parents' homes sat well with expensive modern furniture of the latest design, thanks to her undoubted good taste and an eye for colour and texture.

But despite the enormous pleasure she had always derived from her home, Grace now felt like a stranger and the house like a stage-set without actors, or a sterile picture in a magazine: an empty shell, certainly not a home in the true sense of the word, and she felt alienated from everything around her. Even those personal touches that were in evidence seemed artificially posed, one or two family photographs only, and always in frames that toned with the overall ambience of the room, house plants and flowers chosen for their shade and shape to complement the décor of their surroundings, paintings, originals, of course, but of no personal significance to their owners, rather than the much loved but valueless prints they had started off with in their first home.

What the house lacked—perhaps the only thing it lacked—was the feeling of warmth that comes from the essence of life being lived there, the echo of laughter and loud voices, raised in mirth, love or even anger. But instead, this house seemed redolent of empty lives lived with mutual indifference. It seemed to her to be devoid even of memories: the children had grown up in an earlier home, so there was no possibility of recalling their childlike or youthful presence in the rooms she walked through. Eventually, overcome with a sense of utter exhaustion, the result of her lack of sleep and the emotional stress of the day, she lay down on her bed, pulled the duvet over her and fell into a deep and dreamless slumber.

Later, looking back on that Sunday, Grace felt a sense of embarrassment that she could have been so weak and self-pitying. She remembered how much of a struggle it had been the following morning, as she forced herself to re-establish her usual routine in getting ready for work, so that when she arrived at the health centre she presented her customary efficient and cheerful face to the world. She gave a brief thought to Tom and vaguely wondered how his journey was going, but firmly pushed away any thoughts of missing him. As the day progressed, her panic of the day before began to fade and her impulse to beg him to stay with her, seemed in retrospect a temporary aberration. She reasoned firmly to herself that she should be glad that he was doing what was important to him: she was perfectly capable of living without him for a year or two, had a satisfying life to get on with and would jolly well make the most of the time ahead.

And that is precisely what Grace did! If anything, she became even more wrapped up in her work and pushed her colleagues harder than ever, spending long hours in the surgery and appreciating the freedom she now had at home to do exactly as she wished. She ate only what, when or even if she felt like it. She could read in bed for as long as she liked, watch and listen to her own choice of television, radio and music, and luxuriated in the knowledge that nothing—absolutely nothing—was ever out of place unless she chose it to be! As before, her cleaning lady and the gardener continued to do the bulk of the household chores, leaving her free to make the most of what little leisure time she allowed herself.

There were, however, some petty irritations. Social invitations from couples more or less dried up. Grace could understand it, having herself often complained that single friends were always a pain at dinner parties as they upset the boy-girl, boy-girl, boy-girl seating arrangements, unless you could find another singleton of the opposite sex, which tended to suggest that you were doing a bit of match-making. When she felt the need for company, she would blithely contact single, divorced or widowed friends whom she had more or less lost touch with, and was rather miffed when in some cases they did not immediately accept her invitations or suggestions for shared outings. It never occurred to her that her previous lack of contact had been hurtful and that they resented being called on only when it suited her. So Grace didn't dwell on those occasions when a degree of social ineptness on her part left her rebuffed, but instead moved on to the next name in her diary.

Tom was in touch only very sporadically. Communication with the remote up-country location of his work and accommodation was very hit-and-miss, so there was only the occasional e mail, or even less regular letter or phone call. Naturally, he was totally pre-occupied with the business of acclimatising to the challenging physical environment that confronted him, and adjusting to a very different lifestyle. As far as the actual work was concerned, he was apparently relishing the huge demands it was making on him, and made it clear that his new project was living up to everything it had promised. Apart from the customary polite enquiry about her own work and life, hardly anything remotely personal was ever referred to before the line would break down or a hasty 'Bye, take care of yourself,' would end the call.

A listener might well have assumed Grace was talking to a friend or acquaintance rather than the person she had chosen to share her life with for the last forty years, but as usual, she accepted what had become the normal tenor of their conversations, and the fact that he was thousands of miles away made little or no difference to their cool and emotionless contact. She had become accustomed to living without close physical contact with her husband and minimal emotional interaction with anyone at all. That unfortunate incipient outburst of feeling on the day of Tom's departure had been forgotten and Grace continued to maintain a stoical and restrained face to the world, and indeed for the most part, even to herself.

As autumn passed and Christmas loomed ahead, Grace had to decide what she would do over the festive season. There seemed little likelihood of an invitation from any of her friends to join them, so she made a tentative suggestion to her daughter Jane and son-in-law James that she might pay them and the children a visit. The response was reasonably cordial and she began to make preparations to arrive in Brussels the day before Christmas Eve. She took pleasure in shopping for presents for the three grandsons and one granddaughter she had seen only rarely, but it came as something of a shock to admit to herself that she knew very little about their likes and dislikes. Nevertheless, hoping to do her best to appear as an indulgent and generous grandmother, and to be an easy and helpful house-guest, she was, however, sensitive enough to realise that her unaccustomed presence in their house might be proving something of an ordeal in prospect for her daughter and son-in-law. But the night before Grace was due to leave for Belgium, something happened that meant she would never know how her proposed visit would have turned out.

She was watching the late evening news as she checked over her travel documents and did her last-minute packing, when the name 'Murawi' seemed to scream from the television set. She would always remember in later days how her blood had literally run cold as the newsreader gave a brief account of a breaking news item about an attempted military coup in the African country. There were few details, but mention was made of the presence in the country of British personnel in many of the U.K. funded and run development projects. The remainder of the night passed in a blur of telephone calls and trawling of news programmes as Grace tried frantically to get more information about the unfolding emergency. The journey to Brussels was cancelled, of course, as Grace's son-in-law promised to use whatever influence he had to find out more details.

Some friends arrived at Grace's house first thing in the morning and expressions of concern and offers of help were flooding in. The dreadful truth, however, was that there was very little that anyone could do in a practical sense. The Foreign Office proved to be extremely courteous in a calm and detached way, guaranteeing that everything that could be done was being done, in contact with the British consul in Murawi. But given the chaos in that country and the seasonal shutdown of many parts of the system here in Britain, it was plain that she would simply have to be patient until the smoke settled and the situation became clearer. In other words, do nothing and sit tight—the hardest thing possible to ask, when every one of her instincts was screaming out for action, making Grace alternately rage with frustration and feel physically sick with terror.

Two days later, days when she had hardly slept or ate, despite the best efforts of friends, the news was still fragmented and contradictory. Some British ex-pats had made their way to the British Consul's office, but they had already been in the capital celebrating Christmas, and information about others in the outlying regions was virtually non-existent. Of Tom's particular project and the fate of its workers, nothing was known, although a worrying fact was that the supposed leaders of the coup came from the tribal area nearest his location. The Foreign Office continued to patiently deliver the same advice, couched as always in soothing, diplomatic and ultimately meaningless language which did nothing to give solace or hope to the waiting supplicants. In retrospect, what Grace would find hardest to accept, was that she was completely powerless to affect the outcome of Tom's predicament. All the pleading, threatening and cajoling came to the same in the end: his fate and hers was in the hands of faceless strangers. Those situated in the corridors of power in Whitehall were just as unreachable and intimidating as those who might even now be standing over Tom with a gun at his head, in the furthest reaches of the African wilderness.

Christmas came and went almost without her noticing as she vainly tried to find some reassuring news of Tom. Although some semblance of order had been re-established by the elected government in the capital, the area where Tom had been was in rebel hands and the situation there was fast descending into civil conflict. There had been no news or sightings of Tom and his co-workers, Murawian or British. The best guess was that they had been abducted by some of the rebels who, it was hoped, would treat them well, in the hope that they could be of use in bargaining for a settlement of the conflict. George was in as frequent contact as his location made possible and Jane and her husband were also being a great support, but the imminent arrival of the new baby made travel impossible for them. So it was old friends who were sustaining and encouraging Grace in those early days, but inevitably as the days became weeks, she had to insist on standing on her own two feet and had to try to get some semblance of normality into her life. She had been touched and grateful for the evidence of the affection and esteem that Tom was held in by so many people, many of whom Grace had never met or known about. The waiting game went on, seemingly without end, and it was with some measure of relief that Grace found herself back at work.

The nights were the hardest, and she found herself awake for long spells. She was chastened to think that for years past, she and Tom had shared a bed but with very little physical or loving closeness, while now that she was alone there and Tom might be dead or in mortal danger, she ached for his presence beside her and longed to be able to hold him close. It was in their bed that Grace began to have the first of many unsettling experiences. One night, on the brink of falling asleep, she had the distinct feeling that the mattress dipped on the far side of the bed, just as if someone had got into the bed there. She put it down to her dream-like state, but when it happened again on succeeding nights, she became more and more uneasy and slept less and less. Then she began to notice that when she came to make the bed in the morning, there was an indentation on Tom's pillow, just as if he had lain there all night. She would smooth the pillow carefully, but the next morning there it was again, the shape of Tom's head on the pillow. She calmed herself by reasoning that she must be moving over to his side of the bed during the night, although she was always on her own side in the morning.

The next strange occurrences concerned Tom's car. He had always left for the office before her in the mornings, and she was used to hearing the automatic garage door opening and his car starting just as she was coming downstairs for breakfast. The first time it happened after Tom left, Grace told herself it was her imagination, but when she went out to the garage Tom's Mercedes was parked in the drive with its engine running, the garage door that she had definitely closed the night before was now wide open, and her car still in its usual place in the garage. As she switched off the engine she found herself trembling from head to toe, fearfully peering into the gloomy interior of the garage expecting to see a would-be thief, or hoping that in some way an explanation would present itself. After a few minutes of bewildered confusion, she had to try to pull herself together, change the two cars over and drive off to work.

She had agreed that she would run Tom's car every week or so, and she had taken to using it at the weekend. One Sunday evening as she parked his car, Grace saw that it was low on petrol, so made a mental note to fill it up the following weekend. However, when she drove home from work the next Friday, she was astounded to see the Mercedes parked in the drive! How could that be possible? Initially, as before, she wondered if it could have been stolen out of the garage, but patently that didn't make sense. Who would steal a car just to leave it in the drive? What was even more perplexing was that on checking out the car, she discovered that the petrol tank was full! She thought of asking the neighbours if they had seen anything unusual, but stopped herself. She had become used to people either looking at her with pity as they asked if there was any news of Tom, or even worse, crossing to the other side of the street or dodging out of her way if they saw her at the local shops. Clearly it had become increasingly difficult for friends and acquaintances to know what to say. She didn't dare give them any further reason to pity her or to assume that the strain of waiting to learn of Tom's fate was beginning to unhinge her!

Other things began to happen that made Grace feel she was not actually alone in the house, and while these episodes at first made her made her uneasy, she somehow became able to accept them and even find some comfort in them, as she felt less isolated and lonely in the house. Before leaving for the surgery in the morning, it was her habit to leave everything ship-shape and Bristol fashion, especially on the days when Mrs McDonald came in to clean. But gradually she was feeling that little things would seem to have moved or changed in the course of the day. One of her pet hates was the newspaper being left open or badly folded, and increasingly she would find her copy of the Scotsman left lying higgledy-piggledy on the floor or on the coffee table.

The radio in the kitchen was always tuned to Radio 4, her favourite station, but Tom had invariably listened to 'Sounds of the Sixties' on Radio 2 on a Saturday morning when she would be having a bit of a lie-in, and she would have to re-tune to Radio 4 in time for 'Any Questions'. It was on the first Saturday of the New Year that she found it on Radio 2 when she came down in the morning, just as it had been when Tom was at home. She wondered if Mrs McDonald had taken to reading the Scotsman in her coffee break, but couldn't ask her, because under normal circumstances she would see nothing wrong in that, and she didn't want to appear as if she was being critical. Where the radio was concerned, how could it change from Radio 4 to Radio 2 by itself in the course of the night? This perplexing scenario was to be repeated on every subsequent Saturday thereafter.

Further signs that she had some invisible but benign presence keeping her company started to manifest themselves. Grace had always kept her car keys on the hall table, hanging on a little key holder that George had made for her in primary school, whereas Tom usually kept his in the table drawer. It came as no great surprise when one day she found them in opposite places, and no matter how carefully she re-arranged them, they were always switched back by the next morning. Sometimes she would lift one of the phones in the house only to find the line open as if one of the other extensions was in use, but on checking, all the receivers were firmly in their cradles.

She would find books lying unexpectedly open in various parts of the house, or the last few moments of one of Tom's discs playing in the machine. She would switch on the television and find it tuned to a favourite history channel of Tom's—the 'Hitler Channel' as she called it. Tom had put up a bird feeder just outside his study window and kept it filled with seeds and nuts in the winter. During a very cold spell of weather in late January, Grace remembered about it and decided to fill it up, but was amazed to find it already fully replenished. Even the birdbath beside it was full of fresh water. She knew it couldn't have been old Sandy, the gardener as he had been on his usual mid-winter break since two weeks before Christmas.

One weekend when she was feeling particularly low, in an attempt to distract herself from her misery by keeping busy, Grace decided to tidy out the cupboard in her study. By a happy chance, in the process she came across most of the photograph albums they had compiled when their children were young and their parents still hale and hearty. She spent a happy few hours re-living what were undoubtedly the happiest times of their lives. She marvelled at how young and carefree both she and Tom looked, and how obviously happy the children were and how proud their grandparents were of them all. On reflection, it seemed as if she had actually forgotten those wonderful times. Did the camera really lie and these were only illusions of joyfulness and family togetherness? Christmases, birthdays, anniversaries, christenings, graduations and weddings, the rights of passage that she and her family had gone through together spoke volumes of how successful and gratifying it had all been, and there was evidence of genuine affection and love shared amongst them all in those pictures.

But there were other occasions recorded, less formal and more spontaneous: Halloween nights when the children were resplendent in home-made costumes; a picnic on the beach, Tom all but invisible under a huge mound of sand and little George triumphantly brandishing his spade, proud at having done all the digging and piling himself; Jane in her first school uniform on the first day at junior school grinning happily if toothlessly at the camera; Grace and Tom dancing the jive at some long-forgotten party in the sixties, she in her mini-skirt and Tom in a frilly shirt with long shaggy hair. Prompted by those long neglected photographs, the memories came flooding back until she was laughing and crying at the same time. How she wished Tom was there with her then, but paradoxically she understood that in the weeks since he had been lost to her, she had begun to feel closer to him than she had for a very long time. In celebration of the joyful memories she had just re-discovered, within an hour or two Grace had festooned the sitting room with a myriad of images of Tom and her and their families in a motley collection of frames rescued from boxes in the loft.

The one bright spot in those desperate weeks was when Jane gave birth to a daughter, and Grace at last made that journey to Belgium to spend some happy days with the family, welcoming the new little one and getting to know her grandchildren better. She was moved almost to tears when they told her they were naming the baby Grace after her grandmother. But after returning home she began to understand, with feelings of deep shame, how she had failed her children and her husband: casting Jane and George off unnecessarily soon, in her urgency to see them independent and strong young adults, wasting the precious time she had with Tom, when they should have been growing closer in however many years they had left to them. In her most pessimistic moments of bitter regret, it seemed that this was almost like a rehearsal for widowhood. She had never had any religious faith so prayer was not an option. All she could do was to promise herself and Tom that when he returned their lives would be transformed. She longed to be able to make up for the wasted years, if only there was only something to be done to ensure Tom's safe return.

But she was unable to exert any influence on anyone who was in a position to help. V.S.O. assured her that they were co-operating with the diplomatic and political attempts to start negotiations with the rebels they assumed were holding Tom and the others, but they could not even be sure that Tom had survived the first chaotic days after the coup. But more and more each day she sensed the presence of Tom at home with her: a balm for her aching heart and a consolation for her tortured soul. She would enter a room and feel certain that he had just left by another door. She could hear his electric razor in the mornings and smell his favourite after-shave in the bathroom as she left for work. As she came home each day, Grace was sure there was the aroma of coffee in the kitchen and the kettle was often warm as if it had only just been emptied. Increasingly, these sensations were never accompanied by any feelings other than an intense assurance that one day he would come home to her.

The phone call she had longed for came when she least expected it. An item on the news one cold, bright spring morning, had reported an upsurge in the fighting between the rebels and the embattled government of Murawi, with a warning that this might result in a further delay in starting negotiations for the release of those who were now openly referred to as hostages. So Grace went off to the practice with a heavier than usual heart. It was just after lunch that the receptionist on duty came to her to tell her that one of the national daily newspapers had been in touch: they wanted to ask about her reaction to the news flash they had just seen on the agency wires, that hostages had been freed in Murawi.

Within less than an hour all hell had broken loose as further reports came in, each one in turn seeming more credible. Still she didn't dare to hope, until at last at six o'clock that evening, she had verification in person from the British Consul in Murawi: Tom and all the other British personnel from his dam project were safe and well, but tragically they could not give the same happy news about the Murawian workers who were still unaccounted for. By bedtime, her relief was complete when she had a very short call from Tom himself, his voice sounding tinny and distant, but otherwise very much as she remembered it, happily telling her that he was well and would be home in two days. He ended the call with words that she had not heard him utter for a very long time, which she repeated over and over again, long after the line had gone dead.

A sleepless night ensued, but this time it was happiness and relief that kept her awake, long after the congratulatory phone calls had stopped and visitors had left. In the very early morning, Grace remembered that she had never downloaded the photographs taken during her visit to Jane and the family. She especially wanted to have some prints of his new granddaughter to show Tom when she met him. She was amazed and delighted when she saw the photo Jane had taken of her with baby Grace, because there was Tom, his arm round her shoulders, looking at her lovingly as she cradled the baby girl. She knew it was impossible, that it made no sense whatsoever, but she had to believe the evidence before her. Tom had been with her that day and not just in spirit, but in reality. It was unequivocal confirmation that her sense of Tom's presence during the last dreadful weeks had been true after all.

The nebulous but insistent feeling that he had always been just out of her reach, her sight and her hearing had sustained her through those dark days. No matter how desperate she felt, Grace had clung to the belief that he was coming home to her one day. Or perhaps that he had never really left her, and that the unsuspected bond that connected them during all those years, far from breaking, had grown stronger and stronger during their time apart. Their love and their years together had somehow transcended time and distance. When she at last switched off the computer and walked into the sitting room, she placed the photographic evidence of Tom's love on the piano along with all the other smiling and happy faces of their dear family for him to see when he came home.

On her way to meet Tom at the airport two days later, Grace posted off her resignation letter to the local health authority. Nothing was going to stand in the way of her carrying out the promise she had made to herself and Tom. George, unknown to her, had already arranged leave of absence from his job and had flown in the day before from the other side of the world. Jane and James and the children arrived only just before Tom, and old friends and colleagues materialised at the airport as if by magic. Grace's first glimpse of Tom as he came through the arrivals gate showed that his face had been planed down to its essential features, so that he very strongly resembled the young man she had fallen in love with all those years before. He looked thinner and older and stooped slightly and walked unsteadily, but he was unmistakably her Tom. She took hold of him as if she would never let him go again, and they stood together, laughing and crying all at once.

Then they were overwhelmed as friends and family surrounded them and reached for Tom. As she stood in the midst of the welcoming melee she was suddenly reminded of her mother. When they were all together on family occasions, she would look around at everyone in turn and say, quite simply, 'Aren't we lucky?' Grace certainly felt lucky that day and continued to do so for the rest of her days. When she asked Tom how he had kept going during that dark, uncertain time when he was lost to her, he said, 'I spent most of my waking time concentrating on remembering every thing about you and our home and the family. I would go over in detail all the little things we used to do, all the routines of our days, and I swore that if I could come home to you, I would never again take you or any part of my life for granted again. Oh yes, and I used to try to remember the words of all the pop songs we sang together when we first met, you know the ones I listen to every Saturday morning.'

Truth, Fiction, and the Killer Bean of Calabar

By William Clinkenbeard

Lawrence's fingers were fairly flying over the keyboard now, even if it was only two of them. He punched the keys hard, the way he always did when the story was flowing fast through the riverbed of his mind. Writing was beginning to feel good again. Lately the creative springs seemed to have dried up, and he didn't know why. You could never really pin it down, the creative thing. Sometimes the words and sentences tumbled out of him so fast that he couldn't get them down quickly enough. Yet at other times he sat motionless for hours in front of an untouched keyboard and blank monitor.

The sunshine penetrated the study window to warm his back and to illuminate the neat rows of books in the bookshelf. It also showed up the dust on the screen of the monitor. He should clean it, but that would need to come later. He couldn't allow anything to distract him now that the story was taking shape. He stopped for nothing, not even for the little green squiggly lines that indicated some possible fault, a misspelling or a bit of grammar that the software didn't like. It irritated him anyway, the software. It conveyed the impression that *it* was in charge of his work rather than him. Anyway, he could go back later and correct it all. He had to keep the flow going.

It was precisely then that the doorbell rang. It wasn't the usual sort of half-hearted ring, but a sharp and long one, insistent and demanding. Lawrence finished typing a sentence and reluctantly rose up from his chair, bending over for a last look at the words on the screen. He needed to remember what came next in the paragraph. The bell rang again. It had to be the postman or perhaps a courier with a parcel of some kind. No one else would be calling at this time in the morning. He wished that Judith were there to go, but she was spending the day shopping.

When Lawrence pulled open the door he was surprised to see three people standing on the doorstep, grey-suited men in long black overcoats. He recognised none of them. The first man, clearly the bell ringer, nearly filled the opening with his bulk. He wasn't smiling. The other two stood behind and to the side on the front steps. They weren't smiling either. Who were these guys, Lawrence thought, grasping the door handle more firmly? If these were Mormons or Jehovah Witnesses they would get short shrift.

'Mr. Lithgow?' the man in front asked. He was heavyset and almost completely bald with a wide, knotted nose. He looked aggressive, like an ex-boxer.

'Yes,' Lawrence answered, beginning to feel a little anxious.

The big man flashed an open black wallet showing a badge of some kind and then shut it. 'We're with the security services, MI5. Could we have a word with you?'

Lawrence stared at him, tongue-tied. Half a dozen different scenarios played on his mind. Judith had had an accident on the way into town. She was lying in E&R at the hospital. Ben had been arrested for drunkenness after an all night party at the university. The surly son of the next-door neighbour was a terrorist. He had downloaded some pornography by mistake. There were too many possibilities. He thought now that should have looked more closely at the badge, but it was back in the pocket of the big one. It was as much as he could do the say, 'Aaa … yes, I suppose so,' and open the door wider to let them in.

They moved past him through the open door and into the hall, the big one first, the tall slight chap and finally a smaller man who gave him a friendly but almost apologetic smile. They waited for him in the hall while he shut the door.

The big one spoke. 'Mr. Lithgow, my name is Budge. This is Mr. Crilly and Mr. Lightbody.'

The two men nodded, but no hands were extended.

Budge stood forward, feet apart and firmly planted, as if he were itching for action. Crilly was quite tall with a long face to match. He stood awkwardly and looked around the hall as if bored or distracted. Lightbody was of medium height with sandy hair and blue eyes. A little glimmer of a smile suggested either a sense of humour or disdain.

'We need to talk to you Mr. Lithgow,' the Budge man said. 'Is there some-where we could sit down?'

Lawrence led them into the lounge, his heart and mind racing each other in an attempt to catch up with this alien invasion. What on earth could this be about? He tried desperately to think of some reason why the security services would want to talk to him. He had done nothing wrong that he could remember, at least nothing that MI5 would be interested in. They sat down, unbuttoning their overcoats. Lawrence took the chair in the corner, trying to get as far away as pos-sible.

'What is this all about?' Lawrence asked.

'You're a writer, aren't you?' Budge asked.

'Yes,' Lawrence replied, 'that's what I do.'

One of the other two finally spoke, Crilly, if he remembered the name cor-rectly.

'What kinds of things do you write?' The man had a more academic air about him. But he looked away as soon as he put the question, uninterested or knowing already.

'Short stories mainly,' Lawrence answered. 'The occasional novel. But why are you asking me about …'

Budge interrupted him, 'We'll come to that in a minute, Mr. Lithgow. Just answer the questions please.'

Lawrence felt short of breath, displaced by a rising anger. He bit his tongue.

'What kind of short stories do you write?' Budge asked tersely.

'Well,' Lawrence hesitated, 'how can I answer that? All kinds I guess.'

'You've written a short story about a foreign agent, a woman?'

'You mean *Time for Retribution*?' Lawrence replied. 'Yes, I wrote that a while ago. Why? What on earth is this about?' The three men cast quick glances at each other, as if satisfied that some issue had been resolved.

'If you please, Mr. Lithgow', Crilly spoke up, 'just allow us to ask the ques-tions.'

Budge took over once again. 'In your story, the woman is a sleeper, a Russian agent who is activated in order to murder enemies of the regime by spraying acid into their face.'

'Yes, that's right,' Lawrence replied. 'Prussic acid. It produces cardiac arrest.' In spite of his anxiety he couldn't help but feel a little pleased. Not many people actually ever commented on his stories. It was good when someone took an inter-est, even if it might be with hostile intent.

'Exactly,' Lightbody said, a knowing smile on his face. 'You seem to know quite a lot about poisons and weapons. One might even say that you are an expert in that sort of thing.'

'Well,' Lawrence answered, 'I have to be. A writer has to know what he's writing about. You have to do lots of research. It's easy to get caught out if you make a mistake.'

'And you wouldn't want to be caught out,' said Budge, casting another knowing glance at the other two.

'Look, I still can't see what this is all about,' Lawrence said.

'Mr. Lithgow,' Budge replied, leaning forward in the chair and lowering his voice, 'it surely can't have escaped your attention that several weeks ago a Russian dissident, a former member of the KGB, was murdered in London.'

'Of course I heard about that,' Lawrence answered. 'I listen to the news like everyone else.' It came across a bit defensively, for somewhere in the hinterland of his mind a penny was beginning to drop.

'It was a very sophisticated hit,' Lightbody said. 'His food was sprayed with Polonium 210, a radioactive isotope.'

'Yes, I know that,' Lawrence replied. 'So what? I still don't know what that has to do with me.' He was sounding even more defensive.

'You don't?' Budge said. 'Not a lot of people have expertise on things like Polonium 210.'

'No, I suppose not.' Lawrence responded. No one said anything for a minute.

'Mr. Lithgow,' Crilly said, breaking the silence, 'would you mind if we took a look at your library?'

'My library? Why? I still don't understand. But yes, if you insist,' Lawrence replied. He had better show willing. This seemed to be serious. He got up slowly, feeling reluctant to lead them through to the study. Two thoughts loomed large in his mind. The first was that it wasn't all that tidy. Judith would have a fit when she heard that visitors had seen it in that state. The second was the gnawing recognition of what they might find there.

The sun was still streaming into the study window, lighting up the rows of books. The three men spread themselves evenly along the shelves and began studying the titles. Eventually Crilly said 'This is the section here.' They stood side by side and studied the end of the top shelf.

Budge reached up and extracted a book. 'This is called *Drugs and Poisons in Humans: A Handbook of Practical Analysis,*' he announced. He thumbed through the volume and then studied the contents page.

'This tells you about the contents of specific poisons … how to analyze them and how to put them together. Right?'

'Yes, among other things,' Lawrence replied.

'So this book would be quite useful in making up various kinds of poisons?' Budge asked.

'I suppose so, if you were that way inclined,' Lawrence responded.

'Here's another one,' said Lightbody. Pulling the book down and peering at the title, he read it slowly: '*Poison Arrows*. I take it that this is about the kinds of poisons that can be put on the tips of arrows and darts, perhaps like the prussic acid in your story?'

'No, I'm afraid not,' Lawrence replied, hearing a faint note of triumph sounding somewhere in his being. 'This one is really about how the Crusaders brought spices like ginger and nutmeg back to Europe during the Crusades. I don't really think that you could poison anyone with cinnamon.'

'Oh, right,' Lightbody said, putting the book back into its place.

'Here's another,' Crilly offered, extracting a thick book from the shelf. 'It's called *Germs: Biological Weapons and America's Secret War*. Is this one useful to you in your work?'

'Sorry, I really don't know much about that one. I haven't needed to get into it yet,' Lawrence said dryly.

Budge had taken another book off the shelf and was studying it intently. There was silence for a good minute while he read. Lawrence noted that he mouthed the words.

'Now, this one *is* interesting,' he said. He turned back to the cover and read the title out loud: '*Poisons: From Hemlock to Botox to the Killer Bean of Calabar*. This must provide a pretty extensive list of what you can use to kill people.'

'No doubt that it does,' Lawrence replied, 'but I'm only in the business of killing people in stories. It's fiction, not reality. I'm a writer for God's sake. That's all, just a writer. I get books like this so that I can write convincingly.'

There was no response to his statement. The three men studied him.

'What is this killer bean of Calabar anyway?' Budge asked, still turning the pages slowly.

'It comes from a plant,' Lawrence answered. 'The thing can grow as high as fifty feet and it produces these large brown beans which are poisonous. The people of Calabar used it as a test for witches. If someone was accused of witchcraft they made him or her eat the bean. If the person died they were guilty. If they lived they were innocent.'

'Kind of like the drowning test for witches in this country,' Crilly suggested with a smile.

'Exactly,' Lawrence replied, 'but I imagine there was a higher survival rate with the beans. Some people were naturally resistant to the poison. The beans were also used in duals. The thing was cut in half lengthwise, and the opponents each ate the seeds from their half. Sometimes both died and sometimes only one.'

'And Calabar, that's in the Lake District, right?' Budge asked.

'No,' Crilly interjected, 'I think it's in India, you know "Old Calabar."'

'Sorry,' Lawrence said, 'you're both wrong. Calabar is in Nigeria.' The put-down boosted his confidence a shade.

'Right, Mr. Lithgow', Budge said, 'this has been quite helpful, very helpful indeed. May we take these books away and have a look at them?'

'If you insist,' Lawrence answered, 'but I want them back. In fact, I'd like a receipt for them. I can tell you that you won't find anything in them to incriminate me.'

'We'll see,' Budge answered.

'Look,' Lawrence said, 'you surely don't think that I had anything to do with this former KGB man's death. I write stories, that's all.'

'But you *are* an expert on poisons and weapons,' Lightbody spoke up. 'Even if you are not directly involved, you might be *in*directly involved.' He put emphasis on the *in*.

'That's rubbish. It's totally ridiculous. What possible motive would I have?' Lawrence replied, feeling short of breath again.

'It may be rubbish,' Budge replied, 'but we'll have to check it out. You do seem to have a history of supporting various liberal causes. But even if you were not directly involved you might have influenced this event. Maybe somebody learned from your story. Have you ever thought about the unintended consequences of what people do? That includes writing stuff. All you people who write spy stories and crime novels—I'll bet you never think about how the terrorists might use them. Now, I have to ask you not to leave the country. You'll need to be available in case we want to interview you again. I won't ask for your passport, but please don't try to leave.'

Lawrence was speechless. He could only shake his head from side to side.

Budge continued to speak. 'We'll be on out way now and let you get back to your work, but if you don't mind we'll take a very quick look around the premises before we go.'

That same evening Judith came in from her shopping expedition flushed with success. Distracted, Lawrence tried his best to focus on her story and congratulate her on her new top and pair of shoes.

'So,' she said, 'how was your day? Anything exciting happen around here?'

'Well, yes, in fact,' Lawrence answered. 'It's been a very unusual day.'

'So tell me,' Judith said.

'Could I suggest,' he said, 'that we have a drink first. I feel like having a double whisky this evening. It's been a hard day.'

She looked alarmed and touched his arm. 'Why? What happened today? Tell me.'

Lawrence poured the drinks and told her the whole story. He told her about the visit from MI5 and his interrogation and the inspection of his study. At the mention of that room she raised her eyebrows.

'Oh no, they didn't go into the study?' she said.

'I'm afraid so. And of course they found all my books on weapons and poisons and took away a couple of them to examine.' He told her in detail about which books they had looked at and the ones they had taken away.

'I don't believe this,' she said. 'I cannot believe that these people came into our house and that they suspect you of involvement in that murder. It's absolutely ludicrous.'

'Of course it is,' he said. 'I know that and you know that. The odd thing is that when you are questioned like that and they find relevant books on your shelf you begin to doubt your own innocence.'

'No,' she burst out with her face contorted in astonishment, 'you don't really believe you had anything to do with this.'

'No, of course not,' Lawrence replied. 'I know I'm innocent, and I can't really believe that my story enabled anyone to poison that man. I'm not an expert on killing. There are hundreds or thousands of other people better equipped to aid and abet murder than me, and many of them with serious intent.' Lawrence paused to take another drink and then looked carefully at his wife. 'Anyway, I'm going to stop writing.'

'Come on, Lawrence,' Judith said, 'Writing is so important to you. Why should these men, these three stupid secret agents, put you off?'

'Well,' Lawrence answered, 'for two reasons really. First, I feel quite shaken by all this. My creativity was just beginning to come back and these guys have destroyed it. I don't think I'll ever be creative in the same way again. But more than that, there is no line anymore between truth and fiction. They have merged into each other. The boundary is gone. Any fantasy that I could dream up is not as fantastic as what happens in the real world. It's crazy. I knew that today when these guys went into the garden.'

'What?' Judith said, 'They went into our garden as well?'

'The back garden,' Lawrence answered. 'They went out the back door and into the garden, the three of them in their overcoats, walking around staring at the borders and all the shrubs and trees. They spent a long time standing in front of the Laburnum tree and the Fuchsia vine. It was surreal.'

'But why? What for?' she asked.

'I'm pretty sure,' Lawrence answered, trying hard to suppress a giggle, 'that they were looking for the Killer Bean of Calabar.'

Little Tulla's Legacy

By George Sinclair

Tulla scampered through the low alleyway that connected the eight stone dwellings and ducked as she passed an open window with freezing cold air rushing in. She slipped through the doorway, entered the square room and saw the twelve grown-ups and children sitting around the blazing peat fire in the centre of the room. She managed to find a space as close to Drosten as she could. Drosten was tonight's main storyteller and she did not want to miss a word.

'So what's the story about tonight, Drosten?' she asked cheerily with an innocent smile. Tulla was a pretty six year old with cream coloured skin and flowing golden locks tumbling to her waist. She was always excited to hear new stories, especially from Drosten.

'It's about a giant fish that nearly caught me, instead of me catching it,' replied Drosten with an anxious look as he recalled the feelings he had at the time of the fishing expedition. Everyone listened intently as Drosten began to tell the tale. He had rugged features, prematurely greying hair, and the air of a hero.

'We know that the sea gives us much. Our forefathers used to fish in a nearby freshwater lagoon that has long since dried up and now we fish far out to sea with our boats. It's hard and dangerous work. You'll all remember that last year there were plenty of fish in the sea, and that our boats always came back fully laden. We had enough to smoke and salt to store over the winter, and some days we even had enough to barter with our neighbours on the other side of the island, in exchange for seal pelts.'

'One day I was with Taran in our boat, we were a long way out to sea, when suddenly my line went taut and there was a great commotion in the water. I looked down and there it was, the biggest fish you've ever seen. It was twice as long as me, with two sets of glistening teeth as long as my fingers, a white belly, a grey back and a huge fin.'

'What happened then?' said Tulla, in awe.

'I was pulled into the water and immediately let go of my fishing pole. As my head came up I could see the fish coming straight towards me with its huge mouth open and a myriad of teeth sparkling in the sunlight! *I was terrified!* All I had to protect me was my knife. As it came towards me I could see that it was going for my legs, so I swung them round and faced it directly, with my knife pointing at its nose. It kept coming. I didn't know if I could fight it off, as it was so huge and looked immensely strong. When it came close I slashed at it with my knife and managed to nick it on the nose. Blood oozed out and as it swerved to the side, its fin lashed me like a whip and cut into my arm. In pain, I dropped the knife and the fish began heading towards me again. Just in time I noticed that Taran was holding out a staff for me to get hold of, so I grabbed it and he hauled me aboard the boat, my arm dripping with blood.'

'What did you do then?' asked Tulla, her ears locked to his voice. She pushed against the people beside her with her hands, and rose to her knees in excitement.

'Another large fish came close to the boat. It was attracted by the blood and started to attack the first fish, so Taran and I decided it was time to escape the danger. Dark clouds were gathering, the wind had changed and a storm was heading towards us. It wasn't particularly unusual, but on this occasion the combination of winds and the great waves threatened to capsize us. We battled on and eventually made it back to shore, exhausted but elated.'

'I want to see the scar on your arm,' said Tulla. She rose and moved quickly towards Drosten, but did not see a leg protruding on the floor, and tripped and fell headfirst into the fire. It was particularly large that evening because of the cold and windy weather and she was immediately engulfed in the flames. She screamed in agony as people scrambled to get her out. But it was too late and within a few seconds she lay motionless and silent.

The women began to wail in mortal agony.

The men were quiet.

The next day Tulla's parents and their friends met solemnly to discuss where they would bury Tulla. Her mother, Brigid, could not stop crying, tears streaming down her face.

'Tulla was a good and kind child and once said to me that she would like to be buried inside the sacred circle to protect her spirit,' said Angus, Tulla's father. 'This is where our forefathers are buried and so it's only right and proper. Their spirits will protect her.'

The sacred circle, its sixty standing stones jutting starkly out of the gentle Orcadian landscape, was in the centre of a massive natural cauldron formed by the surrounding countryside and bordered by hill, water and sky.

Preparations for the burial began; the women had prepared the body and the men were starting to dig a hole in the ground inside the sacred circle, near one of the main stones. Uvan, the local priest of Wodden had heard about the accident and that the men had planned to bury Tulla inside the ring, so he went to where the men were digging.

'You're not allowed to bury the girl there,' said Uvan sternly, like a ghost with the eyes of a devil. 'It's against our customs. You all know that inside the circle is reserved for the burial of chiefs and priests.' His voice was strong, yet unconvincing, his eyes winced and his shoulders twitched. *He felt a chill, and realised what he had just unleashed.*

Brigid exploded with fury. 'Who are you to criticise the wishes of a small girl? That is where she said she wanted to be buried and that's where she'll be buried. You'll not stop us!' she screamed.

'You know our customs, Brigid,' Uvan said, shooting an anxious glance at Angus. He could not believe the metamorphosis in Brigid, who had instantly turned into a wild cat pursuing its prey.

'Yes, I know our customs, but you misuse them!' Brigid said, her voice cracking with emotion.

'We're obviously taking different meanings,' Uvan said, realising that a demon was coming out of its hiding place to taunt him. Please, somebody stop her, he thought.

Angus stood in a swirl of confusion, not quite following where the conversation was going.

'You'd better think again,' Brigid said, in a shrill voice.

'As you wish, I understand your feelings,' Uvan said quietly. He did not want a public showdown with a grieving mother, especially Brigid, and turned to the men and said that they could continue.

The next day Uvan went to see Angus. 'If Tulla's body is left inside the ring Wodden will send bad luck to all the community. Is that what you want?'

'So where would you suggest she's buried then?' Angus said, his nerves tingling and questions crowding his mind. Even though he respected Uvan, he sensed that something was wrong.

'She could be buried beside the Comet Stone. Her spirit will be protected there.'

'All right, just make sure that Brigid doesn't find out.'

The next day one of Angus's friends mentioned to his woman what had happened. A few hours later she went to tell Brigid, who listened, her face clouded in disbelief. She immediately ran across the moorland to Uvan's hut.

She barged into it and ran towards him screaming. 'You demon of hell! Why have you done this, have you no decency in you? You know that she was a special child. You know whose blood she has. You remember when we were younger and how wild we were. *Did that mean nothing to you?* Well did it?'

He reeled, knocked back by the words, the blood drained from his face.

His eyes wandered over her face—it was exquisite, not overly beautiful, but possessing full, earthy features that exuded a raw sensuality. They stood silent for a few seconds just staring into each other's eyes as her nubile body sent a familiar longing to his loins. They moved closer together and finally their lips met. They were in a different time, a different world. A time and world where they were both young, free and eager to be with each other. They had met many times in the past.

'Remember when we were young, we met at the shoreline and ran to our special cave, hand in hand. We loved each other deeply, and then Tulla came into our lives. Surely you know that she is your daughter?' said Brigid, staring deeply into Uvan's eyes.

'Tulla is my daughter? I didn't know!' Uvan seemed stunned, but he lied, he did know.

'How could you have been so blind? Why didn't we run away? Our lives could have been so different,' anguished Brigid.

'I wanted to, but my father made me swear on his father's grave that I would become a priest like them.'

Fate had not been on their side. He had been destined to become a priest like all his ancestors and she had been destined to become a sorceress. Their two futures would never meet. They eventually had to part, their hearts broken. What was done was done.

'We cannot live in the past, we must always look to our future,' said Uvan nervously.

Brigid pushed Uvan backwards, *the fleeting spell broken.*

'Let me tell you that you have no future,' she retorted in a blind rage. 'You know that I have powers to change the future. So now I place a curse on you. You will leave this island and never return. You will never find friends or a home. You will wander forever, a lonely man, until you die!'

'I beg you to change you mind,' Uvan pleaded, breaking down with grief, stumbling to his knees, his arms outstretched.

She said nothing ... turned ... and left.

He felt suddenly all alone ... his world empty.

APHORISMS

By Robert Kirk

(Oxford Dictionary: Aphorism: A short pithy saying expressing a general truth; A proverb)

'I've decided, Martha ...' Jim took a long steadying breath then came out with it. 'I've decided I'm going to leave you.'

'Leave me, Jim?' Martha paled. 'But why?'

'Many things, really. I never loved you, you can't cook, you have chronic halitosis and ...'

'And?'

'And I'm fed up with the aphorisms.'

'The aphorisms, Jim? But I thought we had them on the run. That stuff we got from Tesco's, it worked like a charm. The roses seem perfectly healthy now.'

'The *aphorisms*, Martha. You're thinking about aphids."

'Oh,' she said. But Jim could tell she still had only a vague idea of what an aphorism was. He turned and walked towards the stairs. 'I'm going to pack a case. I'll leave first thing in the morning.'

'Please, Jim. Don't go,' she implored.

He stopped and turned. 'Give me one good reason.'

'Well ... a good man is hard to find.'

'That's an aphorism.'

'No it's not!'

He sighed. 'I'm leaving you anyway.'

'But Jim ... a house divided against itself cannot stand.'

'See! You just can't help yourself, can you? That's another aphorism.'

'A leopard can't change its spots.'

'But I can change where I bloody well live.'

Martha stepped forward, grasped his arms, and looked deep into his eyes. 'Time is a great healer.'

'For crying out loud, Martha! Can't you see that you're still doing it? It's like living with a parrot.'

'Birds of a feather flock together, Jim.'

'Well this bird is flocking well moving on. Goodbye.' Jim turned and moved towards the stairs again.

'What about the children?'

'What about them?' he flung over his shoulder.

'The boy is father to the man.'

'You'll make a better father to them than I ever could, Martha. At least they'll have no bother passing their aphorism exams.'

They were now half-way upstairs and Martha was clinging to his jacket.

'Don't bite the hand that feeds you, my love.'

'That's precisely what I should have done the first time you set food on the table. I wouldn't have spent half the night on the toilet then.'

'An apple a day keeps the doctor away.'

They were on the top landing now. Jim tried to enter the bedroom but Martha barred his way.

'Will you let me by, Martha.'

'A woman's place is in the home,' she said desperately. 'The way to a man's heart is through his stomach.'

'The way to my suitcase is through that bloody door. Now move.'

'All you need is love.'

'And don't try to tempt me with sex. That was never much good either.'

'Early to bed and early to rise makes a man healthy, wealthy and wise.'

By now Jim had managed to squeeze past Martha and pull his suitcase from on top of the wardrobe.

'I'll change, Jim. I'll stop using aphorisms. Promise.'

'Don't make me laugh.'

'He who laughs last laughs longest.'

Jim was searching the floor of the wardrobe. 'Where are my suede shoes?'

'Blue, blue ... blue suede shoes.'

'For goodness sake, woman. What have you done with them?'

'A place for everything and everything in its place.'

Jim stopped throwing stuff into the case. Straightened. Looked her in the eye. 'You can't stop, can you? You just keep going on and on and on … like a bloody cracked record.'

'Least said, soonest mended.'

'You still don't know why I can't stand you. After all these years. Fitting a backwards-facing passenger seat in the car so I can't smell your breath. Hanging your picture over the fireplace so the kids wouldn't go near the fire. Living on packets of Smash 'cause you can't even boil potatoes. My god, we've still got the first egg you ever boiled. I nailed it to the bottom of that table leg in the kitchen. It's the only damn thing in this house that's in balance.'

'Jim, how could you be so cruel?'

'Because it's all bloody true, that's how. When you were a kid, all the other kids hated you. Your mother hung a pork chop 'round your neck just so the dogs would play with you.'

'Jim, don't leave me,' she wailed.

Jim pushed her aside and strode out onto the landing.

And that was where he made his mistake. Martha emitted a wail that grew into a yell that became a scream. She rushed forward, shoved Jim between the shoulder blades, and watched him tumbling arse over suitcase down the stairs.

'Jim, oh my darling Jim, what have I done?' she moaned as remorse overtook her. She rushed down to where he sprawled, one leg bent backwards in a way that just wasn't possible with an unbroken leg. His head lay at an odd angle. His eyes fluttered open then quickly closed again as she seized his head in both arms and clasped it to her bosom. A couple of shattered vertebrae made a loud scraping noise every time she rocked back and forth.

'Please forgive me. I didn't mean to hurt you.'

Then she seemed to realise that action, not regret, was called for. Grasping her husband by both arms, she heaved his shuddering body through the kitchen and out through the back door.

'Martha.' His voice was weak. He seemed on the point of death. 'I wish you hadn't done that.'

'If wishes were horses, beggars would ride.'

'I think I'm dying.'

'Live for today for tomorrow never comes.'

She left him there by the rockery while she fetched a spade from the garden shed.

'What are you going to do?'

'Well, I can't leave your body lying here, Jim, can I? What would the neighbours say? And what about the smell?'

She began heaving large rocks from the soft earth of the rockery onto the path.

Jim said something, but the words weren't clear, coming as they did through a throat full of blood.

'What was that my love?' She asked as she grabbed him by the ankles and started dragging him towards the hole she had scooped out with the spade.

Jim swallowed and tried again. 'A rolling stone gathers no moss,' he gurgled.

'You won't do much rolling, Jim. Just to the bottom of this hole.'

Jim's feet scraped on the concrete path as he tried to propel himself towards his final resting place, saying, 'A volunteer is worth twelve pressed men.'

Martha aimed the first spadeful of earth at his face, hoping to shut him up.

'A woman's work is never done,' he managed after spitting out a mouthful of wet soil.

Martha stopped, arrested by a sudden thought. She reached down and tugged Jim's wallet from his jacket. She opened it to find it stuffed with £50 notes and all his credit cards. 'You selfish bastard. You were going to let me bury you with this in your pocket, weren't you?'

'Easy come, easy go.'

A blood-red mist rose behind Martha's eyes. She raised the spade high and brought it down on Jim's skull with a clang that the neighbours surely must have heard.

'Blood is thicker than water,' groaned Jim as the earth around his head turned a deep, soggy crimson.

Martha shovelled energetically for several minutes. 'Better to have loved and lost than never to have loved at all,' was the last thing Jim uttered.

Martha patted the earth flat with the back of the spade then stood back admiring Jim's new home. The rose bush sprouting from the centre of the patch of earth was a nice touch, she felt. She'd tugged it from the flowerbed at the side of the house and replanted it here, knowing it would grow well. After all, it had a ready supply of manure. She'd buried Jim face down just to be sure.

Haggis and Neeps

By Wendy Sinclair

Fergus gnawed at the end of the pencil and tried to concentrate on the workbook on the desk in front of him, but his tummy ached and rumbled a little and he felt ravenously hungry. He looked at the classroom clock. The little hand was nearly at the three and the big hand was fast approaching the twelve. Soon the bell would ring and Miss Baxter, the primary 1 teacher, would set them free.

Tommy Barr sitting next to him had closed his workbook and was tidying his pencils into a blue Superman pencil case. 'What a swot!!' thought Fergus.

At last the bell rang out and twenty-five boys and girls dashed into the cloakroom pushing and jostling each other in their hurry to get their coats, scarves and gloves on. Fergus stuffed his gloves into his bag, pulled the hood of his anorak over his head, grabbed his schoolbag and lunchbox and headed for the door.

'Fergus McIver, put your anorak on properly,' yelled the loud voice of his teacher. Though she was barely as tall as some of the children in primary 7 and was so slim that some might consider her skinny, she had an incredibly loud voice at times.

Finally outside, he dashed towards the crowd of waiting mothers, easily finding his as she had come straight from work and was more formally dressed than most of the others. His mother was a successful lawyer; in fact both his parents worked for his grandfather's law firm but his mother only worked part-time, and always met him from school.

Safely strapped in his booster seat in the car, he looked around for the snack his mother usually brought him, as he always complained of being 'starving' when she collected him. There was nothing there.

'Mum, I'm starving. What can I have?'

'Sorry love, I was in such a hurry this morning that I forgot your snack. There are some rice-cakes in my briefcase if you want them, though.'

'Yuk!' said Fergus. 'I hate rice-cakes. They taste like cardboard.'

So poor Fergus had to wait until he was home to satisfy his hunger.

Entering the house they were greeted enthusiastically by Sammy their pet Labrador. Sammy loved Fergus and Fergus loved Sammy. If Fergus was sad Sammy always snuggled up close to him and made him feel better. He licked Fergus's neck and ear and Fergus had to push him away before he started on his face.

After a glass of milk, two jaffa cakes and a pear, he felt sufficiently satisfied and went up to his bedroom to play until dinnertime. It seemed no time at all until his mother called to him that dinner was ready. She was dishing the dinner on to plates when he entered the kitchen. They always ate together and his father, who was generally late home from work, had his later.

'Today we are having something special to eat as it is November 30th, St Andrew's Day,' explained his mother as she lifted a huge fat brown sausage-shaped thing out of a saucepan. 'St Andrew is the patron saint of Scotland, so we're going to have a Scottish meal of haggis, neeps and tatties.'

Fergus knew that neeps were turnips and tatties were potatoes, but the 'haggis' thing was new to him.

'What's haggis, Mum?'

'Haggis is made from a sheep's inside bits minced up and mixed with oatmeal, then stuffed in a skin,' replied Mum as she cut into the sausage-like thing.

'That's disgusting. I don't want any haggis,' moaned Fergus.

'Don't be silly!' replied his mother, 'You must at least try it.'

Fergus was reminded of the time that his granny had tried to get him to eat porridge. She had spooned a thick, gluey greyish mixture into a bowl, and then poured a little milk on the top. It had looked disgusting as well. So Fergus had told his granny that he had a pain in his tummy (only a little white lie) and he didn't have to eat it.

He sat at the table and eyed the contents of his plate. The orange mashed turnip and the creamy white mashed potatoes looked good, but the brown crumbly stuff looked and smelled revolting. He ate some turnip and potato and hoped that his mother wouldn't notice that he wasn't trying the haggis stuff.

Luckily the telephone started to ring and his mother dashed off to answer it.

Fergus grabbed a handful of the haggis and quickly placed his hand under the table. A warm wet nose nuzzled his hand and a soft furry mouth greedily gobbled the contents. Three more handfuls and it was all gone. By the time his mother returned to the table he was sitting with a clean plate in front of him.

'Well done, Fergus! You see! You shouldn't say you don't like something without even trying it,' said his mother.

Later that evening as he lay in bed, he heard a loud choking noise coming from downstairs and heard his mother shouting to his father. 'Quick! Let the dog out he's going to be sick! Has he been eating things while you had him out for a walk this evening?'

A sly smile crept across Fergus's face, but it didn't last long as he heard his mother say, 'I'm really glad that Fergus liked the haggis; they had a special offer at the shop today. Buy one get one free!'

TURKEY JUSTICE

By William Armstrong

It was three days before Christmas when Jennifer selected the trolley and strode into the supermarket for the big shop. Everything went smoothly until she reached the frozen food section. To her horror the turkey compartment was completely empty. A small notice on the front edge said simply: "Sorry, out of stock due to flu."

Out of stock due to flu! Jennifer's mind grappled with the implications. A modern mother cum career woman, she had little time to absorb the world's problems. Vaguely she remembered seeing something about "avian flu" on the news. However, coping as best she could with little Johnny's tantrums, she'd thought it must be a spelling mistake and most likely something to do with flu in Asia.

Jennifer was debating how she would break the news to the family, when she suddenly realised the supermarket was eerily silent. No ringing of tills, no snatches of conversation in the aisles, and no tannoy requests for staff "to report to the checkouts"! Nothing.

'Stand quite still, ma'am.' The deep, rather hoarse voice seemed to come from directly behind her. Jennifer froze.

'That's fine, ma'am. Now turn around, real slow.'

Jennifer revolved slowly, conscious of the underlying menace in the hoarse tones, and wondering fearfully what she would see. Three huge turkeys faced her in the aisle, one slightly in advance of the others. They were all over six feet tall and built in proportion.

'Thank you, ma'am.' The lead turkey, an imposing figure, gestured with a wing. 'You got to come with us now. This way. Fellas,' in an aside to the others, 'Take the prisoner through the "time gate" while I pull the patrols back.'

'Prisoner!' Jennifer paled visibly. 'Wh … why? I haven't done anything wrong. I only came in for a….' She stopped suddenly, aware of what she was about to say.

'Turkey, ma'am?" The leading gobbler shrugged tiredly. 'If I had a dollar for every time I've heard that I'd be rich. Alright, fellas. Take her down.'

His two companions nodded and Jennifer found herself being eased along the aisle.

'But … my family,' she protested. 'They'll wonder where I am.'

Her escort remained stubbornly silent.

At the end of the aisle a huge trapdoor opened silently in the floor. 'Down the steps, ma'am.' Her right hand escort spoke for the first time. 'Hang on to the rail.'

In a daze, Jennifer descended through the trapdoor, down a steep staircase into a brightly lit underground room. She paused at the bottom, but her escort urged her on.

A big tough looking turkey cock bustled up to them. 'All right, fellas? No trouble?'

'Sir … no sir,' they chorused in unison. The right hand escort coughed. 'Uh … sir, Sergeant Drumstick said to tell you he's pulling the entrance guards back, right now … sir!'

The turkey cock nodded approvingly. 'That's good. Soon as he's got them all back here I'll throw the deactivating time switch. The folks up top'll never know what's happened. Now, take the prisoner through to the courtroom.'

'Sir … yessir.'

Jennifer was hustled down a long corridor to a door marked "Courtroom Entrance". It was guarded by two more massive turkeys, but a muttered 'prisoner and escort' was enough. The door swung silently open and Jennifer found herself in a sizeable courtroom.

A white turkey came forward. 'Are you Mrs Jennifer McLean?' he queried in a not unpleasing drawl.

'Ye … yes,' Jennifer stammered nervously. 'But what …?'

'Jason Turkeytrot, ma'am. Your defence lawyer. Let's get started. We ain't got much time.'

Jennifer paled 'Defence lawyer! But what am I being charged with?'

'Genocide, ma'am. Mass murder of the turkey race at certain seasons.'

'But … there must be millions who eat turkey!'

'Quite so, ma'am. Every year we take one human and try them for "turkey genocide". Just your bad luck to be singled out as the one. Not sure who the presiding judge is. If it's old Tom McFeather we'll be fine. Him and m'father go way back.'

'What are my chances?' Jennifer faltered.

The white turkey shook his head. 'Not good. In my time I've only seen two acquittals.'

'How did they get off?' Jennifer queried, her mind clutching desperately at this ray of hope.

'They were vegetarians. Got picked by mistake. There was hell to pay. Everybody in Records was fired. You vegetarian, ma'am?'

'No,' Jennifer said unhappily.

'Strike that one then.' The white turkey consulted his notes. 'Got a bird table?'

'Yes.…'

'Well, hallelujah! We're getting somewhere at last. Now, if Judge McFeather's on the case we might just get a conditional discharge. Old Tom's a sucker for bird tables.'

'All rise.' The gravelly tones of the turkey usher cut across the muted courtroom chatter. An enormously fat turkey strutted in and settled himself in the judge's chair.

Jason swore softly. 'Damn! Sorry, ma'am, but this is bad.'

'What's wrong?' Jennifer queried timidly.

'This here's Sir Justin Gobble de Gook. One hard judge.'

'Silence.' The judge swept the suddenly still courtroom with a beady stare. 'Is this the human on trial? Who's defending?'

'I am, Your Honour. Jason Turkeytrot. The defendant is a Mrs Jennifer McLean. Married, with three of a family.'

'Plea?'

'Not guilty, Your Honour.'

Justin Gobble de Gook glowered. 'They all say that. Prosecution?'

'Virginia Bronze, Your Honour.' A tall slim turkey hen rose gracefully.

'Your submission?'

'That the accused, representing the human race, is guilty of genocide.'

'H'm. Turkeytrot?'

'Mitigating circumstances, Your Honour. The defendant has a bird table in her garden. Move for a conditional discharge.'

'Objection!' Virginia was on her feet.

'Sustained.' The judge said gruffly. 'No conditional discharge. The trial will proceed.'

Jennifer listened fearfully as Virginia Bronze built a devastating case against her. 'Summing up, Your Honour, my learned friend has conceded that his client has eaten,' here she shuddered theatrically, 'turkey flesh! This is unforgivable and I submit that only the maximum penalty will suffice. Your Honour, that concludes the case for the prosecution.'

'No!' Jennifer shouted wildly, 'You can't …'

'Mr Turkeytrot!' The judge's gruff tones cut across her protests. 'Remind your client that she must remain silent unless called on to speak. If she doesn't I'll have her removed. Is that clear?'

'Yes, Your Honour.' Jason lowered his voice and spoke directly to Jennifer. 'Please, Ma'am. Don't make things any worse.'

Sniffling tearfully, Jennifer subsided.

Jason's presentation was good, but it was obvious he was fighting a losing battle. Even his point about the bird table failed to make an impression. He finished and sat down, pointedly avoiding Jennifer's accusing stare.

'H'm …' Judge Gobble de Gook cleared his throat. 'An open and shut case. Mrs McLean, you are guilty of turkey genocide. You are hereby sentenced to be roasted alive. Take her down.'

'No!' Jennifer screamed. 'You can't. No … no.'

'Darling, wake up. What's the matter?'

'Oh, John, I've just had the most awful dream.'

'Never mind that now. We've got to finish packing and drive to the airport. Ethel and Jim will meet us at the other end. They flew out to Turkey yesterday!'

THE TRAM SHED

By Nick Fair

1945

The bus was on the pit and I had found the oil tin to drain the engine. It was an old oil drum, the ten gallon size, the top had been removed and a heavy wire had been fashioned across the top as a handle. I left it at the front of the bus; I had a rear wheel to change first.

I had slackened off the wheel nuts and I suddenly felt I wasn't alone. After a look around I continued, but a few minutes later a shadow passed by. It was quite clear on the side of the bus; not sharp like a silhouette, more like a cloud had passed over the sun. I could not help feeling there was an aggressiveness about it, but what startled me, the oil drum at the front of the bus went clattering down the pit, as if it had been viciously kicked by someone passing in a temper. This time I stopped and went to investigate and had a good look around, but again there was no one to be seen.

When the job was finished and the bus removed from the shop, the boss came in to see me.

'Well, Andy, settled in again after your spell in the army? Eh, if you don't mind me saying so, you look a little startled!'

'Aye Jim, I'm doing fine, there is just the feeling somebody is playing tricks on me, it feels real creepy in here sometimes.'

It was Saturday afternoon and this was my first week back after demob. The light was good and I foresaw no problems.

Jim Paterson was still the boss. Tam Hilton was now foreman in the shop, but there were a few changes since I left to do my stint in the army. When I asked about Doddy and Anna, I was told they had run off together and Sharky was never seen again.

'Oh Andy, I was talking to Jim Toner; he was asking if you're still interested in football, he said he'd come and see you. Tam Hilton will be here on Monday, he's on holiday this week. See you later.'

After Jim had gone, I was pleased to see a cleaner coming down the shop, it was Lucy Turner. 'Lucy, are you alright? You look a bit pale, are you feeling sickly?'

'No, I'm fine, it's just as I was passing that bus a kind of shiver was running through me. Onyway I hae a lot tae dae.'

I had just come back to the garage after six years in the army, I had been in the R.E.M.E. for the duration of the war, and I came out a corporal and went straight back to the bus depot. I'm not the sort of person who believes in the supernatural, I don't believe in luck or anything like that, the incident in the workshop didn't bother me, but as time wore on I was to encounter other little events that started to get to me.

Lucy was one of the new cleaners since the war and we met on the day I started back at work, and to be truthful, I took a fancy to her. She was a pretty young woman, and had been married and divorced with no children, she was a little shy but not silly. I say this because she figures in some of the things that were about to take place.

When the oil change was finished and the bus was back outside; I was looking at the job sheet to see what was next when Jim Toner came in. He approached me with a smile on his face.

'Welcome home Andy, pleased to see you survived. Sorry, but we did lose a few. Now what I want to know is, have you been playing football in the army? And are you fit for our team?'

'So you have a team again! Did you find the strips, or did you manage to get some more?'

'Andy, that was a mystery that was never resolved, but yes, we got a good second hand set, so what do you think?'

'Down at Aldershot I was playing with a local team, and we did quite well, so when is the next game?'

'We play on Sundays now, so a week tomorrow, can I put you down?'

'Aye Jim, I'll be there'. He turned and faced me with a smile. '"Inspector", if you don't mind!'

Later, a driver, Peter Walker came in and asked me if I could weld a bracket for his bike.

'We can talk about it in this bus, I could do with a seat, and a smoke.'

I never did develop the habit of smoking, but most of the staff did.

We were sitting in the bus and while I was looking at the bracket and he lit up his cigarette. We had only been sitting a few minutes when I felt a slight movement.

'Hey, is this bus sittin on a jack? asked Peter.

'No, I never leave a bus on a jack. Did you feel something too?'

'Aye Ah did, may have been my imagination. Anyway, are ye goin' tae fix my bracket'?

It was when I was welding the bracket it dawned on me that it was the same bus that had given Lucy the shivers, but what the hell, I don't go for that kind of stuff. But we have to go back ten years to clarify what was happening.

1935

As I approached the workshop I was startled by a rumbling, clattering noise, as a tram-car came trundling out and just missed me. I stood for a moment, I was aware it was a tram workshop, but it was the speed that surprised me. I looked in to see if it was safe to enter. A harsh voice from the interior said.

'Whit the f——do you want?'

I entered timidly. 'I was wondering if there was any chance of a job'

The man I was looking at was every bit as ugly as his voice; he stood there with a face of total aggression.

'Whit maks you think we want the likes of you in here? Piss off!'

In the year of 1935, there wasn't much work going anywhere, but you must keep on trying. I turned away feeling a bit disconsolate, I had been doing the rounds since I had lost my first and last job. As I was walking away, I came face to face with two men; one was dressed like he might have been a boss of some kind, the other was obviously a working man. They stopped and looked at me. The man in the suit asked, 'Who are you and what are you doing here?'

'I am sorry sir, I was looking for work, but I have been told there isn't any. Sorry to trouble you.'

I was going to walk past them when the other man said. 'Just a minute Mr. Paterson, who said there isn't any work? I thought that was your job?'

'Well Tam, I don't think we need anyone anyway, do we?'

'It was only last week you agreed I could do with a laddie in the smiddy. Ah canny see onything wrang wie him!'

The two men spoke for a few minutes. Mr. Paterson turned to me and said. 'Come with me and I will see if you are suitable,'

We walked along the side of a long pit until we arrived at the office.

'Right now, tell me you name?'

'Andy Manson, Sir.'

'No, I mean your full name.'

'Sorry. Andrew George Manson.'

'Right. Your age and your address.'

'I'm fifteen and I live at seventeen Greenlaw Road.'

'Now you are only fifteen, have ever worked any other place'?

'Yes sir, I worked for a few months with the blacksmith in Burnside Place but the smith was too old and had to pack it in.'

'Right Andy, I am going to give you a chance, but remember, there are lots of lads out there ready to step into your place, so don't forget you are here to work. Now don't let anyone here bully you. You will be working with big Tam in the smiddy, so if you come with me I will take you along to the tyre shop.'

Now at this stage I thought he was having me on. We all know that a tram doesn't have tyres! However Tam soon put me right on that.

Tam Hilton was the blacksmith who fitted metal rings to the tram wheels; they were sweated on with heat and were known as tyres. I was told to start on the Monday at seven and my pay would be fifteen shillings a week. When I was alone with Tam, the first thing he asked me was. 'Who was it that said there was no work here?'

'I don't know, but he was very coarse and swore at me.'

'Does he have a scar on his lower lip?'

'Yes he had, is that someone I will have to work with?'

'You will only work wi' me, weel, maist o' the time, bit jist watch him; he'll be nasty if he gets the chance. He's Sharky, a constant source of trouble; don't mix wi' him. Now I'll see you on Monday, and you must hae hard boots, it wid be dangerous withoot them.'

And so I started work with the trams, there were a lot of people worked there, but I won't bore you with a lot of names. However, there are some who have to be mentioned. Tam Hilton was the blacksmith and that's who I worked with.

There was a big man, Donald Scottie; he was a soft spoken man, a Highlander from Thurso, single, very strong and very easy to get on with. At that time he would be about forty and his job was labouring and handy-man. He was commonly known as "Doddy". In the shed there were six mechanics, two electricians, two painters and an upholsterer, numerous drivers and conductors. Beside Doddy there were four men who were labourers; one of them was Sharky, and six women who were cleaners. My work consisted mainly of helping Tam, fetching and carrying. I had been there about two weeks when I was approached by one of the drivers, Jimmy Toner.

'Here laddie, you are new here aren't you?'

'Yes I am, I work in the smiddy. Did you want something?'

'Did you know we have a football team here'?

'Yes I had heard, and I hear they are quite good'.

'Well it's my job to run the team. Are you interested in playing? You look fit. Fancy a try out?'

'If it is a team of men I might not be good enough, but I do like to play.'

'Well, we have a game on Saturday afternoon, come along to the high school pitch. The only thing you need is boots, we have everything else.'

So, in a short space of time I had a job and was in the football team. My life was promising, but I still got agro from Sharky. It seemed that he thought he should be in the team and he accused me of crawling to Jim Toner to be picked. I asked Jim about it.

'That bloody animal kicks everything but the ball, he is a liability that I can do without!'

To my surprise Tam Hilton was the goalkeeper, he was quite agile in spite of being forty-two; but he did have tremendous strength. Life for me was great but Sharky was always a thorn in the flesh; I was forever wary of him, and on top of that there was a woman cleaner he seemed to be harassing. It was not really my business, but it did irritate me. I quite liked her. Her name was Anna and she was in her early twenties. She was quite pretty but a little timid, and I could see she was nervous when Sharky was around.

After our first game on the high school pitch, Tam told me that I must wash the gear and have it ironed and bring it back on Monday.

'Would it not be just as well to keep it for the next game?'

'Listen son, this was bad timing, that was the last game of the season, so I have to insist it is all collected and put away till next season. That way, if someone leaves, we will know the kit is safe here'. True enough, on the Monday all the gear came in and Jim and I packed it away in a large wicker hamper, took it into the body shop and put it up on a wide shelf used for storing seats.

'Now listen son, get that lump of tarpaulin and hap it up. It will keep the dust out, it'll be there for two months.'

It had been about three weeks since I had come to the shed and settled in. After finishing my piece, I would enjoy a stroll round the sheds. On this occasion there was an alarming yell, or more of a scream, but before I could get to the scene and find out what was going on, there was a bit of a stramash. Tam Hilton had Sharky pinned against the wall with his hand against Shark's throat.

'You evil twisted bastard; if I ever see you touch that lass again a'll pit yie doon like the rat you are! Get oot o ma sicht, we must be awfy short o men tae hiv you here!'

Back in the shop when Tam had cooled down, I asked him what was going on.

'Anna wis in a tram cleanin' the seats and he cam behind her and started to take liberties. She gave oot a scream and dashed oot and I nailed the bugger as he cam oot the door. I'll swing fur the bugger, he better stye oot o' ma wye.'

'Tam, he's no' worth losing your job for, it would be better if you jist reported him.'

'Aye ye're richt, bit Anna wilnae say onything, gad he's lower than a snake's belly!'

It was good to know that there was somebody there who Sharky had some respect for. However, I got the impression that in spite of the age difference, Tam had a notion for Anna; so had Doddy, but that was none of my business.

1937

It was the autumn when the change took place. What happened then was something that was unforeseeable. The company had a change of policy. They decided to do away with the trams, there was no prior warning and it just about happened overnight. We came in at the usual time on the Monday to find the yard full of buses; the trams had been taken away in the night and parked in a siding out off town. The explanation we got was they wanted to branch out and it would mean laying more tracks all over the place, so buses were the answer. The only significant upheaval was that a lot of tram drivers had to learn to drive buses in a very short space of time, but it also meant the workshop wasn't suitable for buses, so to shorten a tale, one of the other sheds was converted into a workshop until the pits could be filled in.

If you could visualise the inside of a tram workshop the maintenance pits ran the full length off the shed; and there were three of them. Whatever was to be done to a tram, it had to be on tracks, so no matter where they were in the shop, they were over a pit.

The other thing that changed was the fate of the football team. Because of the upheaval, with men away learning to drive and the workshop conversion, it was decided there would be no football this season, so the hamper with all the gear remained on the shelf.

There was a bit of shifting around of personnel. Tam was now not needed to fit tyres to wheels, but as a smith there were plenty of things to do. The difference as far as I was concerned was I was no longer needed in the smiddy. I was put to work with a mechanic named Bruce Weller, a fine man, who also played in the team, so I was quite happy with the move.

'I'm sure the team will start up again when the dust settles,' he would say.

The authorities decided that the now disused pits would be filled in with crushed whinstone from a nearby quarry, but it was too dangerous to have lorries in the shop, so it was to be dumped outside the front door and wheeled in by wheelbarrows. It would be a long and arduous task, but it was the safest way to do it. Bulldozers were not in common use at that time: they would have been handy and time saving. It was arranged that there would be two men on night shift shovelling and barrowing the crushed rock in and dumping it in the old pits. The three pits were only to be filled part of the way, leaving enough room at the end for bus pits. The pits were three and a half feet wide and about four foot deep; they were the full length of the shop which was a full hundred yards from end to end.

With two men needed on the night shift filling in, Doddy and Sharky and a third man, Ben Hutton, the shift was rotated so there would be two on at a time with the third one having a night off. Now when this was going on, the cleaners were working a shift roster, three on nights and three on days with one being off, the management had decided that there would always be at least two women on at a time, mainly for security and safety. I was now classified as a mechanic and had to take my share of night shifts, so while the pits were being filled the maintenance work on buses was still going on, the pits were slowly getting filled up, but it took most of the winter as they had to be levelled out and packed down. When the crushed whinstone was about six inches from the top, they were finished with a heavy layer of concrete.

Now I should explain, the three pits to be filled were to be filled from the door to the back, but they were finished one at a time, the third pit furthest from the busy area was the last to get done; it lay half finished for weeks. Apart from that, the shop was then ready to be a workshop again.

The crisis happened in February 1938 just as the new floor was finished. Sharky never got any better, I was on nights and working under a bus when I heard what sounded like Anna crying. I got out from under the bus and went to investigate. She was sitting in a bus not far from the one I was working on, and was in a state of distress. When I tried to talk to her, she just cringed away and wouldn't answer me, as much as she was coaxed, she would not open up. I left the bus to see if I could see anyone else and met Doddy. 'What the hell is going on? Anna is very upset. Do you know anything about this?'

He took me aside and said. 'Sharky came in half drunk and he raped her. He was just leaving her and tried to squeeze past me to get away. I got hold of him: he is away now with a bloody face!'

'My God, come with me and we'll talk to her.'

We managed to get her to come out and sit in the mess room.

'Anna, we should get the police in, he has committed a serious offence!'

'No, please don't do that, I just want to forget all about it!'

'Anna, if you won't have the police I am going to get Mr. Paterson. I'm sorry, but we can't just ignore this'. And without saying anything else, I dashed away to his house, not too far away. When I explained he came at once and spoke to Anna.

'Anna, we must sort this out. I think you should go home. Andy will take you while I will have a word with Doddy. If nothing else, Sharky will not come back in here. Andy you take Anna home. Now Doddy, tell me what happened, this is a serious business!'

'Well now Mr. Paterson, as I was filling in this pit, there was at this time a dreadful yelling and I went to see what was ado. Anna was crying in the bus and Sharky just squeezed past me. I saw what a state she was in and I went after him. I'm sorry Mr. Paterson, when I got hold of him I smashed his face in and he took off like a scared rabbit!'

'Don't let it bother you Doddy, if he comes back it will only be to collect his cards. Now with Andy away with Anna you will be left here on your own, is that a problem for you'?

'Oh no', said Doddy, 'he will not come here as long as I am here, you just go home to your bed; I will be fine.'

Now all this was being said in my absence. I was with Anna and we had some tea, but she wouldn't budge on going for the police. When I left her it was time to go home, so it was the next evening I got the story from Doddy, but Sharky never showed face again. The pit that Doddy was filling was not to be filled full length; it was to be stopped about forty feet from the end, dressed up with a set of steps to give access, and used for the buses, just like the other two. Doddy had reached the point when he had to stop. The business of Sharky was not spoken about too much and it faded into the distance. A company came and put in the concrete steps and the pit was finished.

Jim Toner came round and talked about the team. 'In three months the season will start. I hope you are all in good shape. I will want a practice game soon to try out some players. Andy, will you get out the gear and see if it is all right'?

Now we had missed a whole season with the change over and surprisingly, the hap was not covered in dust as it should have been, but when I removed it I couldn't believe my eyes: this was not a wicker hamper under the hap—it was a wooden crate. I hauled it off the shelf and found it was nothing but an empty box. I dashed away to find Jim and he came back with Doddy and stood there mystified. 'What in hell's name is going on? Where is our kit?'

I shared the sharp disappointment that he felt, but all that I had to offer was. 'Sorry Jim, I can't put any light on this, but I can tell you where this box came from. Soon after the buses came we had a new gearbox delivered, and this was what it came in. I thought it had been broken up and put in the furnace. It looks like our gear has been nicked.'

Jim went to Mr. Paterson. 'Sorry Jim, it is not really my business, but whoever it was has had a whole year to do it. Sorry, but the chances of a replacement is remote. We might manage to pick up a second hand lot: other than that; sorry, but no more football.'

Doddy came to me and said he had been talking to one of the drivers, Peter Armit. It seems that he, Peter, was having a drink one night some months previous to finding the disappearance of the football gear.

'Hi Pete, gonny buy me a drink'? It was Sharky; sponging drink was quite a common practice for him.

'Now why would I buy you a drink, it has never been known for you to buy a drink for anyone!'

'I think you wid dae weel tae stay on the richt side o me, some day I'll make you aw sit up and tack notice!'

'An' whit the hell dae you think you can dae, they will skin yae alive'.

'Weel tae start wi', there'll be nae mair fitba', I've taken care o that!'

'It would be interesting to see whit you could dae tae stop it!'

Sharky just walked away, smiling and tapping the side of his nose.

'Doddy, what did you make of it? Somehow I can't think of Sharky stealing a load of football gear, and if it was the case, he would surely have been seen.'

'Well Andy, the gear went somewhere, and if I was to suspect anyone, that's who I would pick.'

1939

Now next thing we knew we were at war and any thoughts of football was banished from our minds. I had to report for training and finished up at Aldershot in the transport workshops. The war was over; I was back home in Scotland and returned to my old job in the bus depot.

1945

After the events that seemed to be 'spooky', things were quite normal, but there was the odd occasion, like when Lucy said, 'Andy, I think there was a man looking at me, but I told big Tam and he had a look, but there was nobody there.'

'Lucy, where was this, and more to the point, what did he look like?'

'You see that bus on the pit, well it was the one behind it. I was cleaning the inside and I stopped for a minute and when I looked up it looked like a man at the front of the bus sitting staring at me. I dashed out and got Tam, he came into the bus but there was nothing.'

'Could you describe him? Was he big or little, old or young?'

'Oh I just think I'm being silly. His face was very white, but it was marked as if he had been beaten up. He had a haunted look about him. Sorry, it must have been my imagination!'

A few nights later I was working on over-time, it was getting dark and, one of the late shift cleaners, Jessie, came and said. 'Andy, there's a strange smell of burning; it's out the back!'

The furnace was an old steam boiler that provided both hot water and steam for cleaning the trams, it was not used much now but it still gave the cleaners hot water; it burnt some coal but mainly rubbish and now there was no more steam pressure. So I accompanied her out and she led me to the old boiler and true enough, there was a smell of burning. The cleaner said it was the same as in the war, old clothes were collected for the war effort, we had jumble sales, mainly clothes and sometimes other stuff, but the items of clothing that were 'past it' were burnt in this furnace, but it has not been used for a long time'. I went and opened the iron door and in spite of it being stone cold, there was a distinct stench of burnt clothing.

'Sorry Jessie, I can't think why it should smell like that, we have no choice but to just forget it.'

These little things were starting to get more numerous. Lucy said to me.

'There is a mark on the inside of this bus, but it wasn't there earlier when I cleaned it. I can't think where it came from.'

So I went with her to have a look. It was an open backed decker; no doors, just a platform. Inside the opening there was a chalk mark. To describe it, it was a tick, as if you were filling a form and had to 'tick' the boxes. This tick was about two inches long, and it was the opposite way round, like a tick made by a left handed person.

'Are you sure it wasn't there earlier? Maybe you just missed it.'

'Andy, it wasn't there, and when I was looking at it I thought it moved, and I thought I heard someone laughing. That is why I came to you.'

'Lucy, is this where the bus was when you thought someone was looking at you?'

'Yes, but it was not this bus, I'm getting a bit nervous working here, Andy. It's not the first time I've seen this mark'!

I went to her and held her.

'Lucy, whatever is going on, nothing will hurt you as long as I am here. Just leave the mark there, I want the boss to see it. Go away and do something else.'

I found Tam in the office.

'Would you come with me and see if this means anything to you.'

So he followed me to the bus, but when we looked into the doorway the mark was gone.

'Just a minute. Lucy, come over here. I told you not to touch it, why did you wipe it off?'

She stared at me and looked in the bus, there were no marks, not even a trace of chalk dust.

'I swear to God I never touched it!'

Tam asked us to come to the office.

'Now what is all this about? Lucy, you are seeing faces, you heard someone laughing! And now there are marks that just disappear. Lucy, are you working too hard? Or if there is something bothering you, we will have to sort it out. Now don't let this trouble you, but I'm going to have you working with another woman. You will be together all the time, and I hope this will put an end to it. All right?'

She looked at me.

'Do you think I'm going crazy? Maybe I should just leave.'

Tam walked round the desk and took her hand.

'Lucy, get that nonsense out of your head. It is just a bit of stress. Now you will work with Mary and we'll see what happens. Right now, off you go, and don't worry. It'll be fine.'

When she was away I said, 'That was very fair of you, what do you think it could be?'

'I have no idea. Here, take this.' He handed me a pencil and slid a piece of paper across to me. 'Let me see what that mark looked like.'

As I was drawing it, I said. 'It was a tick; you remember the teacher used it when correcting the papers.'

'Yes, but you made it the wrong way round. That is a left handed tick; is that how it was?'

'Now that you mention it, that is how it was. Let me adjust it a bit.'

I drew another one, but the down stroke was shorter and the tail not rising so high. Tam looked at it and rubbed his chin. 'I have seen this mark before, damned if I can remember where, but it was smaller, and not on paper. I will have to put some thought into it.'

Later that day, I met Jessie again. 'Tell me more about the jumble sales, I wasn't here at the time. Jessie, was it common to get rid of rubbish in the old furnace?'

'Aye, you remember Doddy. He was always burning stuff in it, and yes, it did smell terrible then too.'

'When did Doddy and Anna leave? They were still here when I left.'

'I think it was in the spring of forty-one. Why all this interest in an old furnace?'

'When was the fire last used?'

'It was about a year ago. We were running out of stuff to sell and we just let it go. Are you going to tell me what all this is about?'

'Be patient Jessie. I'm trying to figure out why the smell is still here. By the way, do you ever feel there is something strange about this place, like things that make you feel uncomfortable?'

She gave a little smile. 'You mean like when a driver comes up behind ye and grabs a handful? That isn't really uncomfortable!'

There was another mechanic called Bob Waters: a fairly quiet man, he was working in the pit furthest from the door.

'Hey Andy, I'm taking the gear-box out of this decker, could you give me a hand?'

'Certainly Bob. Are you ready for me now?'

'No, I still have the shaft to take off. I'll give you a shout.'

Now I was doing something else at the time, so I carried on and about ten minutes later I heard Bob give a yell and then: 'Bastard!'

I went down the steps. 'What happened Bob?' I could see his knuckles were bleeding. 'Come out and let us see the damage.'

Once clear of the pit, he wheeled round on me angrily, but seemed to calm down before he spoke. 'I told you I would shout when I wanted you. I got a fright when I found you behind me!'

'Bob, I was working at that bench when you called out. You'd better let me have a look at your hand.'

'Are you telling me that you weren't down the pit?'

I shook my head.

'No Bob, and there is nobody else here. Could you tell me what happened? Just a minute. Your head is bleeding. We'd better go to the office.'

We explained to Tam what had happened.

'Andy, are you saying you weren't in the pit?'

'I was at the bench when he yelled. Bob, tell us what actually happened.'

'I had finished taking off the shaft and was about to slacken off the gear-box studs. I reached behind me to pick up the spanner from the edge of the pit and somebody or something handed it to me! I got such a fright I barked my knuckles on the box and at the same time banged my head. Sorry Andy, it's not the first time funny things have happened, but it is the first time I've been hurt.'

Bob went to the main office to get some first-aid. Tam was a fairly stable person, but now he looked uncertain.

'What the hell's going on Andy? These things are getting more numerous, it is beginning to look like we have a ghost!'

'Tam, I would be scared if I believed in such things. I have always held the opinion that everything can be explained. Before you ask, sorry, I have no explanations, but there must be an answer.'

The following day I was walking past a bus that just happened to be on the floor behind the pit where all the strange things seemed to be taking place. Alec Mercer, who was a painter, was putting a transfer on the side of the bus. I stopped to have a word with him. He had been there since before the war.

'Alec, in all the time you have been here, has there ever been anything odd, like spooky stuff? Maybe an incident of some sort that couldn't be explained?'

'Not in the past, but lately there have been wee things. Nothing serious, but recently I put down a tin of paint and went to get a screwdriver to open it. When I got back the lid was lying beside the tin, and this morning, I was sure someone was at it, having some fun, but, who knows? Now if you were to go and look at the other side of this bus you would see something.'

We walked round and he pointed to a panel that he had just painted, and there, right in the middle was a left-handed tick.

'Have you let Tam see this? It isn't the first time this sign has been seen. Wait there'. I dashed away and nearly dragged Tam away from his cup of tea.

We stood and looked at the mark. Alec Mercer looked at us. 'I don't know what all the fuss is about, it is just a blemish, something must have fallen on it. I'll give it another coat.'

'Alec, the duster you use to put the poster on with, is that it in your hand?'

'Aye, of course it is, and it is quite clean, why do you ask?'

'Doesn't it have a funny smell? Something has.'

He stuck it up to his nose. 'Now that you mention it, it is just like it had come out of a fire, but it was a clean duster! Is there something funny going on?'

'Aye Alec, some very strange happenings!'

There was a short period when nothing unusual took place and we decided to say nothing more about it. Sometime when I was not working, if it was not a football day, I would go to the golf course. It was a thing I took a fancy to in the army, and had joined the local 'Pitmore' course. I had only been there a few times when a man asked if I would like a round with him. 'I'm not very good, just a beginner.'

'Fine, we all have to start sometime. My name is Hendry McNulty.'

I introduced myself and we enjoyed the game. 'You are quite good for a beginner, do you think we could do it again sometime? In my occupation my time off is a bit irregular.'

I inquired about his job and was surprised to learn he was a priest. Now you may wonder how that could have any bearing on the story, but as the situation in the garage developed, I thought he might be able to throw some light on it.

'Sorry Andy, that is something I have never been involved with, but I am very friendly with the Minister from St. Andrews Kirk. I do believe he has had dealings with this kind of thing. If you like I will talk to him.'

So I had a word with Jim Paterson and Tam. There was some discussion and it was agreed that it would do no harm. This had to be resolved.

It was decided the two clerics would come on a Saturday, the shop would be quiet, there was not anyone working on that day except me. On the day the two clergymen came it was a nice sunny afternoon. I introduced them to Jim and Tam and we walked to the centre of the garage floor. The Minister's name was Rev. Hamish Anderson.

'Now I don't want to know what has been happening here. I gather some strange unexplainable phenomena are taking place. What we have to establish is what category these things fall into, is it the place or maybe a person that is causing the disturbance?'

Jim Paterson gave him a run down on the history of the building. He mentioned the incident about Anna and Doddy. 'But we have gone all through the war without any thing happening, it is only in the last three months that things have started to deteriorate.'

'Something must have happened in the last three month to trigger it off!'

'No, there hasn't been anything in that time. I'm sure we would know of any changes. There are always people coming and going, but nothing significant.'

Now it was Tam Hilton who stepped forward. 'Excuse me Mr. Paterson, we are forgetting something.' With that he looked at me. 'Sorry Andy, but you were here when we had the trouble with Anna being assaulted, and these strange things started when you came back. It may have nothing to do with you; it is has all happened since you returned.'

It took the wind right out of my sails. Was it me who had caused the problems? Now I was confused and unhappy. How could it have anything to do with me? I wandered away from them, my head in turmoil. Surely this was not my doing. How could I have brought it on!

Rev. Anderson said. 'Now just a minute, we cannot presume that Andy is directly responsible. Let us look a bit further afield. Now at this time I am getting vibes, but they are not strong. Andy, could I ask you to go to that door and just step outside. We will see if it makes any difference.'

My morale was now very low, almost as if I had been accused of something. Starting towards the door, I'd gone about half way when the weather changed. It clouded over and a darkness seemed to descend. There was a crack of thunder and then another loud bang. This seemed to come from the area where most of the disturbances occurred.

'Andy, come back here. Mr. Hilton, do you think we could go into your office? We may be on to something here.'

We all got into the office. I had to stand as there were not enough seats for everyone.

'Well, I feel this is something that can be exorcised. Can you give me some details about what has been happening? First of all, where is the centre of its activity? Are the things all the same? Andy, you seem to be more involved than the others. Have you anything to offer us at all?'

Thinking about all the things that I could come up with I explained as well as I could. 'Now it all seems to rotate round the spot near that pit at the other side, but come to think about it, I feel now it is focused on me.'

'Right, let's go over to the place you mentioned, we can see if there is anything there.'

I decided not to go, but would stay back and watch from a distance, but it didn't work, as I felt I was being propelled by some force. It was a very strange feeling. I was walking, but I didn't want to.

The group were just assembling when Jimmy Toner came on the scene with Bob Waters. It so happened that Jim, as well as team manager, was also the shop Steward.

'Mr. Paterson, could we have a word please, sorry if I am interrupting something, but this is important.'

'Couldn't it wait for a minute, we are conducting an experiment.'

At that the minister said. 'This may take some time, maybe you should attend to that business first!'

Jim Paterson stopped and hesitated. 'Right you two, go into the mess room, we can talk there. Now Jim, what is this about? Oh you are Bob Waters, yes you hurt your hand. How is it doing?'

Jim answered, 'That is why we are here, the girl in the office has put it through as sick leave, and I would like to know if this was entered into the accident book.'

'Just a minute'. He went out the door and called to Tam. 'Go and fetch the accident book, and bring it in here; and Andy, bring your two friends in and we will have a cup of tea. Will you put the kettle on?'

Tam laid the book on the table. 'What's this all about Boss? I do keep it up to date.'

'When Bob hurt his hand was it entered?'

Tam opened the book. 'There you are; time and date, injury to left side of head and left hand, first aid administered at office. It even has the bus number'.

At that, Father McNulty stepped forward. 'Sorry to interfere, but has this incident anything to do with why we are here?'

'Yes it has!' I went on to explain what had happened.

The Rev. Anderson said. 'Then I'm very glad you came. I may get some help from you, and it makes no difference what faith you are. Mr. Paterson, would you conclude your business? This could be helpful.'

Jim Paterson turned to Jim Toner. 'What is your question?'

'I feel that if he is off injured it should be registered as 'Industrial Injury' and he should be getting full pay. Sick pay is less than half our money!'

For a few minutes Jim Paterson sat with a thoughtful look. 'Yes, I agree with that, I will sort it out in the office.' He turned to Bob. 'Are you alright with that?'

'Yes, I'm more that happy, thank you.'

Jim Toner asked. 'Are these two gentlemen here about the funny things that have been happening?'

Father McNulty answered for him. 'Yes we are. Have you anything to offer?'

Jim smiled. 'I don't suppose so, but maybe you can explain that crack in the floor. It wasn't there this morning!'

Jim Paterson got up out of his seat. 'What crack? Do you know anything about this Tam?'

'Not me, where is it Jim?'

The party was led over to the very spot where most of the trouble had happened. There was a very visible split where the old pit was filled in and the new concrete met. They all stood and looked it. I ventured to say. 'When you asked me to go to the door, there was a peal of thunder, but there was also a loud bang. I bet this was the noise we heard!'

The Rev. Anderson walked on to the centre of the area beyond the crack. 'Could I ask you all to step away, quite a distance, thank you; now if you would refrain from speaking and stand still? He took a bible from his inside pocket, opened it, and looked at it for a few minutes. He closed it and walked first to his left, stopped with the bible held in front of him. He repeated the movement in the other direction.

'Father McNulty, would you come and take my place?' He handed the bible to the Father who repeated the action. As he was standing in the middle of the area, he seemed to shudder slightly. He opened the book and quoted a few words, I think in Latin. He lowered his head as in silent prayer and left the area and joined the others.

The Rev. Anderson asked him. 'Did you feel anything?'

'Yes, it was a strange feeling. It is the first time I have done that; what about you?'

'Could we go back to the mess room and see if we can muster another cup of tea. I feel I could use one.'

Jim Paterson ventured to ask, 'Have you anything to tell us? Is this like a séance?'

'Not quite. Would you let the Father and I have a little conference together? I'm sure we will come up with an answer. Andy, was there any time you felt your life was in danger? The strange thing is you seem to be the centre of his actions. What is the worst thing that has happened to you?'

'It is not what happened, it was what nearly happened. Alec Mercer asked me to help him put up a high platform for an advert at the top of a decker. He used two 'A frame' trestles and put a heavy batten across. He went away to get his paste and I had to go into the bus and on the way out I had to pass under the batten. I was just clear when the whole thing came clattering down. It could have crushed my skull. I feel I was very lucky to escape it!'

The Rev Anderson nodded his head. 'Yes Andy, but was it luck?'

'I'm sorry, I don't understand. It had to be. I could have been killed!'

Now it was the Father McNulty who spoke. 'Andy, you have been here for just over three months. There is an unhappy spirit in this shop; but it has never really tried to harm you. You must realise it has had plenty of opportunities, and I feel this would be a good place to start.'

My mind was again in a tizzy. It never occurred to me that I was not just being lucky. I left them all in the mess room and walked over to the area where it all seemed to take place. As I was standing in the middle of the space, I lifted my arms up in the air and called out. 'Come on then, I'm here now. Do what you must, or tell me what you want!'

It suddenly became quite dark; there was a sudden pain went through my head and I dropped to my knees. I was clutching my head in my hands. The pain slowly went away and the light seemed to improve. All the others were watching. They came to help me, but it was not necessary.

'Now I know what we must do. All of a sudden it became clear as day!'

Jim Paterson was the first to speak. 'Right Andy, in your own time, explain what that was all about?'

'The best explanation I can give you is that there is an imprisoned soul asking to be let out. What happened here before the war is known to most of us, but if you think about it, of the people involved: Anna, Doddy and Sharky, the only one left is myself. I was away for six years; so the spirit had to wait for me to come back, all that has been going on was a message to get me to do something.'

Tam said, 'I was here, and so was Jim Paterson, and I'm sure there are others who were here at that time!'

'No Tam, you were not in this building on that fateful night. Only Sharky and Doddy, who were filling in a pit, and Anna were here. She was the only woman working that night, there should have been two, but the other one didn't show up. I was the only other person here, and as the only one, only I could know how to liberate the entombed spirit!'

'What about Jim Paterson, he should know what went on. I know he was here'.

'Not till after the event, and thereafter, it was only Doddy's version of what happened.'

'Right Andy, no more interruptions. You explain what we want to know, the tick mark, the smell of burning material and all the spooky things that have been going on, and what has that bit of floor got to do with it?'

'Well, we are going to have to lift that patch of concrete, that is the tomb of Sharky, and it must be ventilated.'

'And what are we looking for? What is hidden there?'

'A wicker basket. The one that went missing!'

Jim Toner stepped forward. 'Are you saying my football kit is buried in there!'

'No Jim, your kit was burned in the furnace. That is why we got the smell of burning, Doddy needed the hamper to put the body in. As long as everyone thought the kit was stolen, nobody would think about it being used for anything else. All the other things were only to arouse my attention. Tam, are you thinking now about the tick mark?'

Tam was silent for a moment, then suddenly put his hand up to his mouth. 'God damn'! He thumped the table. 'Of course, the tick was the shape of the scar on Sharky's lower lip. Where is all this leading?'

Father McNulty said. 'If it is what I think you are saying, we must give him a proper burial. His soul has been trapped for over six years.'

Tam asked quietly. 'Tell us what happened Andy. We would like to put it to bed. I suppose we must send for the police?'

'When I was away to get Jim Paterson, Sharky was already dead! The story Doddy told to Jim was that Sharky had already fled. The truth was he was in the empty hamper. Doddy knew that at some time in the night he would get the chance to put it in the pit and cover it up with crushed rock. It was easy with no other person there.'

'But why was my kit burned. He could have buried him without the basket.'

'Jim, don't forget Sharky had boasted to a driver in the pub that he was going to put an end to the football. Burning the gear over a length of time was his way of doing it'.

At that Jim Paterson got up, excused himself and left.

'Where do you suppose he is off to?'

Hamish Anderson replied, 'I would think he is phoning the police.'

Within minutes there was a police car in the garage. A C.I.D. Inspector was looking at the spot with Jim Paterson. 'We will have to excavate this area. Meantime it will have to be taped off. Nothing to be touched until our forensic team has finished.'

As I walked to the door with the two clergymen, I overheard the Reverend Hamish Anderson remark, 'One of yours, I think?'

The Father nodded his head. 'Yes, I'm sure he is.'

'Well the bible in your pocket is one of mine. Do you mind?' He held out his hand. 'That is how I got it in the first place!'

Handing over the bible Father McNulty said. 'Right! You have asked for it. Monday morning at nine on the first tee!'

'You're on'.

THE LONG WEEKEND

By Maureen Brister

I sang softly to myself as I walked along the hospital corridor towards my office. Heels clacking on the floor, newly washed hair bouncing, a hint of a smile playing around my mouth. It was Friday, so of course I was happy. The end of another hectic week in my job as medical secretary to a Consultant Surgeon and his team of Senior House Officers and Junior Doctors. I had worked late last night to finish off some tapes, clear files back to medical records and try to bring order to my chaotic desk.

Keys jingled in my hand in time to the tune I was humming. Shouting good morning to Denise, one of the other secretaries who was already in, I turned the key, swung open the door and switched on the lights.

What on earth….? Slowly I put my weekend bag on the floor and stared in dismay at my desk. I had put out enough hints, goodness knows, about leaving early on Friday and not wanting a load of last minute clinic tapes thank you very much. I knew Dr Jameson had cooperated by my extra hours last night and I thought the SHO's and Junior Doctors had got the message. Obviously some hadn't, given the pile of files and tapes which now covered my desk. The red light was furiously blinking at me from my telephone. Messages, no doubt some urgent, to be dealt with. Damn, damn, damn. Temper was now taking over. I could feel it. I stamped my foot on the ground, tore off my coat and strode along the corridor to the room where most of the doctors did their dictation. Now my heels *really* clacked on the floor. I was furious. Someone was going to get a rollicking. I flung open the door. The room was empty. Of course it would be, the work was lying on my desk. No doubt the culprits were in the canteen enjoying a leisurely breakfast, hoping their pagers didn't go off and interrupt their bacon and egg.

As I strode back to my office Denise poked her head round her door.

'What's going on Cara? All this marching up and down sounds ominous to me.'

'I'm furious Denise. I worked late last night, cleared my desk and what do I find this morning, a load of clinic tapes.'

'But I thought you'd warned your team. Aren't you off early today? Where are you going anyway Cara, you've never actually said? Looking smart by the way.' Denise looked me up and down, smiling brightly.

'Oh, nowhere special, and yes I did give out the message, I thought loud and clear, that I wanted a fairly quiet day. Someone obviously either didn't hear me or chose to ignore me.'

I could hear my voice rising. Calm down Cara, calm down. I took some deep breaths, shrugged my shoulders and smiled at Denise. 'Oh well, better get on with it if I want out of here by three o'clock this afternoon I suppose.' I knew if I made too much fuss Denise would really be curious about my upcoming weekend.

I shut the office door behind me and sat down at my desk. A quick check of the patient files and I knew who the culprit was. 'What on earth is he up to?' I thought.

Telephone messages first, let's get them out of the way. I could hear the other secretaries gathering in the coffee room where no doubt Denise would be regaling them with details of my earlier temper tantrum. A knock on the door and Audrey stuck her head in. Trust her, she'd tried every which way to find out where I was off to and more importantly, much more importantly to Audrey, who I was going with. I half turned in my seat and looked at her.

'Everything OK Cara? Heard about what happened. I'd give you a hand with the tapes but I'm snowed under myself today.' Well *that* was a joke, Audrey didn't know what the words 'snowed under' meant!

'Thanks Audrey. I just need to get my head down and I'll get through it.'

'Who's the doctor in the firing line anyway?' Before I could stop her Audrey had flipped open a file. 'Eric Cuthbert? God, he's a dish, eh Cara? Thought he'd have taken the hint. Oh well, better get on myself I suppose, no rest for the wicked.' Audrey sighed, shrugged her shoulders and disappeared.

I shut the door firmly behind her and inserted the first tape into the audio machine. At least Dr Cuthbert had a clear voice. The transcription would be quick and easy.

Apart from a quick cup of coffee and chocolate digestive, I worked solidly through the morning and by one o'clock had finished the tapes and set all the letters for signature in Dr Cuthbert's pigeon hole. I treated myself to a sandwich and fruit juice then freshened up and went quickly through the offices wishing all the girls a good weekend.

'Not seen much of you today Cara. Have a great weekend,' was their general response. Audrey however was more direct. I might have known she'd have one more go at me.

'That you off then Cara. Plane to catch maybe? You've still got time to put us out of our misery you know. Come on, give us a hint. No? OK we can wait. We *will* find out though girls, won't we? Oh by the way did you manage to see the wonderful Dr Cuthbert and give him a piece of your mind?'

'No, I haven't actually seen him yet Audrey, but don't worry, I will. Anyway must go, see you Monday. Ciao.'

Setting up my phone to answering machine, I picked up my weekend bag, took one last glance in the mirror, 'looking good Cara', and headed off.

I'd booked a taxi to the airport. I had an appointment in the First Class Lounge at 4 o'clock. He was sitting in the far corner, a bottle of wine chilling in the bucket at his side, two glasses on the round table. There was still an hour till take off to Rome, plenty of time to enjoy a relaxing drink. His head was turned from me as I tiptoed up behind him and put my hands over his eyes.

'Dr Eric Cuthbert, what *were* you playing at today?'

He turned round, a broad smile on his very handsome face. God was I lucky.

'Just thought we could keep them guessing a while longer Cara. Did it work?'

'Certainly did, they think I'm after your blood. Little do they know. Pour the wine then. Let's get this weekend under way.'

NEXUS

By Robert Kirk

Carriage doors slammed along the length of the train like someone closing a row of giant coffin lids. A plastic sign with a faulty fluorescent tube buzzed a hesitant welcome to the newly disembarked passengers as they shuffled towards the exit.

'Eric?'

He turned at the sound of his name and found himself under the scrutiny of a man wearing a metallic blue shell suit and carrying a small suitcase. Eric allowed a puzzled frown onto his face, opened his mouth to speak but closed it again as the diesel engine emitted a deafening 'NEE-NAW'. With a series of metallic clunks and groans, the train heaved itself out of the station.

'You are Eric, aren't you? Eric Barnes?' The voice was now tinged with doubt.

Eric swept his eyes over the other man's face, his outlandish clothes, the tiny suitcase dangling from a beefy fist. He took in the scuffed trainers with no laces and tried desperately to identify this stranger who seemed to know him.

'I'm Alistair Murdoch. Your cousin from Perth,' insisted the vision in blue.

Eric's memory whirred through its card index, searching for names and faces that fitted the category 'cousin'. Then it stopped and held up a snapshot from the past. A skinny little boy in a school blazer, squinting against the sun, his cap askew, his shirt collar and tie in 'school boy' mode. Alistair had grown. Out as well as up. Eric studied the face and could now see the ten-year-old behind it, the cousin he'd last seen over thirty years ago.

'Alistair?' He immediately felt foolish for having stated the obvious.

'That's right. That's me.' Alistair swung his suitcase over to the other hand and pumped Eric's arm vigorously. There followed an awkward silence. Eric started to ask shellsuit—inevitably, that was how he'd think of him from now on—what brought him to Kirkcaldy. But he stopped in time, realising that that, also, was obvious.

'You here for the funeral, too?'

'Uh huh.'

'Oh.'

Another uncomfortable silence was avoided when a spot of rain alighted on Alistair's glasses. Eric turned and walked towards the exit. 'Let's find a taxi before this rain gets started.'

After a suspiciously long taxi ride that left them £15 poorer, they stood in awed silence outside their late uncle's house.

'Well, I knew the old bugger had money,' Alistair said eventually. 'But I never expected him to live in a palace.' His soft, high-pitched voice rendered the curse-word amusing rather than offensive. Eric smiled. Knowing their late uncle, the house would be part of a tax dodge.

The two men shuffled self-consciously up to the door, looked at each other with trepidation, then turned their eyes towards the shiny brass plate that said, 'Oscar Mathews'. Alistair prodded the bell push. They heard no ring or chimes, but something must have happened inside for the door jerked open a few seconds later.

'Alistair! Eric! I haven't seen either of you for ages. You're the last two to arrive. Come in and see if you can tell the rest of us what's going on.'

They followed their cousin, Fiona, along the hallway and into what was obviously the library. The room's incumbents were clustered in the centre of the deep red carpet, as if intimidated by the books that ranked along each wall and climbed from floor to ceiling to create a backdrop of multicoloured spines.

'Christ on a bike!' exclaimed Alistair, after he'd wiped his glasses and scanned the room. 'The old git must have been even richer than we thought. These books are worth a fortune.'

'Oh, he was rich, all right,' confirmed Fiona.

'Aye,' came an unexpected voice from behind them. A man with red, curly hair and a foppish manner pushed himself away from the wall behind the door. One hand held a whisky glass while the other brushed a copper curl off his brow. 'Aye,' he said again. 'He was rich because he never gave any of his money away. Especially to family.'

'True,' said Eric. 'Uncle Oscar would buy nothing new if he could get it second-hand.'

'And he wouldn't buy it at all if he thought he could steal it. How's it hanging, Eric?'

'Oh, fair to crap, Dick.'

Dick nodded. It was the answer he'd expected.

Several people in the main group voiced support for his view of their late uncle's character, although one soul with a misguided sense of fair play cautioned against speaking ill of the dead. There's always one, thought Eric as one or two of them drifted over to say hello to the new arrivals.

Thus was revealed to Eric and Alistair for the first time, the presence of their dearly-departed uncle. His coffin rested on a pair of nicely carved oak trestles. Alistair failed to suppress a smile when he saw that the casket had a decidedly second-hand look about it.

'So,' Eric looked around the dozen or so faces. 'Who's in charge, then?'

'You mean, who sent out the invitations, organised the funeral, ordered the flowers and all that?' Fiona's manner seemed whimsical.

'Yes, I suppose that is what I mean.'

She shrugged eloquently. 'We'd sort of hoped you were going to tell us.' She looked around as if to elicit support for her curiosity.

'Yes,' said Dick with a delicate toss of his curls. 'Since you two are the last relatives to arrive, we kind of assumed it must be one of you. Dramatic entrance and all that crap.' He tossed off the last of his whisky and bent to retrieve the bottle from the floor behind him.

Alistair and Eric shook their heads solemnly and in unison. 'I'm afraid not,' said Eric. 'I just received a typed invitation to attend the funeral of one Oscar Mathews at this address.' He eased back his cuff and checked his watch. 'Promptly at 1pm.'

'Me too,' said Alistair.

'We all did.' Fiona failed to hide her disappointment.

'So what's it all about, then?' asked one of the others.

'I don't know.' Fiona turned and nodded towards the coffin. 'But it definitely looks as if the old shite has finally died.'

'Who gets his money, then?' asked Kate.

Eric turned. 'Hullo, Katy. Haven't seen you since ...' All at once he remembered the last time they *had* seen each other. They'd both been drunk and had seen quite a lot of each other. *All* of each other in fact. Five intervening years did nothing to alleviate their embarrassment and the blood that suffused her neck. She suddenly realised her drink needed freshening and moved away.

'Er …, is there anything to eat?' ventured Alistair, partly to fill the uncomfortable silence, but mainly because he was always hungry.

Dick hoisted his replenished glass towards the centre of the room. 'We found some booze and nibbles in the kitchen, brought it in here to save us walking back and forward.'

Eric grimaced as he noted that the plates had been tastelessly spread along the coffin lid.

'So …' He turned his attention back to the others in the room and voiced the question he was sure they all wanted answered. 'Who *does* get the old bugger's money?'

If anyone had been remotely close to Uncle Oscar Mathews, it was Fiona, although she claimed to have detested him as much as the rest of them. And although she was as much in the dark as everyone else, she elected to answer Eric's question. 'Well, unless he made a will, I think we'll all have an equal share.' She lifted a wedge of chocolate gateau from the plate Alistair had brought over from the *'table'*. 'And since he couldn't find anyone desperate enough to marry him,' she went on, 'we're all the family he had in the world.' Perhaps feeling she had said too much, she sunk her teeth into the piece of cake.

The grandfather clock in the corner startled them by striking a single, sonorous note. And although Eric glanced at his watch again, he knew the old clock had always kept perfect time.

It was one o'clock.

Then the unnatural silence was broken by something that clicked and whirred in the far corner. There was a series of barely suppressed gasps as they realised that the TV set and video recorder had somehow been switched on. As the screen slowly blossomed from grey through washed out pastels to full colour, they gasped again. Eric began to feel distinctly uneasy.

'What the f—?' said Alistair, deciding at the last moment that he didn't have the nerve for profanity in his uncle's house. Not that the coffin bothered him, he'd already demonstrated his contempt for that. It was the apparition on the television screen that upset him.

Looking as mean and thin-lipped as ever, the face was recognisably that of Uncle Oscar.

'Hullo, my beloved family,' came the treacly voice from the television speaker. 'If this timer I've rigged up has worked properly, then you, my dear nephews and nieces, will be gathered in my library, drinking my whisky and eating my food.'

Eric heard a soft gagging sound behind him. It seemed that Alistair did have a conscience after all.

'I know none of you had any great love for me. You thought I was mean and tight-fisted.' He paused, pulled a hurt expression, and sniffed. None of his audience was fooled. 'And you're probably all wondering who's going to get my money now that I'm gone.'

'Aye, ye auld goat, we are,' somebody muttered.

Somebody else said, 'Shush.'

'Well,' the image on the screen went on, 'to show that I'm not as mean as you think, I decided to give everything to charity.'

'Greedy auld bast—'

'Shush, will you.'

'I noticed,' continued Uncle Oscar, 'that there's a lot of poverty in Brazil.' Puzzled looks all round. 'And so, I've donated all of my wealth to a charity there.' The image of Uncle Oscar reached for something at his side and drank heavily from a fat, amber-filled glass. 'It's not a charity you'll have heard of before. In fact, this charity is brand new. It's called the 'Benevolent Organisation for Oscar Mathews'.

'I'll shut him up,' said Dick, striding forward with the intention of switching off the TV set.

'No!' Fiona snapped. 'Let's hear what he's got to say.'

On the TV screen, Uncle Oscar's scraggy face assumed an expression that very few people, certainly none of his kin, had seen him wear before. It was … well, it could loosely be described as a smile. But it was the kind of smile Lex Luthor reserved for Superman. It dripped evil.

Their uncle's face faded and was replaced by a shot of blue sea with white-topped waves foaming onto a shimmering golden beach. Almost naked, coffee-skinned girls wobbled enticingly along the sand tossing beach balls to each other.

Eric swallowed. These girls were so well endowed that, when they dropped the ball, it stopped bouncing before they did. The camera panned around, making it obvious that this was a private beach, then swung shoreward to where a white bungalow squatted just beyond the sand. A sign on the gate said, 'Oscar Mathews Sun Centre'. The beach scene faded, leaving them blinking at a dark screen. But they still felt the hot sun on their faces, the sand trickling between their toes.

Uncle Oscar reappeared. 'The house you now stand in, I've decided to let you have, for as long as you and it shall exist.'

They exchanged frowns. What did he mean by that?

'And now, my family, if you look out through the window behind you, you'll see my last tribute to you, my final farewell.' There was a general reluctance to approach the window. Most of them were suspicious to one degree or another. Some were downright scared. Alistair felt acid gurgling in his stomach; a bit of cake wouldn't go amiss right now.

'Oh my god, look!' wailed Kate.

They crowded into the window space and looked along her trembling arm. A hundred yards away was a small hill. And standing on that hill was a familiar figure. One or two of them looked nervously at the coffin behind them, wondering how someone could be in two places at the same time; dead and yet still alive. On the hill, an arm was raised aloft and waved in the manner of a castaway hailing a passing ship. Some twit at the front—Eric couldn't make out who—waved half-heartedly back. Then the distant arm was lowered.

The wizened old man bent and grasped the plunger on a detonator unit. From it, a thin cable snaked all the way to the house.

The name of Uncle Oscar's chosen charity cycled repeatedly through Eric's head. The last function his brain performed was to create an acronym from the name of that charity:

*B*enevolent *O*rganisation for *O*scar *M*athews'.

BOOM

THE ELECTRONIC ELDER

By William Armstrong

Many church members said the whole affair was my fault. Personally I don't buy that. Oh, I grant you it was my remark, made when I was in a somewhat tetchy mood, that triggered the whole sorry mess, but if little Miss McNab hadn't passed it on to Marilyn Rawlings, nothing would have come of it. After all, as I said somewhat bitterly afterwards to the Reverend McKendrick, nobody expects a chance remark, made on the spur of the moment to be taken seriously.

Bruce McKendrick had grinned, that engaging lopsided grin that made all our female church members putty in his hands. 'Sandy, Sandy,' he'd chided gently; 'nobody's blaming you. It was just circumstances. That and four mismatched people. Anyway, you'd been doing the work of two men after Bob Smith died.'

'Well,' I remember saying, somewhat grudgingly, 'I didn't mind. Bob was a personal friend. We served together in the war. He was the best Session Clerk this church has ever had.'

'I know, I know.' In his heyday Bruce McKendrick had been a rampaging front row forward, up there in the top flight, with fourteen caps to prove it. However, the tough exterior belied a sharp analytical mind. If necessary, "the Hulk" as he was affectionately known to his teenage parishioners, could wheel and deal with the best.

Looking back, I can admire the way he handled the situation. The following Sunday he'd drawn me aside after the service, ostensibly to discuss roof repairs. That concluded, he'd turned to other matters.

'You've been covering the two jobs, Session Clerk and Treasurer, for long enough. I've sounded out all the elders and they're unanimous that you should be appointed as Session Clerk. So, if you're agreeable we'll make it official at the next Session meeting.'

'Thanks,' I said, suddenly humbled. It was the position I'd always aspired to in Glenmorlie Church. Now, suddenly, it was mine. 'What about the Treasurer's post?' I queried. 'There'll have to be a handover.'

Bruce nodded. 'That can be arranged,' he said carefully. 'Peter Masterson has volunteered to take the post.'

'Peter Masterson!' I exploded. 'He's an inventor. What does he know about church finance?'

The Reverend McKendrick frowned. 'Sandy Gordon,' he said severely. 'I'm surprised at you. It may have escaped your notice that Peter isn't only an inventor. He also runs his own company. Very successfully, I might add. What have you got against the man?'

'Nothing,' I said reluctantly. 'But he's only been an elder for a couple of years.'

'Time enough,' Bruce said dismissively.' This is the twenty first century now. The church has to move with it.'

And move we did. Within a week the Session had approved the two appointments. 'Session Clerk, A.L. Gordon; and Treasurer, P.J. Masterson.' I spent a couple of nights going through the books with Peter and he was extremely pleased with everything. So he should be, I thought to myself. I hadn't been in banking all those years for nothing.

'You run a tight ship,' he said admiringly. 'I see I'll have to look to my laurels.'

'Thanks,' I mumbled, embarrassed and at the same time flattered. Damn it, why did I dislike Peter so much anyway? I eyed him covertly.

Peter Masterson was tall; over six feet, with a mane of black hair just beginning to silver. In spite of the fact that he was in his mid forties he was still lean and fit. Regular sessions in the gym and on the squash court saw to that. Brown eyes shaded by stylish glasses, plus an engaging smile. All his own teeth, I noted sourly, thinking of my dentures. Oh. He's a charmer all right but ... there was something that didn't sit quite right with me. A feeling it was all a front. A carefully calculated facade.

But why? He was happily married, or so it appeared, though Ann Masterson seemed wrapped up in her riding stable. Rumour had it that she was wealthy in her own right and had financed his company in return for marriage. It was hard to believe, but nowadays you can never tell. She was a tall redhead, striking rather than beautiful, with a stubborn determination to make a success of her business. They had no family.

One thing I had to admire; Peter was brilliant in his field of robotics. His firm was right in the forefront of the market due to his genius.

Forget it, I chided myself tersely. You're letting personal prejudices get to you. Let sleeping dogs lie. Anyway, as I said earlier, Everything would probably have been alright if it hadn't been for Miss McNab. "A douce wee buddie", as my old granny used to say, Miss McNab eked out her small Civil Service with a stint in the local branch of ASCO, the supermarket giant. Polite, hardworking and efficient, Sarah McNab was an employers dream. Even the manageress, Marilyn Rawlings, spoke highly of her and that was the ultimate accolade. Marilyn Rawlings, I can still see her. A tall, curvaceous, blue eyed blonde, with a keen business brain and a determination to use all her assets, both physical and mental, to get her up the promotion ladder.

Marilyn and her husband, John, had come to Glenmorlie some two years previously. John Rawlings was a somewhat colourless individual, pursuing a tenuous career as a writer. He'd had a couple of novels published, but was finding it hard to replicate his early success. I once asked him, 'why Glenmorlie' and he'd just shrugged and said 'why not. We came here for Marilyn's career, as we always do and I just fit in. But,' and he'd grinned wryly, 'it is quiet, which suits me.' An unlikely couple if you ask me.

However, I'm getting ahead of myself, as usual. Joan, my better half, had sent me to get some fruit; apples and oranges as I recall. That was when I had my first encounter with the D-I-Y check out. as I called it.

There they were, four of them, like something from the bridge of the USS Enterprise and, there in the middle of all this technical wizardry, dressed in a blue ASCO overall, was Miss McNab, supervising her electronic acolytes.

I took an instant dislike to the whole setup. The syrupy sweet voice; 'please pass the item in front of the screen. Please press the appropriate icon. Please insert your money. Please take your change. Thank you for shopping at ASCO'. And so on.

Listening to the machine I felt a moment of panic. A feeling that the world was running away from me. Then the blue clad figure of Miss McNab appeared at my elbow. 'Can I help you, Mister Gordon?'

'Sarah', I said thankfully, 'you've saved my sanity. For a moment I thought I'd strayed into another world.'

A smile flickered across her face and I watched admiringly as she went about the task of processing my purchases through the machine. Surreptitiously eyeing the trim figure, the neat ankles and the relatively unlined pleasant features, I rea-lised that Sarah McNab must have been quite good looking when she was young. According to local gossip she'd had one great love; a young pilot who'd been killed in the Battle of Britain. After that she'd devoted herself to taking care of her ageing mother until Mrs McNab's death. That would be about six years ago, I calculated. Since then she'd become more and more involved with the church and was now an elder.

'There you are,' she said, passing me the bag of fruit. 'Oh yes … and your change.'

'Thanks', I said pensively and then, as an afterthought. 'You know, it's a pity we couldn't adapt one of those machines to hand out our hymn books.'

Sarah smiled. 'That would be something, wouldn't it?'

'Bye.' I picked up my bag to a 'thank you for shopping at ASCO,' from the machine.

And there the matter might have ended, if Sarah hadn't relayed my remark to Peter Masterson the following Sunday morning.

Peter latched onto the idea immediately and buttonholed Bruce, pointing out that, even if nothing came of it, we would still be seen as a progressive, forward looking church' especially by the younger generation.

As you might expect, Bruce took the bait avidly. A special meeting of the Kirk Session was convened and Peter was given approval to look at the idea. Mind you, there were some doubts raised, but Bruce overrode them and the proposal went through.

I'm indebted to Miss McNab for the next part of the saga. Peter, she said, came in one morning, bought a few items and then made his way to the self-ser-vice checkout. As luck would have it Marilyn was there, making sure everything was in order and they met. Peter outlined what he had in mind and Marilyn saw the publicity potential at once. A phone call to ASCO headquarters produced immediate results. Senior management, realising they had a publicity coup in the making, were all for it and Marilyn was given "cart blanche".

From then on Peter Masterson was a frequent visitor to the store and, accord-ing to Bruce, the prototype of the "Infernal Machine" as I'd privately christened the idea, was taking shape in Peter's workshop. He estimated it would be ready in about three weeks.

Not wishing to appear lukewarm about the project, I asked Bruce if Peter planned a trial run, before unveiling the machine to the general public.

He nodded. 'Yes. As a matter of fact he intends testing it in church on Satur-day. I'd like you to be there as well.'

'Right,' I said, somewhat mollified that I was being included in the team. 'See you on Saturday then.'

Saturday morning dawned, bright and early. Bruce and Peter were already in the church when I arrived, while, out of the comer of my eye I saw Marilyn's Astra turning into the car park. That did surprise me.

Bruce hailed me cheerfully. 'Morning, Sandy. Come to see Glenmorlie Kirk move into the twenty first century?'

'Let's see if it'll work first,' I said tersely, eyeing the tall black box, sited just outside the door into the worship area. I'll reserve judgment until then.'

At that point Marilyn appeared, looking about her carefully. That's hardly surprising, I thought, considering she's never been here before. Still, there's a first time for everything.

The expression on Bruce's face made it plain he hadn't expected her either.

'All set?' she queried, flashing a smile like a neon sign at Peter.

He nodded. 'Just starting.' He pressed a switch and the machine hummed into life. 'Good morning. Welcome to Glenmorlie church. Please press the icon marked OSS. This is short for Order of Service. Using the same procedure, please press H for a hymn book or B for a bible, as required.'

Peter Masterson motioned to me. 'Go ahead', he sad encouragingly, 'Press OOS.'

Somewhat cautiously I did so. A folded Order of Service slid out of the appropriate slot.

My astonishment must have showed on my face. Peter grinned. 'Go for it,' he said encouragingly. 'A bible, or a hymn book, or both.'

With growing confidence I pressed the appropriate buttons. In quick succession, a blue hymn book and a dull red bible slid out of their respective dispensers. I sucked in my breath. 'It works,' I said in awed tones. 'It really works.'

Bruce McKendrick laughed delightedly. 'Well done, Peter. You've even convinced Sandy. Quite an achievement.'

'Alright,' I conceded grudgingly. 'So this is the way ahead. I suppose you'll launch it tomorrow?'

Bruce nodded. 'It'll certainly be a talking point. Especially with the younger generation. This is something they do understand. Peter will be standing by, just to make sure everything goes according to plan.'

He needn't have worried. The machine behaved impeccably. As for the members, after the initial shock, they all seemed to enjoy the novelty. Even old Davie Johnston, who farmed up at the Mains. 'Aye,' he said, in those booming tones which could be heard above a gale. 'We maun move wi' the times.'

Of course it wasn't long before the press got wind of the story and descended on us "en masse". The national papers gave us quite a spread, while Bruce, Peter and Marilyn had a five minute spot on TV.

It certainly put us on the map. Attendances climbed steadily until the Reverend McKendrick was preaching regularly to a packed church. One channel even broadcast our next Easter service and soon the whole country was talking about the "Electronic Elder", as one smart aleck columnist dubbed it. Oh, it caught the public imagination alright and of course, this huge increase in attendances meant that our financial situation went from just getting by, to very healthy.

And then, three weeks after Easter, something weird happened. It was one of those glorious Sunday mornings, in early spring, when the trees are putting out their leaves in all the different delicate shades of green.

First to arrive, as always, was Mrs Glendinning. Ina Glendinning, a little inoffensive soul, widowed these past ten years. Neat, grey haired and self-effacing, with her purse clutched in her hand and peering owlishly through her horn rimmed glasses. Nervously she made her way to the machine. I was at the door welcoming people and missed the exchange which followed. There was a piercing scream and I dashed in just in time to catch Ina just before she hit the carpet.

Confusion reigned. Somebody brought a glass of water which I held for Ina to sip gratefully. Realisation dawned on her and she clutched at my arm. 'It spoke to me!' she gasped, wide eyed.

'I know, Ina,' I said soothingly. 'It asks you what you want. You know that.'

'No, no!' There was a certainty in her voice which startled me. 'It was after that. It said 'Blessed are the meek for they shall inherit the earth.'

'I think you must be mistaken,' I said carefully. 'It's only programmed to ask you certain questions. Not to quote the Bible.'

'But it did, I tell you!' Ina protested wildly. 'Clear as a bell.' And nothing would shake her story.

Bruce McKendrick was quite upset. 'I'm sorry this happened,' he said worriedly. 'She's obviously hallucinating.' But she wasn't. 'I spoke to our local doctor, who checked Ina over afterwards and he said, off the record, that physically and mentally, she was fine. Peter said it could have been a "glitch", as he called it; but personally I wasn't convinced. Ina was so positive in her story that there was obviously something in it.

Of course we tried to keep the whole thing quiet, but the machine, it seemed, had other ideas.

Joe Skeldon, a local market gardener, who doubled as our church officer, or beadle, if you prefer the Scots version, was the next recipient of its remarks. This didn't come out immediately and indeed might never have, if I hadn't commented on the new Mercedes which suddenly appeared in the church car park.

'That's ma car,' Joe said, somewhat reluctantly.

I whistled admiringly. 'Market gardening must be paying better than I thought. Or have you won the lottery?'

Joe reddened. 'No,' he snapped shortly and that was that. Well, it was for a couple of weeks and then Joe asked if he could have a word in private.

'Certainly, Joe,' I said, somewhat curious as to his reasons. 'Fire away.'

'You …,' Joe seemed unsure how to begin.' Mister Gordon, you were a banker most of your working life, weren't you?'

'That's right.' I knew now that this was serious business. Joe didn't call you "Mister" otherwise. 'Forty years in the business. Why do you ask?'

'Well,' Joe hesitated again. Then, 'you'd know about investing?'

'You mean stocks and shares?' I said cautiously.

He nodded.

'Yes, I've a good grasp of the stock market. In fact, I still dabble in it. I assume you're talking about shares? How much were you planning to invest?'

'A … a hundred thousand,' Joe said hesitantly.

I whistled in amazement. 'Joe, that's serious money. You'd need to spread it around. Don't put all your eggs in one basket.' Curiosity overcame good manners. 'Did you actually win the lottery?'

'No.' Joe frowned and looked away. 'Ach, I suppose I'll have to tell you sooner or later. I won it on the horses.'

'Joe,' I gasped, completely taken aback. 'I didn't know you gambled.'

'I didn't think anybody knew,' Joe said sheepishly. 'I used to place a bet about once a week, when I was in town with fruit and veg.'

'So how on earth did you manage to win that kind of money? Was it luck or information?'

'Information.' He paused, and then went on with a rush. 'It was the machine!'

I struggled to grasp the implications of what he'd just said. 'You mean the "Electronic Elder"?'

'That's right. Ach, I didn't believe it either, but it's true. It all started about five weeks ago. I was giving it a clean with a duster and I switched it on, just to make sure it was working.' He paused.

'And …' I prompted.

'It spoke.' Joe glanced at me nervously. 'Oh, I know it sounds crazy, but it's true. It actually spoke to me.'

'Alright,' I said, trying to keep the disbelief out of my voice. 'So it spoke to you. What did it say?'

'It said.' Joe swallowed ... 'It said, 'Joe I know you like a gamble. Back Heavenly Body. It's running in the 3.30 at Worcester.'

'Wait a minute.' I said sharply. 'How did it know you gambled?'

'I don't know,' Joe said slowly. 'I didn't think anybody knew. But the machine knew. I generally go into town about once a week to place a bet. Anyway, I asked the machine to give again, just to be sure. But it wouldn't. So I was left wondering. The whole thing bothered me so much that, when I went into town, I didn't place a bet. It seemed wrong somehow,' he added defensively. 'However, next day I checked the results at the Worcester meeting ...'

'And,' I prompted.

'There it was. The 3.30 result. First, Heavenly Body, at 10 to 1. A horse with no form at all. Of course I was in church sharp the next day and I was cleaning the machine when it spoke again.'

'Joe,' it said, 'Tm very disappointed in you. Why didn't you bet on Heavenly Body?'

'Well, I wasn't going to lie to something that seemed to know my every move, so I just told the truth; that I couldn't believe what I'd heard.'

'I'm surprised,' the machine said. 'However, I'll give you one more chance. It's a double this time. Chain Lightning in the 2.15 at Kempton Park and Road Runner in the 3.45 at Lingfield. Put a hundred pounds on. The odds are pretty good and you should do well.'

'And I did,' Joe added in awed tones. 'They both won. Chain Lightning at 12 to 1 and Road Runner at 8 to 1.

I calculated the odds. 'You must have picked up a tidy packet?'

'£10,400;' Joe grinned at the memory. 'Well, that was it. I was hooked. Of course I had to cover my tracks. You can't cane the bookies without awkward questions being asked. So ... I took a few days travelling round the various meetings spreading the bets. I've won about £150,000 all told. Out of that I've spent £50,000 on new machinery, new greenhouses and so on.'

'Including the new Mercedes,' I prompted gently.

'I don't see anything wrong with that,' Joe Skeldon said resentfully. 'It's not as though I've done anything illegal.'

'That's true,' I conceded carefully. 'Alright ... I'll prepare a portfolio of stocks and shares for you to invest the £100,000 in. They should bring you in a tidy yearly income. But,' I added warningly, 'we'll have to tell Peter. After all,' I said smugly, 'it's his invention. If there is a "glitch", as he calls it, then it's up to him to put it right. Oh yes … and we'll have to tell the minister. He won't like it of course, so my advice would be to make a substantial donation to the Roof Fund.'

Bruce was taken aback when told of the bizarre happenings and was all for holding a service of exorcism at once. However, Peter asked for a chance to check his brainchild out and, reluctantly, the minister agreed; with the proviso that, if nothing untoward could be found, the service would go ahead within a week.

I could see Peter wasn't happy, but Bruce was adamant and the inventor had to bow to the inevitable. He did say that the check would take some tune, but as he held a key to the church and could come and go as he pleased, I didn't see any problem. So when, on the second evening, I saw the lights on in the church and detoured routinely to check, it didn't surprise me to find him there. However, I was surprised to find Marilyn Rawlings there also. Peter's explanation that her experience of the D-I-Y checkout machines, plus her involvement in the project from the start made her assistance invaluable seemed reasonable. Still, I did feel he was somewhat flustered by my appearance. Marilyn, on the other hand, was completely unfazed and chatted away amicably until I made my departure.

Four days later I had an early morning phone call from Ann McMaster, asking if I had seen Peter. Somewhat surprised, I said no, but that he was probably at the church, checking out the machine. Although sounding somewhat doubtful, she acknowledged that was possible and rang off.

It was only when Miss McNab phoned, asking if I'd seen Marilyn, that the pennies started dropping. Having said no, but I'd check the church, I made a hurried dash along the street. The building was locked, but I, as Session Clerk, was a key holder. Unlocking the door I hurried inside. There was no sign of anyone. Heaving a sigh of relief I turned to go and then something hit me like a ton of bricks. The "Electronic Elder" was missing. Maybe Peter had taken it back to his firm for a check over, I thought hopefully, before phoning there. No such luck. Peter hadn't come in that morning and Jean Forbes, his PA, was equally mystified.

It was only when John Rawlings phoned, asking if his wife at the church, that my suspicions hardened into a certainty that something was wrong. But why take the machine? Hang on though. If that machine continued to forecast winners, Peter and Marilyn had taken a potential goldmine with them.

Eventually, after consulting both Ann McMaster and John Rawlings, we notified the police. Inquiries were set in motion and these led to a small private airfield in the West Country. This proved to be the headquarters of a charter airline, a two-plane job. The proprietor, at first evasive; admitted under police questioning that he had taken a couple, answering to Peter and Marilyn's descriptions, to

Spain. Pressed further, he confirmed that their baggage included a large box, which the couple had warned him was to be handled very carefully.

And that was that. The police spoke to their opposite numbers in Spain, who confirmed the runaways had jetted out to South America; Colombia to be precise, on the first available flight, still with their precious box.

There the trail came to a dead end. At the time relations between Colombia and Britain were going through a frosty spell, and assistance from that country's police force was extremely perfunctory, to say the least. According to them the couple had vanished into thin air.

Back in Glenmorlie, those of us who had been involved were left to pick up the pieces. Of course the press had a field day. Anything where church officials stray off the straight and narrow is meat and drink to them. Bruce, naturally, was furious. 'I trusted that man,' he said bitterly. 'I had faith in him and this is how he repays me.'

'Well,' I said, with just a hint of smugness, 'I always had this feeling that he was just too good to be true. If you remember I did say so at the time.'

'All right,' all right,' Bruce cut in sharply. 'You were right. No need to rub it in. But ... you can't judge people on vague feelings only.'

And that, I had to concede, was true. Anyway the furore over the whole affair died down eventually, and Glenmorlie reverted to the quiet Highland village it had been before the advent of the "Electronic Elder".

It was left to Joe Skeldon to supply one of the last missing pieces of the jigsaw. The portfolio of stocks and shares that I'd prepared for him had done extremely well, and he was now a comparatively wealthy man. Joe was suitably grateful for this and offered me a substantial cash present. However, I declined, suggesting instead that he divide the money between various local charities. This he did, earning himself a great deal of credit in the process. We were discussing his possible expansion into the property market, when he mentioned something he'd picked up from one of his horseracing acquaintances.

'Yes,' he said, eyeing me carefully, 'there's a strong rumour in betting circles that the big bookies have been taken to the cleaners recently. We're talking serious money here. The buzz is that the people behind the coup are American.'

I froze. 'You mean,' I said slowly, 'that it might be Marilyn and Peter?'

Joe shrugged. 'Maybe; it wouldn't surprise me.'

Our suspicions were strengthened a few days later when a cheque for £100,000 made out to Glenmorlie Parish Church, arrived by post at the manse. I could tell Bruce was taken aback when he phoned me. 'It's an American bank,' he said excitedly, 'but there's no other information.'

I gave him the news of the betting coup. 'This is conscience money,' I said. 'It wouldn't surprise me if both Ann McMaster and John Rawlings received something similar.'

An hour later my phone rang again. 'You were right,' Bruce said excitedly. 'I've had both Ann and John on. They've each received cheques for £100,000 plus letters asking them to agree to a divorce. I invited them both to a meeting at the manse tonight and I'd like you to be there as well.' And with that he rang off.

Somewhat unenthusiastically I arrived for the meeting. Ann and John were already there, both looking suitably serious.

Bruce wasted no time on preliminaries. 'This is fairly obviously conscience money,' he said grimly. 'The question is,' he looked at Ann and John in turn, 'what do you two feel about it?'

There was a long pause ... then Ann McMaster spoke. 'Over the past few months John and I have had a number of meetings. I think I speak for us both when I say it's time to draw a line under the whole sorry mess.'

John Rawlings nodded. 'I agree. We'll talk to our lawyers tomorrow.'

And that was it. Within a few months the divorce proceedings had been expedited and everything returned to normal. Well, more or less.

'So' I said to Bruce, 'all the loose ends seem to have been taken care of.'

Bruce smiled enigmatically. 'Almost,' he said. 'They will be next Saturday.'

'How do you mean?' I queried, looking at him in bewilderment.

He laughed. 'Ann and John are getting married.'

Not Men in Kilts

By George Sinclair

I could see wild birds flying like moths in a quandary among the trees outside my study window. I was lying back, slouching in my chair you could say, admiring the view as finches, blue tits and a robin took their turn to eat from the bird feeder in the garden. The overnight frost had made the ground hard, they were hungry and pecked eagerly. I sat at my PC trying to write a story; no words came into my mind, it was completely blank. I sometimes had days like that; was it living in Scotland or was it me?

My dogs started barking. It must be the postman I thought, they always bark at him, so I'll get the letters and junk mail later. The dogs kept barking. I trotted downstairs. The Collie was jumping four feet off the floor and the German Shepherd's bark was deafeningly loud.

'Be quiet dogs!' They both stopped.

I opened the front door and saw that two men in black suits, white shirts and dark ties were standing looking at me. Oh no, not Mormons again, I thought; I saw their mates three months ago and it took me fifteen minutes to get rid of them! One of the men was above average height with dark, unruly hair and the sort of strong clean-cut features that made me think he was an athlete. The other was slightly smaller and stocky, like an American wrestler, with a small scar running across his forehead. These were not your usual Mormons!

'Yes gents, what can I do for you?' I said, looking them straight in the eye.

'We'd like to talk to you for a few minutes, please,' said the first man, with a sharp look and standing as rigid as a statue.

'What about?'

'It would be better if we came inside, so that we can talk in private,'

'No! It took me half an hour to get rid of you lot the last time.' I was about to close the door when the second man spoke, his voice as sharp as a laser.

'Mr McKay, we need to speak to you now!'

'How do you know my name?' I felt his eyes piercing me, but he was silent. They flashed official looking identity badges, but I did not see them properly. 'Please let me see them in my hand.'

'OK,' said the first man grudgingly coming forward holding the cards at a long arm length and keeping a close eye on the dogs, 'but please keep them back!'

I looked at the cards. *The guys were from MI5 and the Secret Intelligence Service, SIS.* What were they doing in Scotland and what could they possibly want from me?

'They look official, but as we all know with identity theft uppermost in everyone's minds these days I'll need to check you out, so I'll take them inside and phone the number on your cards.'

'Is that necessary?' said the statue.

'My dogs think so, do you disagree with them?' The dogs were still snarling and baring their teeth.

'No!' was the super fast response. 'Please feel free.'

I had them on the back foot, and so I ran upstairs two steps at a time and phoned what could have been an MI5 office. Within three rings I was speaking to a nicely spoken young woman. 'Hello, how can I help you?' was her friendly opening phrase. She sounded as though she was next-door, not 350 miles away.

'I've a man from your organisation here and I want to check his credentials.' I gave the woman some details and asked her to confirm others. It all sounded pat, too pat for my liking! I needed time to think, so I went back downstairs.

'The young lady I talked to has never heard of you before, *can you explain that?*' I said with a straight face; well, it was only a white lie.

'That's not possible,' said the MI5 man exasperated, his head twitching to the left. 'If you look at the website you'll get contact information from it. Look, all we want to talk to you about is a conversation that you had with your old colleagues and Chinese men in the Auld Reekie pub in Edinburgh a few months ago. Let me cut to the chase. The Chinese Triads and the Iranians are involved,' a small spittle of froth starting to appear at the edge of his mouth.

How did they know I was there? What could they possibly want to ask me? *The Triads and Iranians are involved!!??* ... Fog shrouded my thoughts.

'OK, that sounds fine to me,' I said, lying through my teeth. 'But first I'll look for contact information on your website.' So I ran upstairs and quickly found the MI5 website. I looked at the biographical note of Jonathan Evans, the new Director General and found it revealing, but I couldn't find any contact information, other than his. The men's patience was probably wearing thin, so I ran downstairs and decided to test them.

'So when did Jonathan Evans join MI5?' I asked.

'1980.'

'What did he do before that?'

'He was at Bristol University.'

Now for the trick question. 'What was his speciality?'

'Policy making.'

'Wrong,' I thought. It was counter-terrorism.

'OK, but I couldn't find any contact information other than his.'

'Why not try e-mailing him?'

'Good idea.'

It was then, as the stocky SIS man turned sideways, glaring at the MI5 man, that I noticed a bulge at the top of his jacket below the shoulder blade and under his armpit. *A gun! Christ!* I ran upstairs again, three steps at a time! I sat and thought for a few seconds. What should I do? … I phoned the police.

'There are two men with a gun at my front door trying to gain unlawful entry.' I gave the policeman my particulars. 'How long will you be?'

'Our team will be with you in five minutes, Sir.'

A minute or so later I heard a faint siren. I sat and composed myself, and yet wondered what questions these guys would ask and how I would respond. Would I end up in a room with a light shining in my face and goons squeezing my neck? What for? What had I done? The siren was now loud and close and the men looked round to see six police coming towards the door. I ran downstairs.

'What seems to be the problem?' said the burly sergeant.

'These two men are trying to force their way into my house and that one has a gun!' I said firmly and noticed that the SIS man was apparently reaching for it. The sergeant grabbed him by the wrist and manhandled him to the ground.

'OK you two, you'd better have a good story,' was the sergeant's gruff statement.

'We're MI5 and SIS officers!' said the MI5 man, 'and we need to talk to Mr McKay urgently!'

'Oh yeah, and I'm William Wallace!' said the sergeant in a broad Scottish accent.

'Sergeant, we really are MI5 and SIS officers. Please look at our ID.' The men handed the sergeant two small black leather folders.

'Say, these are real IDs; I've seen ones like these before. Gentlemen, you have my apologies and are free to go about your business.' The sergeant looked disparagingly and had a knowing smirk.

'Thanks. We need to talk to Mr McKay ... So, Mr McKay, may we now come inside and have that discussion?' the SIS man said.

'Of course, why not?' I felt like a caged animal.

As we entered the lounge, the MI5 man forced an awkward smile and opened the discussion. 'Look, we need to ask a special favour from you. There is going to be a meeting in the Auld Reekie pub in Rose Street tonight between your previous Chinese business colleagues and your old work colleagues. We've had a tip off that the Triads will try something and it gives us a chance to catch them.'

'You're kidding, right? You need me?'

'This is all about a special relationship.'

'What relationship?'

'Remember Mr Chong? Well, he's going to be there. He's very nervous about the situation and needs some moral support.'

Andy Chong and I went back a long way, we'd been at University together and had shared a flat. Sadly, after graduating, we lost touch, but a chance meeting several years later had brought us together again. Our families had met every few years since then with alternate visits to China and the UK. He was now the Director of Procurement with a large Chinese company and we'd met recently at several business meetings. He was visibly sad when I retired.

'We're on the trail of an industrial espionage team consisting of a Chinese Triad gang who've been blackmailing your Chinese business colleagues into giving them technical information on plutonium manufacture, by threatening their families, two of whom have already been tortured and brutally murdered. The Triads have worked a deal with the Iranians to give them atomic bomb capability.'

'But I was responsible for giving the Chinese manufacturing technology for uranium, not plutonium! *Plutonium makes bombs!* So how can the Triads sell what they don't have?' Did they believe me? Their eyes seared through my skull like red-hot pokers.

'They may not have it yet, but we believe that the Iranians are close to getting it.'

'There must be some other route that they are getting the information from! There must be!' I changed the subject. 'Andy wants me involved?'

'Yes. He has specifically asked for you to be present.'

Christ, I thought! Am I getting involved in this—blackmail, murder, Triads, Iranians, atomic bombs!

'I hope that you guys have plenty of fire power if a battle breaks out.'

'We've an armed response team of twenty men that'll surround the area.'

Fantastic, I thought, just what I need—*stress!* After many years in a high-pressure business, and near to burnout, all I really wanted to do was to write and have peace and quiet. 'OK, what time tonight?'

'Eight o'clock.'

At five to eight I padded along Rose Street like a panther, my trainers making no sound. There was still time to back out, but the thought of Andy's problem focused my anger and switched on my adrenaline pump.

I arrived at the Auld Reekie; it had not changed since my last visit. Inside, at the far end was a raised stage with two vertical silver bars that were supporting two scantly dressed young women. A few eyes in the pub were following their movements to the music. They had bags under their eyes and small bruises on their arms at the bends of their elbows. I could see Andy and my old colleagues in the opposite corner and waded towards them through the morass of beer drinking bodies.

'Hi guys, enjoying the scenery then?'

'It's not as good as in China,' Andy said, smiling warmly and stretching out his hand towards me.

'Maybe, but your beer is rubbish.'

Andy laughed. 'I'm sorry to involve you in this, but I feel safe with you around. You were always a tougher cookie than me.'

'No worries, I'll look after you kid,' I said, smiling at Andy and sitting down next to him.

He ordered a beer for me and we began to chat. After a short time, two Chinese men approached us menacingly; they were the same height as us, slightly built and had hawkish features.

'Please come outside with us now,' said one of the Chinese men, emboldened by a bulge protruding from his jacket.

Were these the Triads, I thought? Andy and I nodded at each other and got up to go outside. I let Andy go in front of me. He moved outside the swing door and I was right behind him. As I passed through the door I grabbed the edge and swung it back as hard as I could. It hit the first Triad hard on the face knocking him backwards onto the second Triad. They both fell violently onto the pub floor.

'*Strangle hold,*' I screamed.

Andy and I were on top of them instantly. *Control the head and the body is dead.* My left hand went around the back of the Triad's neck, grabbing the jacket on my right arm below the outside of the elbow; my right hand grabbed the jacket on my left arm above the elbow. The tourniquet was on! I applied severe pressure! The bone on the outer edge of my right arm acted like a steel bar on the Triad's windpipe, cutting off air immediately. His face turned purple. He struggled violently, using up his oxygen too fast. Fool! He soon stopped struggling. His face had become deep purple and he was about to pass out. *But, of course, that was the plan!*

'OK, you can let them go now,' the MI5 man said, gun drawn and his eyes riveted on the Triads.

The two Triads struggled to stand up holding their blood-drained throats and oxygen drained heads, making deep rasping noises. The MI5 and SIS men quickly handcuffed them and dragged them off to their waiting cars, then came back to thank us.

'Where did you learn to do that?' said the MI5 man, with an admiring smile.

'We're not just old dogs you know,' Andy quipped.

'Have you got the Triads that you really need, or are these just the foot soldiers?' I asked.

'These are just foot soldiers, but we'll persuade them to help us find the big guys. We've had news today that the Iranians have changed their tack and are now trying to get plutonium information through the Russian Mafia.'

'So, does that take the heat off us?'

'Yes, thanks for all your help.'

We shook hands and they disappeared into the night. Andy and I decided to go back to the Auld Reekie to join our colleagues, relax, drink and enjoy the scenery.

The next day as I sat at my PC, the memories of the previous day flooded back into my mind. At least now I had a story to write, and perhaps I should delete my website cookies on nuclear bomb manufacture.

LOST AND FOUND ... AND LOST AGAIN

By Anne Ewing

The Fife circle train made its way in turn through the stations of the wee towns in the west of the kingdom, towns which owed much of their existence to the coal measures underlying them. These settlements dated from ancient times, but had, in the course of the twentieth century acquired almost comic cultural connotations relating to their bleak physical characteristics, shading slowly but surely into aspects of real social deprivation, as the coal mines inexorably closed and nothing took their place. The richly varied cultural and educational opportunities that had existed in the community under the auspices of the miners' welfare institutes, the co-operative societies and the schools and churches in the immediate post-war era gradually withered on the vine. Now the post-industrial features of these towns in the early years of the twenty-first century seemed to comprise only combinations of pubs, social, or more accurately drinking clubs, bingo halls, bookmakers premises and occasional shops whose shutters remained in place all day, even during opening hours. These depressing clusters contrasted with and co-existed, somewhat ironically, alongside pockets of new private housing occupying gap sites, or in one case even the actual location of one of the former collieries. Stone walls and elaborate entrances to these estates formed a frontier between new and old, private and public, upwardly mobile and downwardly demoralised. Logo-laden banners fluttered above the sales offices and show houses where gala flags and bunting had once adorned the pit-head premises during the annual miners' celebrations.

Miss Janet Beveridge had done this journey many times and was reasonably familiar with the landscape she passed through. Had she thought about it at all, she would have realised that it was actually completely foreign to her. She had boarded the train in the county town which, had she been asked, and had she given her honest opinion, she would probably have said was a much nicer part of the county. (She still thought in terms of the county of Fife rather than 'the region' or 'the council', titles which had come and gone in the last forty years!) Her generation of Fifers living in old established towns in the centre felt inherently superior to those in the mining towns in the west, and she had grown up with this sense of coming from a more salubrious area and belonging to a better class than her contemporaries in this generally poorer, dirtier and less respectable region. Her father was headmaster of a country school and her mother a tailoress with a client list of exclusively genteel and well-spoken ladies. She was an only child and had a lonely and very restricted childhood. Her parents were both extremely conventional, even for those days, and she was kept on a very short leash.

They had themselves been products of family backgrounds where the inheritance of strictly Calvinist standards remained more or less undiluted. Consequently there was little or no time for, or interest in, the emotional welfare of their little daughter. She had one aunt, on her mother's side, who had broken out of the narrow confines of her upbringing. Mabel was a lady's maid in domestic service to one of the local gentry, until she scandalised the entire community and shamed her own family by running away with the chauffeur! They ran all the way to London where they did the decent thing by getting married and went on to lead a blameless, but sadly childless, life. They did well and became quite prosperous, but although they always tried to keep in touch with the family back in Scotland, they were never forgiven for their earlier impetuous behaviour. Nor did they ever return north of the border, but as the years passed they would invariably send their niece a gift for Christmas. Janet's favourite amongst these presents was a beautiful china doll with piercing blue eyes and lovely blonde curls, which she immediately named Mabeline. Her mother made no secret of the fact that she considered this an unnecessarily expensive and flamboyant gesture, typical of Mabel's frivolous nature, but although Janet was never to meet her aunt and uncle they came to represent another world for her. As did that lovely dolly! Everyone Janet knew amongst her family and friends had sombre brown eyes and mousey hair, including herself, but she always imagined her Auntie Mabel in

London as having blue eyes and blonde hair like the dolly, and she fantasised that one day she would send for Janet who would thenceforth live a wonderful life in the metropolis.

Of course that day was never to come, and as she grew up and was prevailed upon to put away childish things, little remained to relieve the serious and affectionless tenor of Janet's young life. Mabeline disappeared along with other vestiges of her childhood as her parents trained her into a diligent and humdrum life style. In their defence, it was all they had ever known themselves, and nothing in their experience had given them any reason to believe there was anything wrong with their approach. They were gratified that their daughter showed great promise at school. College or university was clearly on the agenda her parents had planned for her, her father because of his background and her mother because she secretly resented her own lack of education and wanted her daughter to have what she had missed. Their family had come through the war unscathed, the immediate post war years of austerity were safely past and it seemed that the way ahead was clear for them to realise their ambitions for their girl. She had gained the required number of higher examination passes to secure admission to Moray House College of Education in Edinburgh, and was about to start her last year at school, the final veneer of accomplishment about to be added, when fate intervened and threatened their best-laid plans in the most unexpected and ghastly way.

Now, more than half a century later, there was no evidence whatsoever of the shocking trauma that visited Janet and her parents that summer of 1950. Had they been alive to see her now, they would have been completely satisfied that she had turned out exactly as they had hoped. She had followed in her father's footsteps and had completed a career of forty years as a primary school teacher in their old home town. She was highly regarded as a great teacher who embodied and inculcated in her charges all the virtues of discipline, respect, probity and industry that her parents could have wished for. If she lacked an ability to relate to her pupils with any measure of affection, humour or sympathy, that was surely a small price to pay for the academic results she achieved with her pupils, even in some of the most seemingly hopeless cases. Those children learned whether they or their parents wanted them to, and in spite of all the factors which might have held them back. Miss Beveridge saw to that!

After she retired, she saw less and less of her colleagues and within a year or two, had lost all contact with the school and her former life. Indeed, she was very lonely, but she would never have thought of herself in those terms. She was brought up to understand that introspection was self-indulgence, and that you had to make the best of things. So, she lived her lonely life and filled her time, if not with people, with the things that had always brought her satisfaction and solace—her books, music and occasional solitary outings to places of historical and cultural interest. So today she was bound for the Royal Scottish Museum in Edinburgh, and a lecture on the Scottish philosophers of the Enlightenment. As she sat primly in her seat on the train, she was the epitome of elderly respectability. Her plain navy blue pleated skirt was matched with a navy and white dog-toothed check jacket over a white silk blouse, caught at the throat by a simple but tasteful Celtic silver brooch. Her well-polished flat, navy leather shoes were teamed with a handbag of the same material. Her hair was neatly permed into a halo of white curls and her make-up limited to a fine dusting of face powder and a touch of lipstick the same shade as the coral nail-polish she wore.

At one of the last stations before the Forth rail bridge, a young woman with a baby buggy got on and sat across from Janet. She made a striking contrast with her older travelling companion. She was dressed in the ubiquitous uniform of the young—denim jeans and a dark hooded fleecy top, her feet shod in blindingly white trainers. Long, luxuriant dark locks with striking scarlet streaks almost hid her face as she stared vacantly out of the window, chewing rhythmically and lounging carelessly in her seat. Janet took all this in with one discreet glance, and having issued a silent instruction with the habit of a lifetime, 'Sit up straight and pay attention!' gave no more thought to the girl. It may have crossed her mind that she seemed very young to have a baby, but in these days, even Janet had become accustomed to the way society seemed able to accept the concept of single teenage motherhood, a far cry and a world away from the situation that pertained in her youth.

As she shifted her eyes to the occupant of the pushchair, she experienced simultaneous and overwhelming senses of shock, déjà vu and stomach-churning recognition that almost had the effect of a physical blow. Staring out of the baby buggy, over the edge of a none-too clean blue woolly blanket and below a froth of blonde curls, were a pair of eyes whose intensity of blue she had only ever seen three times before. The little boy and the old lady gazed unblinkingly at each other solidly for some time, until Janet's eyes began to water, and she shut them tightly as she fumbled for a handkerchief in her handbag. When she opened them again and dabbed discreetly at the tears brimming over her lower eyelids, she was uncomfortably aware that the baby was still staring at her, but thankful that his mother had continued to ignore both her and the little boy.

In the space of those few moments, more than fifty years melted away, and Janet was instantly transported back to a part of her life that she thought she had managed to bury, just as surely as she had buried her parents and her memory of their hurt and disappointment, of her shame and the punishment it had warranted. Now it all came flooding back and she thought she would pass out with the intensity of feeling it had engendered. She couldn't stop looking at the baby in the buggy, and had the feeling that the sense of recognition wasn't hers alone. His mouth was covered by the blanket, but she knew he was smiling by the way his eyes crinkled and his chubby red cheeks bulged. His little arms were now beginning to pump up and down under the blanket, and she had a dangerously irresistible urge to reach over and lift him out of the pushchair. As she felt herself begin to move, the young mother turned and looked at Janet, and years of good manners and social training came to the rescue of the older woman, as she said in a remarkably normal voice, 'What a lovely baby you have!' A sudden smile briefly transformed the surly young face as the girl responded, 'He's not so lovely when he stops me sleeping at night'. 'Oh yes, but I'm sure he's worth it, isn't he?' Janet replied. 'I suppose so,' mumbled the girl and turned back to the window and resumed her chewing and staring. Janet couldn't help noticing that during this short exchange of small talk the young mother hadn't once actually looked at her baby.

Janet turned again to look at the little boy and now she had confirmation that the eyes continuing to gaze unblinkingly at her were the same blue, blue eyes that had looked at her and won her heart more than fifty years before. They belonged to the farmer's son who had taken to appearing, just as she alighted from her high school bus in the village and would walk home with her to the schoolhouse at the end of the secluded lane that ran past the village school. Andrew was a few years older than her and already working with his father on their prosperous farm some distance from the village. He was a real charmer and although she was very shy, unused as she was to attention from anyone at all, let alone a handsome young man who was obviously interested in her, she felt, for the first and, as it was to turn out, only time, the alien and exciting onset of incipient sexual attraction. Now it wasn't only a doll whose blue eyes attracted her, and for the entire summer of 1950 she and her young man had as many times together as they could manage. With great difficulty and much subterfuge, she managed to keep this liaison a secret from her parents, and it wasn't long until, given the young man's persistence and her naivety, the inevitable happened. She had to face up to the fact that she was in the dire kind of trouble that she had heard spoken of amongst her contemporaries, but only ever hinted at by their elders and betters. She was in a state of near collapse with sheer panic, but couldn't bring herself to tell Andrew about her predicament and so immediately cut off all contact with him. But she knew she had no choice but to confess her fall from grace to her parents.

Of course, they were distraught and furious with her, assuming that she had inherited Mabel's wayward tendencies, but very quickly turned their anger and disappointment into fast and decisive action. They only briefly alluded to the identity of the father of her child, but did not attempt to persuade her to tell them who he was. The summer term was almost over and her place at college deferred for a year, a story was concocted to account for her absence for the best part of that time. It was an approximation of the truth: that she was keeping house for a relative up north, whose wife was suffering from a long term illness. The fact was that a distant cousin of her father's, a Free Church of Scotland minister in a remote parish in Inverness-shire, agreed that she could go there and live with him and his wife until her confinement was imminent, when she would be taken to a nursing home in Aberdeen for the birth and subsequent immediate adoption of the baby.

During her time with the minister and his wife, they did their best to convince her that she had committed a terrible sin and that her only hope of ultimate redemption was that she must do her best to accept this solution to her transgression. Thereafter, she must never give any thought to the baby, the result of her wanton behaviour, but rather be grateful that he would have a good life with parents who really wanted him. She should devote the rest of her life to making up to her parents for the way she had let them and herself down. So they would quote appropriate biblical texts at her.

'*Behold, I was brought forth in iniquity, and in sin did my mother conceive me.*' (*Psalm 51*), while other home-spun homilies carried a more basic but equally cruel message.

'*Mind lassie, what ye get up tae in the dark, the Lord sees as clear as day.*'

When her time came, Janet struggled alone, with only a terrifying midwife in attendance, through a protracted and agonising labour. Was this the punishment she had been promised for her sinful and shameful actions? She tried not to think about the father of the baby, but if he did creep unbidden into her thoughts it was as such a dim and shadowy figure that she began to doubt whether he had ever even existed beyond her imagination. It had been made clear to her that she would not be allowed to see the baby, and he was whisked away immediately he was born. Her mother came to visit her the next day, and relented only enough to tell her that the baby was a boy. Tearfully, Janet managed to stammer, 'I would like the baby to be called Andrew, Mother. Will you ask them if that's possible?'

Her mother made no promise, or even reply, to her daughter's request, and no reference was ever made to the child again.

She returned home and in due course went to college, successfully completing her teaching qualification three years later. To that extent, she fulfilled her parents' ambitions for her, but in the remaining years of their lives, while she looked after them as a dutiful daughter as they grew old, ailed and died one after the other, the emotional gulf that separated them widened to the point that she might as well have been living with strangers. Throughout those years, between them hovered the image of that lost baby boy, born of them but never spoken of and remembered by her only fleetingly during the longest and loneliest of nights, as she cherished his memory in her innermost heart.

What her parents never knew was that the night after her mother's visit, she had crept from her bed and stealthily moved through the rooms of that cold, grey, forbidding nursing home until she found the little nursery where only two cots were occupied, one with a pink blanket and the other with a blue. As she peered into her son's crib, her heart was pierced by the bluest of eyes, the exact replica of those of the only sweetheart she would ever know. A precious few moments were all she had as she soon heard the brisk footsteps of a night nurse approaching the nursery. She fled back to her room, sobs breaking from her as she went, weeping the only tears she would ever shed for that little boy. Throughout all the intervening years she had suppressed the memory of the brief time she had with her only child. Only after the death of her parents did she allow herself to wonder what had happened to her baby. Who had brought him up and what had become of him? He would be a man in his fifties now, a father himself, perhaps even a grandfather.

As they pulled into Haymarket station, she came to herself and watched as the girl stood up and grasped the handles of the pushchair. In so doing, she made eye contact with her son for the first time and the baby smiled in recognition of his mother. Joining her at the door of the compartment for the few minutes that remained of their journey, and sensing that time was running away from her, Janet felt a desperate urge to make real contact with the young woman before they reached Waverly station. All she could manage was to blurt out, 'What's the baby's name, dear?' The reply was no surprise, but the extra piece of information the girl added, confirmed in an instant that Janet's instincts had been right, her feeling that she had a connection with the little boy in the buggy. 'His name's Andrew', she said, 'My Mum said that since he didn't have a father, he could at least have my grandfather's name, especially since he looks so much like him.' As she heard these last words, the train lurched to a stop, the doors opened, and the young woman stepped out and started off briskly along the platform.

Janet felt compelled to hurry after her, but instead could only make her way, increasingly unsteadily, towards the barrier, her mind in a whirl of competing delight and despair. More than fifty years of self-denial had come down to a gift of twenty minutes, in which her unspoken, indeed unacknowledged questions, had been all but answered, but as she faltered to a stop, she knew it was too late. The heart that refused to break all those years ago, now gave way to the silent grief and self-imposed loneliness that had been her retribution. As Janet collapsed on the hard, cold tiles of the station forecourt, one or two people rushed to her aid, while most averted their eyes and hurried on their way. Was it a final blessing or the ultimate tragedy, that she didn't catch a last glimpse of the young woman and her son? They were being greeted warmly by a big man who rushed towards them, his blue eyes laughing as he wrapped his arms round his granddaughter and bent to kiss his great-grandson.

REVENGE AT
COTTONWOOD CREEK

By William Clinkenbeard

The State of Nebraska is, as the advert enticing people to relocate puts it, a land of *Endless Possibilities*. It is a worrying turn of phrase, for you might think that where the possibilities are endless the realities are few and far between. However, there is one possibility that enjoys a high degree of certainty. In the middle of the state lies the small town of Cottonwood Creek, the main street of which takes off from US Highway 30 at a thirty-degree angle. If you were driving west on US30 and took your eyes off the road in order to tune in your radio it is highly likely that you might wind up driving down the main street instead. Unsurprisingly, it is called *Main Street*. Highway 30 is just one of five long scratch marks running along most of the length of the state. The Platte River, which meanders a bit, was the first, and the Oregon Trail was the second. Then came the Union Pacific Railroad, then US30 and finally the new four lane divided highway—Interstate 80. Observed from above, the scratch marks as they run right alongside each other might look like a kind of musical score. The people and vehicles dotted on the lines are the notes comprising the song of the plains.

Each of the scratch marks is a highway of sort. The Platte River cuts a wide but shallow silver ribbon through the prairie. French trappers navigated it in the early days searching for beaver, but they must have gone crazy manoeuvring their canoes around the many sandbars and through the shifting channel. Thousands of pioneers heading west to Oregon and California on the Oregon Trail wore ruts into the earth with the wheels of their Conestoga wagons. Some of the Mormons pulled handcarts along the trail when the money for ox-pulled wagons ran out. In the 1860's the Union Pacific railway was constructed along the line of the Platte. Little camps were formed every eight or ten miles in order to supply the gangs of Irish graders and tracklayers. They were temporary settlements, but many of them remained as towns. Towns like Cottonwood Creek still look temporary, little fragile clusters of white timber boxes that might blow away under a strong wind. Interminable freight trains roll over the tracks today, with the level crossings affording ideal venues for suicide. The latest scratch mark, Interstate 80, follows the same course, sucking up some of the life of Cottonwood Creek like a giant vacuum cleaner. Businesses sprang up on the four corners of the highway: a new gas station, a large Wal-Mart, a Pizza Hut and MacDonald's. It wasn't long before the folk began to abandon Neilson's Hardware and Cathy's Café for Wal-Mart and MacDonald's. So if you did accidentally wind up driving down Main Street you might well wonder where everything had gone.

The word that springs to mind when you see central Nebraska for the first time is *flat*. Flat enough to be a pancake or a pocketless pool table, level enough to irrigate the fields for growing maize to feed the cattle. When Pastor Gary Goodall arrived in Cottonwood Creek to take charge of the Presbyterian Church, his wife, who was accustomed to walking the Highlands of Scotland, remarked that it was very flat. It was so flat, she said, that there was nowhere to walk because there was nothing to go up or down or around. And in truth, the inhabitants of Cottonwood Creek do not walk much, unless it is to go the short distance from their car parked on Main Street to the post office or Shorty's Bar & Grill or the Midwest Bank.

The sheriff of Cottonwood Creek was J.H. Bates. The J stood for Jake, but nobody was sure about the H. In any event the sheriff was known as *Jailhouse Bates*. In actual fact, the cell in Sheriff Bates' office on Main Street could hardly be described as a jail. It was a room at the back of the office with a small barred window and an ordinary door with a peephole. An old rocking chair stood in one corner and an army surplus cot along the wall. Sheriff Bates, never a fan of paperwork, often stacked his official papers on the floor until they were past their *Return By* date. He stored his car magazines and old newspapers in the room as well. The girlie magazines were kept safely locked in his desk. On slow days the sheriff sometimes took to the rocking chair to read *The Cottonwood Chronicle* and have a snooze. Once in a while Homer, the town drunk, would be put into the cell to sleep it off.

Sheriff Bates was not an agreeable man, suffering as he was from the short man syndrome. He believed that his high trooper-style hat and dark glasses enhanced his image. Bates was a bachelor, and more than a few ladies of the town reckoned that a good woman would have improved his disposition. The trouble was that no good woman, or even bad one, seemed to be very interested. Bates was cocky, sexist, and an accomplished braggart, making the terms of endearment far too costly for most women. Cathy, of Cathy's Café, couldn't stand the man. When Bates came through the door it was always accompanied by a 'Hi Babe' to draw the attention of all the customers. She had more than once asked him to stop calling her Babe, but it made no difference.

In spite of his unpopularity Sheriff Bates had been successful in being re-elected three times, mainly because he brought money into the town coffers. The secret of his success was speeding. Bates would park his patrol car just along from the Phillips 66 gas station, tucked in behind the massive cottonwoods that lined the highway. It was a mere hundred yards from where the speed limit on US 30 dropped down to 50mph. The Sheriff didn't bother with passenger cars, unless they were travelling in excess of 80 mph. It was the truckers in their big rigs that he liked. It wasn't easy to shift such a heavy load down to fifty miles per hour in such a short distance. Moreover, the incentive to reduce your speed was lessened by the fact that the town was barely a quarter of a mile long. So if a semi passed him at even 53 mph, the sheriff's radar would pick it up. The big semis, the 18-wheeler Peterbilts and Kenworths travelled on Interstate 80 to go cross-country, on their way from Missouri or Tennessee to Nevada or California. But when they pulled off to pick up or deliver part of a load they went by Cottonwood Creek. It was then that they were likely to run afoul of Jailhouse Bates.

The sheriff's speed trap was, however, not popular with Leroy Hansen and Jerry Nabers, who operated the Phillips 66 gas station. They felt that the way the sheriff used the cover of the cottonwood trees immediately behind the station didn't help their business. Bates was always hanging around, either in order to tell his latest dirty story, or to use the gas station restroom to relieve himself. There had been several verbal skirmishes. Leroy Hansen, being a quiet man of genuine integrity, couldn't bring himself to do more than look down through his glasses and bite his tongue. Jerry Nabers, however, didn't have such reticence.

'Sheriff,' Nabers said to him as Bates sloped in one hot day when the west wind was wafting fumes from the alfalfa dryer down the highway, 'aren't there other things you could be doing besides hiding out behind our gas station?'

Behind his dark glasses Bates smiled at him and removed the toothpick from his mouth. 'Hell Jerry,' he said, 'I figured you as a law-abiding man. Surely you want these lawbreakers to taste a little Cottonwood Creek justice.'

'Justice is fine, Sheriff,' Jerry said. 'I don't like speeders any more than you do, but you been here all day and only caught one guy over the limit. You be'in here kinda spoils our business.'

But Bates only smiled again. 'I'll bear what you say in mind, Jerry. Now could I borrow that key to your restroom once more? I got to take me a leak.'

The sheriff wasn't all that popular with the truckers either. Shadowman, as he called himself on his Citizen's Band radio, drove a red Peterbilt 379 between Illinois and Denver. He was big in the shoulders and his upper arms, which were tattooed with mermaids and eels. Dark curly hair poked out from under his CUBS baseball cap. Shadowman was a rough diamond, but courteous to a fault on the roads. To his infinite regret, he had been caught twice by Bates, fined heavily each time, and his desire for revenge had long been simmering. The last time that Shadowman had been done he moaned about it on his radio to anyone who was within range. It was Hero2 who heard and sympathized, for he too had been done once in the same way and he shared Shadowman's opinion of the sheriff. Hero2 was running a Kenworth T600 out of Missouri to Salt Lake City. A tall and skinny man with sideburns and a moustache, he was the quiet type. On the radio they arranged to meet the following week over coffee at the BigT stop just up the road at Kearney.

Shadowman waited until he saw Hero's vehicle pull into BigT and then climbed down from the truck. 'Hey, you must be Hero. How y'all doin'?' Shadowman asked. The two men shook hands firmly, creating a new relationship in the truckers' mobile fraternity.

Over coffee, Shadowman told Hero about his experience and laid out the plan. 'I'm tired of this county mounty in Cottonwood Creek picking our pockets,' he said. 'Are you up for creaming this guy?'

'Damn right,' Hero said. 'The guy's a bastard. He pulled a laugh all the while he was writing out the citation. Yeah, let's do it,' he said, taking a bite out of his doughnut.

'OK,' Shadowman said, 'Here's the plan. We know that the next time we come through he's gonna be sitting out there ready to shoot us in the back. So I go ahead first and shake the bushes. You follow me at about half a mile, but don't let anyone else get in front of you. As soon as he's behind me I'm gonna back 'em up. You stand on it then and we'll make him a bumper sticker. We'll take him down the road for maybe a mile and see how he likes it. Then I'll stand on it and let him off the hook. That sound OK?'

'Sounds good to me,' Hero responded, breaking into a wide smile that showed the gap in his upper front teeth. The truckers returned to their rigs to coordinate their schedules for the next possible date.

It was three weeks later to the very day when Shadowman pulled onto US 30 eight miles east of Cottonwood Creek. It was a hot afternoon, and in Cottonwood Creek the smell of drying alfalfa was overwhelming. Jailhouse Bates sat in his patrol car under the trees beside the gas station. There wasn't a lot of traffic and Bates was close to dozing off, but he managed to keep an eye on the radar whenever he heard traffic coming down the road.

On the highway, Shadowman's huge semi kept up a constant 65 miles per hour. Just before he reached the turnoff to Main Street he picked up a couple of miles on the speedometer. Better be sure about shaking the bushes. Sheriff Bates noted the excess speed and held his breath for a few seconds to confirm the speed. 'Gotcha,' he said to himself, breaking into a grin. He started the engine and pulled out onto the highway. After thirty seconds he was behind Shadowman's rig. He flicked on the flashing light and smiled. This would be a good catch.

It was just after the sheriff smiled that he checked the rear-view mirror and saw a large Kenworth grill coming up behind him alarmingly fast. What was this guy doing? Suddenly Bates saw the brake lights on the truck in front go red. The Sheriff touched his brakes. He checked the mirror again; the semi behind was still coming on, closer and closer. Bates increased speed until he was far too close to the truck ahead. Still the truck behind kept coming. All he could see now in the rear-view mirror was horizontal chrome bars, like some kind of sneering metallic monster.

'Jesus Christ,' the sheriff called out loudly as his eyes moved from the windscreen to the rear-view mirror and back again. He was firmly wedged between the two vehicles. There was a double yellow line on this part of the road as it took a curve to the right, no way of overtaking. Anyway, he had no room to pull out now. The truck in front slowed again, and the truck behind now bumped him gently, but hard enough to move the patrol car forward until it made contact with the rig in front. Bates couldn't figure out what to do. His hands were sweating on the wheel, his heart was racing, and his head was telling him that being squeezed like this wasn't an accident. He could neither step on the brakes or on the accelerator. His front bumper was now touching the semi in front and his back bumper the truck behind. The words on the back of the truck in front were insultingly large: "How's my Driving?" He had never felt this vulnerable and trapped. It was like a pea caught between two, two ... but no words came to mind. Cornfields and cattle flashed by on the right; several cars passed on the left, but no one seemed to be aware of his predicament. His brain wouldn't work properly. He couldn't think of any way to escape.

Just at that moment, the truck ahead picked up speed fast and the one behind dropped back. There was a rest area on the right hand side of the highway and the sheriff pulled into it and jammed on the brakes. He looked out at the road highway long enough to see the driver of the second truck poke his head out the window and give a royal wave of the hand. Bates opened the car door and got out, but his legs buckled. He fell to his knees and threw up.

It was at that very moment that Jerry Nabors happened to be passing on his way back to Cottonwood Creek. He saw a patrol car parked in the rest area, its lights flashing, its door open and a man on the ground beside it. This was an unusual sight around Cottonwood Creek. Jerry pulled in, stopped behind the patrol car and got out.

'Jailhouse,' he asked, 'are you all right? What you doin' here?' The Sheriff was wiping his face with his handkerchief. He tried to get up but the legs still wouldn't support him. 'Damn it,' he said. 'Damn it.' No other words ensued. Clutching the inside handle of the door, he finally made it to his feet and slid onto the car seat.

'What happened here, Sheriff?' Nabors asked, leaning down to study Bates through the door.

'It's these damned truckers,' Bates answered, breathing with difficulty. 'They trapped me, the sonsabitches.'

'How'd they do that, Sheriff?' Nabors asked, just the trace of a smile forming at the corners of his mouth.

But Bates didn't answer the question. 'I'm OK now, Jerry,' he said. 'I got to get back to the office.'

'You don't look OK to me Jailhouse,' Nabors said. 'You're pretty white around the gills and the sweat's pouring off you. Better take it easy for a spell.'

The sheriff shut the car door and reached for the ignition, but he didn't make it. His hand, shaking violently, fell back onto his lap. He closed his eyes and leaned forward on the steering wheel.

'Sheriff, I hate to say it, but I think there is only one thing to do here. You're lucky I got the tow truck this morning. I'll hook you up and tow you back to the office. OK?'

But Jailhouse Bates continued to lean on the steering wheel with his eyes closed. There was a slight nod of the head. Jerry Nabors reversed his truck in front of the patrol car, hooked up the chain, and lifted the front end. He helped the sheriff into the passenger seat of the truck and started up. His next decision would spice the local conversation for several years. Jerry could have driven along US30 back to the Main Street intersection and taken a right in for the short route to the sheriff's office. But for some unexplained reason Jerry didn't take the short way home. He drove instead to the other end of Main Street and turned in. This meant that Jailhouse Bates and his patrol car had to be towed past Cathy's Café, the Cottonwood Chronicle the American Legion and a few other significant places. The sheriff sat back in his seat and kept his eyes closed.

Jailhouse Bates never told anyone the real story about the revenge at Cottonwood Creek. No one would really have known what had happened if it hadn't been for Angie Kroll. Angie was doing her waitress stint at the BigT that very day. It was impossible not to catch the drift of the story when she brought Shadowman and Hero2 their coffee.

'I wish I could have seen his face when I put on the brakes,' Shadowman said, grinning from ear to ear.

'All I know,' Hero said, trying to speak through hysterics, 'is that the sheriff pulled off the road faster'n anyone I've ever seen. Gravel was going everywhere. I bet you that it'll be a while before that guy comes after us.'

When Angie brought a second cup of coffee and pressed them for more details, they obliged very happily. For once she had a good story to share with her friends back in town.

Jailhouse Bates was not re-elected the following year because the income from speeding fines was down, way down. He spent most of his time in the office, thumbing through his magazines in the rocking chair. Eventually he got a job in the Cottonwood Co-op Lockers helping to butcher and pack beef for freezing. People gradually got used to seeing him in his bloodstained white coat and pointy hat, but they never quite got used to his unusual reticence and his hangdog manner.

Meanwhile, there appeared in the poetry section of the truckers' website, an anonymous poem which bore the same kind of quality as most of the poetry on that site:

Highway 30
Is now ever so purty.
Since the sheriff's spleen
Got wedged in between.

EAST, WEST, HAME'S BEST

By Maureen Brister

Sally Reynolds rummaged through the drawers and cupboards of the room she shared with her twin sisters, desperately hoping neither of them would finish their tea and come upstairs to find out what she was up to. She needed to find something to wear, something that would catch the eye of her boyfriend, Joe, and of course, it had to be something she did not own. Sally was well known for borrowing her sisters' clothes. In fact her father said more rows were caused in their house because of this than anything else, and he was probably right. She knew that Helen had recently bought a new twinset, but she just could not find it. Helen must have hidden it. Oh well, she might just have to settle for her sister's second-best twinset! Red had never been Sally's favourite colour, but beggars couldn't be choosers. Joe might like it and that was more important.

Eighteen-year-old Sally lived with her parents, Nell and Alec, and twin sisters, Helen and Lorna, in a semi-detached two-bedroomed council house on the outskirts of Dunfermline. The three sisters had shared the same bedroom for as long as they could remember and until they reached their teenage years, they were as close as peas in a pod. The expression 'Three's a crowd' never meant anything to them. Things changed once the twins left school and began work. Helen and Lorna, now aged 22, changed their attitude to their younger sister when she first began to "borrow" their clothes, the clothes they bought with their hard-earned money. The twins both worked in the Dunfermline branch of a national chain-store. Neither were beauties, but they made the best of what they had. The good looks had been reserved for their younger sister. A lovely baby, good natured, with curly fair hair and smooth skin, she had grown into a stunning teenager and young woman, and she knew it! She had retained her curly fair hair and smooth skin, only now her hair was teased into the latest style and her skin was always covered in what her father took great delight in calling "glaur", much to his youngest daughter's annoyance.

'Oh Dad, it's only a bit of make-up,' she would say, fluttering her mascarad eyelashes at him.

'A bit, you look more like a clown than my daughter. Don't know why you have to put all that muck on your face, can't be doing your skin any good. What do you think Nell?'

Sally's long-suffering Mother would smile gently and shrug her shoulders. 'It's the fashion Alec, just leave it be won't you,' she would say as her husband disappeared behind his newspaper. He just couldn't fathom his youngest daughter at all these days. As a child Sally had been his favourite. She loved to sit on his knee, arms wrapped around his neck, listening to stories about her grandparents and his childhood. It had taken both parents to persuade Sally that she needed some kind of qualifications when she suddenly decided to quit school at age 16. She had eventually agreed to go to night school, learn shorthand and typing and now worked as an office junior in a local legal office. He did not want to go through a year like that again, the battles that had gone on, well he just didn't want to think about it. The twins were a different kettle of fish, they were quiet like their mother, more home birds really, but the quicker *all* the girls got married and left him and Nell to a bit of peace and quiet the better.

Sally was putting the finishing touches to her make-up when her sisters finally appeared in the bedroom. 'Oh Sally, that's *my* twinset,' groaned Helen. 'You'd better not ruin it with any of that make-up. What's wrong with your pink cardigan anyway? Don't tell me, it's in the wash and you just had to have mine.' Helen shook her head.

'You're not seeing Joe again tonight?' asked Lorna. 'That'll be the third time this week. This must be serious. How long's that you've been going out with him? Whatever, it has to be a record for you. You've usually got more than one boyfriend on the go at the same time. Really don't know what you see in this one though Sally, he is so full of himself. If we hear any more about his parents' electrical business and their home in Canada we'll scream. Don't think Mum and Dad are that keen either. We certainly don't like him and he makes it pretty obvious that he doesn't want us around either. Wants you all to himself it seems.'

'You two have got it all wrong as usual. Joe is great fun and I really like him. He only has a month left on his contract at the Dockyard, then he'll be going back to Canada. If you two can keep a secret, I'm hoping that he'll ask me to marry him before then and I can join him there. Don't you breathe a word of this to Mum and Dad though, please don't.'

Sally looked at her sisters, whose eyes had widened at this secret. 'You are kidding us on. You must be. Married … you … and to Joe. That would be a big mistake,' said Lorna.

'What do you mean, a mistake?' Sally bristled at her sister's tone of voice. 'We love each other and I just know he is going to ask me to marry him. Anyway, you won't need to worry about me once I am out of your lives and living in Canada, in a big house with lots of money. You can have the room to yourself, and your clothes for that matter.'

'How do you know you'll live in a big house and have lots of money? We know that is what you dream about Sally, but you just have Joe's word for that.' Helen looked at her sister Lorna.

'Oh you two. Pair of misery guts. Why would Joe lie to me? Why?' Sally stomped off down the stairs, leaving her sisters looking at each other open-mouthed.

The doorbell rang and Sally ran to answer it. Joe Hartington stood on the doorstep. As usual Sally's heart missed a beat. He did that to her every time. She just had to catch a glimpse of him, all 6'2" of him, with his curly black hair and swarthy good looks and she felt a shiver down her spine. He was definitely the best-looking man she had gone out with in a while, and they did get on well, dancing being their passion. The dance hall in Dunfermline was where they met and where they spent most of their time together. The fact that neither her sisters, nor her parents, liked him had irked her at the start, but none of them could give her a good reason for the way they felt, so she just shrugged her shoulders and kept seeing him.

Joe Hartington, 24 years old, was on a year's secondment to the Naval Dockyard at Rosyth, where he was helping to oversee the refit of one of the Canadian Navy's ships. The work was all but complete and the ship would soon be on sea trials before returning to it's base in Halifax, Nova Scotia. Joe would be on that return voyage. So far nothing had been said about their relationship and how and if it would continue when he left, but Sally just knew in her heart that it would not be over and she was doing her utmost to make sure it wouldn't!

'Come on in Joe, I'm almost ready,' she said as he stepped into the narrow hallway. 'Mum and Dad are in the kitchen washing up after tea. Go on in and I'll be with you in a tick. Just got to get my coat,' Sally got up on her tiptoes to plant a quick kiss on Joe's cheek before pushing him towards the kitchen door.

Joe knocked on the door before opening it. As Sally said, her parents were at the kitchen sink, Nell washing and Alec drying. He planted a smile on his face. 'Hello folks, how's it going?'

Nell turned to face him. 'Hello Joe, good to see you. We're fine, aren't we Alec.' Nell stared pointedly at her husband who continued drying the dishes with his back to Joe. What was it about Joe that no-one took to? She couldn't put her finger on it, but whatever it was Sally didn't see it, that was for sure. She was head over heels in love with this man as far as Nell and Alec could tell, and they couldn't do a thing about it.

They had spoken at length about this romance, particularly since they knew that Joe's time at Rosyth was coming to an end and they knew they would have to deal with the fall-out when he returned to Canada. Not for a minute did they think that their youngest daughter was hoping to get married and indeed go to Canada with him. She was only 18 years old for heaven's sake. But she was head-strong, that they did know. Most of the rows in their house were caused by Sally and her opinions which she was never backward at stating. Nell was aware that Joe was standing in the kitchen, watching them warily. Alec had still not acknowledged his presence. Luckily Nell heard Sally's feet on the stair, and the next minute she had swept Joe out of the kitchen, through the door and down the path, shouting to her parents not to wait up, they were going dancing— again!

'Oh Alec, I wish you would at least answer Joe when he speaks to you. It is embarrassing when you don't even speak. Makes an atmosphere.'

'I don't like the boy, and that's that. We've got nothing in common. I'm a grocer and he is in the Canadian forces. His family are obviously well off, all this talk about their large house and successful electrical business. He makes no effort to ask me about my job, does he? No, and before you say any more, I think we need to have a word with Sally. The sooner the better too, before she goes and does anything stupid. I have a feeling we could lose her to this Joe you know Helen.'

'Never. She would have said something to the twins if things had gone that far and they haven't said a word to me. No, you're way off beam there Alec I'm sure. Come on let's finish up and we'll have a cup of tea. The twins are upstairs fiddling about with their hair and listening to the radio, we might even get an hour's peace.'

Joe and Sally were having a great time. The dance hall was packed and the atmosphere was better than usual. There was definitely a dancing crowd here tonight thought Sally. Being so tall, Joe stood out in the crowd and he was a pretty good dancer as was she, so people always made room for them. The red twinset was a hit. Joe had already said she suited the colour, she should wear more red. Sally was in her element.

Later that evening, they were getting their breath back over drinks in the lounge next to the dance floor. Joe cleared his throat and Sally smiled softly at him. 'Come on, out with it,' she said.

The oh-so-confident Joe seemed tongue-tied for once. 'Well, you know that I'll be going back to Canada in a few weeks. Well I was wondering, well just thinking really, that you might like to come with me. What do you think? My Dad has always wanted me to go into the business with him and I'm seriously thinking about it. I've had enough of Naval life for the moment. If you came with me, you could give Mum a hand with the office side of things. She isn't getting any younger and I'm sure she would appreciate a bit of help. Well, say something Sally.'

Sally's eyes were shining and she smiled coquettishly. 'In what capacity exactly would I be going to Canada Joe? I doubt Mum and Dad would be happy about me going as your girlfriend, in fact they could put their foot down and make me stay here. However, if we were engaged, or even married, then that might be different.' Sally couldn't believe she had just said that. God, she might lose him for good. But she didn't think so somehow or other.

'I was coming to that actually. Seems to me you aren't saying no to coming to Canada, and if that is the case then why don't we just get married, hang the engagement. Let's get married Sally, what do you say? I'm sure there's still time to make arrangements before I leave for Halifax, assuming you want to be married in Dunfermline that is?'

Joe was smiling broadly as he gripped both her hands in his. Sally could hardly believe her ears. Things were panning out just the way she wanted. She couldn't wait to get home and tell her stuffy sisters. That red twinset really had done the trick! Telling her parents was another story, but she could talk them round. She would need Joe beside her for back-up, to confirm that they were actually getting married.

'Yes, oh yes Joe. I can't wait to get away from here, meet your parents, live in another country. It will be so exciting. Let's go home right now, tell Mum and Dad. They'll still be up, it's just gone 10 o'clock.'

Half an hour later and they were sitting on the couch in Sally's front room, facing her parents who were seated either side of the coal fire which was burning itself out for the night. Nell and Alec had exchanged worried looks when they saw how excited the two of them were, particularly Sally.

'You two look like the cats that got the cream. What's going on?' asked Nell.

'Well Mum and Dad, it's like this. Joe's asked me to marry him and go to live in Canada, and I've said yes.'

'No, no and no. That's just not possible Sally. Are you out of your mind? Going to the other end of the world to a country you don't know, people you've never met and you only 18 years old. No and that's that,' said Alec.

'Oh Dad, you've got the wrong end of the stick. We aren't *asking* you if we can get married. We *are* getting married, and I *am* going to Canada. I love Joe and he is the person I want to be with.'

'Nell, you speak to her for heaven's sake. Make her see some sense.'

Tears were in Nell's eyes at this turn of events. 'Let's all calm down. We haven't heard anything from Joe yet. What would you like to say about all this Joe.'

'Well I go along with Sally really. I know that neither you nor Alec like me very much although I don't know why. But I've asked Sally to marry me, she has said yes, and I think we should go ahead and make our plans. I have four weeks left in Rosyth, then I will sail back to Halifax and if Sally will join me there, we can be married as soon as I dock. I'll get my parents to start making the arrangements.'

'You'll be married in Canada?' Nell couldn't take this all in. Alec was just sitting opposite her shaking his head. 'Sally, surely you would want to be married here, in your home town, with your sisters as bridesmaids.'

Sally was looking steadily at Joe. 'We did plan to marry in Dunfermline Mum, but given your reaction I think what Joe says makes sense. Maybe we should get married in Canada. In fact yes, I agree with him.'

The twins had by now joined everyone else in the front room and they were all ears. What on earth had Sally got herself into this time? Sounded like they were going to get their bedroom to themselves sooner than they thought! There wouldn't be a lot of sleep in the Reynolds household tonight that was for sure.

'I still say this is a bad idea Sally. It's obvious neither of you have really thought this through. I think we should all sleep on it, and see what tomorrow brings. Hopefully some sense to the pair of you.' With that Alec Reynolds got up, walked out of the living room, slamming the door behind him and stomped off upstairs to bed.

It was left to her Mother to have the final word. 'I have to go along with your Dad. Joe you can't just expect Sally to up sticks and go to Canada. For heaven's sake she has hardly been out of Dunfermline. I know, I know, you're in love and as far as I can see your hearts are ruling your heads. What will your parents have to say about this do you think? Shouldn't you speak to them as well?'

Joe shook his head adamantly. 'They will be fine about it, really they will. They are always on at me to settle down and if I say I am leaving the Navy and joining them in the business they will be over the moon. It's what they have always wanted. There is plenty of space in our house for Sally and I when we are married. Really Nell, it will be fine. Sally and I get on like a house on fire and we love each other. I don't see why you and Alec can't accept that.' Sally was nodding her agreement. Her cheeks had gone quite red and her eyes were shining. She looked every bit the excited bride-to-be. Nell had to admit that. But she was only 18 years old!

Breakfast in the Reynolds' household the next morning was a very subdued affair. Alec and Nell had rehashed their daughter's future in the privacy of their bedroom the previous evening, though no conclusion had been reached. Eventually they had both fallen into a broken sleep, the result of which was bleary eyes and bad tempers over breakfast. The twins were sitting quietly eating their toast and drinking their tea, watching their parents and waiting for something to happen. Sally meanwhile was taking longer than usual over getting dressed for work, probably hoping her father would have gone to work by the time she appeared, thought Nell. But she would have to speak to him some time today!

Eventually Alec got up, put on his coat and left the house, hardly pausing to say his farewells to his wife and the twins. The twins followed him, reluctant to leave the kitchen before Sally appeared, but not wanting to be late for work either. That left Nell to face her daughter. She could hear her feet on the stairs, and then the kitchen door opened.

'Morning Mum, everyone gone?'

'By everyone, I assume you mean your Dad Sally. Yes, he has gone and he is not a happy man. And I am not a happy woman. Honestly Sally we really don't know what has got into you. You hardly know this man.'

'Joe you mean Mum. His name is Joe, and I do know him. No matter what you say I do intend marrying him. I'm meeting him at lunchtime. We thought we would look into flights for me. The quicker we get timescales for everything the better, given your opposition to our plans.'

'We've every reason to oppose your plans as you call it. However I do know you well enough to realise that once you've made up your mind nothing will shift it. You'd better get to work Sally, look at the time, but don't think this is the end of the matter.'

Sally gave her Mum a quick hug and kiss. 'Honestly Mum I don't know what all the fuss is about. Not everyone gets the chance I am getting. Living in another country, with a home to go to and a job in my husband's family business. It all sounds to be good to be true to me.'

'That's what I mean though Sally, it does all sound to good to be true. I know you. You can see a big house, successful business, a bit more money than you are used to at the moment. But that is the story Joe tells you, and it is one that your Dad and I can never quite believe. That is why we are worried.'

Sally Hartington thought of her mother's words as almost two years later she wearily pulled herself out of bed. She could hear her nine-month-old son stirring in his cot at the foot of their bed. He never slept past six o'clock in the morning and once awake he was raring to go. More than his mother was. Her second pregnancy was well advanced, and she was even more nauseous this time around. If only Joe would get up with Michael and let her lie just a bit longer. But life with Joe was anything but happy just now. He seemed uninterested in how she felt or in her at all for that matter. Not that she blamed him; she looked like something the cat dragged in half the time, but whose fault was that?

Their life in Halifax, Nova Scotia, had not gone according to plan. Joe's parents had *not* been ecstatic at their son's proposed arrangements. They were glad to have their blue-eyed boy home and welcomed his input to the business, but a wife on the horizon did not appeal. Joe was their only son, their pride and joy and the apple of his mother's eye. She wanted him to herself, to spoil and here he was telling her that in a few weeks' time his future wife would be joining him, joining *them*. As to where they would live, Joe just seemed to think they should have part of the house to live in and that this person, Sally something or other, would work with her in the office.

An excited Sally had arrived to a frosty reception. Joe was glad to see her and couldn't wait for them to be married, but his mother was a different story. The family did indeed have a lovely home, but Joe told Sally his mother thought they would be better off starting married life in their own place. That 'place' was a one-bed roomed flat near their electrical store and workshop which the family owned, a cold, bare, unwelcoming one-bed roomed flat at that.

Sally had gone along with everything, not wanting to make the relationship between herself and Joe's parents any worse. Privately she thought they would come round in time. The wedding had been a quiet affair. Joe's parents, his best friend Ron and his girlfriend Barbara, were the only people present. They had acted as best man and bridesmaid to a nervous Joe and Sally. After the short ceremony, performed in the local Baptist Church where Mr and Mrs Hartington were members, they had left the four young people to their own devices and returned home. Ron and Barbara took the bride and groom to a local restaurant as their wedding present. A few drinks had melted everyone's reserve, and the four of them had had a good night. Their honeymoon, all four days of it, were spent giving their new home a lick of paint and making it liveable. Mr and Mrs Hartington had reluctantly parted with a few bits and bobs of furniture, but Joe and Sally had had to spend quite a bit of their meagre savings as well. I suppose that had been the first indication that Joe himself was not well off, in fact he seemed to rely on his parents for a lot of his money and given his newly married state they were not particularly forthcoming.

A few weeks into married life Sally realised she was pregnant. Joe was delighted and it did seem that Mrs Hartington thawed a bit to her when given the news. However it also meant Sally's time spent 'helping out' in the shop was limited as she felt so ill for six months that she could only manage an hour or two a day at most. So she never actually learned a lot about the business which had been her intention, and when Michael was born it was just expected that she would stop work, stay at home and look after her son. Ron and Barbara were her only friends during this time and she did not know what she would have done without them, particularly Barbara.

Barbara knew Sally was homesick, but she also knew that she would never admit that to her family back in Scotland. Sally had built her life up into something wonderful so that they could not say 'I told you so.' The reality was something totally different.

The flat Joe and Sally lived in was small, old, too cold in winter and too hot in summer, and with baby Michael around space was at a premium. Joe adored Michael, but the actual looking after him was down to Sally. His parents also adored their grandson, but like Joe, thought Sally should take care of him, the house, the cooking etc. Joe went off to work every morning and came home in the evening expecting a meal on the table no matter how much time had gone into looking after Michael during the day. Barbara knew Sally was unhappy with her life but could see no way out of it as she didn't earn any money and Joe certainly didn't provide her with anything extra. She was just expected to be the 'little woman around the house' and having a second baby so soon had not been in the plan. It certainly bound her to Joe, his parents, and life in Canada and Barbara knew from Ron's comments, that this suited Joe down to the ground.

Sally's letters to her parents were full of tales of their grandson. She often sent them photographs, but these were mostly taken during their visits to Mr & Mrs Hartington's house or outdoors, never in their own home. She would have died rather than let her Mother see where she was living, and she had yet to tell them about her second pregnancy.

Her thoughts often drifted to the life she thought she would have in Canada. It seemed that no matter what she did she could never build up a good relationship with Mr and Mrs Hartington. They just doted on their son and put up with Sally. The best thing about the situation was that she had provided them with a grandson and they certainly loved Michael. She had wanted something better, she had always wanted something better, wanted to show her parents and her sisters that they were wrong in opposing her marriage, but at the end of the day she wished they had locked her in her room and thrown away the key. Let Joe return to his parents alone. Too late now though; she had made her bed and would have to lie in it.

What was it that her Mum and Dad used to say when she would tell them of her great plans for her life? 'Always remember Sally, you're nae better than you should be.' Yes that was it. Well wasn't that the truth at the end of the day. Unfortunately she had had to find this out the hard way.

What Sally did not know was that Barbara had decided to take matters into her own hands. She had not confided in Sally, Joe or Ron, but had managed to copy down Sally's parents' home address from one of their letters and after much soul-searching had decided to write to them herself. She did not go into great detail, but outlined the problems Sally was experiencing with her new life and told them how unhappy she had become. As she posted the letter Barbara crossed her fingers and hoped that Sally would forgive her, but more importantly she hoped that the letter would prompt a visit from a member of her family. They needed to see things for themselves.

Ten days later, Barbara received a letter from Nell Reynolds thanking her for letting them know the situation which had upset both her and her husband. They had had no idea at all from Sally's letters that things were so bad. Sally always sounded so upbeat. They had both decided to come to Halifax as soon as they could, probably within a few weeks and see Sally for themselves. They did not want her to know they were coming, preferring to turn up unannounced so that things could not be made to seem better than they were, and hoped Barbara would go along with this. She was happy to accede to this request. She still did not know how Sally would react to what she had done but in her heart she thought it was for the best.

Two weeks later on a day when thankfully Sally was feeling a bit better and had managed to shower, wash her hair and even apply some make-up, she heard footsteps coming up the outside steps to the flat. A loud knock came to the door and Michael's face immediately lit up. Sally smiled back at him as she moved slowly to the door, rubbing her aching back. 'It isn't Daddy yet Michael. I know that is who you think it is. He is still at work. He won't be home for ages yet. Let's see who it can be.' She opened the door and gasped in amazement at the sight of her parents on the doorstep.

'Oh my God! Mum, oh Mum, and Dad. Come in, please come in. I can't believe it. You've no idea how glad I am to see you both, no idea.' Sally broke down in tears as her parents moved slowly into the kitchen. Michael was sitting on the floor staring quizzically at these two strangers. 'What on earth are you doing here?' Sally managed to ask between wiping her eyes and blowing her nose.

As shocked as Nell and Alec were at the sight of their daughter, they tried not to show it. Nell moved forward to take Sally in her arms and Alec went to pick up his grandson. Neither of them said a word. They were still trying to come to terms with a much thinner, exhausted and obviously pregnant Sally, their first sight of the flat she called home appalled them and although they had decided to come clean and tell Sally that her friend Barbara had written to them, now that they were actually here they were unsure how to handle the situation. Tears were in their eyes.

Alec cleared his throat. 'We had a letter actually, from Barbara, and before you say anything Sally you should know that she had your best interests at heart. She couldn't stand seeing how unhappy you were, she knew your life wasn't turning out the way you thought and that you were not telling us the full story. She was definitely right about that,' Alec said, as his eyes swept round the small untidy kitchen and landed on his daughter's stomach.

Sally wrapped her arms around herself and sat down on one of the kitchen chairs. 'I would have told you, eventually,' she whispered. 'I don't know what to say Dad, but I am glad to see you both,' and she slowly smiled at them.

'Michael, these are your grandparents, your Scottish grandparents, your Gran and Grandad. Have you got a smile and a hug for them? They've come a long way to see you.'

Still in Alec's arms, Michael dutifully smiled up at his Grandad and put his arms round his neck. Alec tightened his grip. 'Hello there Michael. Why don't you show Grandad your toys. Maybe we can find something in this suitcase for us to play with. What do you think?' Alec picked up his case and moved towards what he assumed was the living room.

Nell was still standing in the middle of the kitchen staring at her daughter. 'Why didn't you let us know sooner about all of this Sally?' She gestured at her surroundings. 'And the baby, when is it due?'

'Two months time Mum. I've been going to tell you again and again, but couldn't find the words. I never wanted you to see me like this, living here and looking like I do, I kept thinking things would get better. But they just never do.'

'Well, we're here now.' Nell took off her coat. 'Why don't you go and sit beside your Dad and Michael and I'll make us some tea. Go on, I'll find things Sally.'

Sally shook her head. 'You've no idea how much I'm going to enjoy this tea Mum,' she said, 'I don't think anyone has made me a cup of tea since I got here.'

Fifteen minutes later, Nell carried the mugs and the teapot into the living room to find Alec on the floor with an excited Michael. They had obviously found the toys in the suitcase and were running cars back and forth on the wooden floor. Sally was sitting back in a pretty shabby armchair, looking a bit more relaxed than when she had faced them at the door. 'Here we are,' said Nell. She had had to give the mugs a good scrub and couldn't wait to attack the sink and the cooker, but none of this showed in her smiling face.

'I should give Joe a call, won't he be surprised.' Suddenly Sally stared at her parents. 'I haven't asked how long you are going to be here for and more important where you are going to stay? There is hardly room to swing a cat in here as you can see. There's lots of space at the Hartington's but I don't know how they will react to this situation.' Sally chewed on her bottom lip, suddenly looking worried. 'I'll finish this tea and give Joe a call. Maybe he can speak to his Mum and Dad.'

'Relax Sally. We knew we were taking a chance just turning up like this. There must be a hotel or something nearby that we can book into? Don't get yourself upset over where we are going to stay. It will just be somewhere to sleep anyway as we want to spend as much time as possible with you and this lovely little boy, oh and of course, Joe.' Nell remembered at the last minute to add Joe's name. Really neither of them wanted to face Joe, but they had decided beforehand to put a brave face on things when they did meet him, try to start off on the right foot.

By the end of the afternoon everything appeared to be sorted out. Of course Nell and Alec could stay with Joe's parents. To be fair there had been no hesitation on Joe's part when Sally called him at work. He had not exactly rushed home to greet his in-laws, but he did finish early and was now sitting on the living room floor of the flat with Alec, the two of them building towers of bricks which Michael was thoroughly enjoying knocking down.

Everyone had been invited for supper at Joe's parents and Nell and Alec would then unpack and stay there for the duration of their visit. Nell had made her daughter rest until Joe came home and she and Alec had managed a whispered conversation while Michael and his Mum napped in the bedroom. Their decision had been unanimous. They would both stay for a couple of weeks, then Alec would return to Dunfermline. Nell hoped Sally would allow her to stay until the baby was born and they would take things from there. By that time they could see how the land lay with the Hartingtons and Joe for that matter. They were prepared to take Sally and the children back to Dunfermline if it came to that.

Supper was a slightly nervous affair. Everyone was making an effort to be on their best behaviour. There was certainly no signs from any of the Hartingtons of animosity towards Sally. Clearly Del and Judy Hartington adored Michael giving him a big hug when they arrived at the house. The one thing that was obvious was that there was indeed lots of space in the house for Joe and his family, his expanding family. The Hartingtons lived well, their house seemed to stretch on and on, over three floors. Nell had had a brief tour and had already made up her mind that one floor could easily have been given over to the young couple starting out on their life together. However she had said nothing, plenty of time for that later if need be.

It took a while but eventually Judy Hartington asked the question. 'And what made you two decide to visit out of the blue?'

Alec put down his fork and knife and after a brief glance at his wife replied. 'I had some holidays coming. We've been thinking for a while that we would like to come and see our daughter and of course our grandson, and it just sort of happened, didn't it Nell?'

She nodded and smiled. 'And we're glad we did. Although we still have the twins at home, Sally is our youngest daughter and I'm sure that as a mother yourself Judy you can understand our concern when she left home at such a young age. I have to say her letters are always so full of how well things are going, how much effort you and Del have put into making sure she feels part of your family, giving them somewhere to live. We really just wanted to meet you both and see things for ourselves.' Nell bit her lip. She hoped these remarks had hit home and from the expressions on all three of the Hartingtons' faces she thought they had.

Joe, Sally and Michael left soon afterwards. Michael was asleep in his father's arms as they walked down the path to their car. 'See you both tomorrow Mum and Dad. Come over as soon as you are ready. Michael and I will be waiting.' Sally smiled and waved as she got into the car and they drove off.

'Well, thank you for a lovely meal Judy. If you both don't mind I think Nell and I will get off to bed. It has been a long day, but an exciting one for us. I don't think we will have any trouble sleeping tonight. It's really good of you to put us up like this.' Alec took Nell's hand as they said their goodnights and walked slowly upstairs, leaving the Hartingtons staring after them.

'How do you think that all went Alec? I wasn't too direct was I when I said how welcome they made Sally feel? I just wanted to prick their consciences a bit after what Barbara told us in her letter. Did I go overboard?'

By this time Alec was in the bathroom adjoining their large bedroom, brushing his teeth. 'No, no I think you did just fine there. But I just have to get some sleep Nell, don't know about you but I am exhausted. Michael is a joy though, isn't he? He doesn't seem affected by the situation, thank goodness. Can't wait to see him again tomorrow.' Alec smiled as he climbed into bed. Nell followed him and in the few seconds she took to switch off the bedside light her husband was already in dreamland.

The next few days flew past. As expected, Nell and Alec spent most of their time with Sally and Michael. Sally had accepted her Mum's offer to stay on after Alec went home, in fact she had accepted it almost too readily Nell thought. It was a more relaxed looking Sally that they saw day by day. They took her shopping to buy some things for their new grandchild, though where on earth he or she was going to sleep was anyone's guess. There just was not enough space in the flat, but of course Nell and Alec kept their thoughts to themselves. Joe and his parents were very civil to their visitors. Nell often caught Judy looking thoughtfully at Sally and her father playing with Michael and she thought she could sense a softening of their attitude to her daughter. After one of their shopping trips Judy came over to the flat for coffee and Nell unwrapped their purchases, one of which was a Moses basket for the baby. Nell couldn't help herself.

'Not sure where this is going to go though Judy, but no doubt they'll find a corner for it somewhere in their bedroom.'

'Yes, they are a bit stuck for space, I agree,' said Judy thoughtfully. 'They'll make do though, we all have to start somewhere after all.' And that was the end of that conversation. Could that woman not take the hint?

Both families spent Alec's last day together. It was a much more enjoyable affair than their first meal together, there was much laughter and teasing. Alec and Michael would miss each other loads, that was obvious. He followed his grandad around all the time, just waiting for his attention. Nell and Alec were packing his suitcase for his flight back to Scotland the following day.

'Well I think we did the right thing Nell. I really do. Sally looks so much better than when we arrived and I think she is getting on better with Joe and his parents as each day goes by. We'll need to wait and see what happens when this baby is born, but things are looking up. What do you think?'

'I agree. I just wish you could stay with me, but one of us needs to get back to the twins. Your Mum and Dad will be tearing their hair out by this time and anyway you need to get back to work. I'll write often, and telephone when the baby is born of course. I'll miss you. This will be the first time we have lived apart since we were married, do you realise that? But it is the right thing to do.' Nell shut the suitcase and locked it. 'Let's get some sleep. You need to be up early for that flight. Good of Del to offer to take you to the airport.'

Two weeks later Sally arrived back at the flat after a visit to her doctor. Judy and Nell looked up from the floor where they were playing with Michael. 'How did it go then Sally? Baby OK, still on schedule for delivery on the due date?' Judy asked. Sally sighed as she sat down heavily in the chair. 'Yes, everything seems fine. I just wish it was over. I feel so much bigger than last time. I'm so glad to have Mum around, I doubt I could have coped with Michael without her help. Now that he's on his feet he is never at peace for a minute. Needs constant attention. What I am going to do when you go back to Scotland Mum, I don't know.' Sally's voice broke and tears ran down her face.

Nell got up and went over to her daughter. 'Never mind love, not long now and you'll manage. Joe, Judy and Del will all pitch in, won't you Judy? Everyone loves to have a new baby around.' Nell stared at Judy, who was watching the two of them with a wary expression.

'Actually I should tell you both that Del and I have been talking, and we would love to have you all move in with us. We just need to make some changes to the house which hopefully we can get done before this baby puts in an appearance. Nell is right, there's nothing like a new baby in the house. We haven't said anything to Joe yet by the way, we'll leave that to you Sally. But we hope you'll take us up on our offer. You know, it took Del and I completely by surprise when Joe told us you were coming from Scotland to live with us and to get married. We've always thought the world of our son, and yes maybe it has taken us a while, but seeing you with your own parents has opened our eyes to what we have been missing by not having you all living with us. That's all I'm going to say, except what is it you always say at times like this Nell, something about putting the kettle on?' Judy got up from the floor, smiled at them both and went through into the kitchen.

Sally sniffed as she dried her eyes. 'Well what do you think of that Mum? I can hardly take it in. Do you think she actually means it? What a difference it would make for us all though, more space and having Judy and Del around when you're gone would help me out no end. I can't believe how much more friendly they are towards me since you and Dad arrived. Joe is different too. It's how I always thought it would be.' Nell could only smile and nod. Wait till she told Alec about this. They had Barbara to thank for her intervention, but it looked like things were going to change and for the better. Sally was going to be OK; Nell could feel it. She got up and went into the kitchen to help Judy with the tea.

A Canterbury Tale

By Anne Ewing

He had to admit that life had been good to him, or perhaps more to the point, that he had been good to himself. His work as a leading fund manager in the City of London, where he administered, and latterly embezzled other people's money, had feathered him a very comfortable nest. These people were not individuals known to him. Perhaps the fact that they were anonymous made it easier to rob them blind. He could not put a face or even a name to any of the sums of money he had misappropriated. Had he dared, or even cared enough, to calculate how much money he had stolen, he might have been appalled to learn that the total was eight hundred and thirty five thousand pounds. But since he was devoid of anything remotely approaching a conscience, the figure would have been of only academic interest to him. Indeed he would never know the full significance of that figure, nor would anyone else ever understand that it would determine the date of the merciful retribution, which would be visited on him, or the balancing of his personal account with the world over the best part of a millennium.

If only this fateful calculation, whether it represented mere historical coincidence or providential intervention, could have become public knowledge, he would have had the consolation of knowing that he had become truly famous, and not merely infamous. But the world in general would never hear of his historic demise. And the countless victims of his avarice in particular, would have remained blissfully unaware of his criminality until some future date when their pensions fell due, or if they died an untimely death, and their dependents found that there was no inheritance to be claimed from the plundered estates of their antecedents. He had covered his tracks well and in the process had grown into a fat financial cat at the expense of these hapless strangers who had unwittingly trusted their future security to him. Perhaps he had always known that it couldn't last indefinitely. It was a phone call late on Boxing Day from a long-standing acquaintance in the Financial Services Authority, who had in the past illegally given him some valuable and untraceable tips on insider trading, that alerted him to the fact that a comprehensive and thorough audit of every aspect of his company would take place on the first day of post-Christmas business, December 28th, 2005.

Tarquin A. Barnett had been born fifty-three years before, a few hundred miles to the north, but a whole world away in terms of life experience and aspiration: as Thomas Angus Becket, in Drumchapel, one of the sprawling overspill estates that had been hurriedly thrown up to accommodate the hapless, transplanted occupants of the Gorbals diaspora from the 'no mean city' of Glasgow. Tam, as he was known, had proved to be an intelligent pupil at primary school, and when he surprised everyone by passing his qualifying exam, found himself a fish out of water at the local senior secondary school, until he was fortunate enough to come to the attention of one of his maths teachers, a local labour party activist and leading light in the Workers' Educational Association. He recognised a 'lad o' pairts' when he saw one, and took it upon himself to foster the obvious talents of the young Tam. His parents, Ina and Hughie, were hard-working and honest, but having no experience of formal education, were incapable of helping their unexpectedly gifted son, and so were happy enough to relinquish much of the responsibility for the development of their boy to this self-styled guru. It was thanks to him that Tom won a scholarship to a university where he gained a good degree. Further post-graduate study in accountancy equipped him to move to London and to start working in the City, where he wasted no time in cutting loose from all filial ties with his family and shrugged off any incipient feelings of obligation to his mentor.

Within a few months he had lost all contact with home and set about re-inventing himself, starting with his name and pronounced Glasgow accent. Chameleon-like, he quickly assumed the manners, attitudes and ambitions of the other successful young Turks he saw all around him, and he rose like a phoenix from the ashes of his former and secretly despised life. These included the strictures of hard work and probity which his parents, despite great hardship in their young lives, had made their life's foundation, and the discipline and self-denial that his mentor had tried to inculcate in him. Such virtues had got him where he wanted to be, but he determined from then on to go all out for financial and social success, whatever the cost in terms of self-respect. He soon learned to stifle any pangs of conscience and became adept at using people and situations to his own advantage. He married well, putting his wife's not inconsiderable fortune to good use in setting up his own firm in the City, becoming a pillar of the financial establishment and the epitome of respectability on the surface, while engaging in various types of sharp practice which in time sank into the illegality of downright fraud and theft.

The fruits of this dishonest labour were used to fund the kind of lifestyle he had always longed for. His two children, Jessica and Jeremy, attended prestigious boarding schools and were growing up to be clones of their parents, without getting in the way of their busy lives of work, social functions and entertaining, which were supported by the services of a live-in cook/housekeeper and gardener/handyman. This invaluable pair kept the large and impressive house in Belgravia in immaculate condition and allowed Tarquin and Dinah each to pursue their own individual extra-curricular, and from time to time, extra-marital, activities. Despite his outward appearance of ease and confidence, Tarquin had always felt, in some undefined way, subtly excluded from the club he so fervently aspired to join. He never once articulated to anyone, least of all himself, this feeling of being a square peg in a round hole, a feeling he had first experienced in the early days of secondary school. Indeed this deep-rooted sense of not really belonging may have come entirely from an innate inferiority complex that arose from his humble origins, as no one of his acquaintance had any doubts that he had been born with the requisite silver spoon firmly lodged between his teeth. But then he had never felt that he belonged in his original environment either, and having rejected his background at the first possible opportunity, it would have been all the more damaging to acknowledge that he did not, after all, entirely fit into his newly acquired persona, comfortable and superficially satisfying though it was.

Perhaps it was a subconscious drive to gain some kind of perverted revenge on the financial and social establishment he could not believe had really accepted him, despite all evidence to the contrary, that started him on his nefarious business practices, but had he been able to face up honestly to his situation, he would have had to admit that he was not actually all that good at his job! His early promising academic brilliance had failed to translate into genuine professional success, and the kick-start provided by his wife's financial support soon fizzled out and he had to resort to embezzlement to fund his increasingly expensive lifestyle. The household had just enjoyed enormous and conspicuous Christmas consumption, the cost of which would have been of frightening proportions to most people, but Tarquin as usual revelled in the sheer extravagance and loved the way he could over-indulge his family and the hordes of friends who made the most of his ostentatious generosity, as he dispensed hospitality with reckless abandon. The festival held no religious and little cultural significance for Tarquin and any it might have had for him in his buried past was long forgotten. Perhaps he had a presentiment that the tomorrow to end all the eating, drinking and being merry was at hand, because he knew immediately when he took that fateful phone call as the last of their Boxing Day guests were leaving, that it meant the end of everything that mattered to him.

Had he be been honest with himself, he would have admitted that the persona he presented to the world was an illusion, that the larger than life figure he had become was perched precariously on feet of clay. As a human being, a husband and a father, he was a conspicuous failure, but it would never have occurred to him to examine himself and his life in those terms. Now he could not avoid the conclusion that the imminent examination of his company's books would result in the entire edifice crumbling to the ground in one fell and spectacular swoop, and the effect on his family was the least of his worries. The question now was what to do to extricate himself from the looming catastrophe. A sleepless night later, he made an excuse to visit his office, leaving his wife, already in a bad mood with a raging hangover, and in a foul temper, as she had wanted to discuss their New Year party plans with him. In a curiously detached frame of mind, he wondered, as he proffered his customary dry peck to Dinah's frostily turned cheek, what she would have said had she known she was seeing him for the last time. He gave an equally fleeting thought to what would become of the still sleeping children he glanced at before he made his way downstairs and out of their lives for ever. He had only two items with him in an otherwise empty holdall: his passport and a large supply of sleeping tablets filched from the copious supply of medication in his wife's bathroom cabinet.

He had selected these things quite deliberately, because even in his agitated state, he saw them as alternative means of escape from his terrifying situation. He had some vague notion of making a run for it to a Channel port and out of the country. Unbidden images of Lord Lucan, John Stonehouse and even Reggie Perrin came and went in turn. With the last, as he recalled the time when he had watched that television programme, loving its anarchic humour, he experienced an upsurge of hysterical laughter, as, once in his office, he set about deleting the most obviously incriminating files from his computer. He had no illusions that this would hamper the auditors for any length of time in discovering the full extent of his crimes, but perhaps it would buy him a little window in which to decide his future. Then, as he cleared his safe of stacks of large denomination bank notes, ready cash seeming a better bet than easily traced bank cards (thirty five thousand pounds in total, although he had no real idea of the amount), packing it neatly into the holdall, a feeling of calm came over him and very slowly and deliberately he carefully placed all his credit cards, driving licence and mobile phone in a tidy stack in the now empty safe. After only a short hesitation, he added his passport to the pile, and in so doing, made a decision that would seal his fate. Fleeing abroad was thus abandoned as a solution to his dilemma. Some other means of escape had now to be found. Making sure that he had nothing on his person that could identify him, he closed the safe and looked round his impressive office, before making his way out of the door. As he looked back, he could clearly see himself sitting at his desk, and as he closed the door, he was conscious of his image fuzzily dissolving and slowly but surely disappearing. Once again, remembering his childhood addiction to 'Star Trek', he almost laughed out loud as the command, 'Beam me up, Scotty' came into his mind.

It took him a long time to find a taxi to hail in the deserted Sunday-like streets in the heart of what until now he had considered the centre of his world. Despite the heavy holdall, he felt curiously light-footed as he walked among the monuments to business and financial power which these buildings represented, but their normally reassuring solidity seemed to gradually seep away as his feeling of impending freedom grew with each step. A quick taxi ride through increasingly busy streets took him from the City to Victoria bus station where, by now almost in a trance-like state, he scanned the departure screens. The destination that suggested itself after a few minutes, standing out for some reason from all the rest, was the ancient cathedral town of Canterbury. Somehow he felt drawn to the place as a refuge. He had never been there before. In fact, the only association he had ever had with it was the reading of Chaucer's 'Canterbury Tales' at grammar school. All he could recall of the venerable tome was sniggering with the other boys over the vaguely pornographic passages, which as with similar references in 'Macbeth' were glossed over by their English master. Perhaps it was some long forgotten or barely understood concept of the sanctuary promised by religious buildings, but he had an overwhelming urge to visit the town, and in particular the cathedral.

He knew nothing about the place, indeed until now he would have laughed at the very idea of choosing to visit a cathedral. Beyond knowing that the Archbishop of Canterbury was the highest office in the Church of England, he was scathingly cynical about anything to do with religion at all. Even the historical significance of the famous cathedral and its associations with Thomas à Becket had barely registered with him beyond a vaguely remembered and ironic recognition of the fact that he shared a name with the famous saint. As with much of his education, he had discarded everything he considered unnecessary as he went along, becoming in fact an almost complete Philistine in the process. Nevertheless, he obeyed the increasingly insistent urge, which impelled him to board a bus for Canterbury, along with, it seemed, hordes of other passengers. He had been shocked at the crowds milling around the bus station when he had arrived at Victoria, and even more amazed that so many of them seemed, like him, to be travelling to Canterbury. It was many years since he had deigned to travel by public transport of any kind, and as they set off, he was prepared to find the experience distasteful in the extreme.

Dressed in his very expensive Italian suit and Crombie cashmere overcoat, he certainly stood out from the crowd that seemed to consist largely of women of all ages, most of them laden with full carrier bags bearing the names of various chain stores and fashion boutiques. What he didn't realise was that the chosen destination for most of them was in fact, Blue Water, the huge shopping Mecca in Kent where the bus would call en route to Canterbury. Within a short time, he was surprised to find he was beginning to actually enjoy listening to the loud and insistent chatter of some of his fellow passengers, many of whom seemed to know each other. He was made aware that the main purpose of their shopping was to return or exchange unwanted or unsuitable Christmas gifts. There were hoots of laughter as they described or in some cases showed off the unwelcome gifts from grannies, aunties, parents or frequently, the disastrous gift choices of sadly misguided husbands. He amazed himself by starting to appreciate the humour and cheerfulness displayed by most of these women, and the way they would good-naturedly include him in their chatter.

'You men have absolutely no idea, have you, Lovey?'

'So what did you buy your better half then, Ducks?' These good-natured questions would normally have struck him as intrusive and cheeky, but now he found himself answering their teasing questions in the same spirit.

They were clearly from a social class and economic status that he had seldom come into contact with in his adult life, but despite himself, and perhaps for the first time he could remember, he was aware of the genuine warmth that comes from spontaneous but superficial contact with other human beings. What would be completely natural to most of us was an entirely new experience for him: to relate to other people when there was no advantage to be gained from engaging with them beyond passing some time in unexpectedly congenial company. The coach stopped at Blue Water and the women alighted with a chorus of goodbyes, waving merrily to him as they went. They would never complete the pilgrimage to Canterbury that he was embarked on. Retail therapy, not spiritual sustenance, was their goal, and as he watched them, he had a genuine sense of regret and an unfamiliar ache of loneliness. Part of his mind was reeling with shock at this reaction: How could he feel this way about a crowd of strangers when he had never particularly felt an emotional need for the company of even his nearest and dearest? But he could not deny the strength of the feelings that assailed him as the bus trundled on its way.

After arriving at his destination and as he made his way along the street outside the small bus station, he was suddenly overcome with an overwhelming fatigue as the sleepless night and emotional exhaustion of the extraordinary day he had just lived through took their toll. Breaking the male habit of a life time, and asking for directions to the nearest travel lodge, he checked in and after eating an instantly forgettable meal at the nearby burger joint, he tumbled into bed and slept a deep, dreamless sleep such as he had never had since he was a child.

When he opened his eyes early the following morning, there was no question of wondering where he was or how he came to be in the strange bed in a featureless room. He immediately felt wide awake and got up with a purposeful and business-like awareness of what he wanted to do. He was soon striding out along the road in what he assumed to be the right direction. Within a short time he could see the imposing bulk of the medieval cathedral, its three great towers looming over the town. He was relieved to find an open door, but as soon as he had entered the building his footsteps faltered as the sheer magnitude and splendour of his surroundings enveloped him. This was a new experience for him. He had never really been in a church since those days in his childhood when he had attended the local Church of Scotland for end of term school services, and this was on a different scale entirely. His eyes tentatively took in the grandeur of the carved stonework, the dimly lit side chapels and the elaborate memorials and effigies of the 'Great and the Good'. They had surely earned their places here, and perhaps in Heaven too, if he could believe the testaments to their greatness and goodness there inscribed. His nose wrinkled in response to the atmosphere, which was both musty and dusty, and the back of his throat tickled with the unfamiliar and alien catch of incense.

As he moved slowly through the cathedral, he was increasingly assailed by a feeling of *déjà vu*. He became certain that he had been there before. Normally the least fanciful and most rational of thinkers, he became utterly convinced that he was not seeing this place for the first time, despite what his conscious mind was telling him. He began to feel more and more comfortable with his surroundings as he started to anticipate new details almost before he saw them and it was no surprise that each in turn already seemed familiar to him. Gradually he became aware that the profound and unnerving silence was broken by a murmuring voice, that of a guide addressing a group of obviously bored American tourists in their typical flamboyant garb, who seemed to be remarkably uninterested in the soporific tones of their lecturer. As he passed them, he approached another group, this time of Japanese visitors, who listened attentively to the animated but respectfully hushed tones of their guide as she explained in their own language, the significance of a plaque in the floor. Something in the reactions of her listeners made him realise that this was more than just another tomb, and as they reluctantly moved on in the wake of their leader, he stopped to read the inscription. Only then did he understand that this was the actual site of the murder of St Thomas à Becket on 29th December 1170, and as he read about the way this man of principle had been betrayed by King Henry II, he felt himself becoming intimately involved in and increasingly outraged at the injustice it represented.

This was another completely new experience for Tarquin. Never before had he considered the plight of one individual in the face of overwhelming power. In fact had he been able to review his life honestly, he would have realised that he was almost always the one wielding that power and deciding the fate of lesser beings. As he moved through the cathedral to the shrine dedicated to the memory of its martyred archbishop, and saw the worn steps which had been trodden by thousands of pilgrims in the eight hundred and thirty-five years since his death, he began to understand the influence that Thomas had on countless subsequent generations. His shrine was the object of the pilgrims described in the 'Canterbury Tales' and so many others. Although the historical truth is that religious primates like Thomas were in themselves very powerful men, indeed more like politicians and statesmen than merely humble priests, and engaged in the *real-politic* of their times, Tarquin saw the story of Thomas in terms of 'the good' versus 'the bad'. He was definitely one of the cowboys in the white hats in the old Saturday morning Western serials Tam had watched as a boy. What remained of that simplistic morality in the mind that had subsequently become consumed by self-interest and distorted by greed, now surfaced as he raged internally at the fate of the 'turbulent priest.' As he read some more, he learned that the effect of Henry II's assassination of Thomas was to establish the supremacy of the Crown over the church, a situation that was to be confirmed once and for all by the king's descendent and namesake Henry VIII, when he destroyed the monasteries during the Reformation in 1538, and in the process the original shrine to Thomas. But that earlier Henry enjoyed only a pyrrhic victory. Within three years of his martyrdom, Thomas had been declared a saint, and in the face of thousands making the pilgrimage to Thomas's shrine, as a gesture of penitence, the king walked barefoot through Canterbury in 1174, whipped on his way by the monks of the cathedral.

This image of retribution, whether divine or merely political in origin, visited on the most powerful man in the land, the King no less, gave some degree of satisfaction to Tarquin as he seethed with righteous anger, in support of a saint he had barely heard of before and two days ago would have scoffed at for putting principle before personal gain. By now Tarquin, or perhaps more accurately, Tam, had begun to identify with the martyred archbishop. Like him, he had dared to 'play with the big boys', only in his case it was in the world of finance, not politics. The saint had had the temerity to question the highest power in the land, while Tarquin had ventured to scale the heights of the world of finance and business. While Thomas has suffered the ultimate put-down of assassination at the hands of his king, Tarquin had failed to win the summit of acceptance and equality amongst those he longed to call his peers. The audit that must by now be in full swing in his office was dealing a death blow to all his efforts, as fatal and agonising as the physical assault that had been felt by his alter ego as he fell dying under the swords of his enemies.

Time seemed to cease to have any significance for Tarquin as he continued his tour of the cathedral, but his interest in the other artefacts and images it had to offer waned as he sought out more information about Thomas. As he made his way to the exit, his search still unsatisfied in some way, he found his path blocked by the massive bulk of a large stone urn for donations to the upkeep and restoration of the building. Surmounted by a firmly padlocked cast-iron lid, it was accompanied by a sign detailing the imminent danger of irrevocable damage and disrepair affecting most of the cathedral. The appeal was for urgent and generous assistance, not only from individuals, but from central government. Tarquin vaguely wondered that the Church of England and its vast land holdings could not provide the necessary funds, or whether the Church would accept help from the National Lottery, but as he approached the door, the weight of his holdall made itself felt for the first time since he had left his office more than twenty-four hours before. An idea began to form in his mind as he walked across the cathedral close, following the way-out signs, which as always led through the gift shop and tea-room, strategically sited to tempt the unwary with their ubiquitous array of souvenirs and tourist tat, some in this case unusually tasteful in quality and accordingly expensively priced. Tarquin was immediately drawn to the book section where he bought a book on Canterbury's famous saint.

He made a point of checking the closing time of the cathedral as he left its precincts behind and began to stroll into the neighbouring streets. The pedestrianised shopping street had a distinct post-prandial feel about it, as the Christmas decorations, more pointless and tatty than ever, competed with equally garish *sale* signs at every window. The shoppers here were rather thin on the ground, an indication perhaps of the preferable delights of the Blue Water retail bonanza within easy reach, and appeared limited to the poorer car-less sections of the community: the elderly, young mothers with baby buggies and toddlers and a few lost souls like himself, wandering apparently aimlessly along the narrow street. He found a coffee shop and as he went through the low door he had the impression of entering a glittering Santa's grotto. He instinctively felt the need to duck under an array of shimmering silver and gold stalactites hanging from the ceiling. The desperate strains of Christmas Muzak almost made him turn round and leave, but he was stopped short by the eager young face of a pretty girl cheerfully asking him what he would like. The old Tarquin would have had no hesitation in telling the waitress exactly what he was thinking of her establishment, but in his novel and rather exciting reincarnation, he didn't have the heart to disappoint her, and he was surprised to find how pleased he was to see a warm and welcoming human face, its smile directed only at him. He found he was able to blank out both the awful music and the horrible décor as he had some food and read more about his new-found hero. A few other customers came and went and each time he was conscious of the friendliness and warmth of the young woman. He checked his watch and decided he had just enough time to make it back to the cathedral before it closed for the day. He left the waitress with a huge tip and a delighted if perplexed look on her face. Had she known anything about Tarquin, she would have been even more astounded than she was by the heartfelt hug he gave her.

He took time to call in at an off-licence where he bought a litre bottle of brandy before he hurried back through the rapidly darkening town. He managed to slip unseen into the almost deserted cathedral, and quickly found himself a dark, shadowy corner near the shrine, where he hunkered down to await the closing of the doors. As the last visitors left and the verger made his final round of the now totally silent building, Tarquin rehearsed his next moves. He forced himself to wait for a whole hour to make sure that everyone had gone, by which time it was only just possible to make out the main features of his surroundings by the glimmer of the security lights that filtered through the stained glass windows. Then he found his way to the donations urn and spent the next hour or two carefully and painstakingly executing the first part of his plan. He folded two hundred notes, each promising the bearer one hundred pounds sterling each, and the three hundred fifty-pound notes, before slipping them into the slot in the top of the urn. Thus the thirty—five thousand pounds he had taken from his safe was disposed of, his sense of satisfaction growing with each one. His accountant's brain would have been even more gratified if he had known that the total amount of money that he had stolen represented exactly one thousand pounds for each year that had passed since the murder of Thomas. He would have appreciated the pleasing symmetry of the numbers. But although the £35,000 he was 'donating' was only a fraction of the money he had embezzled, and it was not returning to its rightful owners, he was deeply satisfied that at least this amount was going, hopefully tax-free, to a worthy cause.

He felt certain that Thomas would have been grateful to him, on behalf of the cathedral which must have meant so much to him. As he settled down in his dark corner and opened the packets of sleeping tablets and the bottle of brandy, his thoughts only fleetingly turned to his wife and children, the second family he had abandoned in the course of his life. He had been careful to ensure that their house and most of his moveable estate was in his wife's name, so she and the children would continue to be well enough provided for. However, what all three had already learned and inherited from their husband and father was his business acumen and his less than scrupulous ethics. So his son would grow up to be a swindler like his father, but with the added accomplishments of charm and sexual magnetism. He would live well off the assets of bored and/or desperate rich middle-aged women, while his sister would soon sell her family's story to the tabloids and in so doing enjoy a short-lived celebrity or notoriety, depending on the point of view of the reader. His wife basked in her role of the wronged and tragic widow for a brief spell before setting up her own business as a party planner to the well-heeled contacts she had made over the years. If there was only one thing she was good at, it was throwing a memorable shindig, and with other people's money to spend doing it, she would be as happy as a sand boy. So Tarquin would hardly be missed by his family, and since his real friends did not need even one hand to be counted on, his passing would make little difference to the world.

As he steadily swallowed the tablets, washed down by the alcohol, he sank into a twilight world of half-sleep, in which neither the cold of his stony bed nor the loneliness of his situation penetrated his consciousness. He entered a dream-like state as he slipped away, in which he saw himself lying on the spot where the plaque commemorates Thomas's murder. In the last fast fading glimmer of awareness, he looked up and saw four dark figures, each holding an upraised sword. The swish of their descending blades was the last sound Tarquin ever heard.

Of course he achieved an infamy in death that was exploited by the media for a time. The headlines described his crimes and evoked great sympathy for those he had wronged, including his blameless wife and children. They gloated on the ignominious end he had chosen for himself. The few remaining sleeping tablets and the half empty brandy bottle told their own story. What they couldn't know was that in his dying moments, Tarquin saw himself in the role of saint and martyr, and having lived a notorious and shameful life, he relished the knowledge that he was dying a noble and heroic death. He had in fact become Thomas à Becket, and in so doing re-invented himself as he had done once before. He was a master of self-delusion, but only he knew at the end that ultimately some good would be interred with his bones, while the evil he represented would live after him.

As this nine-day wonder faded from the spotlight, as nine day wonders invariably do, no-one was sufficiently interested to note two seemingly unconnected pieces of information regarding Tarquin's death. One was a footnote in the police report which stated that there were four long slashes in the cashmere overcoat and Italian suit he was wearing when his body was found, lying on top of the Becket commemorative plaque, although the pathologist found no matching cuts on his body. The second was a triumphant item in the Treasurer's report in the minutes of the January meeting of the 'Friends of Canterbury Cathedral' committee.

'An anonymous Christmas donation of thirty-five thousand pounds has been received via the donation urn and will make a substantial contribution to the New Year's fund-raising'.

BUTCHER MAN

By Robert Kirk

The tickle in his throat grew worse and Harry desperately needed to cough. Eventually he could stand it no longer. Still with head bowed and eyes closed, he began one of those under the surface coughs; the kind that starts gently and builds until it's strong enough to dislodge the offending mote. He'd only reached force two on the coughing scale, however, when Janet's elbow in his ribs caused the process to terminate with a splutter.

My God! he lamented inwardly, I never thought, when I admired her body, to check out her elbows; they're like bloody needles. He made a mental note to examine the offending items at the first opportunity. Then he wondered if there would be such an opportunity. He was beginning to tire of this woman and her silly bloody passions. Who would have thought to find Harry Andrews, reporter on the local paper and self-taught cynic, here at a spiritualist meeting? And as a participant rather than in any official capacity?

Certainly not he. Certainly none of his colleagues at the Orebridge Gazette. And he fervently hoped they would never find out either. They would delight in destroying his reputation, built up over a number of years, as a hard nosed sceptic.

The thought caused a fluttering sensation in Harry's bowels and he vowed to himself that this was it: he must finish with Janet. She had a couple of good qualities, both of them inside her jersey, but God did she have some queer ideas. And spiritualism was only one of them.

Only the other week she'd tried to talk him into submitting himself to some oriental person with a handful of long, sharp pins. Janet promised him that the process would cure his dandruff. Too bloody true, it would, Harry had replied. It might also cure him of breathing. And it could be dangerous as well. He'd told her that no one was making any holes in Harry Andrews. He'd keep his snowy shoulders, thank you very much.

A wail from the front of the hall interrupted Harry's muse. He stole a glimpse, although he knew you weren't supposed to, and he would get the elbow again if Janet noticed. He almost laughed out loud. Three chairs had been set up on the stage facing what they liked to call, 'the gathering'. And the lady on the centre chair had gone into a 'trance', her multi-layered chin squashed down onto her chest, her cheeks puffed out, giving her the appearance of a toad trying to turn into a handsome prince. He assumed the noise had come from her.

She wailed again, confirming his guess, and spoke loudly in a deep voice. What she said was, 'Ahh neeka hoara tee.' At least, that's how it sounded to Harry. Then he realised who she was. This was the lady who had a Red Indian Chief as her spirit guide. Every Thursday evening the chief would hover obligingly over the little annexe at the back of Orebridge Co-op tea rooms, waiting his turn to be called down to the meeting. Harry wondered briefly if these spirits had nothing better to do with their time. What, he wondered, would happen if the Chief had been called away on some important matter when it was time for him to do his act? What then, eh? Suppose he had stay behind and stoke one of the Hellish furnaces during a cold snap? Or if he was in the other place—up there— he might be forced to put in some overtime tuning harps or burnishing haloes.

Harry's bout of irreverence was interrupted by a fresh outburst of Red Indian-type sounds from the stage. This time, although spoken with a Hollywood, Sitting Bull accent, they were in English. There were gasps of excitement all around and he noticed a few of the women in the congregation folding their arms and throwing out their chests in subliminal imitation of the medium. All we need now, thought Harry, is for someone to pass round a peace pipe.

'I have a message for you,' the deep voice rumbled. This seemed to be a signal for bowed heads to lift and closed eyes to open. 'For many moons my ancestors hunted the buffalo of the plains.' Heads nodded wisely: the hall was full of people who were authorities on the buffalo herds that had once roamed the American plains. 'We were happy until the blue jackets came and killed the buffalo. They stole our women, our food, and our lands. They—'

The diatribe halted abruptly, on a sharply drawn breath, as if someone had seized the fat lady's throat and begun to squeeze. Harry wished it were so, and he wished it could have been he. But a glance at the platform brought disappointment. Now the voice softened. The chief seemed to have forgiven the white man and was prepared to collaborate. 'There is someone with me now,' boomed the hollow voice. More gasps from the congregation. 'He says he has only been in the spirit world for a short time.'

Harry saw the medium's slitted eyes scan the assembly, looking for a suitable reaction. She was not disappointed, for an old lady in a brown woollen coat clasped paper-white hands at her throat and stood up. On the stage, the woman on the left-hand chair leaned towards the chief and whispered something.

Again came the deep voice of the Indian guide. 'He says he is very happy and has continued in his old job ... something about repairing wheels.'

The lady in the brown coat looked as if she were about to burst. 'It's my Arthur,' she called in a reedy voice. 'Arthur Cartwright!'

The entire gathering sucked in a breath as if they were joined at the throat. What, they wondered, would the message be? Several seconds elapsed. All eyes were on the trembling little woman. All except Harry's, that is. Possibly he was the only one who saw the mediums right-hand woman lean towards her, again whispering from the side of her mouth.

The Chief responded to the old lady's cry. 'Arthur has a message for you, Mrs Cartwright.'

'Yes? Yes?' Her eyes shone with bright anticipation.

'You are not to trust the insurance man!'

There was a bewildered look in her eyes for a second. It was the look often seen on a baby's face as he augments the laundry load: a sort of 'stress overlaid with bliss' look. And then she seemed to accept the message at its face value for she nodded several times, swallowing hard in an effort to stem the tears that swam into her eyes. 'I won't Arthur, I won't trust him.'

All around her, faces broke into smiles. They were gratified that another contact had been made, another vital message passed over the great divide. When they returned their attention to the stage they saw that the chief had departed. Well, the fat lady was slumped in her chair like a rag doll that had lost its stuffing. Or more like, Harry observed cruelly, a blow-up sex toy with the bung removed. So, the Indian must have gone. Suddenly the medium revived, sitting bolt upright, her eyes wide, mouth agape.

Harry slid his cynical gaze to her companion and was surprised at the look of alarm on her face. Then, just as 'Whisperer' reached out a tentative hand towards the fat lady, the flabby jowls quivered and a different voice floated out to them. Again it had an American accent. But this time it had to be a white man for he spoke like one of the characters from Harry's favourite novels. The tone was nasal, the words indistinct, as if the speaker had a mouth full of gum. 'Harry!' it said. Harry snatched a breath, his heart was a dinner gong that had just been struck.

'I want you to write your book now, Harry!' Another stab to his respiratory system. Harry had been toying with the idea of writing a book, a crime thriller. He was an avid reader of Chandleresque novels, the type that invariably starred a private eye working from a tiny office with a naked light bulb in downtown Chicago. Of course, he'd read everything written by the master himself, Raymond Chandler, as well as the novels of Micky Spillaine, Ed McBain and others.

Then common sense returned. There must be quite a few Harrys in the hall besides me, he thought. This contention, however, was not borne out by the swift glance he cast around him. The gathering was almost exclusively female. Anyway, he didn't believe in all that spiritualist crap. When you're dead, you're dead, and that's that, Harry thought.

He felt Janet's eyes on him, sensed her voyeuristic excitement. But he refused to look up. That would be to admit, in a small way, that he thought the voice was addressing him. And that would make him as cookie as the rest of them. Jeez, he'd only allowed himself to be talked into attending this meeting in the hope that Janet would be grateful, more responsive to his physical needs. He didn't expect to become part of the floorshow.

When they tumbled onto the wintry street after the meeting, the air was like a frosty drink, the grass in the park an iced cake. Janet sensed how Harry's mood matched the weather and didn't try to take his arm. They walked stiffly, side-by-side, until they reached her door. If she'd chosen this moment to surrender her virtue to him, asked him in for coffee and a carry on, he would have capitulated. But she didn't.

Harry walked home, buoyed up with a feeling of freedom, not to mention a release from the torments of the flesh. With a bit of luck, he thought, that's the last I'll see of Janet. As he walked, he thought about the voice that had addressed him in the meeting. Oh yes, he accepted now that it had spoken to him. The odds against there being two Harrys at the meeting must be a thousand to one. And for both those Harrys to be contemplating writing a book must be a squillion to one. And then there was that American accent. It was the voice of a Mike Hammer or a Humphrey Bogart: the lip had definitely been off the top teeth. What more proof could be needed that it was his book the voice had referred to? And yet, he still didn't believe in spiritualism. Evidence was one thing, he conceded, but proof was something else.

The steps up to his front door were spangled with frost and Harry's ears tingled as he jiggled his key in the lock. It was going to be a bitter cold night. Perhaps an early retiral was called for, and maybe a glass of whisky? The thought brought a premature glow to Harry's ribs. Within half-an-hour he was settled against plumped up pillows, his favourite Mike Hammer novel against his drawn up knees and a glass of Scotland's finest at his side. He didn't remember putting the book down or switching off the bedside lamp. He wasn't aware of sliding into a restless sleep and a dream so intense that Harry would believe he was awake.

He was on a wet, foggy street. Shop windows, mostly dark, some brightly lit, lined both pavements. Balls of fuzzy light clung to each streetlamp, like halos round the heads of angels. A neon sign in a shop window painted lurid red and green stripes across the pavement.

Harry knew he was being followed. Several times he looked behind but saw nothing, save perhaps for a stray dog snuffling round a litter bin or a car cruising across an intersection. Once he stopped in mid step and his fears were confirmed by the echoing tap of another pair of shoes on the pavement. They had stopped just that fraction later than his. He stood perfectly still and scanned both sides of the street while his heart lubb-dubbed against his ribs. Every shop doorway, every alley seemed to harbour a dark and threatening shadow. Harry caught his breath as something moved. Briefly, he thought he saw a dark shape glide out of sight round a corner. Then his eye was drawn by a movement on the other pavement. This turned out to be the shadow of a tree swaying with the breeze.

Had the other one been a shadow too? Harry didn't think so. But then, why would I be followed? he wondered. And by whom? He dug his hands into his coat pockets and hurried on, quickening his pace as he sensed that his pursuer was still there, drawing ever closer. As the gap narrowed, the echoing footsteps grew louder and clearer. Harry increased his pace again, almost running now as moisture beaded his brow and sweat trickled along his ribs. Only a few more blocks, he told himself. And he mumbled comforting little phrases to himself. Things like, 'Come on, you'll soon be home', and 'Only one street to go, he won't follow you into your own street, will he?'

When it was that the pursuing footsteps faded, Harry wasn't sure. But when he reached his front door he knew he was alone. A shiver that had nothing to do with the cold shook his upper body. He cursed when the key skittered around the lock then sobbed with relief as the door fell open. He was safe now.

But safe from what? And from whom?

The slamming of the door in Harry's dream woke him. He lay staring into the darkened room, the memory of the sound half in his dream, half in the waking world. The slam came again. Sounds of a party across the street wafted through the open window. Rock music, female laughter, some moron with a set of bagpipes while his mate kept time on a dustbin lid.

He began to rationalize his dream. If the slamming of his front door in the nightmare had a connection with reality, so then must the rest. But as he remembered the sequence of visions, reran the film in his head, Harry knew they possessed a starkness that didn't belong in ordinary dreams. He lay for a long time, unable to stop the film that strobed the same pictures through his mind. He heard the same echoing footsteps, felt again the thudding of his heart, the chill running up his spine.

Finally, the weariness that pinned his heavy limbs to the mattress crept over his trunk and stole into his head. Harry slipped from the cruel fingers of the dream and slept soundly for the rest of the night.

Next morning, standing barefoot on the cold tiles in his kitchen and waiting for the kettle to boil, his nocturnal fears seemed silly. The dream had faded from his mind like an old sepia photograph. And when contemplated from the other side of black coffee and three slices of hot buttered toast, the whole experience shrank until it could be tucked away into the back of his mind with a label tied to it that said: product of an overactive imagination.

Harry had a fairly hectic workload the next morning and it was some time after lunch before his mind was able to settle into idle mode. And that was when the notion came to him. He'd just fed a new sheet of paper into his printer and thought, 'Why not?' As the afternoon wore on, Harry's mind fingered the idea more and more. And by the time he got home from work, he was so excited about it he didn't think about dinner at all. Instead, he sat at his computer and rattled on the keyboard in his usual, two fingered style. Scenes from the previous night's dream slid through his mind like glass slivers, too sharp to be stopped. His fingers stuttered over the keys as he remembered the looking glass clarity of the sky, the crackling cold that stung the tops of ears and tips of noses. He registered the crunch of footsteps on frosted pavements, could almost feel the sweat chilling his brow. But there was one thing he couldn't visualise. Because it was something he had never seen—the dark, furtive shape that had followed him most of the way home.

An image appeared from the recesses of his memory. But Harry couldn't be sure if it was something he'd seen or something his mind had concocted from the numerous detective novels he'd read. But he did sense that the mysterious figure had worn a long trench coat belted at the waist. And a wide-brimmed fedora hat. The face, when he tried to recall it, always came out the same; dark, featureless, hidden in the shadow of a hat that was ever tilted forward and down.

Harry eased himself away from the keyboard and read what he'd produced. Perfect, he thought. What better start could his novel have than the terrifying sequence of events from his dream? He flexed his fingers and leaned forward again, only ... his mind was blank. He sat poised, his fingers moving restlessly, threatening to strike the keys at the first inkling of an idea. But none came. He strove to imagine what might have happened next. Murder? Robbery? Perhaps a password spoken in guttural tones, a simple phrase that would send Harry winging off to foreign places to become embroiled in deeds of derring-do, a license to kill folded into his wallet. His mind hopped back and forth between these brief flashes. But they would not gel into anything cohesive. Each path he chose, however promising it seemed at the start, would ultimately turn lacklustre like a ghost that could only exist in the corner of the eye.

Finally he conceded that the moment of inspiration had passed. Harry sighed and switched off the computer, happy that he had at least finished the first chapter. Maybe I'll be inspired again tomorrow, he thought. Who knows?

The dream returned that night, but the setting was different.

Harry was at the discotheque, a place he hated in his waking moments. But now he revelled in the bone-shaking thump of the music, the strobing lights that created a fascinating Charlie Chaplin world on the dance floor. He was well on the way towards inebriation, finishing off his drink with one hand and summoning a passing waitress with the other, when the mass of heaving bodies on the dance floor parted like the Red Sea.

And there he was.

Harry spluttered as his sharp intake of breath pulled the liquor down the wrong aperture. He lowered the glass to the table, peripherally aware that his efforts to attract the attention of the young waitress had been successful and that she stood at his elbow, her face a study of mounting impatience. Harry waved her away, his eyes locked onto the lean, stooped figure at the opposite side of the room. It seemed somehow natural, and not the least incongruous, that the character from his nightmare wore the same ankle-length raincoat, the same fedora hat pulled down over his eyes. Harry sensed a moment of eye contact, even though the eyes under the hat brim were veiled in shadow.

Suddenly, as if the dividing force had been removed, the dancers sloshed together again and the figment of his nightmare was hidden from view. Harry didn't hear the waitress's muttered insults as she walked off to tend to another customer. His mind was a balloon that had suddenly inflated with one thought. Get out of here! Get away. Run, before the bogyman can circumnavigate the ball of heaving flesh that pulsed and throbbed between them.

It seemed that Harry's legs moved before he commanded them to. He was at the exit by the time his brain caught up with the action. This is like a dream, he thought, not really aware that it was. If he had brought an overcoat he couldn't remember, didn't care; he wouldn't have stopped to collect it anyway. Only thoughts of flight were in his head and he almost tripped in his haste to descend the stone steps outside. The temperature had plummeted and the ground was overlaid with a jagged coating of frost that crunched and squeaked at every step. He stepped out briskly, his breath streaming behind him as he tried to slip round the next corner before his pursuer emerged from the building. He dared not glance behind but a sixth sense told of eyes that stabbed into his back. Harry suppressed a moan that began in his throat. The worst thing he could do was show fear. He snatched a quick backward glance but wasn't reassured by what he saw. His eyes registered three or four dancing dark shapes; they might be shadows, they might be … something else. His footsteps pattered swiftly now. He avoided naked concrete, always looking for grass or frost to walk on, anything that might deaden the noise of his passage. He began to mumble like the last time, telling himself how it was all just imagination and that he was nearly home.

Harry became so immersed in his thoughts that the stranger's appearance at his side came as a shock. His peripheral vision glimpsed the tall figure in ankle-length trench coat and wide-brimmed felt hat. He whirled to meet his assailant. But before he could utter a sound his wrist was seized in a grip so strong, Harry knew there was no point in struggling.

'Who are you, what do you want,' he demanded, cursing the shaking voice that betrayed his terror. With a swift movement the shadowy figure slammed Harry's wrist against the coarse stone wall behind him then swung his lean body between Harry and his

'What the hell's going on?' Harry tried to say. But the rigidity of his throat muscles reduced it to a pitiful mewling sound. There came a sharp snick that Harry recognised as the opening of a jack-knife, then he gasped as pain seared from his hand up to his shoulder and then radiated in waves of pure agony across his chest. Tears sprang to his eyes and his knees buckled as shock numbed his body. Harry slid towards a crouch. Abruptly his wrist was released and the shadowy figure slid off along the street to be absorbed by the gloom of a dark alleyway.

Harry's body spasmed with each agonising throb in his hand. He swung his eyes towards the source of his pain, terrified of what he might see.

His brain was still capable of a modicum of logical thought. And that logic tied the sound of the opening knife to the pain he was feeling. An inescapable conclusion, really. Still Harry feared to look. Once he had, there'd be no going back, no pretending it hadn't happened. But he had to know, one way or the other. He distributed the effort by turning his head as he brought his left hand jerkily up towards his face. Then his unwilling eyes locked onto the sight he hadn't wanted to see.

His thumb was missing! Gouts of blood pumped from the wound and splashed onto his chest. The pavement was a study in white and crimson. He stared at the bleeding stump with disbelief, his eyes already clouding over. With a deep sigh, Harry slid the rest of the way down the wall until his body lay on the pavement like a crumpled heap of rags and his mind took refuge from the pain in a dark, deep well of unconsciousness.

Birds twittered and scuttled about their nests in the eaves. Bright sunlight lanced through the window and splashed like butter milk onto the wallpaper. From the street below, letterboxes creaked and clunked as they grudgingly accepted the morning papers.

Harry's eyes opened. What had wakened him? For a moment he lay still. He was anxious but didn't know why. Then he remembered the dream. And with the memory, as if they could only exist together, came the pain. Harry gritted his teeth as the raw stabbing sensation coursed up his arm and spread in waves that explored first his chest, then his groin and finally his entire body. Dreading what he might discover, he pressed his fingers together. The breath he had been holding escaped in a rush as he felt that his thumb was still there. He'd been so certain it would be gone.

Harry groaned as he heaved himself out of bed, staggered to the bathroom cabinet to find some pain killers. But as he prepared to swallow them, he realised that the pain had gone. Suddenly. Completely. He frowned as he returned the pills to the bottle and screwed on the cap.

That was when he felt it. And then he saw it. Running round the base of his thumb was a deep red cut that stung and seeped blood! Swiftly, Harry washed the wound and covered it with a plaster. His bafflement increased when he shuffled into the kitchen to make breakfast and saw the carving knife lying on the work surface. How did that get there? he wondered. He was sure he hadn't left it out the night before. And when he lifted the knife to replace it in the drawer, he noticed that its razor sharp edge was blood stained. Harry shook his head in bewilderment, washed the knife and put it away.

It was in that quiet period after breakfast and just before he was due to leave for work that Harry's glance alighted on the Cycloptic eye of his computer. He remembered how his inspiration had dried up the previous evening. And he realised that it had now returned in the shape of his dream.

Of course! It was the perfect answer. Chapter two had come to him while he slept. He sat down and resumed his novel, his mind, his hands and the keyboard interlinking with each other in one fused unit that was aware of nothing else. The newspaper thudded onto the hall floor unnoticed, the postman came and went, as did the window cleaner and a brace of Jehovah's Witnesses. The world outside the writing automaton that was Harry Andrews did not exist. Neither did the clock on the wall that accused him of neglecting the job that paid his wages. He finished around one-o'clock and, with a rush of guilt, phoned the office.

'I felt sick this morning,' he said. 'Yes, I'm all right now. I'll come in for the afternoon.'

Harry went to bed early that night, anticipating sleep like a child on Christmas Eve. He was impatient to receive the next dream … chapter three.

But chapter three seemed set to disappoint; more or less a rerun of chapter two! The same discotheque with the same pulsating music and stabbing lights. The same tiny dance floor with its huddle of slowly vibrating flesh. And the same nightmare figure with ankle length coat and inscrutable face.

After the inevitable chase and the terrifying click as the knife opened, Harry opened his eyes on a world of hurt. Once more his body was racked with pain and, predictably, its epicentre was Harry's thumb. Resigned to believing that the cut would be opened and bleeding again, Harry tried to lift his hand. But it was stuck to the bed sheets with blood! He craned over and gingerly teased away the sheet, wincing each time the edges of the wound were pulled. Finally the last clinging piece of cotton sheet was unwound and Harry moaned in agony and dismay.

This time, his left thumb was missing! And only the fact that the stump had become entangled in the bed clothes had saved him from bleeding to death.

What he told the doctors in outpatients, he wasn't sure, but he knew it hadn't been the truth. Who would believe he'd lost his thumb in a dream?

Harry was obliged to spend a few days in hospital for observation and remedial surgery. During which time, he was in a state of torment as the dream washed repeatedly through his mind. He knew his mental suffering would end only when he could sit at the computer and commit the next chapter of his book to silicon.

Home once more, he immediately sat before his keyboard and began to work. Even suffering as he was with the discomfort of his bandaged hand, he saw that chapter two could be improved. Now it would be more gruesome, somehow more satisfying.

A little corner of Harry's mind suggested that something was wrong here. It was just too convenient, this tie up between the dreams and his beloved novel. It might have been said in his favour that Harry ignored the warning voice, felt that one must suffer for the sake of one's art. But it wouldn't have been true. Harry didn't even hear it.

Chapter three, when it came that night, was exhilarating and Harry, although he was asleep, began to be aware of the other side, the waking side, of the see-saw he rode. He remembered his novel and he knew he was there, in this dream, to collect the latest instalment for it.

He was at the fun fair. The waltzers were the best he'd ever ridden. They were fast, and the music from fat, powerful speakers could almost be felt on the skin. Car jockeys rode the swooping and dipping floor like rodeo riders, slapping each car into a spin that kept heads pinned back against the seats.

Harry was alone in his car, his arms spread along the cushioned seat top in a way that he hoped looked nonchalant, the pose of the veteran waltzer rider. For the most part he kept his eyes closed and revelled in the thump of the music and the deep rumble of rubber wheels. Then he opened his eyes, puzzled. A feeling of unease had entered his mind. Harry looked around, as best you can while spinning and dipping and carousing round an undulating track. The ride was perfectly safe, everyone knew that. So what was it that had invaded his thoughts, leaving behind a sensation of disquietude?

He scanned the pink faces that ringed the moving platform, the people impatient for the ride to stop and let them on.

It was the briefest of glimpses, but Harry knew there was no mistake. He swallowed heavily and squeezed the soft leather of the seat back with his fingers. The car spun and there he was again. He wore the same ankle length coat, the same fedora hat. And his face was still in shadow. The ride moved on and Harry's view was a whirling vista that encompassed the control booth: the sea: thundering diesel trucks, sheets of green canvas and more pink faces. With a feeling that was half dread, half anticipation, he waited for the same space to reappear, the place where the menacing figure had stood.

But this time he wasn't there!

Harry's fleeting relief ended just as the pain began. Desperately he tried to twist in his seat to see who was behind him, who it was that could pinion his hands behind the wildly gyrating car … and still remain out of sight. But struggle though he might, he could not move his arms; they might just as well have been clamped to the seat with bands of iron for all his flailing and heaving achieved.

As the pain built in intensity, it seemed the music swelled louder, complicit in covering up the assault on Harry Andrews, waltzer rider extraordinaire. It didn't quite drown out Harry's screams. But then, who takes any notice of someone screaming on a fairground waltzer?

Harry stayed in hospital for several weeks this time. He ached to continue his novel while his head swam with visions of the fair: fortunetellers, the ghost train, the waltzers. He nagged the doctor continually for access to a computer. But each time he refused. 'You'll disturb the other patients,' he said. 'And besides …'; he aimed a verbose nod at the bandage that swathed Harry's right hand. But Harry felt sure he didn't need thumbs to hit the spacebar. He could use his wrist, couldn't he? It was just a matter of adjusting his style.

Within a few hours of returning home, Harry had typed in chapter three. He saved it onto the floppy disk that held the previous two chapters and sighed contentedly. The book was going well.

Although …

The little corner of his mind that urged caution was growing bigger and its message almost strident enough to be noticed by Harry. But not quite. Not yet.

When Harry awoke the next morning after being chased through the jungle by someone with a gleaming machete—who caught him—he began to consider that something was seriously wrong.

The ambulance men shook their heads in disbelief.

He should have been dead, they said.

Lucky the raw stump of his ankle became entwined in his pyjama trousers, they said.

The cotton material had formed a makeshift tourniquet. Otherwise he'd have bled to death, they told each other.

Harry, hearing their conversation through a curtain of pain, was beginning to see that it wasn't luck at all. He knew who was behind this, although he didn't know why. Who was this shady character who invaded his dreams and seemed to be carving him up? He was cutting pieces from Harry as calmly as a butcher divides an animal's carcass.

Harry realised where this line of thought was leading and suppressed it. What was he thinking about? Butcher Man—that seemed a good name for him—wasn't real, was he? He was only something from Harry's dream ... surely. But if it wasn't he of the long raincoat and felt hat that was chopping pieces of Harry's body away, then who was it? Could it be that Harry was butchering himself in his sleep? Was that possible ... to inflict such damage on one's self and not wake until it was over?

It was a pale, drawn Harry Andrews who lurched from hospital on a crutch several weeks later. It was a Harry now diminished to the tune of two thumbs and one foot.

It was also a Harry who was under surveillance.

Not unnaturally, the authorities had become suspicious and were treating his stories about accidents in the kitchen with a touch of scepticism. They provided him with a home help, a young and zealous social worker who saw Harry's predicament as his golden opportunity.

'Do I have any say in this?' Harry demanded of the young man standing on his doorstep.

Vincent shrugged. 'I expect you could refuse. But I did hear the word "section" mentioned a couple of times.' He watched the wash of emotions that visited Harry's face, then nodded to a large bundle he'd dumped on the path. 'Brought my own camp bed. Promise I won't get under your feet.'

He waited anxiously, hoping Mr Andrews would allow him to stay. For reasons, Vincent had to admit, that were not entirely altruistic. If he could sort out this case ... well, it was a bloody strange one, wasn't it? ... he could well impress his boss. Promotion. Wage rise. He might even turn it into a book. A block-buster. He pictured Hollywood making it into a film about a one-footed man, framed with his wife's murder and on the run from the police. They could call it 'The Foot I Give'.

Harry turned and walked back into the house, signalling his acquiescence by leaving the door open.

After three fruitless weeks, however, the social services thought they'd wasted enough time on Harry and withdrew their attentions. It seemed the mutilations had stopped anyway. Harry, meanwhile, having decided they would have to stop, had unplugged the computer from the wall. He wasn't sure why or how, exactly, but he did now see that the dreams and his book were inextricably linked. Which one of the two had spawned the other he wasn't certain, nor did he care. All he knew was, if the book stopped, the butchering would stop.

In a way, he was right.

The first night Harry was to spend on his own he felt nervous. Bravado was all very well when the social worker had been sleeping in the next room. But this night, the house was unusually still. He retired early with a large mug of hot chocolate and a Barbara Cartland romance, both chosen for their soporific value. Although convinced that he was safe he had stashed the floppy disk containing his new novel at the back of the desk drawer. Out of sight—out of mind. He would try anything to achieve a deep, and he hoped, dreamless sleep.

He did dream. But not about Butcher Man. No, what Harry dreamed about that night was his computer. He jerked awake at first light, his pyjamas damp with sweat and a feeling in his head that usually meant a hangover. But that couldn't be so. Harry had been on the wagon since his last hospital visit. He gazed dully around the room, wondering what had woken him. Then his bladder complained. With a resigned sigh, he flung back the blankets and plodded through to the bathroom, pain jarring his head with each step. On the way back, Harry stopped, a frown growing on his stubbled features.

The study door was open! He was sure he had closed it last night, it was part of his ritual. Check all the doors, close all the windows, turn out the lights. These last-minute checks were as much a part of Harry's going to bed behaviour as brushing his teeth, or pulling on his pyjamas. He moved towards the open door, a lump of ice beginning to melt in his lower stomach.

Then he paused in mid-stride. The light was on too! Harry vacillated, swaying forward then backward, his body responding to the turbulence that swept through his mind. Finally, he filled his chest with air, accused himself of being a wimp, and barged through the door.

The room was empty. For which Harry was incredibly grateful. Now beginning to accept that he'd been a touch forgetful the night before, he flipped off the light, intending to close the door and return to bed. With the light off, of course, the glowing screen of the computer announced itself, its green luminescence spilling over the desk and onto the carpet.

'What the Hell's going on here?' wondered Harry. A cold shiver tiptoed down the back of his neck, bringing the hairs erect and causing Harry to shiver. Feeling more nervous now, he shuffled forward and peered at the screen. There, in glowing crimson letters, stood the words, Butcher Man.

His book!

A quick prod on the keyboard brought the rest of the text scrolling into view. There were no two ways about it, the computer had been switched on and Harry's novel loaded in. He ejected the floppy disk from the drive slot and checked the label. He delved into the drawer, scraping around the four corners. Harry's heart slammed against the confines of his rib cage. This was his disk! Someone—it wasn't him—had been in here. And that someone had been using the computer. What's more, they had been looking at Harry's book.

A possibility occurred to Harry, one that he didn't care to explore. But he had to know. Even as he hesitated, his foolhardy finger stabbed the keyboard and the text scrolled upwards with maddening slowness.

Chapter 1 … Harry's mouth was drying rapidly, his throat hurt when he swallowed.

Chapter 2 … He suddenly developed a nervous cough.

Chapter 3 … As the end of chapter 3 swept onto the screen, a cold hand closed around Harry's scrotum, causing it to contract and pull his manhood up inside him.

Then, there it was, although it had no right to be there. Harry allowed his finger to slip from the keys and the scrolling stopped. He read … and reread … and read again, unable to accept what he saw. But he had to accept it, or disbelieve his eyes. He rubbed the aforementioned organs with his fingertips and squinted at the screen again. This time he dared to read some of the new text.

He had never seen it before. It was entirely unfamiliar to him.

The headache, briefly forgotten, now stomped its way to a ringside seat in Harry's forehead. There it sat, stamping its feet and causing his eyes to blink in pained response. A tremor built slowly deep inside him, rumbling upwards, outwards, until his whole frame shook. Blindly thrusting out a hand, Harry switched of the machine then stumbled into the hallway. His mind was a snake pit filled with writhing doubts.

Who ... How ... What ...?

Each question ushered out the previous one before the answers could form. He shuddered violently and decided he needed something soothing, something to oil the troubled waters of his soul.

Whisky! A large one!

It is possible for a human being to go without sleep for remarkably long periods. Harry had read of experiments in sleep deprivation during which some of the subjects stayed awake for more than a week. And that was just what he intended to do. Whoever or whatever it was that had broken into his dreams of late, seemed to have two aims.

The first was to have Harry write his novel. What the second aim was, Harry dreaded to think. But it seemed to entail Harry losing bits of his body every now and then. He snorted cynically as he remembered the excitement he'd felt during the early stages of the manuscript. Now he saw that the ideas hadn't belonged to him at all, they had been planted in his mind, in his dreams, by a person unknown who may, or may not, look like the character Harry had dubbed, Butcher Man.

And so, Harry prepared himself for battle. He felt that, if he could refrain from sleep—or more particularly from dreams—for long enough, the menacing figure would give up, leave him alone. There was one insistent little notion that flitted around on the periphery of Harry's thoughts that said, 'But you can't stay awake for ever, Harry. Sooner or later ... you have to sleep. And when you do, you'll dream. And then ...'

But Harry wouldn't give that little thought the house room it desired, turning his thoughts elsewhere each time he glimpsed it at one of the windows of his mind. It was something he couldn't admit, not for the tiniest part of an instant of time. If he did, then he was finished, might as well give in now. Yet the notion was an insistent little bugger, the way all neglected things seem to be. The more he tried to reject it, the more it waved its arms at him, the more strident its voice became. So Harry provided surrogate thoughts, lots of little trifles with which to occupy his mind. It was a brilliant idea, really. He became a rich man, a king who, confronted by the blind beggars on the street, turned his thought towards his fine clothes. He preened himself and fussed over specks of dust for those vital few moments necessary to carry him past that which must not be contemplated.

And it worked!

Of course, the part played by bottles of amber fluid originating in Scotland must not be understated. They helped enormously as long as Harry used them carefully. Too little and the brain stayed sharp, reaching out for new areas of contemplation Too much and they would open the door for his enemy, Morpheus. Harry, literally, had his thoughts in a bottle, and he was determined that no one would open that bottle until he was ready.

He did extremely well for a time, filling his head with crosswords from the daily paper, television game shows and soap operas which he had previously spurned. He listened to the radio, enjoying the endless political discussions. When all that began to bore him, he would retune to what he had previously called 'Radio Stun'. The sort of music they played abounded in anti-soporificness (he doubted if that was a real word. But his brain was liable to do that nowadays, invent new words and phrases. They were mostly nonsense but served their purpose: distraction!).

After the third day, Harry's mind broke through the sleep barrier, that curtain which, when pulled aside, allows us to grasp our second wind, mentally speaking. He no longer lolled on the sofa longing for sleep, but felt more and more alert with each passing hour. His surroundings became brighter, more colourful, more lucid. He didn't realise it then, but he was entering the mental state craved by drug addicts: his mind had started to manufacture its own brand of L.S.D.

It began with the television. Harry was avidly following Question Time, the program that allows an audience to confront a selected panel of public figures. The camera had been panning around the audience when Harry spotted a lean rain-coated figure seated near the back. He wore a wide brimmed fedora hat tugged down over his face. Harry shuddered and stabbed at the remote control. But it wasn't long before the other channels allowed the man from Harry's nightmares into their programmes as well. He appeared in the crowds outside Buckingham Palace waving a tiny Union Flag, in the hushed audience of a snooker game, and even—good God, could that be him at the bar of the Rover's Return, supping beer with Ken Barlow?

Inevitably, all of this nonsense had to end. Whether Harry decided subconsciously that there was no escape from Butcher Man, asleep or awake—or whether his body's ability to do without sleep simply ran out of steam, is irrelevant.

What did matter was; he slept. And the sleep that Harry fell into was one of amazing depth. His mind, free at last, plunged and soared through the waves of dreamtime. Once or twice it rose almost to the surface, as if it meant to breathe, but then down, down, down it would go again, plumbing the awesome depths of Harry's psyche. And guess what it found there. Correct!

Butcher Man!

If pain could be heard then Harry's leg was screaming at the top of its voice. The nerve endings that had once communicated with his foot realised their loss and made plenty of noise about it. When he had managed to screw together the necessary courage, and when it became apparent that he would have to summon help, Harry lifted his head. The bottom of his bed was a mess of sodden blood. It was even worse than last time. And the incredulity of the ambulance men was even greater. They had begun to think of Harry as either a very unfortunate man or a religious nut! He was extremely lucky, they said, to have lost both feet in similar circumstances, and then escape death by bleeding in almost the same way each time.

Last time his pyjama leg had served as a tourniquet, this time it had been the bed sheet. Unbelievable! Their reasoning behind the religious nut theory was this: Johnny, the short fat one, had once read a horror book about a religious sect called the Celestines. They believed that the path to Heaven was through eating each other's bodies. 'It's a bit like cannibalism,' Johnny said, 'but the guy who represents the food is still alive.

'What they do,' he informed his mate, Terry, as they manoeuvred Harry into the ambulance, 'is chop off all the bits the guy can do without. Then the High Priest, he fries them up, and all the others eat them. A finger here, a couple of toes there, and so on. Finally, when they've had all the expendable bits—y'know, the bits the guy can live without—well then he makes the ultimate sacrifice and they all get stuck into his torso.'

Harry heard most of this in the spaces between waves of agony that washed up from his ankle and over the rest of his body. And it says a lot for his sense of humour that his immediate thought was, 'Well, at least somebody got a good meal out of that. I'm getting bugger all, except maybe losing a bit of weight.'

During his recuperation in a cottage hospital on the outskirts of town, Harry conceived the notion that his computer was possessed. Well, look at it from his point of view: it was either the computer or Harry himself that was weird. What would you choose to believe? As soon as he was able, he telephoned the dealer who'd sold it to him and arranged for it to be taken in for a thorough check. And, when the engineers had failed to find any bugs in the system, Harry told them to keep it and give him a new one.

Which he found unpacked and installed, gleaming with innocence, on his computer desk when he arrived home. Beside it stood a box of brand new floppy disks—he had flung the others in the bin. Now, he reckoned, Butcher Man was well and truly out of his life. For over a week he squeaked around the house in his new wheelchair, and he soon became competent.

And he became bored.

He tried to read but found books awkward to hold without thumbs. He'd been fairly good at the guitar but supposed he would have to sell it now. Bugger! He'd just realised he would lose his place on the darts team!

His eyes, casting around for something to do, kept alighting on his new computer. And he had to confess, its attraction was strong, hard to resist. Yes, he did try awfully hard not to switch on old green eye, but he was beaten by a trick. At least, in hindsight, that's what he considered it to be. Surely some evil spirit, if not Butcher Man himself, had a hand in it. After all, it was the first time ever that the writers' magazine he subscribed to, had sported a free CD taped to its cover.

'CHOCK FULL OF USEFUL UTILITIES FOR YOUR WORD PROCESSOR, it said on the label.

'LOAD THIS UP AND TRY OUR USEFUL WORD COUNT UTILITY' it went on.

And, 'JUST WHAT EVERY WRITER NEEDS—A SPELLING CHECKER'

Harry was, in spite of himself, intrigued. A spelling checker, eh? He'd heard about these things, wondered if he could get one for his machine. He spun his wheels towards the desk and fed the new disk into the eagerly waiting CD tray.

Then he froze. His mind quivered as it was besieged by memories: memories of pain and fear and of missing limbs. But then the optimist within him pitched in its tuppence worth. 'Go on,' it said. 'The old disks are in the bin. You've got a new computer, it can't harm you now.'

Harry weakened. Like a fat boy in a sweet shop, his resolve melted. He nudged the CD tray and it slid forward, feeding the silvery disk into the innards of his PC. After a few beeps and burps, a catchy little tune played and a welcoming message on a draughtboard proclaimed, 'SPELL CHECKER'. Harry pressed the keyboard as prompted and after a short introductory message, the program announced its intention of demonstrating how it should be used. It promised Harry faithfully that, if he pressed another key, he could watch as a typical text file was loaded from the disk and then checked for spelling errors.

Harry fell for it! Some inner part of him knew what would happen, sent a twinge of regret through his gut even as his finger sank on to the key. But its warning was too little, too late. Harry gasped as the green words crawled, worm-like up the screen. He didn't read them, didn't have to. It was enough to see that they were headed by …

… CHAPTER FOUR.

The opposite side of the house was where Harry took refuge. 'I've been tricked, I've been tricked,' he muttered over and over. He wheeled back and forth between the two doors of his sitting room, the wheelchair equivalent of pacing the floor, and wondered what he could do. From his study he heard the faint chirrups and beeps as the program chattered to itself. Harry had been in too much of a hurry to escape to switch it off, and he daren't return now.

Night came and Harry's eyes were heavy. But he had formulated a plan. His hot chocolate drink was made and set beside his bed. He completed his toilet, checked the doors and windows, then wheeled through to bed. But, en route, he stopped at the space under the stairs where the electricity meter and fuse boxes were. With a flourish Harry flipped off the main switch.

'Let's see what you can do without electricity,' he sneered over his shoulder. But the computer was silent. When he awoke next morning, Harry remembered very little of his dreams. That he had dreamed he was certain. And of what he had dreamed, he was equally certain. But the particulars of the chase and the gory details of the culmination of that chase were hidden from his conscious mind. Or rather, his conscious mind had other things to occupy it.

Like the numbness that affected his groin!

He extended a probing hand but felt nothing. It's like a jaw after a visit to the dentist, Harry thought. He tried to roll onto his side, thinking he'd been lying on a nerve. But he couldn't move; his body seemed bound to the bed. Further exploration revealed that the sheet had become swaddled around him like a nappy, only much tighter. That's the problem, he thought. Then his fingers encountered the wet, stickiness. He groaned, not with pain, but with mental agony as traces of his dream came wisping back into his head.

He had been climbing a tree, but couldn't remember why. He had slipped as he sensed movement on the ground below him; slipped and been left dangling there as his jacket caught in a branch. With his arms pulled high and his face buried inside his clothes, Harry could see almost nothing of the world outside his jacket. But somehow his other senses told him that Butcher Man was nearby. He heard a loud snick as the knife opened. And then ...

Harry buried his face in his pillow and wept in a way he hadn't done since he was a child. Well, he certainly wasn't a man any more. How can you call yourself a man when …

His self-pity was swept aside as he realised what he must do now. It was all becoming so plain. Butcher Man was some kind of ghost or spirit who had latched on to him during that spiritualist meeting. And Harry could see now what the plan was. By removing Harry a little at a time, that spirit hoped to supplant him in the real world.

And Harry? What was to happen to him? The only logical answer to that seemed to be that Harry was destined for that other place, the place where Butcher Man was now. Harry's breathing became laboured as he thought these thoughts. Yes, it was all so obvious now. Butcher Man was killing him, piece-by-piece, inch-by-inch—his amazingly resilient sense of humour still found time to giggle at the notion that, the last piece Butcher Man had taken had been more than an inch.

But he wouldn't win, Harry would see to that. His determined state of mind and the energy he expended wheeling himself out through the back door and down the garden towards his workshop left him bathed in sweat, even though the night was cold. He stretched up and hit the light switch behind the door. Harry then heaved his wheelchair over the rough wooden floor towards the saw bench. A prod from a shaking finger and the jagged steel blade growled into motion. It wound up in speed until it sang, its wicked teeth a silver blur.

There was nothing wrong with Harry's resolve, or his courage. He was absolutely committed to what he knew he should do. But the problem was one of a purely mechanical nature: the square steel table was too large for Harry. If he had been able to stand he might have managed. But, ensconced in his wheelchair, he found it impossible to get his neck against the blade's whirring edge. For a full minute he tried, heaving this way and that, even sitting with his back to the bench and arching backwards. It was no good. Frustration swelled in his chest until he thought it would burst through the top of his head. Frustration and anger at the thought that Butcher Man had won. He would still be able to use Harry as his means of entry to the real world.

Then Harry remembered how that entry was being effected. Even though there was evidence to the contrary, Harry now realised that he was the one who had typed each and every chapter, awake or in his sleep. And as he glared with hatred at the screaming steel blade, he saw a way to thwart the plans of the creature that had sprung from his nightmare.

It was over before the thought had properly gelled in his head. One quick sweep with both hands clasped together. He was surprised at how quickly the saw blade bit and sliced through skin, flesh and bone. He was amazed at how little noise it made, a little puff of blue smoke the only evidence hanging in the air before him. But the neighbours who heard Harry's screams said it was the most frightening thing they had ever heard.

Johnny and Terry were becoming quite friendly towards Harry now, even to the point of using first names. 'Whoops! Hang on Harry while we take these steps,' they would say. And, 'You should try an electric razor next time, pal. It's safer.' Today, they tried harder than usual. One look at Harry and they knew. Well, after a few years on the job, you could tell the ones that were going to make it and the ones that weren't. Accordingly, they saw it as their duty to make Harry's last few minutes on this earth cheerful ones. Harry wasn't a good audience, his sense of humour finally seeming to have deserted him. He failed to smile at their quips and was ungracious enough to groan when they bumped his head rounding the corner of the living room door. As they progressed along the hallway, Harry suddenly jerked his head forward.

He could hear typing! And it came from his study.

He managed to extricate one bloody stump from the blankets and wave it about. He groaned and pawed at the wall, leaving wide, crimson streaks and causing the procession to halt outside the study door.

'Oh! Almost forgot to tell you,' said Johnny light heartedly. 'Your brother's arrived to look after the house until you get better.' He pulled a face of mock shame at the blatant lie. Harry wasn't going to get better and they all knew it. Johnny stretched out a foot and casually nudged the door open. 'He says he's going to finish some typing for you. Isn't that nice?'

A spider of ice jumped from Harry's heart, to his bowels, to his groin, linking them all with a web of frozen numbness. The tall, rain-coated figure slewed in the chair without removing his fingers from the keys. Although the face was still a dark shadow under the brim of the felt hat, Harry somehow knew the creature had winked. He waited, his imbecilic mouth slack and dripping a skein of saliva onto the blanket, but Butcher Man did not speak. Instead, his fingers rattled over the keyboard. Then he sat to one side so that Harry could read what he had typed. It was:

THE END

Scottish Druid

By George Sinclair

Facts

The world's centre of Druidism was Scotland, or Alba, as it was known then. Dunedin, now called Edinburgh, was the Druids' capital, the Castle rock was their sacrifice arena and the site on which Holyrood Palace now stands was the Druid's Collegiate Headquarters, where all major decisions were taken.

The Druid religion and lifestyle were similar in many ways to those of the early Celtic Church; their fundamental principles of justice, using scientific knowledge and protecting the people were the same. But the Celtic Church differed from the Druids on child sacrifice.

Columba was a great storyteller.

Dunedin 77 AD

'It is time,' said Ferchar, one of the senior Druids, looking at Nechtan.

A wickerwork made in the shape of a man thirty feet high, ten feet wide and mounted on a hollow platform high above him, not far from where he stood, took Nechtan's attention. Inside the wickerwork were thirty children and ten adults, some children were urinating and sobbing, others were screaming, none of them had eaten all day and they were hungry. One child had a particularly piercing scream, Nechtan stared at the boy; his face was contorted with sheer terror. The children were young innocents who had been especially selected by the Druids as being of the right character and age to pacify the gods when they met. The adults were common criminals and would go to Hell.

It was sunset. As he gazed into the eyes of the gathered crowd, Nechtan gave the pronouncement. 'Oh people of Alba, we give thanks to the gods for all the good things that we receive. In return, the gods have requested that we send them these blessed children. Today is our Samhain, the sun's power has waned, and the strength of the gods of darkness, winter and the underworld grow great.'

The children started to scream louder. The criminals were not mentioned—they were irrelevant—a mere nuisance to be got rid of. Nechtan could not believe that the Druids really wanted this practice, performed on a scale that was unsurpassed in horror, even by the most savage tribes on earth, to be carried on.

He took the lit torch from Ferchar and threw it onto the bundles of wood underneath the edifice, and within a few minutes there were large flames licking around the base of the wickerwork. The children and criminals felt the heat; they all started to shout loudly, and tried to clamber up as high as possible. Mayhem broke loose and vicious feet crushed the tender flesh of some of the children. Within a few minutes the flames had engulfed the wickerwork and Nechtan inhaled the nauseating smell of burning flesh. His heart pounded as his eyes took in the unreal sight before him. Within another few minutes the wickerwork was a raging inferno and the screams quietened down to whimpers as the death throws of the children and criminals took over.

Nechtan stared blankly at this Hell on earth. He was shocked to the core. *Numb!* This was a day he would never forget—the face and screams of the boy were emblazoned into his mind forever.

Iona 590 AD

Columba sat silent for some time; he had just had a flashback to a nightmare that had kept haunting him for years. Would he ever be rid of it? He pushed back his long curly brown hair and rested his chin on calloused hands, his elbows on the table. He and his monks were gathered in their hall, sitting around a long wooden table eating bread and cheese. They were drinking beer that had been made only a few days previously. It tasted a bit fresh and some of the monks made faces but continued to drink it. They had been in the fields all day and they would eat and drink anything.

Columba knew them all very well, but they did not know him as well as they thought. He needed to make them understand their legacy so that they could tackle their dangerous future with purpose. How would he do this, he thought? *Could he avoid opening the portal?*

A few minutes later he decided.

'Come, I need to show you a place where you have never been,' Columba said, pointing to the doorway of the hall. Pushing their chairs aside the monks rose and followed him. Some looked at each other and wondered what was going on.

'He doesn't even let us finish our dinner!' moaned Fergus, grabbing his last piece of bread and swilling down some beer.

They scuffled down a dull corridor, squeezed into Columba's private chamber and stood looking at him. Why were they there, some thought?

'What I am about to show you, no man has ever seen before. You must not discuss this with anyone other than those of you in this room ... do you swear?' said Columba.

'We swear,' was the response. A few of them looked at each other, puzzled.

Columba turned and heaved at a thick wooden door. It creaked open and instead of seeing a room they saw a shimmering misty wall. The monks stood in amazement as the mist slowly cleared. They gradually saw that several men were seated in a hall with three raised areas on each side of a marbled floor with coloured patterns. The walls had several pairs of vertical columns, each pair framing a small alcove. One of the men paraded around the marbled floor, talking to the assembly.

'Our northern campaign must quickly extend into southern Alba, and eventually even further north. The Gaelic kings rule the tribes and their advisors, the Druids, burn human beings enclosed in gigantic figures of wicker-men. Polonius has seen it with his very own eyes. Should we let this continue?' said Crastus. He flicked his flowing white robe back with his right hand as he walked slowly and stroked his chiselled chin. He was heavily suntanned and his long silver hair hid an anxious look.

'No!' was the loud response from the gathering.

'So what should we do?'

'Kill them all!'

Columba closed the door.

Gasps and looks of bewilderment filled the room as the monks struggled to understand what they had seen.

'The Druids have changed some of their ways since then,' said Columba. 'You already know that I am a prince of the royal line of the Kings of Tara, but you may not be aware that I am also a Druid.'

The last comment was a revelation to most of the monks and some were visibly shocked.

Brendan whispered to the monk next to him, 'He is said to have won a battle of magic with Broichan, Druid to king of the Picts.'

'My story is centuries old, and has been handed down to me by my father and grandfather, as told to them by their ancestors,' said Columba. 'I now show you another glimpse of our past.' He opened the door again and another misty scene appeared before them. It was another arena with different people.

'All ye bards and Druids of Brude macMaelchon, I plead, like Bran and St Patrick before me, the case for the prime example of Druidism, Jesus Christ, whose blood had a unique mixture of priestly and kingly blood. He is my true Druid and miracle worker.' It was Columba talking to a gathering of Druids. The monks were stunned!

Columba closed the door again. More gasps and looks of bewilderment filled the room.

'Our King in Ireland has sent us here to continue his mission of promoting the principles of justice, using scientific knowledge and medicine for the good of the people, and protecting them. It was for that same reason that princes, nobles and wise men once sent their sons to the Druids in Dunedin, so that they could teach them all they knew. Part of our mission is to restore our world to the grandeur and greatness of those times.'

*   *   *   *

Nechtan was in fighting mood as he addressed the rogue Druids at a gathering in the Great Hall.

'So you want to maintain a high level of child sacrifice, do you? Do you realise that the elders of the community are considering open warfare? They cannot take much more! In addition, the Romans are also concerned and have decided to take severe steps to eliminate the problem at source—they want all Druids eliminated—all of us. I have heard that 'kill them all' was the order of the Commander of Britain to our Dunedin legion commander. Some believe that the order came directly from the Emperor himself. I beg you to change you mind now!' said Nechtan in full fury.

'Why should we change our beliefs on child sacrifice? After all, we have had them for thousands of years and much has been achieved by this method of appeasing the gods. And who are the Romans to dictate to us what we should and shouldn't do?' retorted Ferchar, his eyes bulging with anger.

'We have a successful Druid College here in Dunedin with Druids from many countries participating in our organisation. It has an international reputation for teaching scholars in medicine and science. But we must be seen to change with modern times and the will of the people!' Nechtan said vociferously. 'We must either change or die!'

'Druids are descended from the god of the underworld, Father Dis, and our most important asset is the immortality of the soul. We will not die! *We will live forever!* Ferchar said contemptuously.

Unbeknown to all of the other Druids, Conall, the Chief Druid, had held a discussion with the Romans and come to an informal agreement that the Romans would execute those Druids responsible for condoning child sacrifice and leave the others in peace, if agreement with the rogue Druids could not be reached that day. If necessary, the day of execution had been set for the following day.

However, some of the rogue Druids had heard about the plot and hatched a counter-plot to lay a trap for the Romans who were to be their executioners. The Romans would have to walk through a narrow passageway to get to the entrance of the Druids' College. The rogue Druids' plan was to allow the Romans into the passageway, then block it off at each end, pour oil into the passageway from above and set it alight. The Romans would be cooked alive! Some of the Druids smiled to themselves at the prospect of this.

The Scottish Druid, Nechtan, who was viewed by many as the next Chief Druid, had heard about the plots. In discussion with a few close allies, he decided that if the counter-plot succeeded a situation would be created that would mean a meltdown of society in Dunedin, and potentially the Druid way of life across all of Europe. The Romans would send several legions to annihilate them. He could not allow this to happen. He would try to get both sides of the Druids to reach a compromise. But what kind of compromise? How do you find a compromise between sacrificing children and not sacrificing children?

Nechtan decided he had to play dirty. He asked his friends if they knew of any facts about the Druids who were in favour of child sacrifice that he could use against them. One of his friends informed him that the leader of the rogue Druids, Ferchar, had a mistress four years previously. She had a three-year-old child that was definitely Ferchar's. This is the ammunition I need, thought Nechtan.

That day he confronted Ferchar in a room in the College. 'I am going to recommend that your child is on the list of children to be chosen for the next sacrificial offering to the Gods.'

'*Oh, no, please, no!*' Ferchar retorted.

'Yes,' Nechtan replied coldly.

'Why?'

'Why should he be any different from the other children?'

'Because he's mine.'

'That's not a reason!' And with that, Nechtan walked out of the room.

Later that day Nechtan overheard Ferchar plotting with a few of the other rogue Druids to destroy Nechtan's reputation and force him to leave the college.

'I am going to make sure that Nechtan wishes that he was never born,' said Ferchar to the other Druids.

'How are you going to do that?' one asked.

'Just wait and see, but it will not be pleasant.'

Nechtan thought—I have failed.

*   *   *   *

'Columba, your story of Druidism is very intriguing; it sounds like we have many of their concepts and practices as part of our Celtic Church already. Is that correct?' asked Brendan, his eyes screwed questioningly.

'Well yes, that's right, but it's by coincidence only, as our Celtic Church is founded on ancient eastern teachings that were born of traditions much different from that of the Druids. Druids are not only priests; they are also judges, astronomers, physicians, and the historians of their tribes.'

'But Columba, we do that. Are we Druids also?' asked Brendan, with a puzzled face. He was young and still had a lot to learn and hoped to learn much from Columba.

'No, it doesn't. The Druids have many customs and practices that differ from ours. They practice the art of memory and have developed a verbal tradition for recording their rituals and secrets, and are obsessed with their genealogies. Their decisions are absolute, and those who disobey them are placed under a terrible excommunication. They believe that the soul does not perish, but after death passes from one body to another. They think that this is the best incentive to promote bravery, because it teaches men to disregard the terrors of death,' said Columba.

Some of the monks were again taken aback. They were beginning to realise that they really did not know Columba very well, and were unsure how to react to such radical ideas. They looked at each other in astonishment and bewilderment. What lay ahead of them?

*   *   *   *

Columba was silent. His mind was in Dunedin again, when it was a flourishing centre of trade with international traders from the Baltic and Europe coming into the port of Leith nearly every day. They brought furs, wood, fish, and spices from the east, wine and many other commodities that were popular with the people of southern Alba.

Dunedin was also a unique centre of education. The traders knew this and spread the word throughout their trading area. This was why so many countries sent their young men to be taught by the Druids. When they came they found a truly international city with people from all over the civilised world. The Druids were the magnets to whom everyone was attracted.

Dunedin was buzzing with new people who had come from a far off country, Spain. They were looking for somewhere to sleep. One of them was a man called Josephes. He walked up the hill three miles to the College and asked for advice on whom he should see to request admission. One of the Druids took him to see Nechtan, as one of Nechtan's roles was to check newcomers' suitability for entrance to the College.

'Josephes, I'm pleased to meet you and understand you wish to join our College,' said Nechtan.

'Yes, I do. I've heard so much about it and I'm keen to learn more about medicine and astronomy,' Josephes replied, his face beaming with eagerness.

Nechtan started to ask Josephes a list of standard questions that he asked everyone who wanted to join. He asked about his background, his family, his knowledge, his occupation, and his motivation to join the College. Josephes' reply intrigued Nechtan and he began to realise that this was no ordinary man; his answers were extremely thought provoking and covered many different aspects, some that Nechtan had not even considered. He was eloquent and had an air of tranquillity about him that made Nechtan listen to him very intently. Above all he spoke in an interesting and friendly manner; it was not possible to dislike this man. Nechtan felt an immediate affinity to him; this was a man he would like to have as a friend.

At the end of the conversation, which took three hours, Nechtan said that he wished to consult his superior, and excused himself to request his superior to admit Josephes to the College. Usually, there were two full days of examination, but on this occasion Nechtan did not think that was necessary and his superior concurred. Josephes was delighted when Nechtan told him he had been accepted.

'Can I sleep in the College?' said Josephes smiling and excited.

'Yes, of course.'

Josephes settled into the College routine within a few days. Nechtan had decided to take him under his wing and give him special tuition that he reserved for the best students. During a one-to-one session they talked about their religions and the similarities and differences between them. They soon noticed that there were many similarities and not too many differences. Nechtan then started to ask Josephes some searching questions about his family background, to which Josephes admitted that his father had been Jesus Christ.

The words hit silence.

After a few seconds Nechtan spoke. 'I have heard of this man, he was venerated by tens of thousands throughout the Mediterranean world. It is even believed that he was the founder of the new religion called Christianity,' said Nechtan, amazed by what he had just heard.

'No, I must correct your misinformation about Christianity. It was a man named Saul, who changed his name to Paul who started preaching a different version of Christianity, which should have been called Paulianity. Paul had never even met my father, so how could he possibly know what was in his mind? He corrupted my father's teachings and now it is starting to take hold in some Mediterranean countries. Like my father, I am an Essene. The true Christianity is, in fact, a strict version of Enochian Judaism,' said Josephes.

Josephes then explained that he and his uncle James, Jesus' brother, had come to Britain to preach the true version of Christ's teachings. James and his sons were in England and Josephes had come to Scotland. Josephes' other brothers and sisters were travelling throughout Europe doing the same.

Nechtan stared in stunned silence.

Josephes then explained, 'My father went to Rome seventeen years ago. I settled in Gaul with my mother, Mary Magdalene. Two years later, James, having been hounded out of Jerusalem joined us. The Romans had subjected his friends to brutal harassment, and the Sanhedrin Council had charged James with illegal teaching. He was consequently sentenced to a public stoning and excommunicated, to be declared spiritually dead by the Jewish elders.'

'Then why in your God's name have you come to this Druid's College?' Nechtan exclaimed in an astonished tone.

'You Druids are good men. You have much knowledge that is beneficial to mankind. This knowledge needs to be spread even further than you are currently achieving, and faster. You use memory techniques to gain a basic level of knowledge, however, this takes an individual 20 years to accumulate. This is too slow and you leave no written records,' Josephes said. 'What the world needs now is your scientific and medical knowledge and my religion.'

'It is intriguing that the Druids and the leading Essenes of the Qumran Community both refer to themselves as the Sons of Light. The light we must bring is our mission of not only promoting the principles of justice, using scientific knowledge and medicine for the good of the people, and protecting the people, but most importantly preaching the gospel of Jehovah.'

Nechtan's mind was now swirling with the possible implications of what Josephes was saying. Was he dreaming? Where would this lead?

*   *   *   *

Nechtan had recently taken a secret lover, a young woman called Wylfa with deep brown eyes and long, light brown hair, flowing down to reach her delicate hips. Her beauty was mesmerising. She was of Irish stock, her parents had died when she was young, and had left Ireland to escape the wrath of her miserly uncle who had looked after her, but had wanted to sell her to foreign traders. She ran away and had ended up in Dunedin. Nechtan had known her for some time, but did not know that she had a darker side. She was a prostitute, who earned her living by selling herself to the highest bidder, and there were many who were prepared to pay dearly to spend a night with her. So far, she had managed to keep this hidden from Nechtan.

Shortly after Josephes appeared on the scene, Nechtan told her about him and his revolutionary ideas. With her scheming and devious mind she quickly realised that this was a business opportunity that could not be missed. She was friendly with some of the Romans in the nearby camp. Friendly is an understatement; she had a full-blown trading business with them. She was a brothel madam, and had a row of twelve houses that served not only the male population of Dunedin but also the Roman soldiers who often came to be "serviced". Nechtan would have been humiliated, disgusted and sad if he had found out about this situation.

A few days later, a Roman Centurion, Pietro, visited her house.

'Is your mistress in?' he asked the young girl. 'I wish her to be my consort.'

'Yes, she's in. And, of course, she'll be delighted to see you,' was the courteous response.

Pietro was a coarse man, but strong, with scars on his face and arms and a deep baritone rasping voice. Wylfa preferred nubile young men who were more flexible in their attitude to sex and their physical ability in bed, but Pietro presented her with the business opportunity. After she had serviced him, they were lying and talking. At first it was idle chitchat, then Wylfa changed the subject to Nechtan and Josephes. She weighed her words carefully like the true professional she was. Pietro listened intently, saying nothing. He had heard of Jesus Christ and knew that the Roman authorities wanted to capture him and all his family and friends. They were the Desposyni, the dispossessed. He could not believe his luck, this could be another promotion and a better lifestyle coming his way.

In the next room, another woman was servicing a local community leader, Gabran. He could hear some of the discussion between Wylfa and Pietro and asked his woman to keep quiet so that he could hear the conversation better. Gabran was a friend of Nechtan. They shared many common views and often talked about subjects that they were both interested in. Gabran would now have to inform Nechtan about Wylfa's secret life, which he knew would greatly upset him. But as she had betrayed both Nechtan and Josephes to the Romans, he would be doubly upset. Nechtan would be furious! *What a bitch,* thought Gabran.

Pietro decided not to report the story to his Legion Commander, but to plan the necessary action and take total control of the situation himself. He would tell his Commander once he had successfully carried out his plan.

Pietro did not, however, count on the ingenuity of Nechtan for spotting a conspiracy; he had seen many before and knew how to operate, and win. The Scottish Druid was a master schemer and tactician; he had many friends in the community and his many spies would willingly give him information that would benefit him. In return he would secretly keep their children off the sacrifice list.

✳   ✳   ✳   ✳

Nechtan was silent when Gabran told him the story of Wylfa and the Roman. His silence soon turned to rage. He threw clay goblets and wooden chairs everywhere, and they smashed into pieces. Gabran let the rage expend itself for a few minutes then spoke quietly to Nechtan.

'You must flee to protect yourself or the Romans will kill you and Josephes.'

'Not if I persuade them it would be better to kill the Druids who condone child sacrifice. I need to rid the world of Ferchar and all his cronies. They are a menace to all mankind!' replied Nechtan, his blood at boiling point.

That night, Nechtan sent a message to Pietro through one of his many spies, and he agreed to meet Nechtan.

'Why do you want to have your fellow Druids killed?' asked Pietro, inquisitively.

'Two reasons—one, they are evil men who sacrifice children, which I now abhor and I know that you Romans also abhor. And two, I wish to save the life of Josephes—he is a good man and should not die. You could explain to your superiors that he escaped,' said Nechtan, with a pleading look on his face.

Pietro knew that his superiors did not know about Josephes so that would not be a problem.

'This will cost you dearly,' said Pietro, seeing his promotion and improved lifestyle vanishing into thin air.

'There is some gold that I have access to. I will give you what I can,' replied Nechtan gratefully.

'Then we have a deal.'

The next evening Nechtan arranged a meeting with the entire group of rogue Druids on the pretext that he wished to discuss it with them again. As soon as they were gathered, Pietro and his soldiers rushed into the room and massacred all the rogue Druids. The Roman swords were covered in blood, the floor was a blanket of mutilated bodies and blood ran through cracks in the floor. A few Druids were still moaning, but they were swiftly dispatched by the soldiers. The silence was only broken by the soldiers cleaning their swords.

*   *   *   *

Columba concluded his story to the monks.

'Agricola advanced into Scotland and drove the Druids and their followers before him to a sacred site called Mons Grampius. During the battle 30,000 Britons were killed and the last Scottish Druid stronghold was destroyed. However, genocide is rarely 100 per cent successful, and there were some survivors. Nechtan, Josephes and a few others went to Ireland to continue with their mission. It continues to this day,' said Columba looking at the amazed monks.

Columba then explained to the monks that Nechtan was an ancestor of his, but he was sure they would not believe that, in fact, *he was a reincarnation of Nechtan.*

WELL, YOU DID SAY GHOST WRITER

By William Armstrong

I sleep nude. It's no big deal. At least it wasn't until that French fireman crashed through my bedroom window in Nice and I had just time to grab a towel before he carried me down the ladder. Even then it wouldn't have been more than a one edition wonder if the towel hadn't caught on one of the rungs. A run of the mill rescue turned into a press feeding frenzy. There were full frontal shots, rear and I mean rear shots; in fact, shots from all angles.

Jim Hendrickson, my agent, was ecstatic. 'Babe,' he said almost reverently, 'that shot of your legs was real class. And the cleavage! That was something else.'

On the other hand, Aunt Kit, my Scottish godmother, was appalled. 'Look at you!' she shouted furiously, waving a copy of one of the more sensational dailies. 'Tits draped over his shoulder and his cheek against your bum!'

Aunt Kit, I thought inconsequentially, you're slipping. At one time you wouldn't have stopped at "bum".

'But it was an accident,' I protested. 'The towel caught on the ladder. There was nothing I could do.'

'I don't believe you,' my godmother said frostily. 'I bet that disgusting little agent is at the bottom of it. What you see in him I don't know.' And with that she flounced out.

Only that he's one of the best in the business, I thought to myself. Jimmy didn't believe my protestations either, but his attitude was one of admiration at being upstaged by a client.

Not that he was averse to grasping the opportunity presented. Oh no. 'This is your big chance, doll.' He always called me either "doll" or "babe". That was another thing Aunt Kit detested about him. It didn't bother me. But then, I was an up and coming starlet, climbing the ladder of success and, in the process, using every artifice to assist me.

Now, I'm a mega star of stage and screen. Mention the name, "Virginia Walters", dahling, and the red carpet is rolled out immediately. Throw in the odd "Jinny and I go way back", and they'll crawl on broken glass for you.

However, I'm getting away from the fire, the incident that kick-started my career. Jimmy might not have thought of it, but he wasn't about to look a gift horse in the mouth. 'Babe,' he said soberly, 'this is your big break. This is your escalator to success. We're on the way up. You were just a bit player in that lousy flick they were shooting in Nice. Since then my phone hasn't stopped ringing. I've got photo shoots stacked up for months, two film offers; supporting roles, but good, and a coupla TV interviews. I tell you, doll, we're off and running.'

'Great,' I said. 'So what's next?' I looked at my agent and friend. The stocky red-faced figure with the shock of black hair brushed back, the pseudo American drawl—Jimmy had spent several years in the States—plus the eternal cigar he chomped on all through a conversation.

'I've got it all figured out. You're going to bring out your biography.'

'Jimmy,' I protested, 'I'm only twenty-one. How am I going to fill a book on my life so far?'

But Jimmy had the bit between his teeth now. 'Nothing to it, doll. That young footballer, Ray Cooney, he's only nineteen and he's got a contract worth three million for three books. You'll need a ghostwriter though. Guess we'll have to advertise.' So we did. Discreetly of course. We had one or two inquiries from "wanabees", but Jimmy was playing it close to his chest and he rejected them. 'This has got to be done tastefully,' he kept saying. 'Bet if we asked Medusa,' his private name for Aunt Kit, 'she'd agree with me.'

And, just for once, she did. 'Dahling,' she drawled, in those cut glass, upper crust tones; 'I hate to say it, but that obnoxious little creature is right. Now is the time to bring out your biography. Only,' she added darkly, looking down that long patrician nose. 'Be selective.'

And that, I thought with a slight shiver, is the rub. There are areas in my life which only Aunt Kit and a few of her trusted staff are privy to.

However, I digress. Our search for a ghostwriter had fizzled out like a damp squib. Then one night I woke suddenly with a feeling I wasn't alone. As my eyes adjusted to the gloom I made out a shadowy figure perched on the end of the bed. Fear sharpened my reflexes and I shot up and switched on my reading light. Incidentally, don't believe those scenes in films where the heroine sits up clutching the bedclothes to her bosom. When panic sets in modesty takes a back seat.

Anyway, there I was, being looked over by a phantom. Not bad either, I thought critically, even if somewhat ethereal. 'What ... who are you?' I demanded; 'and what are you doing in my room?'

The ghost leaned forward and leered at me. 'I must say you're an attractive little thing. I, my dear, am Lance McKenna, at your service. One time ghost writer to celebrities. I'm here in answer to your advert.'

'But ... you're a ghost,' I protested.

'How very perceptive of you, young lady. But you did say ghost writer.'

'True,' I admitted, eyeing the apparition. He really was quite good looking. About six feet two, with broad shoulders, a shock of grey hair and a neat nicely trimmed moustache. He was dressed in a tweed hacking jacket, check shirt, cavalry twill trousers and tan brogues. Eyes a shade too close together, but you can't have everything, even in a ghost. 'Still, I didn't foresee ...'

'That a spirit would apply? Well actually this is part of Saint Peter's new rehab programme.' He produced a pack of cards and riffled them absently. 'I was a writer in my day. A very successful one I might add. The cards and the ladies were my downfall. It was mainly the ladies. A jealous husband caught me *in flagrante delicto* with his wife and killed me.'

'How awful,' I gasped.

McKenna shrugged. 'Fortunes of war, my dear. But,' he looked at me critically and I was suddenly conscious that I was naked from the waist up; 'I wish you and I had been around at the same time.'

'However, to business. I have to help solve three problems to expiate part of my sins. Yours is the first and, according to our research department, the easiest.'

'So,' I said, 'and the others?'

McKenna riffled the cards again. 'I'm not allowed to say, but I will be moving up the social scale. Now, about your biography. I'll deliver two chapters each week to you. Pass them to your publisher.'

'That's all?'

'Oh yes. It won't be difficult. Of course I'll have to leave out that episode in your teens. The one where Lady McGregor straightened you out.'

Cold shivers ran up and down my spine. Only Aunt Kit, aka Lady McGregor and her few trusted retainers knew that story. Early in my teens I'd experimented with drink and drugs, and only the timely intervention of my godmother had prevented me becoming a basket case. Whisked off to her mansion in Wester Ross I'd been subjected to a regime of iron discipline and cold turkey treatment which, though brutal, had worked.

'How did you …?'

'It's all in your file, my dear. But don't worry. I'll bury it neatly.' And he did. The chapters, which arrived every week, were well written and interesting.

I'd told Jimmy I was writing the book myself and he was really impressed. 'Jeez, doll, I never thought you could do it.' He flipped through the latest chapters. 'You've really got talent.'

Aunt Kit also got on the bandwagon. 'So,' she said grudgingly, 'you're not just another blonde bimbo after all.'

It was round about then that I met Matt Jackson, the latest British heart throb and the country's answer to an industry dominated by male Hollywood film stars. We fell for each other immediately. Matt was, and still is, a man who puts women on a pedestal and I'll ignore that crack about being able to see their legs better. The trouble was I had feet of clay and I was afraid to tell him. This was the real thing at last.

At the same time my ghost writer completed the biography and it was published to critical acclaim. "Brains and beauty can go together after all" was the caption I liked best, but the general consensus was very favourable and sales rocketed. I complimented McKenna at our next meeting and he preened himself, still shuffling his infernal cards.

'Anyway,' I said, 'It's been a pleasure doing business with you. I imagine you'll be moving on to your next assignment?'

He looked at me speculatively. 'Yes, though I'd like to continue our weekly chats. The trouble is I've developed certain feelings towards you.'

Damn! I thought. I should have worn a nightie. The last thing I need is an amorous ghost leering down at me when Matt and I are making love. 'That won't be possible I'm afraid,' I said stiffly. 'You're probably aware that I'm getting married and naturally my husband and I would like some privacy.'

The atmosphere chilled suddenly and McKenna fixed me with a piercing stare. 'You obviously haven't thought this through. It wouldn't be difficult for me to inform your prospective husband of your brush with the drug scene.'

An icy hand seemed to grip my heart. 'You wouldn't …' I said slowly.

McKenna leered. 'Try me. Now, I'll give you a fortnight to think it over. Then I'll be back for my answer.' There was a puff of smoke and he was gone.

I cursed myself for my carelessness. But then, I thought, who'd have dreamt of an amorous ghost. Jinny, my girl, you're in a real jam. It's a pity you can't fight fire with fire ... wait a minute, maybe you can.

It was well into the second week when I woke to the now familiar, but still unsettling feeling, that somebody, or something, was in the room with me. Switching on the bedside lamp I stared at the tall figure standing by the window.

'Good evening.' There was a hint of authority in the voice, though the tone was friendly. 'Cardinal Jacques Lemaine, at your service. I'm here in answer to your advertisement. You require the services of a ...' he hesitated fractionally ... 'ghost buster. Personally I deplore the use of such modernistic jargon, but senior management say we must move with the times. However, before I go any further, would you mind covering your ... ahem ... upper body. I'm beginning to understand why young priests have such difficulty keeping their celibacy vows.'

'Oh ... sorry,' I said, hurriedly wrapping myself in the duvet. I eyed the cardinal covertly. He was an imposing figure in his flowing red robes. Strong patrician features and a mane of silvery hair. Around six feet tall, with the build of someone who, though getting on in years, still kept himself in trim. Not a person to trifle with.

'Well now.' He seemed more at ease since I'd covered my breasts. 'How can I be of assistance?'

Briefly, I outlined my problem.

Lemaine's face darkened at the mention of McKenna. 'I thought as much. He's one of Saint Peter's protégés in this new rehabilitation programme of his. Personally I have considerable reservations about the whole thing. However, I am empowered to act in such matters. When is McKenna due to return?'

'In three nights' time,' I replied.

'Very well, I'll deal with him then.'

The two spirits seemed poles apart and I viewed the impending confrontation with considerable unease. You've sown the wind, I thought soberly and you might just reap the whirlwind. Hopefully not.

As it turned out, a long hard day on the set of my latest film ensured that I was sound asleep when Lemaine and McKenna appeared. I woke to the sound of a furious, if low voiced argument. Resisting my impulse to intervene, I lay still and, feigning sleep, listened to the exchanges.

'You've broken the rules,' Lemaine said icily. Ghosts are not supposed to become involved sexually with the living and well you know it. I could have you taken off the programme.'

'Saint Peter wouldn't like that,' Lance McKenna protested sulkily. 'Anyway, I knew it wasn't possible. All I did was look. After all,' and his voice took on a challenging, more confident tone, 'she is beautiful. Can you honestly say she doesn't have any effect on you?'

'Ahem' … there was a long pause, then … 'no.' For the first time in the exchange the cardinal sounded unsure. 'But,' his voice gathered pace again, 'there is no future in this for you. Your brief is to assist the living and earn remission of your sins. Personal pleasure is precluded.'

'That's unfair,' McKenna protested weakly.

'Tell that to Saint Peter,' Lemaine retorted, somewhat smugly I thought. 'He set the rules for your rehabilitation.'

There was a long silence after this. From beneath lowered lids I could see McKenna wasn't happy. 'Alright,' he conceded reluctantly. 'I don't suppose I've much choice.' 'None, I'm afraid,' Lemaine said briskly. 'Now, let's look at your other tasks.'

The discussion moved on to McKenna's remaining two assignments and there was a good deal of low voiced conversation regarding them. Some of the snatches I picked up intrigued me.

'I thought that spin doctor chap would handle their memoirs?'

Mckenna shook his head and lowered his voice even more. '… wife isn't too keen on him now. Not since he brought out …'

'Ahem … 1 see. What about your final assignment?'

Lance McKenna shot a glance in my direction and, leaning forward, whispered something that caused Lemaine's voice to rise sharply.

'You're quite sure?' he queried.

McKenna nodded.

The cardinal frowned. 'Exercise extreme caution,' he said sternly. 'You're talking about the succession …' he broke off as McKenna shook his head warningly, then lowering his voice, went on softly, 'I didn't think she would publish her memoirs. However, as regards the matter in hand. Do I have your word that you will not attempt to see this young lady again?'

McKenna nodded. 'Yes,' he said, somewhat grudgingly.

'Very well, I suggest you leave now.'

And, in a puff of smoke, McKenna did so.

Time to make my entrance I thought, sitting up and remembering to keep the duvet round me. 'What ... what happened?'

Lemaine looked at me severely. 'You will have no further trouble from McKenna. As for yourself, young lady, I suggest you wear the appropriate night attire in future. It might save complications. Now, I'll bid you goodbye.'

The inevitable puff of smoke, white this time and he too was gone.

Two months later, Matt and I tied the knot and, to everyone's surprise, I took to married life like a duck to water. A year later the twins, Donald and Dougal arrived. Aunt Kit doted on them immediately, while Matt was over the moon. Among other things, he insisted on putting their names down for his old school. Personally I couldn't have cared less, but it pleased my husband and that was all that mattered.

Well, the years rolled on, as they do, but our marriage stood the test of time. By now the boys were in their second year at Mart's old school, while Aunt Kit and Jimmy had gone to the big theatre in the sky.

Then suddenly the blow fell. The boys were expelled. They'd been caught running a poker game. Subsequent investigations revealed that most of the teachers were in hock to them. Matt was appalled, while I, with a sinking feeling, remembered those long fingers riffling the cards.

'Right,' I said when I got the boys alone. 'How did it all begin?'

Neither would answer.

'Alright, I'll tell you what I think happened. You met a poker-playing ghost and he taught you the game.'

They gaped at me. 'How ... how did you know that?' Donald stuttered.

'Never mind,' I said sharply. 'What else did he teach you?'

Two bewildered faces stared back at me. 'Nothing.' That was Dougal. 'He said it was payment for an old debt.'

I mulled that over and came to a decision. 'Right, off you go. I'll try and square things with your father.'

Watching them shuffle out I heaved a sigh of relief. After all, I thought, remembering how McKenna had died, it could have been much worse.

For Whom the Bell Tolls

By Maureen Brister

It was just before 9 o'clock in the morning on the first Monday in July when fifteen-year-old Gillian Evans walked slowly into her local newsagent's shop. Her Mum had managed to secure her a six-week summer job here and though she had had a short meeting with Mr and Mrs MacDonald who ran the shop Gillian really had no idea what would be expected of her. A tall, skinny, very shy girl, who wanted to earn some extra pocket money, she knew this would not be easy for her, dealing with customers face to face. She was easily embarrassed and blushed at the slightest thing. Her parents, however, thought this job would be good for her and bring her out of herself, whatever that might mean. Anyway, deep breaths, here she was, reporting for duty as agreed.

Mrs MacDonald saw her from the back of the shop and hurried forward. 'Morning Gillian. Nice to see you're on time on your first morning. Hope that's a sign of things to come. Now, let's get you settled. Did you bring an apron? Oh good, you can get really dirty from handling the newspapers, and these wooden floors need a good scrub at least once a week. Did Mum not mention that? Oh don't worry, it'll be just fine. Now, you'll know Jessie of course. In with the bricks is our Jessie. Knows everything there is to know about this shop and its customers, so she's the very person to show you the ropes.'

Mrs MacDonald finally paused for breath. Gillian and Jessie eyed each other behind the counter. Of course she knew Jessie by sight, a plump homely girl, a good ten years older than Gillian, still single, living with her parents. The newspaper shop had been her one and only job since leaving school as far as Gillian knew. Not a lot of ambition there then thought Gillian as she blushed averting her eyes at her thoughts. Damn, she knew this was not going to be easy.

'Hello Jessie,' she said tentatively. Jessie nodded back. 'Aye Gillian. I'll just show her the till will I Mrs MacDonald and generally where everything is behind the counter then I'll have my break and leave her to it. She'll cope. Top of her class at the High School so I'm told, this should all be a dawdle.' Jessie looked straight at Gillian and gave a small smile as she saw her face fall and go pale at the thought of being left alone behind the counter.

In fact, Gillian's stomach was churning. She was glad when she heard Mrs MacDonald say, 'Now don't you worry Gillian, we'll just be in the back room, we'll be right out if there's a problem. You aren't really on your own, not yet anyway.'

By lunchtime her head was swimming. She was sure she would never get the hang of the till. She thought that tills these days were meant to show the amount of change you had to give back to the customer, but Mr and Mrs MacDonald were still in the dark ages it seemed. At least their till did nothing like that, you still had to calculate things out. Unfortunately! The two customers she had short-changed had found out the hard way that maths was not her strong point! She would definitely need to keep her wits about her. As for that shop bell, it was giving her *the* biggest headache. Everyone announced their arrival, loudly. For all the times she herself had been a customer in the shop she had never really noticed the bell, but now she definitely did.

The reason the MacDonald's took on extra help during the holidays was the number of people who still liked to come to this seaside town on the east coast of Scotland, either for their annual fortnight's holiday or just for days out over the summer months. There was a local fair on the Links for the whole of the school holidays. The paper shop was well situated just opposite the path to the beach and with its pails and spades and beach balls hanging colourfully outside business was brisk, even on days when the sun did not shine.

By the end of her first week Gillian and Jessie were on reasonable terms. Jessie was not a great chatterbox, she liked to keep herself to herself, but she was friendly enough. Gillian was quiet at the best of times, so things ticked along nicely. At least she had not made any other ghastly mistakes with the till but she knew she would never be comfortable with it for the duration of her time there.

The shop was kept going, there was never really a quiet spell. Mr MacDonald popped in and out but left things mostly to his wife and her two assistants. He liked to see things set up at the start of the day and was always on hand before closing to "do the balance" as Jessie called it. That was when Gillian would sweat, she was sure there would be a major discrepancy one of these days and it would be her fault there was no doubt about that. She always breathed a sigh of relief when she saw Mr MacDonald's face break into a smile at the end of his counting.

The week before the annual Highland Games the sun shone from clear blue skies and the normally cool sea breeze dwindled to nothing. Joy of joys, the warm weather meant the shop door got propped open first thing in the morning and stayed that way throughout the day. No bell! Heaven, thought Gillian.

Two Boys' Brigade camps from Glasgow joined the other holidaymakers in the town. One lot were billeted at the local Parish Church Hall just up the street, the others were camping out on some farmland at the back of the town. That meant the paper shop was selling lots of postcards, comics and sweets to the younger members, cigarettes to the older boys and newspapers to their leaders. Jessie noticed that one of the younger leaders of the camp at the farm was never out of the shop, he seemed to be buying for the whole group and would always hang back till Gillian was serving.

'See that one there,' Jessie nodded over to Gillian one morning when they were both in the back shop, 'he definitely fancies you.' Gillian immediately went bright red as she looked out at the shop. She knew exactly who Jessie was referring to. 'Never mind your blushing, oh aye, I've noticed him looking through the front window waiting till you're behind the counter before he comes in. Made a mistake this morning though, got Mrs Mac instead.' Jessie eyed Gillian from under her eyelashes, noticing the effect her words had had on the younger girl. 'You've not got a boyfriend have you? Bet you anything he asks you out before the end of the week. Not that I'd have anything to do with him if I were you, you know what these folk from Glasgow are like and he's only here for a week.'

Gillian smiled softly to herself as she collected her boxes of sweets from the stock room. She had actually noticed this young man. He wasn't bad looking and she thought maybe Jessie was right, maybe he did fancy her!

On the Tuesday morning in he came while Jessie was on her break. Gillian could see from the corner of her eye that she was watching intently from the back of the shop, teacup in hand, poised half way to her mouth. 'Daily Mirror please,' he said and handed over the money. 'Just right, thanks,' said Gillian putting the money in the till and looking at him under her eyelashes. 'Ever get any time off from here?' he said. 'Tomorrow afternoon is my half day,' Gillian heard herself say. Her heart was thumping and she could feel the usual flush come to her cheeks. That would surely put him off. But no. 'OK, what do you usually do on a Wednesday afternoon then.' 'Go swimming. I have a season ticket for the pool.' 'Mind if I come along? Name's Frank by the way,' he said. 'I'm Gillian,' she stuttered. 'No that would be OK. I'll see you here about two o'clock tomorrow?' 'See you,' said Frank and off he went.

Jessie was out in a flash. 'What was all that about? Ask you out did he? Told you he would. Hope you told him where to go. Cheeky thing.'

'Well actually I didn't. He's coming to the pool with me tomorrow afternoon Jessie,' said Gillian.

'I'd watch him if I were you. What age do you think he is, looks older than you that's for sure. Cannae trust these Westcoasters,' Jessie muttered.

Gillian was beside herself with excitement for the rest of the day. She supposed this could be called a date, and if it was it would be her first. The question now was whether to tell her parents or not. She could just hear them asking all kinds of questions and probably at the end of it all saying she couldn't go. She wouldn't say a word, see how things went.

There was no sign of Frank next morning. Gillian ran home at lunchtime, bolted down her food and got her swimming things ready. 'What's the rush Gill? Got a hot date?' her Dad said, smiling broadly at her and winking at her Mum. 'Ha-ha, very funny Dad,' said Gillian deliberately slowing herself down.

She was just about to set out for the pool when her Aunt and cousin arrived. 'Oh goody,' said Karen, 'you're off to the pool, I brought my swimming things just in case.' Gillian who would normally have been glad to have Karen along for company as they were almost the same age and got on well together, couldn't believe it. Today of all days. She had no choice but to take her along otherwise she would have to do some explaining to her mother and they would never get anywhere, certainly not by two o'clock!

Gillian briefed Karen on the way to the newsagent shop. Karen was wide eyed at the story. 'What did Aunty Jen and Uncle Dave say? Are they OK about it?'

'Well actually.... I haven't told them. You know what they're like Karen. He'll probably not turn up anyway.'

But when they rounded the corner on to the High Street, there was Frank as he said he would be, rolled up towel under his arm. Gillian swallowed. 'What is it?' Karen whispered looking at her cousin. 'Is that him Gill? What age did you say he is? He looks so much older than you, and ... oh Gill, he's smoking! Are you sure that's him?'

'Shut up Karen, of course it's him.' But Karen had echoed her thoughts exactly. Dressed in a short-sleeved white shirt and long trousers, Frank looked years older than her, especially with that cigarette in his mouth. She hated to say it, but Jessie might have been right! Please please don't let him offer her a cigarette. What had she done? Maybe they could just turn around and run home, but no, he'd seen them now. Suddenly Gillian felt just like the schoolgirl she was. She still had her ankle socks on for God's sake. With all the kafuffle in getting out of the house she had forgotten to take them off at the front door and stuff them inside her towel. Did he even know she was still at school? He had probably never seen her out from behind the counter.

'Hi Frank. Sorry we're a bit late. This is my cousin Karen. She sometimes comes with me to the pool on a Wednesday afternoon. Hope you don't mind me bringing her too.' Gillian could see by Frank's face that he did mind. Oh boy, did he mind.

Off they set, through the path to the beach and on to the swimming pool. Not a lot of conversation on the way. Gillian's mind was all over the place. She didn't want to go through with this now. In fact she wanted to go home to the safety of the kitchen where she knew her Mum and her Aunty would be having a fine chat over a cup of tea. This was awful. She had no idea what Frank wanted or expected, but there was no way she was getting changed into her swimming costume and letting him see her in it. There was one way out. They got to the entrance to the pool. Gillian flashed her pass at the booth and went through the revolving gate as Karen and Frank paid. 'See you in five minutes' said Frank. Gillian nodded as they headed into their respective changing rooms. They were no sooner inside and Karen was headed for a cubicle when Gillian hissed 'No Karen, come on, quick, we're going home. Hurry, before Frank comes out. Hurry,' she yelled at her cousin. Gillian and Karen ran out of the pool, up the path and home arriving red faced, completely out of breath and with Gillian by that time in floods of tears. Her Mum and her Aunt were just about to have their afternoon cuppa when the two girls burst in on them. 'What on earth's the matter, what happened?' said her Mum. Neither girl could speak. Eventually Gillian was able to tell the story. Her Mum looked horrified, but her Aunt just laughed. 'No harm done Jenny,' she said to her sister as they sat the girls down with their tea and biscuits and wandered through to the kitchen. 'Gillian was out of her depth, but luckily realised it and came home. She'll need to face this Frank person tomorrow probably, in the paper shop, but the experience will have taught her a lesson. She won't be doing that again in a hurry, and neither will Karen. She was pretty upset too. They have to learn these things and some choose to do it the hard way.'

Next morning Gillian dilly-dallied over her breakfast almost making herself sick at the thought of the morning ahead. Frank was sure to come to the shop and want an explanation for her disappearance the previous afternoon. She didn't have one, except that she had been dead scared when she saw him waiting for her, all of a sudden her bravado had vanished and she wanted the earth to open up and swallow her!

After running all the way down to the shop on the first dreich drizzly morning in ages Gillian arrived ten minutes late and out of breath! Ding, ding! That blasted bell. No chance of sneaking into *this* shop. She started to prop open the door behind her but Mrs Macdonald shouted from the back. 'Not today Gillian, leave the door shut, horrible morning out there.'

What a start! Jessie eyed her suspiciously but was happy to see her and hand over so that she could get a break. Ten o'clock came and still no sign of Frank. In fact no sign of any of the boys from his camp. Funny, thought Gillian. Just before lunchtime the leader of the other camp came into the shop for some cigarettes. "Did you hear what happened up at the farm last night?' he said. Jessie shook her head, looking sideways at Gillian who was blushing furiously at her side, her heart beating so fast and so loud she thought everyone would hear it. 'Apparently some of the cows broke out of the adjacent field and rampaged through the tents and equipment. The group had to pack up this morning and head back to Glasgow from what I hear. No choice. Luckily no one was hurt, but I wish I'd been there to see it. Must have been something eh. They'll not choose that farm to camp on again I bet.'

Amid the laughter between the other customers and the staff Gillian heard Jessie's voice. 'So did they all go then?' she asked. Gillian held her breath, refusing to look in Jessie's direction but with every bone in her body tensed waiting for the reply. 'What, oh no, now that you mention it I did hear that one of them stayed behind. Some unfinished business or something. Don't know what was meant by that though.' Just at that the doorbell gave an extra loud ring.

BEN'S FRIEND

By George Sinclair

We arrived in darkness. From the outside, the large mid-nineteenth century house had seen better days, the walls were crumbling and it looked spooky. I stared at it for a few seconds and a single word entered my mind—ghosts! Did I really believe in them? I wondered if there were any in the house. The front door squeaked open as we stepped inside; my mind was racing to guess what we would find. The floorboards creaked and I could hear strange noises coming from a room at the end of the corridor. I wondered what it could possibly be, surely not real ghosts, I thought? We sneaked along the corridor and gingerly opened the door.

To our relief, it was other members of the club who were busy organising their climbing gear for the next day. The quantity and variety of items displayed on the table and floor was staggering. There were caribiners, pitons of all shapes and sizes, chalk bags, ropes and ice axes with curved heads that could kill with a single stroke.

After handshaking and joke telling my friend and I sorted our gear and picked our bedrooms. In most cases it was three to a room, and we soon settled into our beds. As I was getting into mine I noticed a musty smell—the room had dampness in it and the thought of ghosts lingered in my mind.

Next morning the smell of cooking filled the air and my mouth started to water. We all needed a good thick lining on our stomachs for the tortuous day's climbing and I always enjoyed a tasty breakfast, so I grilled sausages and bacon.

Dave was standing beside me frying eggs and black pudding in what looked like a pint of fat.

'That looks good Dave, but don't you worry about the effect the fat will have?' thinking of all the fat clogging Dave's arteries.

'Well, I knew an old lady who lived till she was 108, and I once asked her what she put her good health and fine old age down to. She told me that she had bread with lashings of dripping and plenty of salt every day. I always wonder if nutritionists would change their theories of eating if they knew her,' was Dave's response.

The large kitchen was filled with all types of mountain people. Essentially, there are three types. The ramblers who keep to low level walking, the mountaineers who challenge the high peaks, and the special breed called "tigers"—those who lived for, and sometimes died for, rock and ice climbing.

'Where do you fancy going today? Anywhere special in mind?' I asked Dave.

'Oh, I haven't decided yet. I guess we're spoilt for choice in this area. Where are you thinking of going?'

'I was considering climbing Ben Nevis. I haven't done it yet and would like to do a big one today, as the weather looks great.'

'I've climbed the Ben several times, but I could do him again,' Dave said affectionately, as though Ben Nevis was a personal friend that he knew well. 'He can be unpredictable and deceiving at times, so we'll need to be careful. This time I'd also like to try his mate, Carn Mor Dearg.'

'Sounds fine to me, let's give them a go.'

The decision was made. We took Dave's car to the base of Ben Nevis and started up the "tourist route", armed with crampons, ice axes and a rope. It was 9 a.m., the start of a day with daggers of sunshine thrown in all directions and not a breath of wind in the air.

'How do you rate this climb, Dave?'

'In strenuous terms, reasonably hard. It gets wearisome at the end when we come back down. Technically, it's easy, as the terrain is straight forward, except for the Carn Mor Dearg arête,' Dave said with a slightly anxious look in his eyes. Why was that I wondered?

The two mountains combine to form one of the most outstanding walks in Britain, with mountain scenery to die for, and some have! I had experience of climbing in the Rockies at 12,000 feet in winter on my own and at 11,000 feet in the Italian Alps with a friend, but on both trips suffered life-threatening incidents—being hit by a tornado in the Rockies and nearly falling into a crevasse in the Alps. So I have a simple, well-developed axiom that I remind myself of every time that I climb—my life is in my hands in the mountains. That thought always helped me to plan well. Nevertheless, a foreboding feeling about today's climb was lingering around me. Perhaps it was the usual nerves. I hoped so, and tried to shrug it off.

Two miles on, the path split into two, near a lochan.

'We could continue climbing the tourist route; it would take us to the top in a few hours. But we need to continue east and go into Corrie Leis on the east side of Ben Nevis to reach Carn Mor Dearg,' Dave said.

We soon approached Corrie Leis and gradually reached the snow level—the near end of the Corrie had a light covering of snow but it looked as though there was much more further in. A few climbers were finishing breakfast outside the mountaineering hut, enjoying the sunshine and looking at one of the faces of the Ben. As we got closer we noticed a mixture of friendly and serious faces amongst them.

'Where are you climbing today, guys?' I asked, with genuine interest.

'See the North-East Buttress over there … that's the one for us,' was the friendly response.

'It looks covered in ice, and may be tricky.'

'That's exactly why we're doing it. No pain, no gain!'

'Good luck and be careful,' I said, as we moved off towards the snow-covered flank of Carn Mor Dearg. When we were out of earshot I turned to Dave. 'These guys are up against it today. Do you think they'll make it?'

'There's a reasonable chance; they'll have to be careful. They've got the right gear and look fit, so let's hope they've enough experience.'

As we started to climb the western flank of Carn Mor Dearg, the purpose of the rope began to bother me. 'What's the rope for Dave?'

'It's a small precaution, as it might be difficult on the CMD arête.'

Great, I thought! I wish that I had known that earlier, I don't like surprises. Usually I read about the mountain and the area so that I know what I'm getting into.

We sank in the fresh snow to our knees as we climbed, lifting our legs clear and placing them higher up the slope as we took the next step forward, using our snow poles as aids to push us up. The steep climb was tiring and we had to take several short rests. Our hearts pounded and our lungs worked like blacksmith's bellows! I felt a trickle running down my back. Worryingly, there was frozen snow beneath the new snow—excellent avalanche conditions. Looking up, I noticed that there were two climbers a good distance above us, to our right. Then we heard it—a loud dull crack! That was the sound that all climbers feared! It meant only one thing—*an avalanche!* The other climbers were above the line where the avalanche had started and it was heading down straight towards us.

'*Move!*' screamed Dave. 'Get over there! Quickly!'

A primitive signal of self-preservation emerged from deep within me, propelling me forward. With only a few seconds to spare, we scrambled to our left pushing the snow as hard as possible with our quivering legs, no time for lifting them! Our snow poles pummelled the snow. We were moving fast and frantically, dazed and numb and robotic, not thinking about what was happening, not thinking about anything except survival! Seconds later the enormous slab avalanche thundered past, taking hundreds of tons of snow and ice with it. The windblast nearly knocked us off our feet, and then a cloud of ice particles whooshed past, stinging our faces as if we were being thrashed with nettles. I held my breath to prevent inhaling the ice particles and thus avoid severe pain in my lungs. Had we been caught in the deluge we would have been thrown down the mountain, tossed around like rag dolls, trapped in solidifying ice, suffocated alive, and finally … *a peaceful nothingness!* It was a close call! I breathed deeply a few times to relieve the tension. As if in a dream, we stood and looked at each other for a few seconds. Our faces had gone pale, like snowmen in a snow wilderness. I felt drained of energy, empty. Dave was paralysed by terror and shock and disbelief.

Dave's fast reactions had saved us. I owed him my life, and now looked at him through different eyes. 'Are you OK?' I asked quietly, trying to appear calm.

'Yes, that was closer than I'd have liked! What do you think, should we carry on?' Dave was severely shaken by the event and was having second thoughts about continuing. His voice carried no judgment or challenge.

I was also shaken, but nevertheless decided. 'It's too good a day to waste, so let's bite the bullet and keep going,' doubt lingering in my mind. Was it the right decision I thought?

We looked above us and saw that the other climbers were safe, so we pressed on up the slope. This time we moved towards our left, away from their fall line as they had probably caused the avalanche, so I thought of a few names to call them.

We finally reached the top and the views were stunning! I was awe-struck at the 2,000 feet cliffs of the Ben to the west and what appeared to be 15 feet snow cornices at the top of them. To the north was the inspiring landscape around Loch Lochy, to the east Aonoch Mor where people were skiing, and to the south the Mamores. This was mountain scenery made in Heaven, especially when covered in snow.

It was time for lunch, our sandwiches, crisps, chocolate and coffee were scoffed greedily to replace the calories we had already burnt off. We rested for a while, quietly enjoyed the vista and dozed for a few minutes in the brilliant sunshine.

The CMD arête was beckoning. 'Let's move on before we get cold,' Dave said, standing up.

We made our way along the top of the Carn Mor Dearg ridge, towards the arête. It was a "razor back" of repute. As we approached it, we stopped to put on our climbing harnesses, fit crampons and tie the rope to our climbing harnesses. Dave tied the knots as I viewed the arête with trepidation—it looked awesome. One slip and we would be in serious trouble. We started to walk with ice axes for extra protection. Dave was the front man, his disposition now intensified, his focus total, he inched forward taking one step at a time. Time seemed to slow down!

Suddenly, *Dave disappeared over the edge!* 'Shi ...,' he screamed. His right crampon had slipped on a narrow icy rock, making him topple over. I quickly shoved one of my ice axes deeply into the snow, but did not have enough time to wrap the rope around it. It became taut instantly. Dave's weight at the other end of the rope was trying to pull me over the edge. A violent rush of adrenalin tore through my veins. The survival instinct kicked in! My muscles strained to hold onto the ice axe with both hands. How long could I hold on? I tried to dig my boots into the snow but couldn't. Was this why I'd had that feeling of foreboding?

'Are you OK, Dave?' I shouted.

'Yes, I've a small foot hold, but I'm not sure how much longer I can hold on.' His words terrified me.

I struggled to get my second ice axe into the snow for better anchorage, but my body position would not allow it. We were goners, I thought!

'How far down is the drop?' I shouted to Dave.

'Not too far, a hundred feet! If there's a snowdrift at the bottom we may be lucky enough to get off with a few broken bones. Unless, you land on top of me that is!'

Oh Christ, what am I doing here, I thought? Why had I not listened to my gut? I could have been skiing safely on Aonoch Mor, and I wished I was there. I wasn't, I was here, starting to fall down a hundred foot cliff, to God knows what! Fear of death gripped my whole being. A vision of my life sped past my eyes in a few seconds. My hands were slowly slipping, slipping, slip ... *Does it end now?*

'Hang on!' a loud voice bellowed close by.

I will never forget these two words. The climbers that I had nearly sworn at had come back to our rescue. They both got hold of the rope, tied it around one of their ice axes that was buried in the snow and hauled Dave to safety.

'Are we glad to see you guys? We owe you,' I said, lying back, relief setting in.

'That's not a problem, so which pub are you going to tonight, you can pay us back there?' replied the tall one, named Jim.

'Our pleasure, I hope you're good drinkers!' said Dave smiling. I'd heard that Dave could drink most people under the table and hoped to see him in action tonight.

With the CMD arête gladly behind us, we looked up and saw the steep massive slope of the Ben. It was also covered in deep snow and so the bacon reserves started to kick in. Half way up the mist came down—the climber's nightmare! We kept going.

As we reached the top of Ben Nevis we saw that a few people were standing around the summit hut, talking, eating and drinking.

'I guess there's ten feet of snow on top of the Ben,' said Jim.

I was puzzled. 'How did you work that out?'

'Well, the snow level is adjacent to the base of the hut and the hut is 10 feet above ground level.'

'Your school was a good one then?' I said with a wide grin.

Jim smiled at me and laughed.

The mist was floating around creating a dream-like, ethereal environment. Dave looked at his watch; it was 6 p.m. He turned to me and said, 'as the mist is still down, we'll have to navigate off.'

'So how do we do that?' Anxiety quickly replaced bullishness at reaching the summit.

Dave explained the route. 'So you'll be the front man, for a change, and I'll steer you with the compass.'

'Thanks Dave, I always wanted to be a front man!' I said sarcastically.

'You need to be at least 20 feet in front and keep going at a steady pace.'

As visibility was down to 20 feet, I would at least see the edge of the snow cornices with 5 feet to spare. Fantastic! What if I don't see the edge till it was too late? The hair on the back of my head started to rise. My heart thumped. Sweat started to trickle down my neck. This time it was fear, not effort!

'Let's get roped up,' Dave said.

As we started to walk through the mist I realised that it was extremely difficult to make sense of the terrain. Disorientation had set in. I couldn't tell whether I was going up, down, left or right. Dave, as rear man, could at least tell left and right by using the compass and me as the bearing marker. He occasionally shouted, 'go left' or 'go right'. I counted the first 200 yards. The sweat was still trickling. Dave ensured we stayed on the right bearing. That was the slowest 200 yards ever! Each step lasted a lifetime. Or so it seemed.

'The next 500 yards at 288° are important because there are 1500 feet cliffs on the right,' said Dave. The words hit silence for a few seconds.

'Our rope is not long enough!' was my terse response.

As we were walking along I realised that I had lost count of the steps. God, what am I doing here?

'Dave, have you been counting the steps?' My nerves were fraying.

'Yes, I'll send you the bill and, be warned, I'm not cheap!'

'Thank God! How does two pints sound?'

'Just fine for starters, but remember that my favourite malt whisky is Macallan cask strength,' said Dave, nonchalantly. He had fully recovered.

'The next 500 yards at 308° are more dangerous because 1500 feet cliffs are still on the right, and 500 feet cliffs are now on the left,' Dave quipped. The Ben was in a merciless mood.

My heart was at explosion level! Sweat ran down my neck and forehead. My fear demon had come back and was laughing at me! *I can't handle this!*

I saw a dark shape a short distance away, and stopped. What was it? I shouted to Dave for advice.

'I'll anchor the rope to both my ice axes, and you try to walk slowly towards it. I'm not sure that we're on the correct bearing,' said Dave.

What? My body froze! Stay calm, don't panic. I breathed deeply a few times to relieve the tension. Was this the edge? I summoned courage from God only knows where. As I got closer to the dark shape I saw that it was only a boulder above the snow and not the peak of a buttress at the cliff edge. Thank goodness! Strangely though, there was a man sitting on the boulder. He looked tired and cold. As I got near to him and looked him in the eye, I felt a strange tingling feeling.

'Hello, are you alright?' I asked.

'Yes, I'm fine,' he said calmly. 'I'm just sitting here enjoying the solitude and contemplating which way to go. Are you lost by any chance?'

'As a matter of fact we are,' I said sheepishly, wondering why he'd picked such an odd place to contemplate.

'Don't worry, I know how to get off the plateau, so just follow me and we'll soon be away from danger,' he said with a knowing smile.

So Dave and I set off following our newfound friend.

'What's your name?' I asked.

'Alex Campbell.'

We chatted on the way down and as we got close to the turn off near the lochan, Alex mentioned that he was going to the mountaineering hut. We thanked him for his kindness towards us and bid him farewell. From there on it was a doddle—an easy walk down the rest of the "tourist route". The mist lifted half way down and it was starting to get dark. It was 8.45 p.m. as we walked off the Ben.

After a shower had replaced the sweat and tiredness with freshness and vigour, we could hear the call of the local pub summoning us. The pints were flowing freely and tales were being told. The guys we had met in Corrie Leis were there—they had got into a spot of bother on the North East Buttress, luckily, they had managed to extricate themselves. We repaid Jim and his friend with several pints and when we started to tell them about meeting Alex, an old man sitting in the corner interjected.

'Did he have worn hill walking clothes with a tear in the jacket?' he asked.

'Yes,' said Dave. 'He also had grey scrambling gloves with holes at the finger tips and I'd have sworn that he had frostbite on one or two of his fingers.'

'Sweet Jesus!' said the old man. 'Alex Campbell disappeared on the mountain four years ago today, and some say that he wanders the Ben trying to help lost climbers. He's known affectionately as Ben's friend.'

THE DREAM RING

By Robert Kirk

Lesley ran her gaze over the goods on the market stall. A tray full of knitted woollen gloves lay next to a wicker basket containing cheap cosmetics. A cardboard box that had once contained trainers was crammed full of packets of ladies tights. The packets looked scuffed and worn. Then she saw what she was looking for in a cream snowball box, right at the back of the stall.

'Twenty Lambert and Butler, please,' she said, tugging her purse from her pocket.

The stallholder reached over an expanse of sweets and chocolate bars towards the cigarettes and flipped the cellophane wrapped packet on to the counter in front of Lesley. His face and voice were expressionless. 'Four fifty five,' he said. Then his cheeks crinkled into a humourless grin when he saw the five pound note she proffered. He sucked a breath through his teeth and shook his head. 'You're my first customer. Haven't you got the right money?'

'Oh ... I don't think ...' Lesley fumbled in her purse. 'Sorry, that's all I've got.'

His thumb and forefinger pecked the note from her hand and he scrabbled about in a shoe box under the counter until he discovered a fifty pence coin. 'Do you have a five pee?'

'No,' Lesley said, with a quick shake of her head.

'Oh. Well, it looks like ...' He craned his neck and looked around the other stalls, hoping to find someone who could give him change. Seeing no one close by, he languidly scratched the back of his neck and scowled at her.

Lesley looked at her watch. 'I'm going to be late for work,' she said. 'If you give me the fifty, I could drop the five pence in when I'm passing tomorrow.'

The stallholder's raised eyebrows said, "*No chance!*"

Lesley was reluctantly handing back the cigarettes when her eye fell on a tray filled with cheap costume jewellery. She poked among the assorted brooches, clasps and the like, hoping to see something she could buy for forty-five pence. Picking up a ring with a large tiger's-eye stone, she tried it on the little finger of her left hand. It fitted.

'How much is this?' she asked.

'Oh that,' said the stall keeper. He held out his open hand until Lesley placed the ring in it. 'That's some old thing my kids found in a field in North Queens-ferry. Let me see.' He twisted the ring back and forth several times.

'There isn't a price on it,' supplied Lesley.

'No, neither there is.'

He looked at the tray to see if the price tag had fallen off but it wasn't there either. Lesley looked at her watch again. 'Look, I really have to be going.'

He sighed and scratched his jaw, then held out the ring. 'Here, take it and that's me and you square. Okay?'

'Thanks.' Lesley said, pushing the ring back onto her finger but he only grunted and started tidying his wares. She turned and ran towards the library building, stuffing the packet of cigarettes into her pocket.

'Good morning, Lesley,' chimed her supervisor. 'Would you do some first aid today?'

'Right, Mrs Shaw,' Lesley said breathlessly, tugging off her jacket and scarf. She pushed through the heavily varnished brown door into the small room that was known by all of the library staff as "Casualty". This was their workshop; the place where they repaired damaged books or prepared new ones for the shelves.

Lesley hung her jacket and scarf on a vacant hook behind the door and turned to survey the broken spines and torn covers that sagged against each other on the shelves. The damaged books always reminded her of a row of old-age-pensioners sitting on a park bench. 'All right,' she said, 'who's first?' And she reached for the nearest book, a heavy, dark blue tome entitled, *A History of Fife*.

As soon as her fingers touched the book, however, she felt a slight dizziness and the room seemed to swirl round her. Lesley groaned and sagged drunkenly against the bookshelf. Strangely, the giddy sensation faded immediately. Puzzled, Lesley grasped the book again and, once more, her vision swam and the air before her eyes seemed to waver. She let go the book and normality returned.

What's going on? she wondered.

Pulling a chair over to the workbench, she sat and stared at the row of books. She still felt a bit light-headed and her eyes watered. Fishing her hanky from her sleeve, Lesley blew her nose. I shouldn't have run that last hundred yards, she thought. And I'm not taking enough exercise. She also felt guilty about the cigarettes. If her parents found out …

Then the ring gleamed as it caught the fluorescent light. Lesley stared. Was she seeing things? Were the colours in the stone moving? She took it from her finger, laid it on the bench then blinked several times and rubbed her eyes with her fingertips. She looked at the ring again. No, it looked quite normal. Thinking her eyes were playing tricks on her, she approached the shelf once more. She reached out to the dark blue book.

And this time, when she touched it …

Nothing! Everything was normal.

With a sigh of relief Lesley lifted the large volume onto the bench. She examined the cover and spine, and idly riffled through the book looking for torn or loose pages. Then she realised she'd lain the heavy book on her new ring and she quickly retrieved it, screwing it back onto her finger as she flicked through the book. Immediately, the dizziness returned. This time her hand was resting on the book, at a page of text. And then that text began to swim before her eyes. No, it wasn't before her eyes, it was behind them—inside her head. She knew this for certain since she had closed her eyes when the dizzy spell began.

She opened her eyes again and gasped when she saw that the colours within the tiger's-eye stone were swirling lazily over its surface. She dropped her head into her hands and, as if someone had flipped a switch, the dizziness went.

Lesley looked at the ring. The movement was like snakes slithering over, under and around each other. And while she watched, the movement slowed and finally stopped.

Strange ideas were coming to her now. She knew it made no sense, but the fact was, the giddy feeling and the movement of colours within the surface of the ring were linked.

But wait. There was another factor at work here. Nothing seemed to happen if she wasn't touching the book. Or if she touched the book with her right hand—the hand that wasn't wearing the ring.

She reached out tentatively towards the page of text. And instantly the words and letters from the page jumbled around in her brain. She snatched her hand away and the vision ceased abruptly. Then she had a crazy notion. Was it just text? What would happen with pictures or photographs?

Lesley flicked over the pages with the fingers of her right hand until she came to a picture of the Forth Rail Bridge during its construction in 1889.

Her heart fluttering with trepidation, Lesley laid her open left hand on the page. Instantly, her head reeled and nausea seized her stomach. She tried to lift her hand from the book but her dizziness had pitched her head forward onto her outspread fingers, increasing the pressure on the page. Her eyes closed as the room seemed to spin faster and faster ... and then ...

... the giddy feeling went. In its place was a cold biting wind and a great clamour of sound. Lesley's eyes flickered open and then she gasped, fought back a scream of terror.

She stood in the open air on the crest of a hill. Stretched out below her was a jumbled patchwork of stitched-together fields. Barley, yellow rape, grass.

And beyond the fields, half-a-mile away, lay a wide river and a huge structure that she knew very well. For a moment or two she tried to convince herself that she was still seeing a photograph, that she was dreaming or hallucinating. But slowly she began to accept the reality of the situation. She couldn't deny the springy grass beneath her feet or the sharp bite of the wind through her thin cardigan.

Below her lay the Forth Rail Bridge, solid and real. But it was not as she knew it. Judging by the missing beams and the clang of steel on steel, the growling of huge cranes as they worked and the metallic drumbeat of riveters, the bridge was still under construction. She had somehow been transported to the place—and time—shown in the photograph.

How long she stood staring at the bridge, she later wouldn't be able to say, but her trance-like state was interrupted by the sound of children's voices. Then, over the crest of the hill they appeared. There were three of them, two of about seven or eight years old and the third, an older girl of maybe eleven or twelve. When they saw Lesley their steps faltered, their chatter ceased and the two younger ones moved closer to the girl that Lesley assumed was their big sister. Not one of them spoke to her. And rather than call a friendly greeting or wave, as you might expect, they simply stared, their eyes were filled with fear.

Lesley wasn't surprised by this; she felt the same fear tug at her own stomach.

But why? Why should they feel this way? It was beyond explanation; not something based on logic, but an instinctive feeling of dread that they all shared.

Then Lesley began to rationalise her fear. She was reminded of how she felt when she looked at the faces in old photographs. The sad expressions, the tired eyes under shawls and working men's caps had always seemed to her to be ... somehow alien, as if those people, if they had ever existed, were not like her, were perhaps not even of the same race. Or not even of this world. She looked at the children's faces now and felt that same cold dread. And she was sure they were feeling it, too. Their eyes looked empty, their faces gaunt. It was as if ... Lesley hesitated before allowing the thought to form. It was as if ... they had no soul behind their eyes.

With this thought, the cold dread turned black and became terror. Lesley knew, and she was aware that the children also knew, that something was terribly wrong. To Lesley, the children seemed alien and frightening and she knew they felt the same way about her. They stood and stared at her, their faces slowly draining of colour, their alarm showing in the way they shivered.

Lesley could stand it no longer. She turned and walked rapidly away, not stopping or slackening her pace until she had placed several hundred yards and several hillocks between herself and the children. But as she walked away from them, one thing added to her feeling of dread and made her realise that she was the one who was out of place, the one who had brought the fear and the sense of wrongness to this place. One of the younger children turned wide eyes up to her sister's face and said in a hushed voice, 'Is it a ghost, Maggie?'

Now that she was alone, Lesley wondered about her predicament. How did it happen? What had brought her here? But she knew it must have been the ring. The swirling motion within the tiger's-eye stone had been real and must have been caused by her wearing it while her hand was in contact with the photograph in the book.

What she wasn't sure about was, would it take her back to her own time?

She unscrewed the ring from her finger and stared into the huge tiger's-eye stone. Yes, sure enough, the browns and blacks whorled and swam around the stone's surface. Yet, even as she looked, the movement began to slow and turned sluggish. Giddiness brushed over her again. I'm going back, she thought, and immediately panicked. How could she be sure this had happened, that she had really been here, that it wasn't all just a dream?

Casting around, she saw a poppy nodding its head to her and made a desperate lunge for it. Triumphantly, she pocketed the bright red flower then staggered as the full force of dizziness washed over her. She felt the ring slipping from her fingers and tried to drop it into her cardigan pocket beside the poppy. Whether it went in or not, she wasn't sure and she quickly forgot about it as she reeled like a drunken man, teetering in an effort to maintain her balance.

Then the wind abruptly died. She felt warmth on her skin and the hard wooden stool beneath her. The last vestiges of dizziness faded and she opened her eyes, terrified that she might have been transported to some other place—or some other time—than her own. But she was in the library first aid room, and there was the book, still open at the same page. She turned and studied the rest of the room, the books on the shelf and the calendar on the wall. It had today's date circled. Lesley heaved a long relieved sigh. She rose and made for the door, smoothing down her windblown hair as she went. Her steps were hesitant, slightly off-balance, as if she'd just stepped off a fast ride at the fair.

Mrs Shaw turned as Lesley entered and her face assumed a worried look.

'Goodness, Lesley ... are you all right? You look ill. And you're shivering too! I hope you aren't catching flu or something.'

Lesley swallowed and shook her head slowly. She still felt somewhat bemused by her experience and Mrs Shaw's voice seemed to come from a long way away. No, she thought, I'm not ill. But she was surprised to discover that Mrs Shaw was right, she was shivering and she remembered how cold the wind had been as she stood there on that hill overlooking the Forth Rail Bridge. She wondered if she should tell Mrs Shaw what had happened to her, but ... would she be believed? Unlikely, Lesley thought. I'm not even sure I believe it myself anymore. Then she remembered the poppy in her cardigan pocket. Of course! That would prove it.

Lesley plunged her hand into the pocket but ... it was empty. They were both gone, the poppy *and* the ring. Not only could she not prove where—or when— she had been, but she could never go back!

To her surprise, and to her supervisor's, Lesley began to cry.

'Yes, Mrs Shaw,' she sobbed, 'I think I may very well be catching flu.'

Run For Your Life

By William Armstrong

Father was restless. He got up, stretched, scratched for a moment, then disappeared down the entrance tunnel.

'What's …,' I began.

'Shush,' Mother snapped. 'Just stay out of his way.'

Father reappeared. He was a big Border hill fox and the tunnel fitted him snugly. 'It's quiet oot there.'

'Of course, it's quiet,' Mother snarled. 'What did you expect when they banned hunting? A good thing too. The Hunt had a lot to answer for.'

'Prince says there's talk o' shootin' the hounds.' He sat down and began checking for fleas.

'What does that great clodhopper know about it?' Mother exploded angrily. 'All he's ever done is chew grass and carry Farmer Johnson to the hunt.'

'Prince is a'right,' Father said defensively. 'He aye tipped me aff when they were gaun tae hunt roond here.'

Mother bristled. 'A lot of good that was, when Johnson's terrier caught you under the henhouse.'

'Aye.' Father grinned reminiscently. 'That was some fight. He nearly chewed ma ear aff. Mind you,' he added reflectively, 'Ah marked him as weel. He's still limpin'.'

'That reminds me,' Mother said sharply. 'What was that strange scent on you when you came in this morning?'

'Weel,' father shuffled his paws uneasily. 'Ah ran intae wee Vera last night.'

'That stuck-up little madam. Her that's always yapping. Thinks she's too good for the rest of us. Hasn't she found a mate yet?'

'She says she's lookin' for a male wi' charisma,' Father smirked.

'For heaven's sake!' Mother rolled her eyes. 'Don't tell me you fell for that old line. Thank goodness this isn't the mating season, or you'd have your work cut out providing for two litters come the spring. Anyway,' she added, *sotto voce*, 'two can play at that game.'

'What's that supposed tae mean?' Father growled belligerently.

'Well,' Mother paused, savouring the moment, 'I came across a strange scent the other day, and I followed it. Turned out it was a big male who'd come up from England. Jeremy, he said his name was. My, but he was handsome,' she went on dreamily. 'And so well-spoken. None of your coarse Border dialect there. Breeding always shows. He said his parents had been hunted by the Beaufort Hunt. And you know who rides with them! Imagine being hunted by royalty! Pity it wasn't the mating season.... Still, he said he'd be around for quite a while.'

'Ah am what Ah am,' Father said grimly. 'Your fine friend'll no' be aroond lang if Ah catch him. Damn red settlers. Comin' up here and carryin' on as if they owned the place.'

'Jeremy said he'd decided to take a break during their hunting season. He's looking for a range around here.'

'Is he though? He'll be lucky. Now they've banned hunting' here, every Tom, Dick an' Harry'll be movin' up frae the sooth.'

'Father,' I said hesitantly, 'what's it like? Being hunted, I mean?'

'Weel onyway.' Father settled himself comfortably on the sandy floor of the den. 'There's naethin' quite like it. Tae run fur your life wi' a' these dogs and riders behind you, knowin' that one slip might be your last. Bein' hunted is the greatest thrill there is.'

'Speak for yourself.' Mother said tartly. 'The only time I was ever really hunted, I was terrified.'

'What happened?' I queried excitedly.

Mother smiled. 'Your father saved my life.'

'Gosh!' I gasped. 'How did you do that?'

Father raised a deprecatory paw. 'Naethin' tae it really. Your mother's parents were urban foxes. They lived on the edge o' a big toon. Very lah-di-dah,' he added contemptuously.

Mother scowled. 'Very refined,' she riposted snootily.

'Weel, onyway,' Father resumed, 'their den was discovered, and they were dug oot an' shot. It's hard tae believe,' he went on wonderingly. 'People shootin' foxes. What's wrang wi' this country?'

'But how did you save Mother?' I persisted.

Father looked suitably modest. 'She was up on the hill behind their den, and saw it a'.' He shook his head. 'Imagine seein' your parents shot. So she made a run for it. The hunt was ower that way and they picked up her scent. Ah was aroond an' cut across her trail. That drew the hounds aff an' Ah took them on a lang run doon tae the Border. Managed tae gie them the slip, then Ah doubled back and traced her next day. Ah was lucky really.'

Mother looked at him for a moment. 'It wasn't luck, Ray,' she said quietly. 'You were ...,' she broke off as Father sat up, suddenly alert.

'It's the Hunt and they're headin' this way,' he barked excitedly.

'It can't be!' Mother gasped. 'Hunting's banned.'

'Ah tell you it is,' father growled urgently. 'We cannae stay here. The terriers'll be in and you know what that means. We lost his sisters that way. Ah'll slip oot an' lead them aff. Then you take the cub up tae the Big Woods. Wait there until it's dark, then come back here.' And with that he was gone. We listened intently: A sudden crescendo of noise, shouts, the baying of hounds, and above everything, the brassy blare of the horn, then three quick bangs, before the noise receded and finally died away.

Mother waited a long time before slipping out to check. 'Right,' she called, 'it's all clear now.'

We hid in the Big Woods until nightfall, then made our way cautiously back to the den. All was quiet, but there was no sign of Father. Much later, he limped in, tired, bedraggled and exuding an air of gloom.

'Ray, dear.' Mother growled softly as she nuzzled him. 'Are you all right? I thought I heard guns ...'

'Oh, you heard guns right enough,' Father snarled savagely. 'Ah never thought Ah'd see the Hunt shootin' at foxes. Onyway, that's it. We're movin'.'

'But where?' Mother gasped in amazement.

'Sooth,' said Father grimly. 'We're gaun tae England. At least the Hunt doon there doesnae shoot you ... yet!'

No Smoke Without Fire

By Nick Fair

There was a tremendous explosion; two of the windows on the upper floor were blown right out, followed with a large billow of flame. The firemen beneath the windows were showered with glass. Mark Lewis, the section leader, dashed over to see if any of the crew was injured. They had scampered away and stood looking up at the flames now leaping high in the air.

'It's all right Mark, we all got clear. I think Alex Weir has a cut on his hand. Christ! That was a near thing; it sounded like a gas bottle going up!'

Just at that another man came dashing round the side of the building, pulling off his facemask. 'Hey Mark! Alec Cowan is in there, he had just entered the side door before the explosion!'

'Right! Steve, put the hose up to the windows, you others follow me.'

Inside the door they found the floor from above had come down and they could see Alec's leg from under the debris, Mark had a quick look around. 'Right, he is caught under that beam! Now boys, get round it, we might be able to get it up.'

The four men took hold of one end and tried to lift it; it did move, but not enough.

'Willie, go and get Steve, that might be enough to get it up.' When the two men arrived they again got hold of the beam, with a concerted effort they managed to get it up high enough but Alec was unconscious. As luck would have it, two policemen appeared on the scene. Mark yelled, 'Quick, get his legs and pull him out!'

In a very short time Alec was out and clear of the building, an ambulance had arrived and the medics took over; meantime the fire was intensifying and the crew tackled the blaze as the ambulance dashed away with Alex.

The second fire wagon arrived and the fire was soon under control. The second tender was not always too quickly off the mark; this was because it was mainly manned by part-time crewmen, it took some time for them to be assembled, nonetheless they were usually very sharp at turning out.

The two wagons returned to the station and as normal they were immediately prepared ready for the next call out. The two crews retired to the common room. The station Commander, George Hutton came in to address them. He was grim faced and somewhat downcast.

'Gentlemen, this is a part of the job I don't like, I'm very sorry to tell you that Alec Cowan didn't survive, there is no easy way to say these things, he was barely alive when he arrived at hospital but his injuries were multiple, he died without regaining consciousness. He was a good man and dedicated to duty. He will not be easily replaced. Sorry, I wish I had something better to say.' With that he withdrew. There was a deadly silence in the room. One man said. 'Poor bastard, he never had a chance!'

Mark stood up. 'Come on now, we did the best we could; the explosion took us all by surprise! Steve, are the wagons ready to roll?'

'Yes Mark, they are ready to go.' Steve said quietly.

Mark looked around and said. 'Right men, thank you all for a job well done, the part-time crew can now stand down.'

When Steve got home the first thing Sandra asked was: 'Is it true what I've heard? I get uptight every time you go out. Who was it?'

'Sorry Sandie, it was Alex Cowan, he never had a chance. Come on now, settle down, you know this is my job, it is what I want to do.'

'I know, but what will happen to me when your turn comes? You know I can't manage on my own. I can't help worrying.'

'Would you like me to make a cup of tea? It is time for your medicine.'

This was the usual line of conversation when something went wrong ever since Sandra was diagnosed with a malignant tumour. It was on her spine which couldn't be removed, which had now given her a limited life span. When the doctor first told him of her condition his first reaction was to quit work and just look after her. He had taken a month's compassionate leave, but long before the month was up, he was nearly going up the wall. He knew that was not the answer, they were getting on each other's nerves. So it was agreed he would go on working until her condition became unbearable. That was about a year ago without any serious mishaps so he lived in the hope that it would last, but he knew that the time would come. He shuddered at the thought.

'Come on Sandie, here's your tea; let's see if there is anything good on the television'.

Steven Wardie was a fireman in the town of Lamasmuir, a medium sized town in the Scottish borders. The fire station had only two fire wagons, but it was supported by other stations in some of the larger towns in the surrounding area.

Steven was now forty-four years old; he had been a fireman for some twenty years and prior to that worked in one of the tweed mills in the town. Married to Sandra with two children, a boy and a girl in that order, now grown up and married. James, the son had gone to Australia at an early age, married and settled in Perth. The daughter, Sylvia, married an Englishman and was now living in Cornwall

Things were quiet for a few days with no serious incidents. After Alex's funeral, there was a meeting called in the common room.

George Hutton stood before them. 'Now gentlemen, we have had a sad loss and he will be sadly missed, but things have to go on, Brigade has sent us a replacement.'

With that he went to the door and opened it to allow a woman to enter. She was tallish, about five nine, slight built and walked with a straight back. She was attractive without being glamorous; her hair was short and neat, a sort of dark chestnut, and she looked about twenty-five.

'I would like to introduce Joyce Harding. She is not here as a trainee; she has transferred from Dumfries to be near her father who is now infirmed and lives here, I hope you will welcome her and give her the co-operation she deserves.'

Now Simon Springer, the only one that had been there longer than Steve Wardie and a few years older spoke up. 'Hey Boss, just a minute, that's a woman! We canny hae a bliddy woman on the station, they bring nothin bit trouble and bad luck!'

George looked at him for a few seconds. 'Right Simon, let's hear your objections, this better be good.'

'Well you know the trouble they caused on the auld sailing ships. When they were manned with men it was fine, but wimen had to get on board, they were drinking lime juice and spreading scurvy all over the place, and what about the 'Titanic'? That was a woman's fault'.

George was looking at him patiently. 'All right, what the hell did a woman have to do with the sinking of the 'Titanic'? I can't wait to hear this.'

'It's a weel kent fact that the navigator was havin it aff with a woman and not looking where he was going.'

Some of the crew was laughing. George had his hand on his forehead. 'Is there any more before we go slightly mad?'

'Weel in the old west in America it wis lawless with bank and train robbers, shooting and stealing cattle, and the worst one was a woman!'

'Oh dear, now who would that be? Make this a good one.'

'Come on, everybody's heard of 'Jessie James!'

Now everyone was laughing. But this whole thing was lightening the mood and helping to put the disaster behind them.

When the laughter died down Simon stood up and walked down to face the newcomer. He looked at her for a moment, held out his and, after a few seconds had passed he said. 'Joyce Harding, you are a fine looking woman, and by the hand I am holding, I know you are strong in mind and body. On behalf of the crew I wish to welcome you to our team. Now if you would come and join your new colleagues we will get on with the meeting,' the other members of the crew started to clap their hands as he led her to a seat.

George said. 'Fine. Now I'm sure you will accept your new colleague and give her all the assistance she will need to get into our ways. Is there anything else you want to talk about before we go?'

Once again it was Simon. 'I would like to make a suggestion sir.'

'Oh God, what is it this time Simon? I do wish the alarm would go; what is it you are suggesting?'

'I think all fire engines should be painted white!'

'Dare I ask why? Fire engines have been red since they were created, why change now?'

'Well if they were all white they would get the same privileges as white vans, we all know that they don't have to stop at red lights, they never give way at roundabouts, they can ignore speed limits and pedestrians have to jump, and even on crossings; the drivers treat everyone as if they shouldn't be on the road!'

'Simon, have you ever thought of standing for parliament?'

'Oh, do you think I would be a good M.P.?'

'No! But then you would be a problem to someone else. Now I think we should break up and go back to duty.'

With the meeting closed the crew were giving the new member their full attention. In front of all the staff Alex Weir was openly flirting with her. He was young, fairly good looking and known as a ladies man. He was winking and gesticulating like he was on a good thing. She looked straight at him. 'Excuse me, could I ask your name?'

'Yes it's Alex, Alex Weir, and we are delighted to have you with us.'

'Alex could I ask a favour of you?' She said sweetly

'Certainly, anything!'

'Please don't try and get into my knickers, there's already an arsehole in there!'

Sandra Wardie was at this time slightly disabled and walked with a stick. She was working in the kitchen when the doorbell rang.

Answering the bell, she found a man on the step with a briefcase.

'Good morning Mrs. Wardie, I am from the Security Association and I've come to check that you are nice and secure in your house!'

'And what is it you want to check? I don't think there is anything wrong with my house.'

'Actually, it is only your doors and windows, which is the usual weakness. Would you mind if I had a look?'

'Well there's no harm in looking. I would be happier if my man was here, but do come in.'

After a quick look at the doors and windows, he sat on the settee, opened his briefcase and started looking at some papers.

'Mrs. Wardie, I see you have no alarm system installed! A person in your condition should be covered by an alarm. Now it so happens that my company have a range of alarm systems that will easily cover your needs, and because of your disability, you would come in for a very substantial discount.'

'Just a moment and I will put the kettle on.'

She walked out through the kitchen and tapped on the door over the fence. As she was coming into the room again a man entered the front door.

'Right mister, whatever you are selling, put it back in the case and leave! Now before you protest, you can walk out the door or be propelled at high speed!' When the salesman hesitated the neighbour moved forward and the safety expert made a hasty retreat.

'Thanks Bert. I wish I hadn't fallen for that.'

Steve found his wife having tea with Bert and asked if he could join the picnic. Bert explained what it was all about, suggesting a spy hole in the door might be a good idea.

'Sandie, I have said before that a dog would be good company for you. You would feel a bit safer with one at your heels when you open the door.'

'Well I'm not sure; we will have to talk about this'.

Next day Steve was at the station and was cleaning one of the engines with Joyce. The alarm sounded. The crew scrambled and was on their way.

The fire was one flat up in a block of flats. There was smoke billowing out of a window. Mark called out for two to mask up, the others to prepare water hoses. Joyce started to dress in smoke apparatus when Mark said. 'No Joyce, not you, Simon will change, Joyce will help Steve with the water.'

The two men went up the stairs and had to force the front door. They were met by a huge pall of smoke; after investigating Simon went down and reported to Mark. 'The flat is empty; the fire is a settee, and it can be controlled by an extinguisher!'

'Right Simon, you attend to that, Steve and Joyce, wind up the hoses, it's nothing serious!'

When it was all over and they were tidying up, Steve said to Mark. 'Don't you think you could have given Joyce the chance to get some action? It would have broken her in.'

'Steve, I'm surprised at you, you know better that to question an order; she will be in action soon enough! Joyce, come over here, now you were about to put on gear without being told? You must understand that I decide who does what and when, all right?'

'Yes sir, but I am experienced.'

'Well that's fine, but I will try you out at the station first.'

They had no sooner returned to the station when another call came. Road traffic accident, down the Peebles Road.

Arriving at the scene they found a car on its side and another still upright, but badly damaged. The Police indicated that they had managed to get the couple out of the car on its side, but there was still someone in the other car and the doors were jammed.

Mark dashed over and surveyed the car. 'Right! Cutting gear, power shears and metal saw!'

The gear was pulled out and lying on the ground. Joyce was about to pick up the shears and stopped, looked at Mark. He walked over and asked. 'Which of these can you use?'

'I am confident with both, sir!'

'Good, take the shears and we will see what's to be done!'

Looking through the shattered windscreen he said. 'There are two people in there, start cutting from the other side; I will get Steve to bring the saw.'

Between them they had the roof off in a short time. A doctor was on the scene and looked down the hole.

'The woman is conscious; so get her out first; the man looks to be in trouble.' He turned to the medics. 'Get the woman out, we will have to cut the driver's door off!' He asked Mark. 'Is there any danger of fire?'

'No I don't think so, it seems to be stable. Will I start to cut the door?'

'Yes but be careful; he is locked in with the wheel!'

Joyce cut it right at the doorpost and the door swung open, they manoeuvred the man out and he was taken away in the ambulance.

'Well done Joyce, you obviously know your stuff; right gang, lets tidy up, our job is finished here!'

It was just two evenings later, the alarm sounded and the first engine was dispatched and the part-timers were alerted. It was quite late and the streets were quiet; the fire was in the Co-operative in the main street.

When the fire wagon stopped at the front of the shop, Mark could see lots of smoke but as yet no flames. 'Right, Alex Weir and Joyce, kit up for smoke, Simon and Steve, see if you can find a way in.'

When Joyce and Alex were ready, Steve came back and said the building was secure and all locked up.

'Right Steve, you and Simon force the front door and when Joyce and Alex are in we will start with the hoses. The police said they have sent for the manager.'

With the noise of shattering glass, the door disintegrated and the two masked figures went inside; meantime a car pulled up and a man got out and was standing near the door of the shop. A policeman approached him and then spoke to Mark.

'That is Mr. Hitchins. He is the manager of the shop, and he is asking if he can go into the shop?'

Mark went over and spoke to him. 'Sorry sir, until it is found to be safe, we cannot allow anyone to go in, at this stage, it would be too dangerous!'

By the time the second engine arrived, the hoses were laid out and waiting to hear from the inside members. While the second wagon was getting ready, Alex came out and hurried to inform Mark that the fire was centralised in the clothing area. The hoses were pulled in by Steve and members of the second wagon.

The fire was a serious one and when it was under control a policeman spoke to Mr. Hitchins and said a joiner was on his way to secure the premises; Mark also spoke to him. 'Sorry sir, I hope you will understand my refusal to let you enter. We are finished now; I don't think there is too much damage. I will make out my report and you will get a copy, again, sorry about the mess. Good night sir.'

The following evening the crew were going about their normal tasks and were unaware there was a man in talking to George Hutton.

After some discussion the two men left the office and went downstairs and spoke to Mark.

Mark did not look too happy but called all the crew to line up for inspection. 'I'm sorry men, I don't know what this is about, the boss wants to have a word with you!'

The first thing George asked was. 'Is this the crew that was on duty last night at the Co-op?'

'Yes sir, but there were part-timers called out, they are not here!'

'Right gentlemen, stand at ease, this is Detective Sergeant Wilson, Lothian and Borders C.I.D. And he wants to have a word with you.'

D.S. Wilson came forward and stood in front of them.

'I'm sorry I have to ask questions, but there has been a complaint about last night. I have always had the greatest respect for the Fire Service, but it has been reported to us that while you were in the store attending to the fire, one of your team was seen to go to the fire engine, return to the shop with a pair of bolt cutters and a crowbar. He was later seen leaving the shop with the cutters and the crowbar under his arm and carrying a case of whisky; he returned to the wagon, deposited what he was carrying and went again into the shop and this time he emerged carrying a case of liqueur. The whisky missing from stock this morning has been identified as 'Grant's Special', and the liqueur as 'Drambuie'; now Chief Officer Hutton says it is sometimes necessary to remove anything that can be regarded as inflammable, but this was not reported and has not been returned to the store. Sorry, but it is now classified as theft.

Simon Stringer, who was the fireman's representative, stepped forward and said. 'This is a serious accusation; can the person identify the man that was supposedly seen?'

'Now Simon, let's slow down and see where this is going, I'm not any happier than you about this. The whole thing maybe just a misunderstanding,' George turned to the Sergeant, 'What's the next step?'

'I have the Manager in the car outside. Now I know I can't legally have an I. D. parade in here, but it would give us some guidance.'

Simon got the team together and asked them what they thought. It was Steve that suggested they let it happen. 'At the moment we are all suspects, I think we should line up and see where it takes us!'

So the Sergeant went out and brought the manager in. The crew were in line and before Mr. Hitchins made a move, Simon stopped him.

'Excuse me, before you start pointing a finger!' He turned to Mark. 'Is it not so that everyone on the scene was wearing a helmet?'

'Yes of course, it's a must at all operations!'

Simon said in a very positive manner. 'Sergeant, I want that man to turn his back on us now!'

D.S. Wilson stood in front of the man and made him face about.

'Right, I want you all to get dressed as you were last night, including helmets.' Simon then nodded to the Sergeant.

The man again faced the crew, looked along the line and then walked along looking at each one as he passed. He stopped at Joyce. 'I think it may be this one; the size and build are about right!'

George Hutton stepped forward. 'Would you take your helmet off please? Thank you, he looked at the manager, 'is this your suspect?'

'Oh dear, it's a woman; sorry, it must be someone else.'

Simon immediately said. 'Excuse me, what difference does that make?'

Mark said. 'It doesn't matter anyway; she was inside wearing smoke gear, and she was in there with Alex Weir until the second wagon arrived!'

Mr. Hitchins looked again at the line up and pointed to Alex. 'This one is about the same height, not quite so thin. I'm sorry, but seeing you all dressed up makes it difficult'. Looking at Steve. 'That's the only other one of about the same height. Sorry Sergeant, it's the best I can do!' He turned and walked away.

The Sergeant faced Steve. 'What were you doing and what were your movements at the time?'

'Generally laying out hoses, looking for the hydrant. What I wasn't doing was running about with cutters and moving cases of whisky. If you are going to ask me to prove it, sorry. For the last twenty years my mind has been on fighting fires, so the ball is in your court!'

The Sergeant walked away with George, had a word and returned to the men. 'Sorry about all this. I want you to carry on with your duties and I will see to the next step. Again sorry, I don't believe it was any one of you.'

Mark said to Simon. 'That was a mess: four members in a line up, and three of them don't fit. We will have to wait and see if the boss is going to suspend Steve!'

George came and spoke to Steve, 'We're waiting to see what the Sergeant is going to do. The report will go to Brigade and I personally don't think they will suspend anyone on the strength of that farce we just witnessed, but it is still a serious business about the whisky. Steve, just carry on; the truth will out.'

They were still talking about it when the alarm sounded. The crew scrambled to the wagon and the part-timers were paged.

Arriving at the scene, they found it was a lower flat in a two-storey building. There was a lot of smoke visible at the windows. A neighbour said she didn't think there was anyone in. There were two doors, one for each flat. The same neighbour pointed out that the door to the lower flat was at the side of the building.

Mark called out. 'Simon, Joyce, smoke gear; Steve, check and find out if the door is locked!'

Steve hurried round to the door, tried it and it opened. He flung it wide and could see a woman with a child in her arms and holding a toddler by the hand at the end of the passage. He was about to shout for help when a burst of flame leapt out of a door halfway down the hall. He acted instinctively and dashed straight in past the flames. Tearing off his jacket, he put it round the shoulders of the woman and started to edge her to the door. The heat increased and he had to draw back.

As it turned out two of his colleagues appeared at the door with a hose, seeing the situation, turned on a fine spray. As Steve felt the cold water he eased the woman out and Mark ran over to her. 'Is there anyone else in there?' She just shook her head. Two medics took her away and the fire was dealt with. The damage was confined to one room and after checking out the flat the fire engine returned to the station, Steve was rushed to hospital and kept in.

The following morning Steve was lying in a ward when he was visited by George Hutton and Joyce.

Steve looked at George. 'Is my wife all right? She isn't well!'

'Yes. Mark went round to assure her you were fine, just in for observation. By the way, we bought grapes for you, but Joyce said you may not be allowed to eat, so she ate them!'

Joyce sat on the edge of the bed. 'I think you are in trouble, going into that house without the proper gear, I think they will punish you with a medal; seriously, how long do you think you will be in here?'

Steve cast his eyes down. 'I think I have a touch of smoke in my lungs. They are making tests this afternoon. Joyce, could I ask you to go and see Sandie? You don't have to mention what I just said.'

She smiled and nodded her head. 'Yes, I will go straight from here, you take care.' She leaned over and kissed him on the cheek.

Steve was off for a week. When he reported back he was told he would not be operational until the doctor gave him the all clear, but he could work around the station or man the telephone.

Now this meant paging the part-time firemen. They had a simple system: if it looked like the second wagon would be needed, he would call them all, but sometimes they were not all available, so they took the first four that turned up, and they went out with a full time fireman.

After a few days there was a call-out. Number one wagon dashed right out, and the spares were paged. When the second wagon was about to leave, a call from the first engine reported a false alarm. The second crew stood down and the first lot parked up.

This was the kind of situation when most of staff was in the common room and nothing to do. It was put to use for meetings. On this occasion the topic was the missing cases of liquor.

Alex Weir said: 'Say what you like, I have known Steve for a few years and I can't believe he had anything to do with it!'

Now there were two part-timers sitting together: Brian Sweeney and Jack For-syth, who had each been with the Brigade for a number of years. 'What do you think Jack? Is Steve the kind of man to behave in that way?'

'Well it's hard to say,' Jack answered, 'but I believe in the thought "No smoke without fire", but don't quote me on this!'

Now Mark Lewis overheard this conversation. At first he thought it was a remark in poor taste, and he was about to remonstrate with him when a thought came to him. He hurried away and spoke to the boss.

'I'll only be away for a short time. An idea has come into my head, and it might answer a question!'

'Well don't be longer than you need be because you are on duty.'

Mark got into his car and drove to the Co-op shop. 'Can I have a word with the manager please? It's quite important.'

'Just one question Mr. Hitchins; think carefully. The night of the fire, were you there before the second wagon arrived? Can you remember? It might be important!'

'Oh yes, I can clearly remember the second engine coming alongside and stop-ping. How is this important?'

'Mr. Hitchins, can you remember which fire engine the man came out of?'

The manager looked up at the ceiling and stroked his chin before answering. 'All the crew from the first one were already working, the man with the cutters came from the second engine! Yes, I'm quite sure. Is it the kind of answer you want?'

'Yes Mr. Hichins, so long as you are sure. This is why you had so much trou-ble identifying the man: you only seen the crew from the first wagon. Thank you, this will clear a man's name!'

When Mark returned to the station, the part-timers were away. He hurried into the boss's office. 'I have solved a problem. It clears Steve, but it doesn't say who is guilty.' He went on to explain what had happened. George was relieved about Steve, but he still had a thief on his squad. 'I suppose we are now looking at a part-timer, any ideas?'

'Sorry boss, is it all right to tell Steve? It will be a load off his mind.'

George nodded his head. 'Yes, and I will contact Sergeant Wilson, but it means we start all over again.'

Steve was now relieved that he had been cleared of the theft but was still concerned about his chest. He settled into the routine of regular dayshift, answering the phone and doing some of the paper work.

Lately there had been a series of fires that seemed to come in a pattern. A hay-loft on a farm, a primary school on a Sunday when it was empty, and a railway carriage in a siding near the local station.

George Hutton came to see Steve. 'I'm very pleased you were cleared of that thing about the whisky, but I am not happy about these fires; they seem to come up regularly. Have you had any thoughts about that? It looks to me as if it was to benefit someone!'

Steve looked at him. 'That is a strange thing to say, but I feel it is happening in such a way that there aren't any casualties; nobody gets hurt, yes, this is curious!'

'Steve, if you come up with any thoughts about this, bring them to me. We have to tread carefully, I'm sure you understand.'

When the boss had gone, Joyce stuck her head in. 'Coming for a cup of tea Steve? You can tell me how Sandie is keeping.' Steve switched the telephone to the extension in the canteen. Over a cuppa, they chatted about things in general.

'These fires, you know the ones I mean: you must be having thoughts about them; I feel there is something strange going on. Do you feel it?'

'Joyce, someone sees a fire and calls us; it is up to us to put it out. Now if I was a policeman, I would be thinking: does anyone benefit from them? But for the world of me, nobody comes to mind. There doesn't seem to be an answer so let's change the subject. How is your dad?' She looked at him, her face clouding over. 'He is not doing very well. The doctor was in again today, but it's hopeless!'

He reached over and took her hand. 'Joyce, we are both in the same boat. We live and hope it will not happen too soon; our friendship will keep us going.'

As she was wiping a tear from her eye the telephone rang, Steve dashed over and listened. He immediately pressed the alarm button and everyone sprung into action. Steve wrote on a pad and handed it to Mark. 'Fire in an empty shop in

Dewar Street; I'll page the staff to come in!' As the off-duty staff started to appear he checked them in. When there were five on board they followed on.

Steve went back to the canteen; there wasn't anything he could do now. George Hutton came in and sat beside him. Steve made a pot of tea and they had a cup. 'Steve, what do you make of these fires? We seem to be getting a spate just now, have you any thoughts about it?'

'Boss, I feel there is a pattern there; I just can't put my finger on it. It isn't at the same time of day, nor the same day of the week; sorry I can't think of anything!'

'I had a word with Sergeant Wilson. He says he has had forensic on it and they say is isn't accidental. In each case there is some form of forced entry. There hadn't been any fire problems here for years, and now we are averaging about two a week. It looks like somebody is trying to keep us working, but nobody is benefiting. Steve, you make lousy tea!'

The next morning Joyce dropped in to the duty office to have a chat with Steve. 'Joyce, how are you fitting in now? Any problems?'

'No, not really, I find the part-timers are a bit off hand. Maybe there is a bit of jealousy, me coming in full time. One man in particular is very stand-offish, but it doesn't bother me. I have tried to be friendly with them all. Never mind that, how is Sandie? Bearing up I hope?'

'Well she will never be any better; I'm just pleased I have a good neighbour who looks after her.' Steve put his head down in deep thought, Joyce slipped away to get on with her work.

Sergeant Wilson called at the station; he was met by Simon Stringer. 'I would like to have a word with Steve Wardie, is he in?'

'Is this something I should be in on? You know I am the Rep here, and if you are here to question him he is entitled to representation.'

'Come off it Simon; it's just a chat, come in if you want!'

'No it's all right, he's in the duty office.' The Sergeant and Steve spoke for some time. 'Steve, if you were a policeman, what is the first thing you would look for?'

After a bit of thought Steve said: 'I suppose it would be motive, but who benefits from a fire in an empty shop? I have been thinking, but sorry, nothing comes to me.'

'Well there must be something, Steve. Firemen don't get anything extra for attending a fire do they?' Steve just shook his head. 'If they are kept back over their time they do get paid; no, that is not on, overtime isn't the answer!'

'Maybe it has nothing to do with us, just some maniac who likes to see a fire, or possibly anyone who has been rejected for the service!'

'We haven't had a Pyromaniac here for many years, and I don't believe we have one now; there is an answer to this and I mean to find it. See you later Steve.'

A few days later Joyce said to Steve, 'Would you like me to come home with you and visit Sandie? There is going to be a MacMillan nurse in with my dad and they prefer to be alone.'

'Yes, I'm sure she would like that, you can have tea with us.'

After she had been there for some time Joyce said. 'I think I should be going, the nurse may have left. Are you giving me a lift?'

'Yes, go and say cheerio to Sandie and I will see you outside.'

As they were travelling through town Joyce suddenly said. 'Look, there is a fire over there; drive over!'

There was indeed a fire, Steve parked the car and they both got out. The Blue Watch were in attendance, which is the opposite shift. As they watched, there was a commotion near one of the engines; a great fountain of water shot into the air, in the semi darkness it looked quite spectacular, the firemen were dashing about in the area trying to sort it out.

'Steve, what the hell is happening, let's move a little closer and see.' They got as near as they could go without getting involved. After a few minutes Joyce said. 'Look! There is somebody at your car!' They dashed over but the man was gone.

'Joyce, look at this, he has scratched the bonnet; just a minute, it says 'SCAB'; what in heaven's name is going on, why would anyone think that!?'

'Steve, take me home, my dad will be getting worried, and you better report this to the police.'

The following morning Steve intended to call Sergeant Wilson, but he never had the chance; D.S. Wilson was at the station.

'Tell me Steve, why were you at the fire last night but not taking part? It was quite a sight when the hoses burst.'

'Well to start with I wasn't on duty. We were just passing. Why were you there?' The Sergeant hesitated. 'As things are, I come out to all 999s, especially for fires. Steve, have I got this right, the other watch isn't called out when they are off duty, but the part-timers will come out at any time, does that sound right?'

'Yes it does!' but Steve saw a glint in the Sergeant's eye. 'I think we have cracked it; do you see what I'm getting at?'

'No I haven't caught on, what is it?'

'Before I say any more, can you give me a list of what the part-timers do for a living?'

'That's a funny question, but I can tell you. We have six call-out men and a waiting list to join us; I'm not sure it's correct to pass it out.'

'Come on Steve, this could be important; names now please!'

Steve sat and looked at him, and then he suddenly twigged. 'I follow your thoughts. Two of them work night shift at the mill, and we try not to call them out at night. One man is self-sufficient; he does it for the excitement. That leaves three, Sweeney, Forsyth and Parker; now Sweeney is a road sweeper, Forsyth is self employed as a taxi owner and Parker works with the Parks department; is that what you wanted to know?'

The Sergeant just smiled and left.

It was still early in the morning and Joyce showed her face at the door. 'You have a funny look on your face; have you something to tell me?' Before he could answer, the phone rang. Steve picked it up and immediately pressed the alarm button. 'Joyce, you better go!' He paged part-time staff. When he passed the note to Mark, he went and spoke to the Chief who was talking to D.S. Wilson.

'What is it this time Steve, another bogus call out?'

'No sir, a warehouse on the south side of town. It's storage for large drums of paint and chemicals, and we may have to call out other stations!'

'Damn, get in touch with Gala and ask them to send what they have. Steve, have you paged everyone we have? Keep me informed; better still, I will go to the scene!'

The fire was quite massive, eight engines from four stations in attendance. It seemed that when they thought it was coming under control, it would burst out again. It was about six in the evening when the fire was finally mastered; Mark was winding up when there was a radio message from Steve. 'We have another fire, Langside Farm. It will need both wagons.' So instead of heading for the station both the engines headed for the farm.

Steve would have stayed on but he had a phone call saying Sandie was very poorly. He went straight home and found Bert kneeling at the settee; Sandie was lying down on it. 'Sorry Steve, I tried to contact you but couldn't get through, so I've phoned for an ambulance. Steve, it looks very bad; if you are needed at the station I will go with her!'

Steve knelt by Sandie. 'Sorry love, we are having a lot of trouble and things are desperate!' His shoulders slumped and his head went down; he started to shake. Bert put his arm round his shoulders. 'Come on Steve, you do what has to be done. I will look after Sandie!'

'Bert, there are fires all over the place. If you don't mind, I should go back. Call me if you need me!'

Steve left the house with a heavy heart; He knew he should be with her; he would leave as soon as he could.

Back at the station he heard two bodies had been recovered from the warehouse and five men were in hospital. His thoughts at this time were for Joyce. She had been at the first fire for about ten hours and now she was at another.

The engines returned at about midnight and when Steve saw Joyce he said. 'Come on, I will run you home, you look all in!'

She was sagging at the shoulders. 'I still have to tend the wagon.' But as she was saying this she was leaning against the side of the engine.

Mark said. 'Joyce, go while you have the chance and Steve: you should be at the hospital. Get going, and we will deal with this!'

On the way to her house she started to cry. 'Equality or not, that was more than I could take!'

He stopped at her door and they both got out of the car. She handed him the key. When he had opened the door she just stood there. He stepped forward and took her in his arms. 'Come on Joyce, this has nothing to do with being a woman. There wasn't a man there who didn't feel the way you do; now go and see your dad and I will put the kettle on!'

Next morning Steve went to the hospital. He found Bert still sitting at Sandy's bedside. 'Oh Bert, have you been here all night? You look shagged out!'

'It's not so bad as it looks. When they sedated her I fell asleep on the chair, but I will go home now, and don't forget, I will be there when you need me!'

Steve felt very humble: friends like that don't come easy. A doctor came to him and said, 'Her condition is more to do with anxiety than her spine. I'm sure it is your job that is doing the damage. Try and spend a bit more time with her. We'll keep her in for a few days, when she is fit you can take her home!'

Steve sat with her for a while and reflected on what the doctor had said. Sandie was still sedated so Steve returned to the station. When he had reported in he went to the locker room and found Joyce looking for something in her locker. He went and spoke to her, about to tell her what the doctor had said when he noticed his own locker. He went over and found the word 'Scab' scratched on the door. Before he could say anything Joyce said. 'I think there is someone in there!' She pointed to a little anti-room at the end of the locker room. They both went to investigate. It was shadowy in the poor light, but they could see someone in the corner. Steve pushed the door open and in the extra light they could see a man: it was one of the part-timers.

'Brian Sweeney, what are you doing here, and what's wrong? You look upset!'

Sweeney had his back to the wall. 'Aye, you bastard, you have everything and I'm just shite!' His eyes were blazing and his features were distorted. Steve took a step forward and in a flash Sweeney pulled a knife from his pocket. Steve stopped in his tracks as Sweeney pointed the knife at his chest. It seemed as if he was out of control. Joyce stepped quickly in front of Steve and faced Sweeney. 'Sween, if you are going to hurt anyone, it has to be me; now put the knife down and tell us what's wrong!'

Sweeney looked at Joyce and then at Steve. His head was going down. He dropped the knife at Steve's feet, who picked it up. 'Sween, this is very sharp; do you have a sheath for it?' Sweeney, with his head still down handed him the sheath and Steve covered the blade with it and put it in his pocket. 'Come on now Sween, tell us what this is all about; what have I ever done to you?'

Sweeney lifted his head, his face awash with tears. He was totally devastated. 'I'll tell you, It's plain blind fuckin jealousy. You have everything, I don't even have a friend. I'm too ugly. I was born ugly, never had a pal. At school I never got to play, nobody wanted me; I became the school bully and was hated by everyone!!'

Joyce said, 'When I came here I tried to be friends with everyone. You didn't want to know me, and you didn't give me a chance!'

Steve now realised that Sweeney was always alone. 'Sween, I have smoke on my lungs and I'm about to lose my job. My wife is dying and I've been accused of stealing whisky, but you say I have everything!'

Sweeney covered his face with his hands, shuddered and slumped against the wall. Joyce put her hand on his arm, 'Come on now Sween, all this can be sorted out, give life a chance.'

Sweeney lifted his head, looked straight at Steve. 'You have her; I have never had anybody; I have been alone all my life!'

'We are good friends and that is all. Joyce is easy to get on with.'

Sweeney pointed to him. 'You spent a night with her. I know you did; it was after the big fire!'

'Brian Sweeney, listen to me: on that night Steve offered to take me home. I was totally exhausted and could hardly stand up. My dad is very ill, Steve took me home, told me to go and get ready for bed. When I had my pyjamas on he had made some tea and toast. I went to see my father; Sween, he ordered me to bed and he sat with my dad'.

'Are you saying he was with your dad all night?'

Tears welled up in her eyes. 'He was holding my dad's hand until half past three in the morning. That is when my dad died.'

Sweeney didn't know what to say. He was choked with grief. Another voice was heard; it was Sergeant Wilson.

'Sweeney, you seem to spread unhappiness like confetti at a wedding on a nice day. I have been hearing what you were all saying.' He held out his hand to Steve. 'I'll take the knife; it's done enough damage!'

Steve handed it to him. 'I don't believe he has ever used it. It is just a prop that goes with his life style.' The sergeant put it in his pocket.

'You say he never used it, but I think it is what he used to slash the water hoses, and he had to use something to scratch your car. 'Well Sweeney, have I got it right?' Sweeney nodded his head. 'I suppose I will be blamed for the whisky and the fires, you might as well make a complete sweep, somebody has to be the culprit!'

The sergeant looked at him. 'Did I say anything about whisky and fires? I've already got someone in custody for that. Now George Hutton isn't making any charges about the fire hoses, said he would write it off as an accident. It would be bad publicity for a fireman to be charged with a thing like that. What about you Steve? He scratched your car, are you going to charge him?'

'No. I will get it re-sprayed, but I suppose he is finished with the fire service?' The sergeant spread his hands out. 'Well yes, George won't take him back now. Right Sweeny, you better come with me.'

Joyce said, 'Do you have to lock him up? It hardly seems fair.'

'Who said anything about locking him up? I'm giving him a lift home; he isn't charged with any of the things that's been going on.'

'Before you go Sergeant Wilson, who have you got locked up? We will find out anyway.'

'The man with the taxi. He wasn't making enough money, so he arranged some call-outs. Jack Forsyth!'

On the way to the door the Sergeant said to Sweeney, 'I heard you say you never had any friends, just look behind you. What the hell do you think they are!'

After Mr. Harding's funeral, George Hutton was speaking to Joyce. 'What are your plans now? A return to Dumfries? I hasten to say you are very welcome to stay here; the men have got used to having a woman around.'

'I would like to stay here. I am going to help Steve to look after Sandie. She'll get out of hospital soon; they do have a spare room.'

'Well don't forget you have to notify me of any change of address, and that will include the room number!'

Joyce just smiled.

THE WEST-CENTRAL FIFE PRIZE FOR FICTION

By William Clinkenbeard

Eric

The thing was actually coming to pass. He wasn't able yet to excavate a phrase for it from the recesses of his mind, so it was still just the "thing". He had half-expected it, but only vaguely, a mere possibility lurking in the hinterland. He had now to face facts and be rigorously honest. His integrity as a writer was at stake. She deserved the prize. Her story was the best, better than his. But the fact that she would be walking off with the prize was going to trigger off so many time bombs in his life. He knew this and it worried him.

This whole saga had started off when Eric had been depressed. The cause of his depression was clear to him. He had expected his short story to win the competition and it hadn't. Not even second or third place, not even a mention. It was especially humiliating because of the way his entry into the competition had occurred. It was accidental really. He had only happened onto the online intimation of the writing competition. It was, after all, just the quarterly magazine published by his old university. According to the terms, you were to write a piece of about a thousand words on nostalgia or personal biography. Eric had reckoned that the competition wouldn't be all that keen. Surely there wouldn't be many entries, at least entries written by anyone of his calibre. He was fired up, had never felt so confident. He only spent a day on it and sent it off, reasonably satisfied with his work. It wasn't great, but it would do nicely. He felt that he had captured the essence of his first job after finishing university. Two months later the results were published online. His story did not appear, and neither did his name. This was the trigger for his depression.

It seemed to ignite in Eric a slow burning of the truth, the whole truth and nothing but the truth. And the truth was that he had never won anything for his fiction. The novels he sent to publishers were always returned attached to polite letters indicating that the work wasn't their kind of material or that their lists were closed for the year or providing some other creative excuse. The short stories he submitted to national competitions were never heard of again, and there was never an explanation. It was like launching a precious word-rocket fabricated from your own being into outer space where it trailed through endless galaxies and was forever lost to you.

He didn't think his writing was that bad. On two occasions he had entered national competitions for short stories. When the winning stories were published he read them carefully and decided that they weren't as good as his. He was sure that he could be objective enough to judge this. The friends who had willingly looked at his writing agreed with him. They read his stories and had pronounced them very good and worthy of being published. 'That's great, Eric,' they said. 'That ought to be in print.'

But this particular rejection struck him as somehow worse than the others. This had to be because the scale of the competition was smaller and he had been surer of himself. So losing was really tough. In his mind Eric reasoned that there were only two solutions. He could give up writing altogether, for what was the point if you weren't any good at it? The trouble was that it was the one thing he enjoyed, the single activity that produced meaning and pleasure. The second possibility was to start thinking about some other way of being rewarded for his efforts. That seemed to be the better way.

So that was how it all started, the reason for establishing The West-Central Fife Prize for Fiction several years ago. He needed some kind of win to keep him going, a shot of literary adrenalin. So his bright idea was The West-Central Fife Prize for Fiction. It would be an annual prize awarded to a writer in the area producing the best short story. The defined geographical area needed to be large enough to provide sufficient scope for a number of authors. On the other hand, it needed to be small enough to exclude certain writers who might enter and win easily, people like Ian Rankin and Christopher Rush. They were Fifers certainly, but they were already established writers. They didn't face a dispiriting struggle to get their work published. Their names were enough, just their names. The mere mention of the name blew publishers away, whether the writing was good or not. The quality of their latest work was irrelevant. So it would be a mistake to allow them to enter the competition. Anyway, they had their rewards. The setup was that Eric himself would announce the competition, receive the submissions and do the judging. He knew that on the surface it might look slightly incestuous, but he was a fair and objective person and would be rigorous in his judgements. He scoured Dunfermline for a prize to award. Finally he found a silver quaich, not inexpensive. It would do the job.

When Eric was finally satisfied with these arrangements he put an advertisement in the weekly edition of the *Dunfermline Press*, a very small one which read: *Wanted: Short Stories of 5000 Words or less for the annual West-Central Fife Prize for Fiction. Submissions to … etc.* He then waited for the stories to roll in. But when the deadline came at the end of the first year he had received no submissions, except of course for his own work that he had finished and handed in to himself on time. He read the story that he had submitted quite critically. It was definitely the best … well, the only one of course, but still the clear winner. In planning the prize-giving ceremony Eric thought about having champagne, but finally decided against it. With the best will in the world he couldn't see how he could drink a whole bottle by himself. A dram of fine single malt from the quaich would suffice. He realised, of course, that he couldn't invite Elsie to the ceremony or even tell her about the competition. She would think that he was completely loony.

The following year, once again no other submissions dropped through the letterbox, so he awarded the prize to himself again. It felt good to hold onto the prize for two year's running. The idea was really working; he was feeling more positive about the writing.

The third year, Angie, a journalist at the *Dunfermline Press*, spotted the advert in the paper and phoned him for an interview. It turned out to be rather tough going for Eric.

'Hello,' Angie said, 'is this the person that deals with the short story competition?'

'Yes, it is,' Eric responded, surprised and pleased that his effort was getting some recognition.

'Who am I talking to?' she asked.

'This is Eric,' Eric said. 'I run the competition.'

'Oh good,' Angie answered. 'I'm Angie from the *Dunfermline Press* and I'm interested in doing a piece on this. Would that be OK?'

'Great,' Eric responded, feeling a sense of elation beginning to surge through his body. 'Glad to know that the newspaper is interested in our little competition.' In the background he could hear the clattering of keyboards and formed a vision of the *Washington Post* newsroom in *All the President's Men*.

'Now,' Angie said, 'we might send out a photographer later to take a few pictures. But first let me just ask you some questions. The advert specifies the West-Central part of Fife. That geographical area seems quite small. It's only a little part of Fife. Why is that?'

'Well,' Eric hedged a little, 'we feel that potentially there is a hotbed of creativity in this little part of Fife. But there have been very few great writers emerge from it yet, so we wanted to encourage them.'

'But the way you define it,' Angie said, 'it can't be more than about fifteen miles by twenty miles in size. Isn't that pretty small creative hotbed? Surely it is more like a single bed than a king-sized one.'

'Oh,' said Eric, 'I think you'll find that it is larger than a single.'

'Right,' Angie said after a long pause. 'Let's move on. How many short stories were submitted to you last year?'

'Oh there were a number last year,' Eric answered. This was true in fact; the number was three, all submitted by Eric.

There was another long pause. 'A number,' Angie finally said. 'OK, let's move on to the judging. Who reads the stories and does the judging?'

'Well, Eric answered, 'I am the chairman of the panel that judges all the stories.'

'Right,' Angie responded, sounding somewhat confused, 'and who is exactly is on the panel? You must have some well-known literary figures.'

'I'm sorry,' Eric said, 'but I can't divulge that information. I don't feel that it's fair to the members of the panel. I wouldn't want them to be lobbied by the writers.'

There was silence down the line. Eric was beginning to think that he had lost contact when the reporter came back on.

Angie said, 'Right, Eric, I guess that I've got all I need for the moment. Thank you very much for the interesting interview, and I hope your competition goes well.'

'Oh, you're welcome,' Eric answered. 'Thank you for your interest. I'll look forward to seeing your article.'

Eric stayed at home for several days, but no photographer from the paper appeared to take his picture. He faithfully bought the *Dunfermline Press* on the next four Thursdays, but no article on the competition appeared. No one submitted any work that year either, except for Eric, who put in two stories, But after lengthy consideration he judged that his work wasn't good enough, and so the cup wasn't awarded.

But that was all some time ago, and now this "thing" has happened. Another writer actually sent in a story, a good one worthy of the prize, Jessica from Auchtertool. Now Eric had a problem. Someone else had submitted a first-rate short story. What was he going to do?

Jessica

She found the Albert Hotel pinched into an acutely-angled corner in North Queensferry. The red steel girders of the Forth Rail Bridge towered over her like an amusement park ride. Every few minutes a miniature train would rumble across. With some hesitation Jessica pushed open the door and found herself standing on a faded rug lying over a scarred timber floor. Old black and white pictures of the building of the bridge decorated walls that had probably once been colourful. A short, balding man with dark rimmed glasses met her in the corridor.

'You must be Jessica,' Eric said, smiling and stretching out his hand. He took her arm to lead her into the public bar. They stood beside a round table holding a briefcase.

'Can I ask you why the award ceremony is here, at a hotel in North Queensferry?' Jessica asked. 'I mean, it seems like a strange place for this kind of event. I was rather expecting it to be held in Carnegie Hall in Dunfermline.'

'Well, Carnegie Hall is great,' Eric said, 'but it's really too big for this occasion, and it is very expensive. This place has a certain intimacy about it.'

'Yes, I can see that,' Jessica said, glancing around to discover only a bar with a bartender, a number of empty tables and two other couples at a table near the window. 'Are there many people here for the prize-giving?'

'There's a few here,' Eric answered. 'Now let me get you a drink.'

They sat down. The bartender was looking without looking. Across the room the two couples sat with drinks, absorbed in their conversation. Across the hallway in the restaurant a large group of women were dining.

'There's no one here at all,' Jessica said when Eric placed her gin and tonic on the table. 'This just isn't what I expected.'

'Yes, I'm sorry that more people haven't taken the opportunity to be here,' Eric replied. 'You can never tell about these things. It often depends on the weather. In any event, I want to congratulate you on your story. It's very good indeed. It was a close decision in relation to the other stories, but your story won the day. The panel liked it best.'

'What were the other stories?' Jessica asked.

'Well, the runner up was a story entitled *The Mysterious Monk of Inchcolm Island*. It was very good, but the panel preferred yours.'

'Does the author get a prize for second place? Is he here?' Jessica asked hopefully.

Eric looked around the room. 'I think that he was planning to be here, but no, I don't see him. Anyway, there is only the first prize, and I think that I should award it to you now.' He leaned down and opened his brief case and extracted a silver quaich. Eric rested the quaich on the fingertips of his right hand and elevated it for her to admire, turning it slowly to reflect the light. He then thrust it towards Jessica and said, 'Jessica, it is with the greatest pleasure that I award you the West-Central Fife Prize for Fiction for the year 2006.' Handing her the quaich with his left hand, Eric extended his right hand in order to shake hers. Bewildered by the ceremony, Jessica took the quaich and held out her hand.

'Would you care to say a few words?' Eric asked.

'I don't really know what to say,' Jessica said, looking around at the bartender, the empty tables and the two couples in conversation. 'I guess that I should say thank you for this really ... really unusual award.'

Elsie

Elsie and Jane had finished their round and were having a glass of wine in the lounge at Aberdour Golf Club. Some late afternoon sun revealed the features of Inchcolm Island. Just beyond it the BlueStar Ferry was making its way up the Forth. Jane was seriously quiet for a moment before looking up at her friend.

'Elsie,' she said, touching her arm, 'there is something I need to tell you and I don't know quite how to broach the subject.' She hesitated and studied the scene out the window for a moment.

'Well,' Elsie responded, 'go on Jane. You know you can talk to me. What on earth is it?'

'It's about Eric,' Jane said. 'I was in the Albert Hotel in North Queensferry the other day. It's was the Ladies Lunch, you know, the Flower Club. Anyway, through the door I could see into the public bar. Oh, I shouldn't be telling you this.'

'Go on Jane. What is it?'

'Well, Eric was there.' Jane paused and took a breath. 'Eric was there with a female. She was young and quite attractive. They were talking and then I saw them drinking out of a quaich. Oh, Elsie, it's probably nothing. I'm sure you know all about it. But I just couldn't stop thinking about it.'

'Jane, thank you, I guess,' Elsie said. 'I didn't know about it, but I'm going to find out about it quite soon.'

'Eric,' Jane said that same evening, sounding very serious and very deliberate, 'I'm sorry, but I really have to ask you something important. You were seen the other day. I won't say by whom, but she saw you, in the Albert Hotel in North Queensferry. You were with a woman, a young woman. I hear that she was quite pretty. You were talking and drinking, the two of you. Eric, are you having an affair? And I warn you that if you say "No" your explanation needs to be pretty damn convincing.'

978-0-595-47086-0
0-595-47086-6

Printed in the United Kingdom
by Lightning Source UK Ltd.
124358UK00002B/133-324/A